The Augathella Girls: Volume 1

Annie Seaton

ISBN 9781923048317

Outback Roads:
The Nanny

ANNIE SEATON

The Augathella Girls: Book 1

Dedication

This book is dedicated to my loyal readers who love exploring the outback with me.

The Augathella Girls series.

Book 1: Outback Roads –The Nanny
Book 2: Outback Sky – The Pilot
Book 3: Outback Escape – The Sister
Book 4: Outback Winds – The Jillaroo
Book 5: Outback Dawn – The Visitor
Book 6: Outback Moonlight – The Rogue
Book 7: Outback Dust – The Drifter
Book 8: Outback Hope – The Farmer

Augathella Characters

Callie Young	School teacher/ nanny
Braden Cartwright	Owner of *Kilcoy Station*
Rory, Nigel and Petie	Braden's sons
Sophie Cartwright	Braden's sister
Jock Evans	Sophie's partner
Kent Mason	Owner of *Lara Waters*
Kimberley Riordan	School deputy principal
Bob Hamblin	School principal
Jon Ogilvie	Contract cattleman
Jim Anderson	Local garage owner
Jacinta Mason	School teacher
Jen, Nat and Kristie	Callie's best friends

Chapter 1
Spring
Brisbane - Friday

As Callie waited for her cue on the raised weather set she glanced over at the news desk. Greg Broadbent, her fiancé and Channel 8 sports broadcaster, had just wound up the sports news for Friday night. With the weekend coming on, and all the associated football codes heading for September finals, Greg's sports report had gone over time—as it often did—and the director's voice had just come through her earbuds telling her she'd lost ninety seconds of her weather segment.

'Speed it up, Calista. None of the pretty sunsets or "have a fabulous weekend" stuff, tonight. Just give 'em the forecast, and cut it short,' Rowan said. She could almost hear his teeth clenching. But Greg was the network's golden-haired boy and he could do what he wanted without penalty.

'Right, got it,' she said.

Damn Greg. As much as she wanted to marry him, his selfish behaviour drove her crazy. She'd wasted an hour preparing her script for the weekend weather wrap-up and trimming it to exactly sixty seconds. The ratings and viewer feedback had proven that her personal touch and comments on the Channel 8 weather segment contributed to the consistently high ratings of the news, sport, and weather hour. Not quite the poster celebrity that Greg was, but her segment was pulling good ratings too.

Greg had been flippant about her careful planning. 'You worry too much, Cal. It's the sport, they want,' he'd said last night. 'And your pretty face and boobs stop the viewers switching channels before the current affairs crew come on. They can look out the window and see the weather for themselves, so it doesn't matter what you say.'

She knew what she should have said to him when he'd dropped his sexist pearl of wisdom, but they'd been in a bar celebrating the ratings improvement with the network guys and Greg had turned his attention away from her to Maxine, the makeup girl, before Callie could protest.

Now thanks to Greg and his blatant disregard for the director, the last minute of the weather would have to be shelved. That was three times in the last month.

'He's a bloody cowboy.' Rowan's voice was short, and it was obvious that Greg was going to cop a serve from the director as soon as they were off air. No matter how many times he was told to wind it up, he'd flash that ten thousand dollar dental-work smile, and go over time.

That dental work meant even though he and Callie were engaged, it was "unofficial" until Greg could afford a ring.

'Forty-five seconds, Calista.'

She took her position on her mark, and stared at the teleprompt where her script waited.

Callie frowned as she scanned quickly through the rainfall and temperature forecast for the greater Brisbane area, and the rest of the Sunshine State for the weekend. Very little sunshine was predicted for the weekend with *la Niña* moving in, but it wasn't the forecast that was making her unsettled tonight. Greg had been strange all week, and she intended having a serious talk to him at dinner tonight. Being Friday, they would go to *his* favourite Italian restaurant at Paddington.

Greg was a stickler for being organised and having a plan. Spontaneity was not in his vocabulary, but Callie was tired of waiting for the plan for an official engagement and wedding date.

It was time to get a firm commitment from Greg; there'd been enough of this "soon" or "at Christmas" for the past two years. Callie's biological clock was ticking louder and faster every day. Jen, Natalie, and Kristie, her three best friends, had seven kids between them already.

Yes, seven!

She wasn't even sporting an engagement ring, and every time she suggested Greg move into her house so he could save the huge rent that he was paying for that luxury riverfront apartment near the Botanic Gardens, he had come up with one excuse or another.

He knew how keen she was to start a family, and her frustration at his "we have plenty of time" attitude was building.

Coffee yesterday with the girls, with only two babies in prams—the rest of the kids were at school or day care—had been a wakeup call, and had added to her discontent.

Her best and long-time friend, Jen, had leaned forward over her soy latte, and picked up Callie's newly manicured hand. 'God, Cal, I'd almost give away one of my kids for a manicure like that. Love that red.' Jen held up her neatly trimmed and unpainted nails. 'I haven't had time for a manicure for three years!'

'Getting married at thirty plus means there's still money for manicures and eating out. Love the matching lipstick too.' Nat's eyes had narrowed as she'd stared at Callie. 'Maybe Calista's the one with the right idea.'

Kristie had shaken her head. 'You're just trying to make her feel better, Nat. I've been wondering how long until we hear a wedding date. I need to lose five kilos.'

'I'm waiting to see the ring that lives up to the manicure,' Jen chipped in.

'Hey, you three.' Callie waved a hand in front of three tired, but happy faces. And yes, she was manicured, but it was for work appearance only. She would happily forgo the hour with Maxine every Monday morning, listening to how drunk the makeup girl had got on the weekend and who she'd slept with. 'I'm still here. And I'm perfectly happy with the way things are.' Despite the lie, she kept her voice upbeat. 'We're unofficially engaged, we just haven't got the ring, or set a date yet. But it won't be long now. And I promise you three will be the first to know.' She turned to Kristie. 'And *you* don't need to lose any weight.'

'Are you, sweets? Happy, I mean?' Jen's voice was low as both Kristie's and Nat's babies started grizzling at the same time. 'And why not? You know my thoughts on Greggie boy. He's not the one for you, trust me.' She shook her head. 'Great teeth, but that's about it.'

Callie had shrugged again. 'It's too late to be looking elsewhere.'

Jen stared at her. 'See? I rest my case. If you really loved him, you wouldn't even think of saying that.'

'No, you misunderstood me.'

'Did I?' Jen had always been shrewd.

'Calista!'

Callie jumped and brought her thoughts back to the weather program as the director's voice filled her ears.

'For God's sake, Calista. Stop daydreaming, ten seconds and you're on. Camera one. Jack, ready to swing in. Sweep from Greg after the ad. Boyd, be ready to switch to the synoptics charts when Callie is thirty seconds in.'

Callie straightened and looked over to the news desk where the set lights reflected on Greg's perfectly coiffured hair. Yep, Jen was right,. It was time.

Tonight was the night. They would set a firm date for the wedding.

I can wait for an engagement ring.

##

'So a wet weekend,' Callie finished up four minutes later. ''Stay dry, folks and have a great weekend. See you on—'

Her words were interrupted by Rowan swearing loudly and static in her ear buds. 'What the friggin' hell is he bloody doing now?'

Callie looked across to the monitor behind the floor manager. Both cameras had panned to Greg who was kneeling in front of Maxine. Maxine, their make-up artist.

Greg. Callie's mouth dropped open as he opened a ring box and held up a huge sparkling diamond in front of Maxine.

Suddenly the sound switched from her back to the news desk and Callie drew a sharp breath.

'Maxine, my love. Will you marry me?' Greg took her hand.

'Oh, sweet cheeks,' Maxine purred in her annoying little girl voice. 'Of course I will.'

For a few seconds shock held Callie rigid. Then without thinking, and paying no attention to the cameras, she stepped down off the weather set and strode across to the news desk.

Rowan's voice was gleeful in her earbud. 'Follow her, cameras two and three. Oh, ratings heaven, guys.'

'You lowlife, double-timing piece of shit. What the hell are you playing at, *sweet cheeks*?' Pushing between Greg and Maxine, Callie shoved at his shoulder with one beautifully manicured red fingernail and was not one bit remorseful when he overbalanced and fell onto his Armani-clad backside.

'You've hurt him,' Maxine squealed and dropped to the floor beside Greg—who looked ridiculous—as Callie turned away fighting a mix of tears and temper, just as both cameras zoomed in for a closeup. Of *her* face.

Chapter 2
Kilcoy Station - Sunday

Braden Cartwright tilted his head to the side listening as he sat at his desk entering the day's cattle weights into the spreadsheet. He could have sworn he'd heard a car door shut, but he hadn't heard a vehicle come into the house yard. He turned back to the computer and then jumped when the back screen door slammed.

'You there, Bray?'

He stood and stretched before he made his way down the hall to the kitchen.

As he closed the study door behind him, he frowned as his boys' excited voices came from outside.

'Soph, what's happening? I wasn't expecting you guys this weekend.' He rubbed a hand over his unshaven face as he walked into the kitchen. 'Have I stuffed up the dates again?'

His sister was standing at the fridge unloading an esky full of food onto the empty shelves.

'What's wrong? What are you doing?' he asked as she kept her back to him.

'No. You didn't stuff up the dates. I'm filling your fridge because I knew there'd be nothing here. What the hell do you live on, Braden?'

'I was going to the pub for a steak in a while.'

'Before or after you drank the six pack that's in here?' Sophie's back was ramrod straight and her movements were jerky. 'And then you were going to drive forty ks home in the dark after more beer and a steak?'

'Yes, I was. What's wrong with that? I have to eat. What's going on? Is everything all right? Are the boys okay?'

'Yes, your boys are fine.'

'So what's happening? Is Jock with you?'

Sophie closed the fridge door and turned to him. Her eyes were ringed with dark mauve shadows and her usually smiling lips were set in a straight line. 'What's happening is that it's time for some tough love. There's no easy way for me to do this, and it's caused me a lot of sleepless nights.'

'Do what?'

'I've brought the boys home because Jock and I are moving to Innot Springs.'

'What?' Braden stared at her.

'Jock's giving up the helicopter mustering. He's been offered a job managing a property.'

'Where the hell is Innot Springs? I've never heard of it.'

'On the Atherton Tablelands.'

'What! That's too far to take the boys away.'

'Yes, you're damn right it is. It's eleven hundred kilometres north and that's why they're here now. They've come home. Almost two years away from their father and their real home is too long. I've given you as much time as I could, Bray, but it's time for you to take responsibility before Rory, Nigel, and Petie think that Jock and I are their parents. Petie's starting to call me Mummy. It's way past time that they came home to you.'

'Now hang on, Soph.' Shock rippled through Braden. He'd never seen his sister like this before. She was usually full of joy; this angry person was not his giggly little sister.

Although not so little any more. He was thirty-one, so that made her twenty-three.

'No. *You* hang on. I know what you've been through and I—we, Jock too—have gone above and beyond for you. This is the only way to do it. If we stayed at Augathella, you'd talk me around and the boys would stay with us. Jock and I have our own lives, and he's given me an ultimatum. It's him or the boys.' Her voice shook. 'I'm only twenty-three years old, Bray, and I can't do it anymore. I spent my twenty-first birthday changing Petie's nappies.'

Braden ran his hand through his hair as disbelief took hold. 'Look, I—'

'No! You listen to me for a change. I'm not budging, no matter what you say. It's two years since Julia left us.' Sophie's voice shook. 'Yes, she left *all* of us. Not just you. The boys and me too. And we are slowly learning to live with it. You can't wallow here by yourself forever, Braden. Working yourself to death, living on beer and pub food.' She came over and held his arm, her work-roughened fingers pressing hard into his skin. 'You have three sons out there and it's time to start being a father again to those beautiful little boys. I can't do it anymore.'

'When?' he managed to choke out. 'When are you moving?'

'Now. The removalists are coming for our furniture tomorrow. Jock'll be over in a while to pick me up. Kent's getting a new pilot for the next muster.'

Before Braden could speak, the back door opened and three small bodies tumbled in, followed by three puppies.

'We're hungry, Aunty Soph. Hi, Dad. Look at our new puppies.' Rory, his eldest at eight, lifted an ugly brindle pup and put it against his face. 'This is Bumper.'

'And mine's called Tweedle, Dad.' Nigel held one of the other pups up high. He squealed as a stream of wee trickled down his arm. 'You little bugger!'

'Nigel. Language.' Sophie held Braden's eyes steadily as Petie, the youngest at almost four, walked across to her and clung to her leg.

Braden crouched down and kept his voice even. 'Who's got a hug for Daddy?'

Rory and Nigel raced into his open arms, but Petie held back.

'Good to see you, fellas,' he said as both boys planted a sloppy kiss on his unshaven cheek.

'We're coming home to live with you, Dad. I can help you with the cattle. Nige and I are so excited.' Rory's voice was full of self-importance. 'But Petie's being a sook. But don't worry we'll look after him when you haven't got time.'

Braden nodded and swallowed back the emotion as he held his sister's eyes. Eyes that were awash with tears as she nodded.

'Yes, you are coming home.' He moved away from the boys and reached out to Petie as Sophie gave his youngest a gentle push in Braden's direction. 'Rory and Nigel, you go and get your stuff out of Aunty Sophie's car and then you can choose what rooms you want. We live in this side of the house now. When you choose, I'll move your stuff over.' He swung Petie up into his arms, and his eyes stung with tears as he buried his face in the hair that smelled of the baby shampoo Julia had used on the other two when they were little. 'Now tell me, my little man. Do you have a puppy too?'

'I do.' Petie's voice was as gravelly as ever.

'What's his name?'

'*Her* name is Apricot.'

Braden hid the smile that tugged at his mouth. 'Apricot, hmm.' He met Sophie's eyes over the top of Petie's head. She nodded again and wiped the back of her hand over her eyes.

##

As the boys lugged their stuff in from the boot of the Camry station wagon, Sophie helped Braden make up their beds in the room they chose.

'We've been calling her Cottie,' Sophie said. 'Easier to call her in from the yard.'

'Dad, Nigel locked the toilet door on his way out and I'm busting,' Rory yelled down the hall.

'Use the one in the laundry.'

'Petie's in there doing a poo,' Nigel called from the bathroom.

'Go out on the grass then. But just this once, Rory. Nigel, you get a screwdriver and unlock that door.' Braden rolled his eyes as Sophie's grin appeared for the first time. 'I can't get you to change your mind, can I, sis?'

'Nope. You'd better get used to it, Bray. Petie still needs a hand wiping his bum. You go and help him and I'll finish making the beds.'

Braden took off down the hall, tripped over a puppy outside the laundry and then slipped in a wet patch outside the open toilet door.

'Apricot had an accident, Daddy. But I'm *such* a good boy. I can get on the big toilet by myself now.' Petie's blue eyes—so like Julia's—were wide. 'And I can wipe my own bottom too.'

'You *are* a good boy.' Braden quickly dealt with Petie's needs and lifted him down. 'Go and wash your hands. I'll be right behind you.' Braden shook his head as he followed Petie to the bathroom. He was still shellshocked and took little notice of the mud on the floor. As he supervised the handwashing and scrubbed his own hands, a bloodcurdling yell came from the kitchen. He and Sophie arrived in the doorway at the same time. Nigel sat astride Rory, pummelling his brother's chests with his fists.

'You're a dobber.'

'Get off your brother and go and sort out that locked toilet door right now, Nigel Cartwright.' Braden reached down and grabbed Nigel by the scruff of his shirt, and tried to hold his temper in.

Nigel took off up the hall, muttering under his breath.

'You'll have to watch his language, Braden, I don't know where he's picking it up, but he's had a cake of soap in his mouth a couple of times lately.' Sophie crossed to the esky and put the lid back on it. 'There's Jock now. We're going to leave my car here and take the Land Cruiser. I thought if you take my suggestions on board, you could do with a station wagon. She's a bit old but good enough to get into town, and there's a booster seat in the back for Petie.'

'Suggestions?' he asked cautiously. What suggestions? Did I miss something?'

'No. We didn't get a chance to talk. I have a list of sites here for you to get on and look for a nanny. And some other staff. With the insurance'—her voice wobbled again—'I know you can afford it, Bray. You need help here. You can't do it by yourself. I'm sorry we're moving away. I really am.'

He nodded slowly. 'Thank you. I'll look at it after the boys go to bed.'

Sophie held her arms out and when Braden held her she put her head on his shoulder. 'I'm sorry, it was a very hard choice to make. I'm going to miss you and the boys so much. Even though you're a cranky pants, remember I do love my big brother.'

'I know, sis. And I love you. I owe you the world for what you've done.' Braden leaned back and held Sophie's shoulders gently as he looked down at her. 'And don't worry. You're right. It's time. Now that the shock's passed, I'll be fine. We'll cope. I want you to be happy too.'

He waited a moment as he looked closely at her. 'Are you sure you want to move so far away?'

Her reply came slowly. 'It's where Jock wants to be. So, I guess if I love Jock, I'll be going.'

Chapter 3
Fortitude Valley, Brisbane - Tuesday

'And your experience with children, Ms Young?' The woman behind the desk scanned the resumé Callie had put together over the weekend after she'd searched Jobs Online and emailed to the agency yesterday afternoon. She'd been stunned to get a call first thing this morning inviting her to interview. The response had been much quicker than she'd expected.

'I see you have a primary teaching qualification. Were you ever employed by a school?'

'Yes, I worked at Barfield State School for three years after I graduated.' Callie reached down into her bag and pulled out the folder with the original references inside. 'These are references from the principal, the deputy principal, and my supervising teacher.'

The woman nodded and took them; there was silence as she read through them.

'And why did you leave? It looks like you were highly regarded.'

'I was offered a job with a television network that I thought was better hours and pay, and that I'd enjoy.' Callie stared at the clock on the wall.

'And now you want to go back to working with children?'

Callie nodded. 'Yes.'

I should never have left teaching, she thought.

But Greg had been persuasive and told her that it would mean them having holidays at the same time, and a better salary, once she worked her way up at the television station. He'd hated that she had more holidays than his four weeks a year.

She'd met Greg at a riverside bar near Queen Street one Friday night a few months after her parents had died, and her grief had left her confidence at a low ebb. He'd asked her out and they were soon a couple. At the time she had deferred to Greg to make the decisions, and when he suggested she leave teaching and take a job that he'd wangled for her at Channel 8, Callie had foolishly listened to him. Over the three and a bit years they'd been together, they'd been to heaps of weddings, including those of her best friends, and watched them settle into homes and start their families.

That was all Callie had ever wanted. Her parents were both gone, and she'd been an only child and she'd yearned to be married and raise a family in her beautiful house. Three kids was her plan, but she could never engage Greg in a conversation about a timeline for their future or how many kids he wanted. He was more interested in talking about their financial future and always dragging her off to investment advisers to invest her money.

Her money.

'Plenty of time, Calista. No need to rush. We need to get our investments in place.'

But there wasn't plenty of time and she'd wasted three years of her life with that lowlife. Thank goodness she'd not given into any of the schemes he and the financial adviser had come up with. In hindsight that was when he'd started to pull back a bit.

Jen had been right all along, and Callie knew she'd been naive. She'd dreamed of her happy family in the future, and if she was totally honest, Greg had never been a part of the image in her head.

Now the only image she had of him was him on his knees proposing to Maxine on television.

Her stomach churned and Callie bit down on her lip, pushing away the nausea that threatened. She felt like such a gullible fool.

Rowan had called her into his office when she'd put in her notice yesterday and said, 'Calista, the ratings have gone through the roof. You're a star. The CEO has refused to accept your resignation. He's offered you a pay rise.'

'No. And please don't call me Calista. You know I prefer Callie.'

Rowan's eyes narrowed and his voice was cunning. 'More than Greg's salary. A lot more.' He sat back and folded his arms.

'He humiliated me.' Callie's hands clenched on her lap. 'And I totally humiliated myself. And in front of most of Queensland. I'm sorry, Rowan, but I'm out of here. I'm not going on air again.'

Rowan's assistant, Julia, had tapped on the door. 'Callie, you're trending on Insta and the vid has gone viral on Tik Tok. It's got over a million views already. International too. You're famous. You're hash tagged *#wrong forecast*.'

'Name your price, Calis—Callie, and I'm sure the CEO will meet it.' Rowan smiled at her.

'No way. If you think I can front the public ever again or work with *him*, you are kidding yourselves.' She'd almost spat the words as she looked through the glass door of Rowan's office and watched Greg cosying up to Maxine. The bitch had put on an Oscar-worthy performance on Friday night when the camera was on her, but had stopped crying as soon as Rowan had called cut, and the seven o'clock current affairs show broadcast from the next studio, filled the screen.

'Whatever they've offered we'll top,' Rowan stated. 'And give you a sports car, and maybe look at finding you an apartment on the river.'

How ironic.

'I have a sports car and I already have a perfectly suitable house on the river, thank you.' Rowan didn't know she was very comfortable financially, and he probably didn't need to, but his smug expression changed to surprise.

'Anyway, they?' Callie had frowned. 'Who's they?'

Julia pointed to Callie's desk. 'You've had calls from most of the major networks in the country.'

'No. No chance at all.' She turned to Rowan. 'Just get them to make up my pay, and take off whatever notice I had to give.'

'Who's going to do the weather segment tonight? You'll lose your standing in the entertainment industry, Callie.'

'Maybe Maxine could,' Callie had said sweetly as she'd headed to her office to pack up the few personal items she had in there.

'Ms Young?'

Callie lifted her head and stared at the agency woman across the desk who was holding her references out to her. 'Sorry, what did you say?'

'I said, you have excellent references. If you are happy to wait here, I just have to make a call and I can give you a decision.'

'What, today?'

'Yes. But I have one more question, and then I'll be honest with you. I'd hate you to change your mind if you do decide to take the position.'

'Yes? What's the question?'

'We interviewed all day yesterday, and we didn't have a single person interested in the position, so I'd rather be up front with you before I call the employer.'

'What's the problem with the job?'

'The isolation. It's a large cattle station in remote outback Queensland, with the closest major towns four hundred kilometres away. No shops, no restaurants or clubs, no cinema. Is that a problem for you?'

Callie smiled and shook her head. 'Not one bit. The more remote the better. But I do have one question for you. Is there television reception out there?'

The agency woman frowned. 'I really don't know, but I can ask for you when I make the call.' She stared at Callie for a moment. 'I thought you looked familiar. Didn't you work at Channel 8?' Callie's stomach sank as the woman's face broke into a grin. 'I know! You're the Tik Tok weather girl. Why on earth do you want to go to the outback?''

'I've decided to go back to teaching.' She leaned forward and spoke firmly. 'The further away from Brisbane the better.'

The woman closed her mouth and left Callie in the office.

Chapter 4
Kilcoy Station - Tuesday

By noon on Tuesday, Braden was exhausted. It wasn't that the boys had been naughty or extra demanding, but the number of things he had to keep in his head were wearing him out.

Had they all had enough decent food to eat?

Had Petie been to the loo by himself? Note to self, check his underdaks.

Had Nigel and Rory done the schoolwork he'd given them after morning tea? It was awfully quiet in the schoolroom on the veranda behind the living room where they were doing the morning's school work. Sophie had organised Distance Education from Brisbane for them, until Braden could chase up school of the air. She'd driven them to the small state school at Augathella from their place and Petie had gone to kindy two days a week, but it was too far from *Kilcoy Station* for Braden to take them into town every day.

Ring School of the Air.

Another job to add to the growing list.

Don't forget to send the online grocery order.

Don't forget to pick it up.

Feed the dogs and put them outside for a toilet break.

Remember to bring the dogs in. He'd seen a few snakes on the move last week.

Warn the boys about not leaving the house yard.

Don't forget to call Sophie at eight tonight to tell her everything is okay.

It wasn't okay, because the agency hadn't had any luck finding a nanny so far, but he wouldn't worry her.

He also wanted to have a chat about Jock, and make sure she was doing the right thing, moving away with him. Braden knew he owed his sister big time. Sophie was right; maybe he'd wallowed for too long and given up responsibility for his boys too easily, but Julia leaving them so suddenly had left him unable to function for the first couple of months.

Okay, maybe he was weak, but losing Julia had been a huge shock and had shattered him; since he'd stopped taking the sleeping pills two years ago he still had nightmares most nights.

Don't go there. No point.

Afterwards Sophie had stepped in and offered to take the boys for a while, until Braden got himself sorted. To be honest, he found it hard to even look at them, because blue-eyed Rory and Petie looked so much like their mother. He had put the little energy he had left into the cattle station, and the months had raced by. Then a year, then two years. Every time Sophie had brought the boys over to see him, it got a little bit easier, but—

Braden lifted his head and listened. The house was way too quiet. When he'd come in earlier, he'd heard Rory and Nigel talking, but now there was an ominous quiet.

Damn it to hell, what were they doing?'

He pushed the chair back and hurried down to the schoolroom. It was empty. With a frown he walked quickly down the hall to the TV room where he'd left Petie watching cartoons. That room was empty too and the television was off.

Shit, where are they? His temper eased as a tendril of worry pushed its way up into his throat and he swallowed.

I can't do this.

You have to.

'Rory! Nigel! Where are you? Petie!' Braden bellowed as he pounded down the hall. He pushed open the kitchen door and stopped dead. Three innocent—and vegemite-covered—faces stared at him.

'What are you doing in here?'

Petie's bottom lip quivered.

'Petie was hungry.' Rory put his arm around his little brother and nodded at Braden. 'You were busy, Dad, and it was lunchtime so I made sandwiches for us. Do you want one? Aunty Soph taught me how to make vegemite or peanut butter sandwiches because I can use the butter knife to make them. I'm not allowed to use a sharp knife, although I reckon I could now that we're home. What do you think?'

Guilt stormed through Braden. He walked over to the table, gently touched Petie's shoulder and crouched down beside Rory.

'Mate, you're a champion. Thanks for making sandwiches for your brothers. And yes, I'd love you to make a peanut butter one for me, but you probably don't know—because Aunty Soph always told me it was gross—that I have strawberry jam with my peanut butter too.'

'Ew, that's gross, Dad. You won't catch me eating it, but I'll give it a go for you.'

'I want jam too, like Daddy,' Petie piped up, his little face clearing into a wide smile.

An ache formed behind Braden's eyes, and his chest tightened; as he stood there he vowed he would do the best he could for his three boys.

They were good kids, and they deserved more from him. It was way overdue. He had to get his head together and focus on them. They were his number one priority.

'Guys, I—' He jumped as the house phone rang. 'I'll just get that and then I'll make chocolate milkshakes. Don't go away.'

He hurried back to the study and picked up the phone. '*Kilcoy Station*, Braden Cartwright speaking.'

'Oh Mr Cartwright, I was hoping you'd be there. It's Siobhan McPherson from Jobs Online. I have an extremely suitable candidate for you.'

'Great. When can she—he—start?'

'We haven't discussed that yet. It's really up to you to decide if she is suitable. Callie was a primary school teacher, and she presents as a very sensible and competent young woman. I can email the application and references now that we've completed the interview.'

'Ms McPherson, if you're happy, I'm satisfied. I'm sure you've had much more experience in filling jobs that I ever have. Just tell me what I need to do.'

'Ah, before that, there is one question she wanted me to ask you. Do you have television reception out there?'

Braden rolled his eyes. God, no one wanted to come this far out, and as soon as there was a suitable person, she was going to knock it back because she couldn't watch the soapies. He cleared his throat. 'In good weather, tell her we can pick up Imparja from the Territory, but there's no other free to air TV, I'm sorry. We have a DVD player and internet access *most* of the time. Via satellite.' He knew his words were tumbling over each other, but he was desperate to get someone out here as soon as the agency could send someone. 'Oh and Netflix, of course, when the internet reception is good.'

'Okay, I'll let her know. I won't be a moment. Please hold the line.'

As Braden waited, he could hear murmured voices. It was only a moment before Ms McPherson came back on.

'Ms Young has accepted the position. We just have to complete the paperwork and I'll email it to you. Once you approve it, I'll give her your contact number and she can call you directly with any questions. I told her there is some urgency and she's happy to head out to Augathella tomorrow.'

'Where does she live?'

'Brisbane.'

'I'll organise a flight for her. That'll be quicker.'

'Just a moment.'

Braden waited again as the muffled voices sounded in the background.

'No, she wants to drive. She has her own car, and prefers to bring it with her.'

'Tell her . . . wait . . . can I please talk to her now? I'll sign the paperwork and get it back to you, and it'll save time if we can make the plans now. Ms McPherson, I'm desperate.'

'I can't see a problem. I'll email you the papers now while you speak to her. Here she is. This is Callie Young.'

Braden waited until a tentative voice spoke. 'Hello?'

'Hello, Ms Young. I'm Braden Cartwright. Thanks for speaking to me, and thanks for agreeing to work out here. I'm really pleased that you've accepted.'

'I'm grateful for the opportunity, Mr Cartwright.'

'I'd like to get you out here as soon as we can. I have a mate I can organise to pick you up at Archerfield Airport and bring you direct to *Kilcoy Station*. Can you come tomorrow?'

'I can, but I am going to drive out.'

'There's no need. There's a car here for you to use. A station wagon.'

He widened his eyes when she spoke firmly.

'I will *not* be told what to do, Mr Cartwright. I'll drive myself out to Augathella. When you send the forms back to Siobhan, please also attach directions. And please email me if there's anything else that I'll need out there. If I need to bring anything.'

'You do know how far it is, don't you?'

Her reply was a while coming. 'Yes, I do, but I prefer to drive.'

'Okay, I'll expect you about Friday or Saturday then.'

'Ah, okay. I'll see you then.'

Braden hung up, downloaded his email and signed the forms without looking at them, and sent them straight back. Now he had four days to spend in the house with the boys.

They'd make the most of it. He could see what Rory and Nigel were up to with their schoolwork. He could afford to take four days off the property—until the nanny arrived. He'd get a couple of extra stockmen sent over for the rest of the week. There was a mob to be moved in before the big muster, but it could be done on horseback.

He picked up the phone to leave a message for Kent Mason, his mate, and the station manager at *Lara Waters*, the neighbouring property. Braden's head stockman, Jim had gone over there with the cattle truck this morning.

Kent picked up straight away.

'Hey, Kent. Just a quick one, mate. When Jim arrives with the truck, can you let him know I'll be caught up for the rest of the week. Ask him to organise a couple of extra blokes to come back over with him for a few days, on his way back through town this afternoon.'

'Will do. Everything okay there?'

Braden nodded silently as noise carried down the hall. The sound of his boys' giggles lightened his heart and he couldn't help smiling.

'Yeah, mate. Actually very okay. My boys have come home.'

'Great news, Braden. It'll be good to see them. It's been a while.'

'How about you? A bit of a shock that Jock's moving.'

'Yeah, he mentioned something vague the other day, but I didn't realise they were moving away until he finished up yesterday. Muster pilots are in short supply as always. If you hear of anyone around the traps, let me know.'

'Mate, the only traps I'll be in the next few weeks is in the house. Cooking and looking after the boys.'

'True. I'll come over for a beer one night. You'll miss Soph.'

'I will. But we'll get used to it. And I'll hold you to that beer.'

'Great, I'll look forward to it.'

Braden was thoughtful as he hung up the phone. Kent and Sophie had gone out at high school and they'd been tight for a couple of years afterwards. Braden had been disappointed when they'd broken up; Kent would have made a great brother-in-law. He'd never thought much of Jock but it wasn't up to him to pick his sister's partner. Life was so uncertain, you had to go for what you wanted.

When you wanted it, he thought.

Braden shook his head as he headed for the kitchen to make the three promised milkshakes.

Stuff it. He'd make four. There'd be no beer drinking here while he was looking after his boys.

Chapter 5
Brisbane - Tuesday 5.30 p.m.

'Jen, I need a favour. Are you free for a couple of hours?' Callie said when Jen answered the call.

'I am. Damien's just home from work, and both the kids are bathed and ready for bed. I was going to call you and ask you out for a wine tonight anyway.'

'Maybe after.'

'Are you okay, love?'

'Never been better.' Callie stood on the wide front veranda and watched a couple of honeyeaters drinking nectar from the blooms hanging over the fence. The garden was a riot of colour and she was so going to miss her home. She swallowed. 'I need you as soon as you can get away to keep a look out for me.'

'Huh? A look out? What are you up to?'

'I'm retrieving *my* car. The one *I* paid for.'

'The Mazda Roadster? You go, girl. That will tick Greg off big time.'

'That's the one. And a few other things too. And Jen, I have lots to tell you. I'll wait in the foyer while you knock on the door.'

'Are you really okay, Cal?'

'I am. I'm doing what I should have done two years ago. Meet me at the entrance to the gardens. I'll grab a City Cat.'

'Okay, I'll be there within the hour.'

Callie walked down to the river and waited at the Milton ferry terminal. It didn't take long to travel the four stops and walk to the gate of the gardens. Jen was already there waiting for her.

'Thanks, Jen. Did you have any trouble getting a park?'

Jen gave her a quick hug. 'Damien heard me say we were going for a wine and he dropped me in. I'll get a taxi home.' She stepped back and looked at Callie. 'So what's the plan?'

'I have to get into the apartment block to get down to the basement garage, and that won't be a problem. Greg's at work, but I want to be sure Maxine's not there. There's a couple of things I need to get—'

'As well as the sports car?' Jen asked drily. 'The one he called "*our* car" and wouldn't let you keep at your place, even though *you* paid for it.'

'That's the one. *My* car. And all the other things I paid for over the three years, and some of Nan's good china that he took a liking to.'

'You go, girl! I know that TikTok garbage must be hard, but it'll be a flash in the pan. When do you go back to work?'

'I don't. I quit. And I'm going back teaching. I've got a job already.'

'Wow, that's excellent. Which school?'

Callie pulled a face. 'Ah, not in Brissie.'

'Up the coast?'

She shook her head. 'No. I've taken on a nannying position at Augathella. Or rather on a property out that way.'

'What! Augathella? Isn't that way out in the outback?' Jen's mouth dropped open. 'That's the last place I'd expect you to go. You're such a city girl, Cal. What about your lovely house?'

'Sure is "way out in the outback". New horizons and all that. Plus there's no TV reception out there, so the family I'm going to help out will be part of the tiny handful of people in the whole world who didn't witness my humiliation.'

'It wasn't humiliation. It was giving Greg what he deserved. Good riddance to him, and a lovely public one.'

'It's still a bit raw, and a bit embarrassing. I'm going to lie low for a while where no one knows me. You've got no idea how many people have laughed at me. Even the woman who interviewed me at the agency had seen it.'

'It wasn't *at* you, Callie. It was with you, and how you showed that jerk up.' Jen laughed. 'Or should I say pushed him down? You were superb. And don't you worry; slimy, sleazy Greg came across exactly as he is and so did that skank.'

'Oh, God. Did you see it live too?' Callie rolled her eyes.

'I did. You were on fire. Must have been great for the ratings.'

'Apparently.'

'I was waiting for them to put a soundtrack on it. You know that Helen Reddy song. Would have made a perfect theme. You were *invincible.*'

'I still get all prickly hot when I think about it. And then I get so angry at Greg.'

'Hold that anger, sweetheart. There's no need for you to take off. It'll blow over. What are you going to do with your house if you go?'

'*When* I go. Lock it up and leave it empty. It'll be there when I decide to come back to the city.'

'As long as you do.'

'I will. And I'll get a job in another school in a year or two. When I'm not the famous *#wrongforecast* weather girl.'

Jen glanced at her as they walked to Eagle Street where Greg's apartment was on the second top floor.

'I can see where you're coming from, but I'll miss you. Tell me a bit about this job you're going to.'

'It's a nannying job. Some teaching too, I guess.'

'You guess? Have you got a statement of duties?'

'Not yet.'

'And what about the family. Are they decent? Have they got references?'

Callie chuckled. 'I was the one who had to have references.'

'Well, do you know anything about them?'

'Not a lot,' she admitted.

Jen put her hands on her hips. 'Honestly, Cal, you are so trusting. You're going to the outback!'

'And that means what?'

'You've seen the movies. *Wolf Creek, Razorback,* and then there's all those people who go missing out there. That new series on STAN. What was it called?'

'*The Tourist.*' Callie rolled her eyes. 'But you're exaggerating.'

'No, you're trusting too easily again. I might be mean, but think of Greg and how you trusted him. He's stuffed up your life and your career. And one of my friend's sisters went out to a nanny job, and she was expected to look after the kids, the house, the cooking and the washing and ironing. Apparently the wife did nothing but sit around all day and play at being lady of the house.'

'Did she leave?'

Jen grinned. 'Um no. It sort of worked out. She ended up being wife number two.'

'You're making that up.' Callie nudged Jen with her elbow as they approached the luxury apartment block.

'Okay, maybe a little bit. But she did end up with the farmer. So where do you want me?' Jen asked.

'I called the station and asked to speak to Maxine, to make sure she was there, but they said she's on leave. I want you to knock on the door and make sure she's not in the apartment, and then, if the coast's clear, I'll go and get my things while you keep watch.'

'Is there much?'

'Just my Nan's Wedgewood dinner set, and a couple of pieces of Venetian glass that Greg took a fancy to. Three trips down to the car max.'

Jen shook her head. 'Lowlife. I was right, wasn't I? I can think of worse names too.'

Callie sighed. 'You were. And don't you worry, I've called him a lot of things over the weekend.' She pulled out the key to the apartment as they approached the foyer on the river side. 'Ready?'

'Yep. Let's do this, and then we'll go have a drink. Damien said he'll put the kids to bed.'

'Thanks, Jen. You're a good friend. And you're lucky. Damien is a great guy.'

Jen nodded. 'He is. And I'm a friend you'll learn to listen to next time when I tell you *your* guy is a jerk of the first order.'

'There's not going to be a next time!'

Jen waited as Callie inserted the key. 'I'll ring you when it's all clear.' She chuckled as the door opened and they stepped into the foyer. 'I just wish I could see Greg's face when he discovers you've taken *your* car.'

Chapter 6
The Warrego Highway - Thursday 9.30am

Doubts niggled at Callie a couple of times on the first day of driving west in her red sports car. Maybe it had been a bit of a knee jerk reaction, and her decision to go so far away from Brisbane—where she'd always lived—might have been a bit over the top. It had been hard pulling the door shut on her house, and the little honeyeater had looked at her balefully as if he too wondered what the hell she was doing.

'Me too, little bird,' she'd said wistfully. 'The only thing I know about the outback is what I've seen in the movies.'

Her doubts as to whether she'd made the right call vanished when she stopped at Toowoomba for her first coffee and the girl in the coffee shop had recognised her and asked for her autograph.

Her bloody autograph!

So I did the make the right decision, and I'll stop worrying.

With no family to worry about and having once led an independent life—before Greg—told her she could do this.

'I can,' she told herself over and over again as her little red sports car chewed up the kilometres. 'I will do it.'

Braden Cartwright had attached the directions as promised and when Callie had printed them out at home, and pulled up Google Maps on her laptop her heart almost stopped beating. No wonder he'd offered to fly her out there. It was such a long way.

She didn't know anything about the job, the place, the children or the setup out there. When Jen had asked for details and Callie couldn't give her any, Jen had frowned.

'Do you know what you're heading for?'

'Not exactly, but it's a bona fide agency, so there's nothing to worry about.'

'You ring me as soon as you get out there. If you have any doubt, turn around and come straight home.'

'Yes, I promise.' She'd pulled a face at Jen, but appreciated her best friend's concern and took it on board. Maybe she *should* have got more details.

Glancing down at the sat nav on the dashboard, she calculated how long it was before she would take her next break.

A long time between towns.

Hmmm.

Chapter 7
Chinchilla - Thursday afternoon

Eight hundred and thirty kilometres of driving, Google Maps told Callie as she peered at her phone screen. When she'd set off, she'd followed the instructions about which road to take and where to stop for fuel and coffee, although she thought Braden Cartwright had been a bit presumptuous telling her where to stop the first night. And not only telling her where to stop, he'd *also* booked and paid for the motel room. Callie was tempted to ignore it and find her own accommodation. She woke up to herself in time and realised she was letting Greg's behaviour dictate her reactions to a person who was simply trying to ease her way out to her new job.

It had been very kind of her new employer to map out a route, and book and pay for the accommodation, although by the time she'd swung her car into the highway motel car park, her back and legs were aching from being in the car so long. She could feel how far she'd driven that day.

After Toowoomba when she left cityscapes behind, the landscape had turned to yellow and gold. Flat paddocks and straight roads, passing the occasional road train—the first Callie had ever seen—had made for a pretty drive that had gone very quickly as she'd focused on her driving. On the second day of driving, the morning mist had lifted by the time Callie reached the little town her new employer recommended for a break.

The old fashioned grocery store had a coffee shop at the front and she ordered coffee and cake to take away. When the woman handed her the coffee without any recognition or any smart "TikTok girl" comments, Callie relaxed and sat outside feeling quite anonymous. It was a beautiful clear day, so before she headed west again, she put down the soft top of her roadster.

The drive to Chinchilla was uneventful but she was tired by the time she pulled up for the night. As she locked the car door and headed for the reception office of the Highway Motel, she nodded.

Good job, Callie, she muttered. No one need know it was the longest distance she'd ever driven. Once she was out on this outback station, seemingly far flung and not close to any town according to the map, she'd have to be careful not to show her lack of country awareness and experience.

Not to mention knowledge. Callie had lived in Brisbane her entire life. Apart from two flights to Sydney to visit her Great Aunt Pattie—her only living relative—and then one memorable trip to the resort on Pentecost Island in the Whitsundays with Greg, she had never left Brisbane.

She frowned as she thought of the trip to Pentecost Island and blocked the memory.

Decidedly unpleasant. The resort and the staff had been wonderful but Greg's behaviour had been appalling. She'd considered breaking up with him then, but had stupidly let him talk her around.

'I'm stressed, love. When I'm away from the studio, my confidence goes and I'm scared they'll replace me,' he'd said.

Refusing to think of anything more to do with Greg and blocking the image of his proposal to his new woman from her thoughts, Callie dragged her overnight bag from the back seat and headed to the office.

The bell above the reception office door tinkled as she pushed it open and stepped into the icy air-conditioned foyer. Even though it was only September, it was hotter than she was used to at this time of the year, and Callie appreciated the cooler air as she stepped inside.

After five minutes of ringing the bell on the desk, and shivering in the cool air, Callie contemplated going back to her car, and continuing her journey; there were still a couple of hours before dark. A brief thought popped in unbidden; maybe she could just keep going and make this a road trip? Maybe she could ring Mr Cartwright and tell him she'd changed her mind. She could keep driving and go to any of the destinations on his map, and then keep just heading off into the wilds, maybe even to the Northern Territory.

No one would know her there, surely. Hopefully they didn't get the Queensland weather show in other states. Despondency took over as she remembered that Tik Tok was worldwide. Callie turned for the door, but a woman rushed in from the back office before she opened it.

'Oh my gawd! It's you!' The squeal filled the room, and Callie froze under the intense stare. 'Oh my gawd, oh my gawd. It really is you. You're famous!'

'I beg your pardon?' Callie tipped her head and gestured to the computer behind the desk. 'I have a booking for tonight.'

'Calista Young?' The girl ran her finger down a page in the open book on the desk.

Callie nodded.

'I recognised your name straight away. I was really hoping it was *the* Calista Young. A cool name, and such a cool thing you did. You're that awesome weather chick who clocked her two-timing boyfriend on TV. Oh my gawd, we've watched it a hundred times, and we cheer you every time. Wait until I tell the girls you're in town, girlfriend! We'll meet you at the pub tonight, for sure.'

Over my dead body, Callie thought as the girl chewed bright pink bubble gum with her mouth open. She didn't look old enough to go to a pub. Despair crawled up Callie's spine. What chance did she have? Even in a tiny town like this in the middle of nowhere, they knew about her. She forced a smile to her face.

'Could you please let me know how much Mr Cartwright paid for my room tonight?'

Once she was checked in, she went to her room, and managed to avoid the receptionist, and the suggested trip to the pub. She rose as soon as it was light the next morning, left the room key in the box outside the office and headed west again.

Chapter 8
Mitchell - Friday

Just after noon, Callie yawned and looked at her watch as she approached a town called Mitchell. A broken night's sleep on a lumpy mattress with something scratching at the walls in the motel at Chinchilla every time she turned the light off had been followed by another long drive. She still had two hundred kilometres to drive until her booked accommodation for tonight and she needed to take a bit of a break before she drove the last leg. As she drove into the small town, a bridge crossed over a pretty river edged with tall lacy-leaved trees, and she noticed a public footpath along the edge of the water. She'd buy some lunch and a coffee, and stretch her legs. Sit by the river and have a rest.

The landscape had changed today; the rolling fields of yellow and green crops around the Darling Downs had gradually changed to paddocks with short scrubby trees and wide expanses of red dirt the further west she drove, but this river was pretty. For the first time, Callie regretted not doing any research on her destination. Her mind had been taken up with the fiasco at the network, and she realised she had to consciously put it behind her. But despite being very different to the sub-tropical landscapes and huge shady trees she was used to, this landscape held a different beauty.

The door of the bakery opened with a loud creak and the woman behind the counter looked at her curiously; Callie waited for the recognition and the smart comment. As she handed the takeaway coffee over, the woman gestured to her car that she'd parked against the high gutter outside.

'Nice car, love.' Her voice was gravelly as though she'd smoked too many cigarettes in her day.

'Thank you.' Callie handed over twenty dollars and waited for her change.

'You staying in town or just passing through?'

'Just passing through. I'm heading for Augathella.'

The woman handed over the change and shook her head. 'You haven't seen the forecast?'

'No.' Callie flinched and waited for the punchline to follow. *#Wrongforecast.*

How many times was she going to have to put up with hearing that before someone else took over the news?

'I haven't.' Her voice was cold as she stared at the woman.

'Well, put your radio on in your car, love. Charleville 603 AM.' The woman folded her arms. 'Just came over the news. Big dust storm heading this way.'

'A dust storm?' Seemed like she'd judged the woman too harshly. Callie smiled as she waited for the reply.

'Yeah. Apparently it's a doozie. You'll want to put the top up on that fancy car of yours, and find yourself a cabin down at the caravan park. The pub's full tonight because the Telstra blokes are in town.'

'Thank you. You really think I should stay here and not keep going? I'm booked into a motel at Augathella tonight.'

'You ever been in a dust storm?'

Callie shook her head. 'No. I'm from Brisbane.'

'Yeah, if you drive into it in that fancy car, you could get stranded on the side of the road. Not much between here and Augathella. Not a good move.'

'Thank you. I'll stay in town here then. Where's the caravan park?'

'Back the way you came into town. On the river just before the bridge.'

'Thank you. I appreciate you telling me.'

'You tell Pat that Rosie said to give you the cabin with the garage. You can put your car away and it won't get scratched when the storm hits. And you won't be stranded in a pile of dirt. '

'Thanks heaps.'

'From the city, aren't ya?'

'I am.'

The woman's grin widened and she chuckled. 'Good to get the "right forecast" for a change, hey love?'

Callie rolled her eyes and hurried out the door. Carefully placing her coffee in the console, she put the soft top up, did a U turn and headed back to the river.

Two hours later, her car was securely away in a fibro garage and she was safely ensconced in a cabin as the afternoon turned to night.

Chapter 9
Kilcoy Station – Saturday

'Daddy, when is our new teacher lady coming to stay?' Nigel kicked the dirt under the clothesline creating a flurry of red dust that settled on the wet white sheets in the washing basket.

Braden flung a double sheet over the outer wire of the Hills Hoist. 'Shit.' Red dust drifted down on the rest of the washing. He'd forgotten about yesterday's dust storm, and hadn't thought to wipe the clothesline first. Not only that, one of the boys had opened the window in the bedroom where he'd been going to put Calista Young, and now it was covered in a thick layer of brown and red dirt. Braden had decided to put her in the donga where Sophie and Jock stayed when they were mustering; they wouldn't need it any more. The nanny would have a bit more privacy there, with her own shower and loo, plus a small kitchen to make a cuppa. It had a nice small veranda along the back that looked out over the house dam.

Yeah, it was a good idea.

'Shit's a bad word, Dad.'

'Sorry, Nigel. Haven't you got a job you should be doing?'

'Nuh, I've done them all. I wiped up and put the cups in the cupboard. Rory hasn't done his jobs but. He's on the iPad.'

'No one likes a dobber, mate,' Braden said as he gave up on the washing. He shoved the now dirty wet whites back in the basket to take back to the laundry and put them through the washing machine again. A waste because the tanks were getting low again. The spring rains hadn't arrived yet. 'And to answer your question, the new teacher was staying in town last night, so she should be here before lunch. That's why we want to have the house clean and tidy, and the washing done.'

'Why do we have to have a teacher here? Why can't you drive us to school like Aunty Sophie did?'

'Because I have to go out and work with the cattle.'

'Why? Why can't you pay someone to do that? Uncle Jock said you were rich enough to hire anyone you wanted.'

'Did he now? When did he tell you that?' A slow burn began in Braden's gut.

'No, he didn't talk to us kids. Only to tell us to piss off when he was watching the big TV.'

'Language, Nigel.'

'Fair suck of the sav, Dad. I'm not swearing, I'm only telling you what he said.'

The anger eased as Braden tried not to laugh. *Fair suck of the sav?* Where the hell had that come from? He hoisted the washing basket onto his hip and put his free hand on Nigel's shoulder. 'Come on, we'll go find the other pair.'

'I used to listen to him yelling at Aunty Sophie. Don't tell her that's where I learned all my swear words. He knew lots and lots, Dad. Do you want to hear some?' A cheeky face grinned up at him and a pang of emotion squeezed Braden's heart.

'Hmm, did he? And no, I don't want to hear them. Forget them until you're grown up.'

Petie and Rory were curled up on the lounge together when Braden took a quick look inside on the way to the laundry.

'Five more minutes, men, and then we have some more chores to do after morning tea. You can help me make the bed in the donga and put some milk in the fridge for our nanny.'

Braden was ashamed of the state the house was in. Being there by himself with very few visitors—when Kent came over for a beer, they always sat out on the veranda—had meant the house needed a good spring clean. He hadn't been in the donga since last winter before Jock stayed in it. Sophie had been away in Brisbane for some reason or another, and Jock had kept to himself at night.

The least he could do was have a decent place for Calista Young to stay. Then once she was settled they'd sort out her role. Jeez, he hoped she was happy to cook occasionally.

After Braden put the whites back in the machine—this time they could go in the clothes dryer—he went to the kitchen and filled the kettle.

'Morning tea, guys.'

There was a flurry of bodies through the door and almost before he could blink, the three boys were at the kitchen table.

'Poppers and fruit first, and then if you're still hungry you can have the last of that cake Aunty Sophie made.'

'Will the new nanny make cakes too?' Petie asked.

'I don't know, mate. I have to find out exactly what we can ask her to do.'

Braden put out the drinks and fruit for the boys, and the rest of the cake. He turned a blind eye when they reached for the cake first.

Some battles weren't worth fighting. Making a quick cuppa, he snagged the last piece of cake, beating Rory to it by a whisker.

'I've got to go and make a quick phone call, and then we'll all do some work together. If we get it done fast, we might put some of those party pies on for lunch.'

'A party for the new lady, Daddy? Can we have more cake?' Petie's eyes were wide.

'We'll see.' Braden went to the study and dialled Sophie's mobile.

Please be in range, he thought. There was no service outside Augathella for mobiles, and he was sure it would be the same all the way up through Central Queensland. When he'd been mustering on the road, he could remember that occasionally they would come across a small town, or a large property where there was a Telstra tower and they'd all make their phone calls home while they had service for about five kilometres.

He was in luck. Sophie picked up on the second ring.

'Bray, what's wrong? Are the boys all right?' Her voice echoed down the line.

'They're fine. Where are you?'

'Just past Charters Towers. First time we've had service for a few hours.'

'Good timing then. I wanted to ask you a couple of things.'

'Kids are okay?'

'Yes, we've settled into a good routine, although they've nearly eaten all that food you brought over. I wanted to ask you what a nanny does.'

'What do you mean, what she does?'

'Well, you know. Can I ask her to cook? Shop? Make beds? Or is she just here to teach the boys?'

'I don't know, Braden. What did you put in the ad?'

'I dunno. Something about taking their lessons and looking after them. Just general stuff.'

'Well, I guess you're going to have to sit down with her and see what her expectations are. When is she arriving?'

'Some time this morning. As far as I know she should have been in Augathella last night, but we had a pretty bad dust storm on Thursday, so she might have got held up a day.'

'Okay, so when she arrives, sit down and have a good talk and come to an agreement.'

'Okay, I will. You okay, sis? You sound a bit flat.'

'I'm missing the three terrors. Are they really okay? You're not just saying that?'

'No, I'm not. Surprisingly we've coped really well. No major dramas, not too many fights and Petie's slept through every night.'

'Who's he sleeping with?'

Braden chuckled. 'Guess?'

'You?'

'You always were the clever one,' he said.

'Give them all a hug and a kiss from Aunty Soph, will you please, Bray?'

'I will. Take care, Soph. I'll talk to you soon and let you know how the nanny's going.'

'Did you read the rest of my suggestions?'

'No. I haven't had time.'

'Read them, and at least get a housekeeper.'

Braden laughed again. 'Sounds like I need to read it. Take care, Soph. Love you.'

'Love you, too.'

Braden hung the phone up thoughtfully. Sophie sounded unhappy; he knew her well.

Chapter 10
Augathella, Saturday 10am

Callie stayed over in Mitchell and left after breakfast. It had only taken a couple of hours to reach the tiny township of Augathella, and she was pleased that she had navigated a coffee shop and a petrol station with not one iota of recognition. This far west was looking good for her.

Anonymity, that was what she wanted. She was now Callie Young, ex-school teacher and governess or nanny or whatever the position was she had taken up. It was all very vague, and her thoughts hadn't been focused when she'd applied. She'd had the interview, accepted the job and taken off.

In *her* car.

As she'd packed the car after the non-eventful car retrieval the night before, she'd left after having a wine with Jen, her phone had pinged with an incoming text.

From Greg.

She read the first few abusive words, then closed the message and deleted it. And took much satisfaction deleting him from her contact list.

Her anger was directed inwards; she had been so gullible.

No more. From now on, she was her own boss and no one was going to tell her what to do with her life. Or her car. Or her career.

As Callie drove through the morning and closer to her destination, a niggle of uncertainty began to tug at her.

The isolation and the vastness of the landscape was not what she'd expected. After she'd turned north at a small town called Morven the traffic had almost disappeared. Occasionally she would overtake a four wheel drive vehicle towing a caravan.

She shook her head. People actually came out here for holidays? For pleasure?

Each of the caravans had a call sign on the back, and the signs made her smile.

Val and Ron. Give us a call on Channel 18.

Harry and Marge. Adventure before Dementia. Channel 40.

Peter and Cheryl. If the van's a rocking, call the police. It's not us. She'd chuckled at that one as she'd followed the vans into Augathella. She'd parked the car and gone for a walk to stretch her legs and delay her imminent arrival at *Kilcoy Station.*

The giant meat ant sculpture in the park at Augathella made her grin too. She'd heard of the Big Banana and seen the Big Pineapple. But a Big Meat Ant?

Hmmm. Where the hell had she ended up?

After leaving the park, Callie did as much shopping as she could in the newsagent and grocery store she found in the small row of shops in the main street. She'd packed some curriculum materials, but hadn't given any thought to what supplies her students might— or might not—have. Her lessons were still on a hard drive attached to her laptop, and she'd packed her printer for printing out worksheets. Pens and pencils, and some exercise books and stickers would be enough to get started until she saw where they were up to. She'd been in such a state before she'd left Brisbane, she hadn't even asked how many children, how old they were or what sex.

Not that it mattered. She'd taught from prep to Grade 6 when she'd started out as a teacher and even though she'd been out of it for a while, she could summon up her curriculum knowledge quickly. Excited anticipation replaced the nervous niggle; it would be good to be teaching again.

Callie left town at the western end, following Braden Cartwright's instructions and took the south western route on the Charleville road. After seven kilometres, she turned again onto another road, relieved when she saw a sign that said *Kilcoy Station*, twenty-two kilometres.

Almost there—she should make it by lunchtime. Biting her lip, she realised it would have been polite to call and let them know she would arrive today. Pulling over on the soft red dirt at the side of the road, she took out her phone, and dialled the number but there was no answer. She left a brief message: "Callie Young here. See you in an hour or two."

She set off again but the state of the road began to make her nervous. She'd never been on a road like this before; ungraded and so corrugated her car bumped and slewed left and right even when she was going really slowly.

She'd left Augathella with the top down, but as the sun rose higher in the sky, her scalp began to burn, and she pulled over to put the soft top up. As she pulled over to the side, there was a large thump, and she got out to see what it was.

Walking around the car, she sussed it out and there was no sign of any damage, but Callie almost cried when she saw how dirty her usually shiny red sports car was. Hopefully she'd be able to wash it, although the dry cracked riverbed she'd crossed at the edge of town made her wonder about the water situation out here.

She straightened her shoulders, got back in, and pushed the button to bring the soft top up so she wouldn't burn, but nothing happened. Pressing it again, she frowned and then started the car, and tried to get the top up again.

Nothing.

With a sigh, she reached into the back for the red and white striped bandana that matched her T-shirt and wound it around her head. It was getting awfully hot; the sun had burned her legs below the cuffed leg of her white shorts already. The condition of the road improved for a while, and Callie drove another twelve kilometres before a loud clunking started.

Clunk, clunk, clunk.

She slowed the car down to a crawl and tipped her head to the side. There was definitely something wrong. With the car, that was. As well as the situation she had found herself in. She tried to ignore the noise for a while, telling herself she was within ten kilometres of her destination. Ahead, the road was a straight unbroken line of red, and in the far distance she could see a line of low blue mountains to the south west. Low tussocky trees were scattered in the red sandy soil as far as she could see.

But there was no sign of life. No cars. No houses. No cattle. No wildlife of any kind to be seen. For a moment, fear tugged at her; it was the first time in her life she had been alone in the true sense of the word. At the same time, the noise coming from beneath the car got louder and suddenly the driver's side dipped and there was a loud wrenching noise.

'Well, Calista Young,' she said, trying to inject some courage into her voice. 'I guess this is what you call a breakdown.'

Reaching across for her bag, she pulled out her RACQ membership card, and her phone. The garage back at Augathella had the RACQ sign out the front. Squinting in the bright light, Callie dialled the number on the card and waited.

And waited.

Waited for any sound at all. Her phone was dead. With a frown, she put her hand over her eyes and looked at the screen. The service icons had disappeared. It was the first time they'd ever been completely missing from the screen.

Either her phone was dead, or there was no phone service out here.

In either case, she was in trouble. There was obviously not going to be any traffic along this road, so there was only one course of action open to her.

Callie sat there for a moment biting her lip, then turned the key and looked at the digital odometer reading. It had been twenty-two kilometres from the turn off to the *Kilcoy Station*, and by her calculations she had come at least seventeen of them.

So at worst, she had a five kilometre walk ahead of her. A walk on a dirt road, in forty degree heat, without a proper hat.

At least she had plenty of water.

Okay, she'd moved to the outback. She needed a survival kit to get her to the farmhouse or the station or whatever it was called.

Leaning over her seat, she opened her suitcase on the back seat and pulled out her nylon backpack. She threw in her purse and phone, a change of undies, a clean pair of shorts and a T-shirt, her toothbrush, and two bottles of water. The small amount of food she'd bought at the grocery store wasn't perishable so it could stay. Reaching for her makeup bag, she pulled out the lipstick that matched her red nails and outlined her lips. She would not turn up looking like a hobo.

For a couple of minutes before she set off, Callie stood beside the car and frowned; she looked long and hard at her laptop. It was too bulky to carry. Weighing up the risk of leaving it on the seat in the burning sun, and in full view of anyone who might come past against the hassle of carrying it for an unknown distance, she tried to decide what to do.

In the end she slipped the external hard drive into her backpack. If the worst came to the worst, she'd still have her files. Surely the laptop would be right out here until the Cartwrights could bring her back to the car to get her stuff.

With a frown, she realised if anyone else came past they could help themselves to everything in the car. Her two suitcases, and her laptop.

No, she wasn't going to risk it.

Taking care to watch where she walked—although her white high top converse sneakers were soon as red as the dust on the road—Callie walked into the scrub at the side of the road. Over a slight rise and about thirty metres from the car there was a wide ditch. She turned and looked back to the road. Unless you walked over the slight rise, you'd never know the ditch was there.

She hurried back to the car, retrieved her two suitcases, slung her laptop bag around her neck and carried them over. She carefully placed them on this side of the ditch under a slight bank. There, the worst that could happen now was that her car would get stolen, but there was little chance of that happening because the wheels wouldn't turn. Hopefully the Cartwrights could bring her straight back here and she could retrieve her belongings quickly.

Callie looked up at the clear blue sky and figured it wasn't going to rain. The only problem would be the sun on her laptop. She rearranged her two suitcases, standing them up and putting the laptop bag in the shade between them. Pocketing the car keys, she slipped the backpack over her shoulders, tightened the bandanna around her head and headed back to the road.

The road was straight and red as far as she could see. Presumably there'd be a gate or a sign to turn off to *Kilcoy Station*. She took a deep drink from her water bottle—the water was already lukewarm—and set off down the road towards her new job.

The sun was unbearably hot on her head, perspiration trickled down her arms and legs, and red dust covered her shoes. As she walked, Callie summoned up and muttered every swear word she could think of and applied them to Greg.

Her mood and language worsened and Callie's cursing was the only sound until a huge crow flew from the high branches of a gum tree. It cawed at her as it swooped close to the road and glared at her scathingly.

'Don't mess with me,' she yelled as she glared back. She hated bloody crows; she had done ever since she'd read that Merlin book by that New Age author guy. She couldn't even remember the name of the author or the book, but she'd hated crows ever since. Callie shuddered as she remembered the story had started in a roadside ditch.

Hopefully it wasn't an omen.

Nevertheless, the interaction with the crow took her mind off snakes, wild buffalos, vultures, and any other life-threatening creatures she could encounter on her walk in this arid and remote outback. She kept a close eye on the crow until it flew away with one loud raucous squawk.

Callie pulled out her phone and took a video of the landscape as she walked, using some not quite so rude words to express what she thought of Greg Broadbent at this moment. Words that were suitable for recording and for the ears of her friends who would be waiting to hear that she had arrived safely. She'd send it off as soon as she had service and she knew that Jen would reply straight away, with a **Come Home!**

Maybe she'd do her own Tik Tok video one day and call it Life after a— no, she couldn't put *that* word on social media.

Revenge was a sweet thing. Her imagination kept her mind off her current predicament as she strode west. Her mood improved with every step.

The same *couldn't* be said for her appearance, she thought as perspiration trickled down her arms and legs.

Chapter 11
Kilcoy Station – Saturday 1pm

After the boys had eaten the party pies Braden found in the freezer—thanks, Soph—he looked around the kitchen, satisfied with how it looked.

A glimmer of guilt lingered. It hadn't looked this clean and sparkly for a long time. Over the past months, his habit had been to wash up on Sunday nights to clear the way for the coming week. That was about it. There was no need to clean up, because he was the only one who ever saw it. But today. . .

Pretty spiff.

No cattle drench on the bench tops, no bits and pieces that usually accumulated through the week. You could actually see the grey and white marble swirl colour of the benchtops and they were gleaming.

For the first time in a long time, Braden smiled as he thought of what Julia would have said.

Just what he'd thought.

Pretty spiff, love. He could almost hear her voice, and the usual grief didn't slam in.

'Dad, what's happening?' Nigel stood in the doorway with a cranky face. 'Rory said I can't turn the TV on.'

'What's happening is that we're going to town to get a few more groceries before the new teacher lady arrives. You've eaten almost all the food Aunty Sophie cooked.' He looked up at the clock with a frown.

He hoped the new nanny hadn't changed her mind; it was after one already, and he thought she would have been here before midday.

'Okay. Can we have hot chips in town?'

Braden opened his mouth to tell his son that they'd just demolished a whole box of party pies, but he bit his tongue. 'Sounds like a good arvo treat to me, Nige. Go and get your brothers. Tell them it's time to go.'

##

Ten minutes later, Braden and the three boys were in the twin cab ute. It was the first time they'd left the house since Sophie had dropped them off.

Braden was almost to the cattle grid near the main gate when he remembered that he'd meant to turn the pump on to bring some water down from the artesian bore to top up the tanks.

'Shit,' he muttered and immediately regretted it as giggles came from the back seat.

'Daddy said "shit" again,' Nigel said with glee. There'd been a few occasions this week when his language had been noted. And always by Nigel.

'I'm sorry. Forget I said that,' Braden said as he turned back to the shed.

'Aw, Dad, aren't we going to town now?' Rory whined.

'Yes, we are. But I have to turn the pump on. Just wait there.' He left the car running, jumped out and hurried across to the main pump switch and turned it on. By the time they got back, the water would have come down the channel to the garden tanks and he could put the sprinklers on and give the lawn—such as it was—and the gardens, a good soaking. The place would look a bit brighter. He was going to do everything he could to keep this nanny here.

Braden frowned; that was if she was okay. If she was okay, and then if he got himself organised over the weekend, he might even get the pool cleaned and filled.

'Right, men! Let's get to town and find this new teacher lady.'

Chapter 12

Callie's feet hurt—her Converse walking shoes appeared to be made more for appearance than comfort. Greg had insisted she buy a matching pair to his for when they went for their walk along Moreton Bay before breakfast on Sunday mornings. They were rubbing, her toes were stinging, and that was only half the problem. Her neck and arms were a lather of perspiration, and her throat was as dry as—

She stopped feeling sorry for herself and stared ahead intently as a puff of red dust appeared in the distance. It looked like she was about to be passed by a car. The first one she'd seen since she'd driven out of Augathella an hour ago.

Callie moved to the side of the road, reached up and retied her bandana, and then took a swig of water while she waited. Water trickled down her chin and she grimaced as she wiped it away and her hand came away red.

As the vehicle approached, she could see it was some sort of high farm ute. She straightened her back as the dust-covered twin cab slowed and parked in the middle of the road.

'Gidday there, you've taken a wrong turn,' a deep voice called to her. The guy who had his elbow half out of the open window looked at her curiously. 'No point hitchhiking on this road. It doesn't go anywhere and you won't see any other cars come by. Lucky we were heading to town. Do you want a lift back to the highway? We're heading that way.'

She stared at him, but he continued talking before she could reply. 'There's not a lot of room, but we can fit you in if you don't mind a squeeze.'

Finally she found her voice. 'No, but thank you very much for the offer. I do need to keep going this way. I'm expected at *Kilcoy Station*.'

***

Braden frowned as the sweaty, dust-covered woman replied politely, her voice posh, and her words clearly articulated. He stared at her, looked more closely and then shook his head.

No. No way. It couldn't be the nanny.

This young woman was nothing like he'd expected.

'Why are you hitching to Kilcoy?' he asked carefully.

'I'm hitching because my car broke down about three kilometres back, and they were expecting me there a couple of hours ago. A Braden Cartwright.'

'Shit,' he muttered as he realised she *was* the nanny.

'Dad said shit,' Petie squealed with delight.

Braden opened the ute door and jumped out to stand next to the woman. At the same time Nigel and Rory leaned out the driver's window.

'Is that our new teacher lady, Dad?' Rory asked.

Nigel was out to impress in his inimitable way. 'What's all that red shit on her lips?'

Braden turned and roared. 'Nigel Cartwright! That's it. You've been warned. No more television for you for a week.'

The girl took a step back. '*You're* Braden Cartwright?' she said, staring at him with horror on her face.

Braden took a deep breath. 'Sorry I yelled, but yes, I am.'

Her hands went to her hips and he wondered if it was to draw attention to her lithe figure and fancy clothes.

'Now just wait one moment. I didn't think you had television out here,' their new nanny said, rolling eye-linered and mascaraed eyes. 'That's it. I've had more than enough today. Just take me back to my car, and I'll organise to get towed into town.'

'Just a minute. Look, I'm sorry, just wait.' Embarrassment flooded through Braden. 'Let's start again.' He gestured with a sharp jerk of his hand for the boys to stop hanging out the window, before he held out his hand to her.

'I'm assuming you're Calista Young. Welcome to *Kilcoy Station*. I'm Braden Cartwright. I apologise for my son's rudeness, I apologise for my reaction to his swearing, and no, we don't have television out here. The kids watch DVDs on the television.'

Although why the hell television, or her preference for not having one, was so important to her accepting the job, beat him. Maybe she was into some kind of weird religion.

Her expression cleared slightly as she lifted her hand and pushed back a stray strand of dark hair that had fallen from beneath the striped fabric wound around her head.

'Okay, I'm sorry too. I'm tired and hot and sweaty.' She reached out and shook his hand. 'And yes, I'm Callie Young. Nice to meet you.'

Braden held back a groan; her fingernails were like talons and painted the same red as the lipstick outlining her full lips.

The nanny? A teacher? Maybe he should have looked at her application and references, and not left it up to that woman in Brisbane.

He had no one else to blame but himself. This one looked like she should grace the front page of a fashion magazine, and not be in the remote outback teaching his three boys.

But Braden tried to be fair. There was no point prejudging her. He'd learned that before, but it was still a bad habit of his. And besides, they needed her. Today.

He turned to the car and glanced into the back. Petie had drifted off. He lowered his voice. 'Rory, Nigel, get in the back with Petie. Now.' Although quiet, his tone held a warning note, and both the boys were smart enough to pick up on it. 'And keep quiet and still. Don't wake him up.'

Petie had had a rough night, and because he'd slept in Braden's bed again, so had Braden. That was one of the reasons he was short-tempered today. Lack of sleep, worry about the muster, and some niggles of concern about Sophie after listening to what the boys had said about Jock.

What was it the experts said? *Out of the mouths of babes.*

'Come around and jump in the front, Ms Young. I'll take you back to your car, and we'll pick up your luggage, and have a quick look at the car. I assume you have luggage with you?'

'Callie, please. I do, but I took my two cases, and my laptop out of the car. I didn't want them to be stolen.'

'Where are they?' He looked at the side of the road where she'd been waiting, but there was nothing there.

'I put them in a ditch just off the road, away from my car.'

'There's no fear of that on our road. It doesn't lead anywhere apart from our station, so there's no through traffic. The occasional truck does—' Suddenly her words registered. 'Hang on, what did you say? You put them in a ditch?'

She nodded.

'How wide a ditch? How far from the road?'

An elegant shrug. 'Around thirty metres.'

'Quick, run! Get in the car.' He grabbed her arm, and pushed her as gently as he could towards the passenger side.

'Bloody hell, Dad. You're gonna be in trouble.' Nigel's voice came from the back seat as she climbed into the passenger seat.'

'Zip it, Nigel, and that's two weeks with no TV now.'

As soon as the passenger door closed, Braden pushed the clutch in, changed into second gear, and planted his foot on the accelerator.

'What's the matter?' Her glare was as cold as the posh voice. 'Where are we going?'

'The drain is an irrigation channel.'

'It's okay. There was no water in it,' she said smartly.

'That's right,' Braden said as he crunched into third gear. 'It would have been dry an hour ago but I turned the main pump on back at the house when we left.'

'It's okay. My car is about five kilometres from the house, or at least that's what I worked out from your sign.'

He tried to keep his tone patient as he explained how the irrigation channels worked. 'The water is tapped from the artesian basin below us, and it services many of our cattle stations. Our garden tanks are a bit low, so before we left I turned the pump on. That feeds our water from the bore through the channel along the side of the road to the station. It travels about ten kilometres before it gets to our place.'

'But the drain was bone dry.' Her voice wasn't as confident now. 'It looked like it had never had water in it.'

He flicked a glance at her. 'It only takes a couple of forty degree days to dry it out and crack the mud here. How long ago did you put your stuff in the drain?'

She frowned and looked down at the expensive watch that was on her now sunburned wrist. 'About twenty minutes ago. At most.'

'You might be lucky. The water mightn't have reached it yet.' Braden changed gears and accelerated harder. The wheels spun, and then after the tyres got traction the twin cab lurched up and down the corrugations. 'It's pretty dry, so it'll take a while to come to the surface and make its way down the channel.'

He tried to sound positive, but the first three kilometres of channel had a concrete base and sides and the water would gain momentum in that first bit before it turned to a dirt channel.

Braden peered ahead and after a few minutes a low red car appeared on the side of the road in the far distance. That'd be right. Fire engine red to match her nails, lipstick and clothes.

'That's my car just up there.' She pointed to the vehicle he'd already spotted.

A bloody sports car. He kept his face expressionless and didn't comment.

Stretching high in his seat Braden glanced to the side of the road. 'The water hasn't come this far yet. You might be in luck. But we'd better be quick. It won't be far off.'

'How deep does it get?'

He turned his head and stared at her. 'Over a metre.'

She looked away from him and didn't say another word.

Two minutes later the ute slewed to a stop.

'I can hear it coming,' Braden said as he pulled the hand brake on and flung his door open. 'Nigel, Rory. Come with me, and watch out for snakes. Callie—Miss Young—please stay here and keep an eye on Petie for me.'

He didn't wait for her answer as he took off towards the irrigation channel.

Chapter 13

Callie opened her mouth to answer her new boss, but before she could speak he and the two little boys had taken off and disappeared behind the slight rise in the scrub.

Petie? Who was Petie? She'd spent the last five minutes staring ahead as the ute had gone tearing back along the dirt road she'd walked.

Now she turned to the back seat for the first time as a noise came from the seat behind her, and her gaze settled on a little boy in a booster seat set in the middle. He was staring at her and his face crumpled with distress as she stared back.

'Oh, please don't cry, sweetie. Are you Petie?'

Stupid question, Callie. There was no one else in the back seat.

'Where's my Daddy? Are you the teacher lady?'

'Daddy had to go and get my bag.' Callie pulled a face. 'Because I left it in the drain and it might be wet. Will we go and see if he saved it?' He nodded slowly, but his face was wary. 'And my name's Callie, and yes, I'm the teacher lady.'

'Yes, find Daddy.'

She unclipped the seat belt and opened her door, looking down to check the ground was clear before she jumped into the red dust.

Braden Cartwright's warning to his other two boys about snakes hadn't gone unheeded.

The red dirt was clear, but her brows drew together in a frown as she looked at the side of the road and saw some slithery marks. They certainly weren't footprints. She'd get the little boy out of the back before he started to cry, and they'd be very careful as they walked over to see if her bags had been saved. She looked over to the scrub, but there was no sign of the boys or their father. She shivered as she thought about how she had walked through there before without really watching where she was going. Greg had been in her head; she had to get over her anger.

Opening the back door, she reached over and tried to find the clip that secured the belt into the seat, but she couldn't see it.

'Hang on a minute, Petie, silly Callie can't find the seatbelt.'

His little giggle made her smile. 'Silly Callie,' he repeated.

'Yep, silly Callie, who put her bags in the drain, and silly Callie who can't undo your seatbelt.'

A little hand grabbed hers as she felt along the side of the seat.

'This side, silly Callie.' He pulled her hand over his legs and let go when her fingers encountered the belt holder.

'Ah, thank you.'

With a loud click, the catch let go, and Petie leaned forward in the seat.

'Can you get out or will I lift you out?' she asked, holding her hands out to the little boy who wasn't much bigger than a toddler. In a flash he slid off the seat and ducked under her arm and was out the door. Another puff of red dust filled the air as he landed in the dirt.

'Okay, so you know how to get out.'

He waited beside the ute. 'I'm a big boy. I'll be four on my birthday.'

'I'm pleased to hear that.' Callie held out her hand. 'Come on. We'll go find your dad and the others.'

He looked up at her. 'Carry me, please. Daddy said snakes. I don't like snakes. They bite and bite you hard.'

Callie shivered again and wiped her damp hands on the side of her once white shorts, reached down and swung him into her arms. At least she'd had toddler experience with Jen's kids, and he was almost kinder age. She knew how to deal with kids that age with her eyes shut almost. By the look of things, she'd only have two boys to teach; Petie was too young for the classroom by a good two years. But it would be fun having a little one around; she'd loved minding her friends' kids.

Any chance she might have of having her own kids was gone; she was going to ignore that ticking biological clock. She would never trust a man again.

Petie sat comfortably on her hip with one hand holding her shoulder as she turned towards the scrub where the ditch was.

'Look, there's Daddy.'

Callie followed the direction he was pointing and a jolt of worry hit her. She could just see the top of her employer's head through the low trees as he ran along the side of the ditch about a hundred metres along from where they were parked. There was no sign of the two boys.

'Uh oh. Not looking good,' she said with a groan. Could the day get any worse?

***

Braden scrambled up the bank, one suitcase in his hand and the laptop case under his arm. He'd managed to get them out of the channel with about thirty seconds to spare as the first surge of water had come down from the bore. He put the suitcase and the laptop bag on the ground in front of the boys. 'Don't move, you pair. Wait right there.'

'Look, Dad. There's another one!' Rory leaned over the bank.

'It's floating, like a boat!' Nigel yelled, excitement in his voice.

'I'll get it. And don't go near the water. Guard them.' By the time Braden had thrown the suitcase and the laptop up to the boys, the water was up to his thighs and the other suitcase had started its journey along the irrigation channel.

He raced along the edge of the channel, his work boots squelching as he kept his eyes on the other suitcase as it bobbed along on top of the quickly rising water. If it sank, they'd have no hope of finding it.

Braden was out of breath when the handle snagged against a dead tree that had fallen across the channel about three hundred metres along. From up here it looked as though the tree trunk was broad enough for him to shinny along so he wouldn't have to go into the water to reach the suitcase and get any wetter than he already was. He scrambled down the bank again; the dirt was softer here and his boots slipped the last metre, and he grabbed one of the protruding branches just in time to stop himself falling into the now-deep water.

He tested the stability of the tree trunk with one foot and it didn't budge, so he dropped down into a crouch and inched along the tree with his arm stretched out for the red—*of course it was bloody red*—suitcase.

'Got it,' he muttered as his fingers closed over the handle. At the same time there was an ominous creak and the trunk rolled beneath him.

Braden kept a firm grip on the handle of the suitcase as he slid beneath the muddy water, and took a deep breath as the weight of the suitcase pulled him under.

Of all the stupid places to put her stuff.

What sort of idiot put luggage and computers in an irrigation channel? He kicked hard, and as his head broke the surface a Coke can and an empty chip packet floated past, worsening his already bad mood. Even this far out of town, there was rubbish in the channel.

Determined not to let go of the suitcase now that he had hold of it, he let the water take him along until the bottom of the channel rose and he could feel solid ground beneath his feet. He moved across and hoisted the red suitcase up the bank. As he clambered after it, he noticed the Louis Vuitton insignia on the side, and an engraved name plate that said G. Broadbent.

Who was this woman?

His thoughts boiled and he cursed Sophie as he tried to climb the bank in his sodden boots. This nanny person had turned up in a low-slung sports car, with her long red talons and colour co-ordinated clothes and designer shoes. Expensive luggage that had someone else's name on it.

How did he even know he could trust her? How did he even know she was who she said she was? The first thing he'd be doing would be asking for some sort of ID. And more fool him, he'd left the three boys back there where she was. And the keys in the ute.

All she'd have to do would be offer hot chips and the boys would be in the ute with her in a flash.

The curse that came from his lips was the worst yet, but Nigel wasn't in earshot. It took two attempts to get to the top of the bank and by the time he succeeded, his long pants were streaked with red mud, his boots were damn near totalled, and his mood was as filthy as his boots.

Braden focused on his breathing as he trudged back along the track at the top of the channel. He would keep it together until he and Miss Whoever She Was Callie Young could have a conversation in private. He didn't want to upset the boys.

'Dad! You got it.' Nigel and Rory were standing where he had told them to wait fifty metres away. *She* was beside them.

Braden frowned and broke into a loping run, as best as he could with his boots slipping up and down, and the damn suitcase slapping against his legs. It felt like it was full of bricks; it was a wonder the damn thing had floated. He'd told her to wait in the car with Petie. She wouldn't know that the little terror could undo his belt by himself, and that he had a fascination with water.

'Where's Petie?' he yelled, scanning the channel as he ran.

She turned as he called and relief surged though him as he realised that she was holding Petie on one hip. His red T-shirt had blended with her red shirt from a distance.

'He's here, Dad,' Rory called back.

'Thanks, mate.' Braden lifted his spare hand and acknowledged Rory's call. 'Stay calm,' he muttered to himself. 'Shit.'
And watch your language.

Chapter 14

Callie's heart sank when she saw the tight smile on Braden Cartwright's face. He looked decidedly unimpressed, not to mention very wet. His hair was sticking up in spikes where he'd run his muddy hand through it. The last thing she wanted or needed was a cranky boss.

She injected a bright note into her voice, and plastered a wide smile on her face. 'Thank you *so* much. I really appreciate what you've done.'

He nodded. 'I'm sorry one got wet. We weren't quick enough.'

'No, it's fine. Totally my fault for putting my luggage in an irrigation channel. My first outback lesson.' Callie waved a dismissive hand. 'Anyway if one of them had to get wet, that was the best one.'

'Why, because it's not yours?' His expression held disdain, and she knew he was thinking less of her by the minute. He'd obviously seen Greg's name on it.

'Yes, they're both mine. I meant because there were winter clothes in that one and they'll wash and dry out by next winter.' As soon as the words left her mouth she regretted them. It sounded like she had decided to stay for the long term without even knowing anything about the job, or the boss and his wife, and the kids. Or seeing if she was suitable to her new employer.

She glanced down at Petie still snug on her hip; so far the three children had been polite and well behaved. If you discounted the comment about her lipstick.

Early days, Callie. If it didn't feel right, she could leave. She didn't owe the Cartwright family anything and so far she was as unimpressed with Braden as he seemed to be with her.

The man occupying her thoughts held out his arms to Petie but the little boy shook his head. 'No, Daddy, you is muddy. I like Callie.'

That brought an eyebrow raise.

'Okay, then. Let's get back to the ute. We can take Miss Young to the donga and she can get sorted while I have a shower.' He turned to Callie. 'I'll come back and sort out your car later.'

'That's not fair, Dad!' The boy, Nigel, stamped his foot. 'We were going to get hot chips in town.'

'Sometimes, mate, circumstances change and we have to adapt.' To his credit, the father's voice was calm.

Nigel started to bellow. 'I want hot chips.'

This time it was Callie who raised her eyebrows, but she walked over to the angry little boy, and put her hand on his shoulder. 'I'm sorry, Nigel, it was my fault for being silly.'

'Silly Callie,' Petie echoed.

Nigel looked up and glared at her. 'It is your fault and *you* can bloody well fix it.'

Callie's mouth dropped open, and she wasn't sure how to reply; she didn't have to as Braden looked over at the older boy. He gestured to the laptop bag. 'Are you right to carry that for us, Rory?'

'Yes, Dad.'

Nigel's squeal pierced the still air as his father reached down, picked him up and threw him over his shoulder like a sack of potatoes. 'You and I will have a talk back at the house.'

It was a silent group who trudged back along the track to the twin cab ute. Callie carried Petie, Rory carried the laptop, and she was most impressed as Braden carried a suitcase in each hand with his son over one shoulder. Her thoughts were in a whirl; this wasn't the way she had expected to arrive and be greeted at the cattle station. But at least it wasn't a public humiliation and she could cope. Her car breakdown and then putting her bags in an irrigation channel hadn't been witnessed by the whole world. Okay, so her new boss might think she was a ditz, but she could cope with that. It was better than being seen as a bitch by a million or so viewers.

They reached the ute and Braden put the suitcases down, and Nigel slid to the ground. He stood there looking mutinous. Opening the back door, Braden held his arms out for Petie. 'Rory. You go around the other side and get in. Nigel, you wait until Petie's strapped in and get in this side. I don't want to hear one more word from you until we have a little talk in my office.'

Callie opened the front door and climbed into the passenger seat while both suitcases and laptop were loaded into the back of the ute. She had taken the suitcases from Greg's apartment when she and Jen had gone there earlier in the week.

Greg had found the copycat Louis Vuitton luggage online the week before they'd gone to Pentecost Island, and he'd asked her to pay for them because he'd been a bit short that week.

'I'll pay you back next week,' he'd said.

Pah! There were a lot of things that Greg had said and done that she should have taken as a warning.

He'd never paid her back the seven hundred and fifty dollars so the suitcases belonged to her. The anger that bubbled briefly as she thought about her lowlife ex disappeared when Braden Cartwright opened the ute door.

Callie's mouth dried and she pushed away the totally inappropriate thoughts and reaction that slammed through her.

He'd removed his sodden boots and socks, *and* his wet shirt. Her eyes moved up from his bare feet and settled on a broad tanned chest.

She swallowed and looked away as heat filled her cheeks. Not only broad and tanned, but he was absolutely built. The only place she'd ever seen a perfect specimen like that was in her dreams.

She couldn't help the grin that tugged at her lips. Although there had been that time Jen and Nat had dragged her to that male stripper troupe show for Kristie's hen's night. Braden Cartwright would have fitted right in.

Callie stared straight ahead as he started the ute, not game to turn and look at him in case her eyes dropped to that gorgeous chest again.

For God's sake, wake up to yourself! She closed her eyes and chastised herself.

She'd already presented herself badly enough without salivating over a married man *and* father, before they'd even arrived at the cattle station.

Besides being totally inappropriate, she firmly reminded herself, she was off men for good.

For life. They were not to be trusted.

##

The wheels of the ute rattled over a metal grid when they reached a locked gate at the end of another long straight road. Callie stared at a large sign warning that *Kilcoy Station* was private property.

Braden pulled up. 'Rory. Your turn.' It was the first time he'd spoken since they'd set off, and Callie was finding the silence uncomfortable, but she'd be damned if she was going to break it first. The occasional sniff had come from the back seat and she wondered if Nigel was crying. Even though he was a naughty boy, her heart went out to him. When she'd been teaching, it only took tears to soften her, and the naughtier kids in the class had soon picked up on that. She'd try not to do that here: Nigel was obviously a handful.

The passenger side back door of the ute opened and Rory ran to the gate, unlooped the chain and pushed the gate back and Braden drove them through.

'We're almost to the house,' Braden said as he waited for Rory to shut the gate and get back in the car. 'We have the gates to keep the cattle out of the house yard.'

'Where do you do the milking?' Callie kept her eyes ahead, feeling embarrassed as she wondered if he'd noticed her eyes widen when she'd looked at his chest.

Oh God, how embarrassing.

A rude splutter came from the back seat, and Braden raised a warning finger. 'Nigel.'

'Ah, we don't have a dairy, we raise cattle for meat,' he said. 'Plus we breed bulls.'

'Okay.'

Soon a house came into view and Callie's eyes widened again when she saw the size of it. A long one-storey brick house with a high-pitched green roof sat in the middle of a large fenced-off block. It was one of the biggest houses she'd ever seen. High colonial windows broke the brick every few metres and she wondered how many rooms could be in a house that size. On the other side of the fence was a large shed with the same green roof. Callie looked around, taking in the rest of the buildings scattered around the paddocks past the house. As they got closer, she was surprised to see the mess covering the dead lawn. Old drums and various pieces of equipment sat on the dry brown grass.

'Dad, I need the dunny.' Nigel unclipped the seat belt and leaned over the back of his father's seat. 'I'm in a hurry.'

'Okay, Nigel and Rory, you can both jump out now. I won't be long.' He flicked a glance at her. 'Then I'll drop Callie over to the donga.' Braden's voice interrupted her perusal of the property; it was very different to what she'd expected.

'Okay, thank you,' she said slowly, wondering if she would look stupid again if she asked what a donga was.

Then again, she had no experience of the outback, so maybe huge houses on cattle stations like this one were the norm.

And dongas, whatever they were.

As they stopped at the back of the house where the yard was much tidier, she spotted two small buildings across the dead grass about a hundred metres from the house.

'We have two dongas and they're both empty at the moment,' he explained.

Callie nodded. *Donga, okay, some sort of apartment.*

'Ms Young will come back over and see you in a while. You can show her the schoolroom and your rooms.'

Flicking a quick glance into the back seat, Callie regretted it straight away when Nigel poked his tongue out when she turned to look at him. The two boys jumped out of the car and pounded up the back steps. The screen door banged shut behind them and there was silence.

She stared after them, her heart sinking. This was going to be an interesting job. Nigel was obviously a strong-willed kid and Callie wondered what the parents' discipline was like. There'd been no sign of Mrs Cartwright yet. Braden hadn't mentioned his wife, and no one had come out to meet the car.

Maybe she was away, but she'd thought he would have mentioned that. She was pleased that she had separate accommodation at least. Jen was right; she should have found out more about the setup out here before she'd taken off from the city.

'Get yourself settled in and unpack while I have a shower. Anything you want to wash from your suitcase, put aside and I'll show you where the laundry is in the main house when you come over.'

'Okay.'

'I checked the one with the single bedroom for you. When the muster starts, we'll use the other one with two bedrooms to put up some of the contract staff.'

'Thank you.'

'Being here will give you a bit of privacy and means you don't have to be in the house. You won't feel like you're on duty all the time. Plus—' he grinned and glanced over to the back seat where Petie had started to sing a song about baby sharks at the top of his voice— 'It'll give you a break from the three terrors.'

'Yes, we need to have a talk about what you expect,' Callie said as he pulled up near the steps of a building with unpainted timber walls. A white front door was flanked by two dust covered windows. A single white plastic chair sat on the veranda.

'Yeah, we do. Once you get settled come on over to the house and we'll have a chat. I don't expect you to start today. You'll be tired after the drive from Brisbane.'

'Okay. How long before you'll be ready to meet with me?'

'Give me half an hour.'

Callie frowned. It was all "me", no mention of an "us".

'There's tea and coffee in the cupboard in your kitchen, and some fresh milk in the fridge. Towels in the bathroom and if you want the air conditioner on, the remote's in the top drawer in the kitchen. I hope it's clean enough. It didn't look too bad when I brought the milk over and made the bed. You can tell me if there's any problems or if there's anything else you need when you come over.'

Still no mention of a wife.

'Okay.' Callie reached for the car door handle. She looked across at him and kept her eyes away from his bare chest as he opened his door too. She didn't think he'd done that on purpose. She hoped not anyway. His shirt had been sodden.

'I'm sorry I caused you a hassle today,' she said. 'Please don't worry about going out to my car again. I'll call the RACQ later. There is phone service here, isn't there?'

For the first time, his face creased in a genuine smile and she thought what a good looking man he was. Rugged and tanned, but he had a nice face. Kind.

Braden got out and walked around to her side of the car. 'Ah, sort of. We hook up via satellite, so I'll try to get your mobile and computer connected to our network later. If we can't get you set up, there's a house phone hooked up to the satellite. You're quite welcome to use that whenever you need to.'

'Oh, okay.' She picked up her small backpack and turned, sliding her legs down the side of the seat, and jumped to the ground next to him. 'See you in a while, Petie.'

She waited at the bottom of the four steps while Braden took her two suitcases and laptop case from the back of the ute. He carried them up to the veranda.

When he came back down the steps, Callie looked past him and stepped back so he could get past her to his ute. 'Is there a front door key?' she asked.

'No. They're never locked. Don't worry, it's safe out here. We never lock doors.'

Hmm, she thought, not very happy with the idea of not being able to lock her door at night.

'Okay, I guess I'm used to the city. I'll have to get used to being in the outback.'

'If it makes you more comfortable, I'm sure we can sort something.'

'It's okay. I'll get used to it.' Callie watched as he went back to the ute, climbed in and started the engine.

Or put a chair against the door.

There were a lot of things she was going to have to get used to. Back with kids, teaching, being with strangers, no working phone, not to mention the isolation.

And this prefab hut was very different to her elegant house in Brisbane.

Even though she'd known she was coming to the outback, she'd not considered the vast distances and the isolation or the rough way she was going to live. It had taken forever to come down that rough road where she'd left her car and had almost lost her luggage. Embarrassment heated her cheeks as she realised how unprepared she was and how stupid she must have looked.

They didn't lock doors and she'd put her luggage in a ditch to keep it safe. Oh well, it would give the girls a laugh when she told them.

With a shrug, Callie headed to the steps as the ute took off in a cloud of red dust. She smiled when Petie waved to her. He was a cute little kid, but she wasn't too sure about the other two. The older one—Rory—had spent a lot of time quietly watching her.

But there was no need to worry about that. As long as she had the parents' support she could handle them. It might have been a while, but she'd dealt with kids with worse behaviour than Nigel when she was at Barfield State School, and his father had reacted appropriately when he'd been rude.

Pulling a face as she walked up the steps to the narrow veranda, she tried to get her responses into teacher mode. After all, that's what she was here for. She was good with kids, and she was usually a good judge of people. Well, she had been once until Greg pulled the wool over her eyes. So she'd be very wary with anyone she met out here. She still hadn't made a call on Braden Cartwright, but her instincts were saying she could trust him.

Keep to herself, not talk about her life or background, while she got herself settled and then decided what she wanted to do with the rest of her life.

Stuff the biological clock. Family and motherhood were no longer an option for her.

Until she'd learned how to be a better judge of people, Callie wasn't going to trust anyone here. Not even the Cartwright family, no matter how kind Braden seemed. He'd probably just been trying to make a good impression saving her luggage; anyone would.

Greg wouldn't have dived into a dirty channel, she thought.

With a shrug, she pushed the door open, and was met by a musty smell overlaid with disinfectant. The donga was basic. One bedroom, a living area with a small television, and a compact kitchenette on one wall. There were two doors at the back. Pushing the first one open she was met by a functional but clean small bathroom and toilet. The other door opened up to a bigger veranda with two plastic chairs and a table. The wind ruffled the water of a small dam not far from the back fence.

Callie stood for a moment looking out over the flat arid land to the west. The sun shimmered in the dust as it headed towards the horizon. There was an eerie quiet and there was no sign of any life. No cattle, no cars, no people. One single tree sat between her donga and the horizon.

And that suited her just fine. Isolation was what she'd wanted, and isolation was what she'd got. Her spirits lifted a little as Callie turned back inside to her new home.

If donga meant small and plain, that's what she was in, but she would cope. It was a bit disconcerting to think this was home for the next who knew how long. It was very different to her beautiful house in the leafy suburb back in Brisbane. That graceful old Queenslander had been her grandparents' house, and they'd left it to her. Dad had always encouraged her to sell it, but she'd hung onto it.

'You can travel, love, and you'll never have any money problems if you invest your cash wisely,' he'd said. 'It needs too much work to hang on to.'

'No, Dad, I love that house. I'll rent it out for the time being, and I'll live there one day when I can afford to do it up.'

She'd never dreamed that day would come so soon. When her parents had been killed in that horrific accident on the Autobahn in Germany Callie had moved out of the family home and sold that.

Not being able to handle being there without her parents, she'd put the proceeds of the sale and her inheritance into doing up her grandparents' home, and she'd moved in when it was finished.

Greg had tried over and over to talk her into selling it and invest the proceeds in a share portfolio, but that was the one place she had managed to hold firm. Maybe that was when he had started to lose interest in her—or her potential as a gravy train.

And now thanks to him—or if she was fair—thanks to *her* bad choices, her beautiful home on an acre across the road from the Brisbane River was sitting empty while she was out here in a "donga".

Callie pushed away the negative thoughts as she had a quick shower, and then left the wet suitcase out on the small veranda— there'd be time for that later—and headed across the hard dirt to the main house.

She would be fine.

Chapter 15

Braden settled Rory and Petie in front of the TV with a sandwich and withstood the angry glare from Nigel as he took him to his room after he'd been to the bathroom.

'You can read a book while you eat your sandwich, and then when I've had my shower, we're going to have a chat in the office.'

'Whatever,' Nigel said sullenly.

Braden put the plate with the sandwich on the chair and held his temper as he closed the door. The last thing Nigel needed was temper, and Braden's temper had been on a knife edge since the boys had come home. He loved his sons and he loved having them home—he knew it was where they should be—but he carried so much guilt he worried he wouldn't be enough for them. His anger was at himself for abandoning his boys. Since they had come home—or since Sophie had insisted they come to him—Braden's mind and heart had been forced out of that dark place where he had hidden any feelings for the past two years. He had handled his grief so badly; the boys had suffered more because of his actions.

Before Sophie had taken the boys to their place, and on the too few occasions he'd seen them when she'd brought them back to the station, Braden had known that Nigel was the child who had struggled most with Julia's death.

A surge of fresh guilt rose from his chest as he sat on the side of his bed and dropped his head into his hands, uncaring of the red mud on his trousers. He'd thought that his middle son had improved, and Sophie had told him that Nigel's night terrors had stopped over the past year, but his son's behaviour today told him differently.

Maybe he should have taken the boys to grief counselling like Sophie told him he should.

But he'd thought they were too young.

Shit, he hadn't even gone to the one appointment he'd made in town with the visiting counsellor. Damn it all, he had enough problems dealing with the situation himself. What was the good of talking to someone you didn't even know? Braden carried his own guilt close to his heart and couldn't see the point of sharing it. It wasn't going to bring Julia back.

Nothing would ever bring back his wife and the mother of his children. If he'd known what that day was going to bring he would have stopped her going out to that bloody horse. The first thing

Braden had done when he'd come back from the hospital was ring Kent and ask him to take Taffee away.

At least with his boys back home with him he could make sure they were safe. Keep them safe and then work on their happiness—and Nigel's behaviour. Show them how much he loved them and make up for being an absent father.

Braden stood slowly and rubbed his hands over his face before he headed for the shower.

##

Ten minutes later, scrubbed clean of red mud and without the sour smell of the bore water coming from his hair and skin, Braden headed for the kitchen via the boys' room. Rory and Nigel had twin bunks and Petie's bed was across the big room under the window. They'd chosen the room with the bunks so they could be together. Petie played in there with his toys, but spent most nights in Braden's bed.

Braden had closed up the house at the other side of the breezeway where the master bedroom suite and the boys' old room were. He never went in there. Julia's clothes and possessions were untouched. Strangely the boys hadn't shown any interest in going there either. One day soon he'd tackle it and have a sort out. That was way past time too.

As he walked down the hall Braden frowned and stopped outside the boys' bedroom door. It was closed. Opening the door quietly, he stuck his head in the room.

'Nigel?' He frowned as he looked around; there was no sign of his son. The noise of the television blared down the hall and Braden pursed his lips and headed to the living room.

Disobedient little tyke.

Rory and Petie were sprawled on the floor. But there was no sign of their brother. 'Has Nigel been in here?' he asked.

No response as the blare of the cartoon filled the room.

'Rory!' This time his voice was like a gunshot and he immediately regretted it as Rory jumped and Petie's eyes widened.

'Sorry, guys. Have you seen Nigel?'

Rory stared at him for a moment and then shook his head. 'No, Dad. He's in our room.'

'He might have gone to the bathroom again. How about a Paddle Pop when I come back?' he added by way of an apology.

'Is Nigel in big trouble, Dad?' Rory asked tentatively.

'No, mate. He just needs to learn a few more manners.'

'Maybe you need to give him a clip under the ear when he's naughty.'

Braden froze and stared at Rory. 'I don't think so. You know Mum and I always said that hitting kids to get them to be good was a bad way for parents to behave. And where did you hear that expression anyway?'

Rory put his head down and mumbled. 'Doesn't matter.'

Braden crouched down in front of him. 'It does to me. I don't ever want you to think that I would do or say that.'

'Uncle Jock used to clip Nigel. He told him he was a waste of space.'

'Did he now?'

Rory's eyes glistened with tears. 'I thought you might have changed and might be like Uncle Jock too. I don't want you to get cranky. That's why I've been really good since we came home. Uncle Jock said you didn't want us home, and I'm cranky with Nigel for stuffing it up. You won't send us back there, will you, Dad? If you do I'll be really angry at Nigel for saying "shit" to the teacher lady.'

Braden's heart broke. It was a physical feeling that pressed hard on his chest. He plonked his bum on the floor and held his arms out to Rory. 'Come here, mate.'

He put his arms around his boy, and blinked moisture away from his eyes as Rory's arms crept around his neck.

'Before I go and find Nigel—and no I'm not going to clip him— I want to tell you something very important. I love you guys, and I'm sorry it took so long for me to bring you home. It took me a long time to get over what happened to your mum. I'm really sorry it took me so long. I have a lot to make up to my three special boys. Things are going to change now. We're going to have a teacher for you, and I'm going to get someone to come and help us cook, and someone to help us in the house and garden. And I'll be here as much as I can. I love you three. You guys and Aunty Sophie are my life.'

'Can I start to come out to the cattle with you? I'm eight now.'

Braden ruffled Rory's hair. 'I think that's a good idea.'

'Me too, Daddy?' A little hand tugged at his T-shirt.

'We'll see. Maybe Miss Young will bring you out after your school hours when I'm working the paddocks close to the house. How would that be, Petie?'

'That would be good.'

'Now give me a big hug, both of you, and I'll go and get Nigel.'

'And then our Paddle Pops,' Petie said.

'You don't miss a trick, do you, mate?' Braden pushed himself to his feet. 'I'll be back in a minute. Nigel and I just have to have a little bit of a talk.'

Anger seethed through him at the things Rory had said about Jock. He would follow that through later when the boys were in bed.

Braden headed up the hall. The toilet door usually left open was shut. He stood outside and tapped on the door. 'Nige? You okay? You in there, mate?'

There was no reply.

Braden tapped on the door again and when there was no response, he turned the door handle. It was locked.

'Nigel! Unlock the door! Or answer me!' Worry rippled down into his stomach and formed a hard lump.

Braden turned and raced to the kitchen and flung open the second drawer under the counter beside the stove. As he scrabbled through the assortment of bits and pieces—string, bottle tops and sticky tape—in search of the screwdriver he knew was in there, there was a tap at the kitchen door.

'Hello?'

'Yes!' he answered impatiently as his fingers curled around the yellow-handled screwdriver. He looked up as Callie Young pushed the door open. 'Sorry. The boys are in the living room.' Then he realised she didn't know where that was so he hurried over to the door. 'I've got a bit of an emergency.'

'Can I help?'

He almost didn't recognise her because she looked very different to the hot and red-faced woman with the red bandanna wrapped around her head.

Callie Young had showered and damp, dark brown hair hung in ringlets on her shoulders. Fair skinned, delicate shoulders that had been left bare by a strappy sundress. And all the makeup was gone from her face. Her cheeks were flushed a slight pink. He hadn't realised what a pretty girl she was.

Braden immediately killed that thought. 'I've lost Nigel,' he said gruffly. 'I'm worried he's in the toilet and crook. The door's locked from the inside.' He held up the screwdriver. 'Can you keep an eye on the other pair for me. Just follow the sounds of the TV. I said they can have a Paddle Pop. Rory'll show you where they are.'

Before she could answer, he took off back up the hallway.

Chapter 16

Her boss's greeting that he had an emergency and to please sit with the boys and get them a Paddle Pop worried Callie. He had looked distressed as he'd disappeared with a screwdriver in hand.

As instructed, she followed the noise of the television and finally found Rory and Petie ensconced in two small bean bags on the floor of a large room where a DVD was playing at full volume.

'Ah, hello,' she ventured, but wasn't heard.

A second time. 'Hello, boys.'

Finally her loud teacher voice, 'Who wants a Paddle Pop?' gained an instant response.

Two heads flew around to see who was offering Paddle Pops.

Rory's expression was confused, but Petie recognised her straight away. His, 'Yes please, silly Callie,' brought a smile to her face.

She held out her hand. 'Maybe we could turn the TV off for a minute and you can show me where they are?'

Rory picked up the remote and pointed it at the television set like a seasoned pro. 'The Paddle Pops are in the freezer in the laundry.'

'Can you show me where the laundry is?' Callie asked with a smile. 'And then when you have them, maybe you can show me the schoolroom where we'll be doing your lessons.'

Petie took her hand and let her down a hallway followed closely by Rory and two pups. They reached the end of the hall where there was a door in the centre of the house. Petie tried to reach the handle but it was way above his little hand, even though he stood on his tippytoes. Callie leaned over and opened the door, surprised to see a wide concrete breezeway in the middle of the house.

She hadn't realised that the house was virtually split into two and wondered if maybe someone else lived in the other side.

'The freezer's over here,' Rory said. 'We're allowed to have the Paddle Pops out of the top basket.'

The boys led her to a big utility room at the back of the breezeway. Two washing machines, a clothes dryer and two large chest freezers filled the space. Assorted coats and hats hung on a large board on the adjacent wall, plus there was an assortment of boots neatly lined up beneath them. Now that she knew the washing machines were there, she'd sort out her wet clothes later.

A quick glance told her there were only men's boots there. No sign of a woman.

Rory opened the lid of the freezer on the left and pulled out three chocolate Paddle Pops. 'One for you too?' He looked at her cautiously. 'If you want one, that is?'

'No, thank you, but maybe bring that one for Nigel and we can put it in the freezer in the kitchen for when he's ready. I'll have a cuppa with your dad while we talk about my duties.'

'The scissors is in the kitchen,' Petie explained as Callie tried to tear open the shiny wrapping around the frozen treats.

Rory looked at her thoughtfully. 'So you're gonna stay? Even with Nigel being bad?'

Callie tried not to look hesitant. 'Looks like it,' she said. 'I've unpacked, and then I have to get my car fixed in town.'

A couple of minutes later, the two boys were sitting at the kitchen table eating their Paddle Pops and Callie put the third Paddle Pop in the freezer at the top of the large fridge. She was surprised to see it was almost empty. Half a bag of frozen peas sat on the shelf.

'Nigel won't be allowed to have that one,' Petie said as chocolate dribbled down his chin.

Rory shook his head. 'Probably not. He's in trouble with Dad. He's always naughty. Uncle Jock even smacked him a few times and Aunty Sophie got really cranky at him. Not at Nigel, at Uncle Jock, I mean. They had a fight about it.'

Callie raised her eyebrows, unsure of who Uncle Jock and Aunty Sophie were.

'I'm *cwanky* at Nigel too. He's being naughty,' Petie said. 'He's doing it on purpose.'

'Let's have a wash, and go outside and then the puppies can have a run around. Is that okay? Would your dad let you do that?' Callie didn't want to do the wrong thing straight up. She'd already had a bad start with Braden Cartwright.

'Yes, there's a fenced off bit out the back near their kennels. We're allowed out there as long as we look out for snakes.'

'What are their names? The puppies, I mean,' Callie asked as she picked up the facecloth that was hanging over the sink.

'Bumper and Cottie,' Rory replied. 'Nigel has one too. Cottie is the only girl so when they grow up we have to be careful that she doesn't have babies.'

Callie nodded carefully. 'Fair enough.'

'Aunty Sophie gave us our pups when we came home.'

'They're very cute.' Callie said, and wondered who Aunty Sophie was as she wiped Petie's face and hands with the cloth. She had lots of questions but it wasn't the right thing to grill the kids. She'd save them up for the interview with the boss. She turned to wipe Rory's sticky fingers, and looked up as loud footsteps pounded down the timber floor of the hallway from the other end of the house.

Braden came to the door running his hand through his hair, his brow wrinkled in a frown.

'Has anyone seen Nigel? He locked the toilet door and I thought he was in there, but when I got it open, it was his usual party trick of locking the door and shutting it from the outside. I've searched all the rooms and looked under the beds and in the wardrobes, but there's no sign of him.'

Callie shook her head. 'We went out to the laundry, and he wasn't there. We were about to go outside. Should we look out there, or try the other side of the house?'

Braden's voice was terse. 'No, it's all locked up. We don't go in there. Come and help me look outside. He won't be far away.'

But Callie could see the worry etched on his face. She was starting to wonder what the family setup was here. Had she made a big mistake?

Chapter 17

Nigel

Nigel pulled his knees up to his chest and tried to keep as still as he possibly could. Tweedle snuggled into his chest and gave a little huff in his sleep.

He'd done it again. Ruined things for everyone. He thought about running away, but there was nowhere to go. He was too little to go all the way to town, and if Tweedle ran away they could both get lost. Dad would be proud of him for thinking that.

If they lived in a town he could have found somewhere to sleep, he and Tweedle could have found food to eat; it would have been an adventure like those books Aunty Sophie had read to him at night. Someone might have adopted him. He could have had a mummy again, and a daddy who was proud of him.

Nigel blinked as hot tears pushed out of his eyes. He'd stay here for a while and see what happened. At least Dad wouldn't be angry like Uncle Jock was. Dad never hit them.

Another tear squeezed out of his eyes. He didn't want to cry. He hadn't cried when Uncle Jock had got cross, but he'd had Aunty Sophie to cuddle him then.

She didn't smell as nice as Mummy had, but her cuddles had made him feel better.

And now he'd messed everything up again. Aunty Sophie had been their mum for a while but she'd gone all funny when Petie called her Mummy, and then she'd decided to bring them home. Now they were home with their real dad.

Uncle Jock had said, 'About bloody time too.'

Nigel had missed Dad and they had all been excited when Aunty Sophie said they were coming home to their big house. And when they got their puppies, he'd been really happy.

But it was yucky without Mummy here. When he'd cried, Aunty Sophie had told him all about the lovely place where Mummy lived now and that she was watching down on them from up in the sky.

Now he'd gone and opened his big mouth—two times—and the new nanny would leave. He'd hoped that she'd want to stay and be their new mum. But now Dad would have to look after them all the time. But that wasn't too bad, because Dad wasn't as sad anymore. And Dad made the best milkshakes with ice cream.

Another two bloody tears—Nigel bit his lip hard, *don't* say bloody, it's a bad word—rolled down his cheeks and he lifted his fist and rubbed at them.

Tweedle woke up and barked once.

'Ssh, go back to sleep.'

Nigel closed his eyes and it wasn't long before he drifted off too, the little pup snuggled up under his chin.

Chapter 18

Callie followed Braden and Rory to the big shed behind the house on the opposite side to the dongas. A couple of small buildings were on the other side of the shed, flanking another long building with a verandah at ground level.

Braden must have noticed her looking around.

'That's more accommodation,' he said, 'but it's empty these days. We use contract stockmen mostly now. The permanent guys live in the original house at the back of the property where the cattle yards are.'

'Is the house fairly new?'

'Yes. My grandparents bought the property back in the nineteen sixties, and moved into the house that was already there. We built the new one.'

We? But she didn't ask.

'Could Nigel have gone to the old house?'

'No, it's about ten kilometres away. There's a back entrance to the property that joins the Charleville road. We don't use it anymore.' He shook his head. 'The road, I mean.'

'How big is the station?' Callie asked. She looked down at her sandals. She should have put boots on; her white sandals were filthy already.

Braden pushed open the two wide doors of the machinery shed, and the large space flooded with late afternoon light. If they didn't find Nigel soon, it would be dark. Petie was holding her hand firmly.

'Where do you want us to look?' she asked.

'I'll call him and then we'll look behind the machinery, up in the rafters—there's a couple of ladders—'

'He likes being in the excavator, Dad,' Rory said.

'I know, mate. We'll look in all the machines. You walk around and call Tweedle.' He turned to Callie. 'Watch where you walk here, sometimes there can be snakes in here. They chase the rats that get in the hay.'

'Oh, uh, okay.' She froze and looked down at her bare legs and flimsy—dirty—sandals, but reached down and scooped Petie up off the concrete floor. 'How about I carry you?'

'Yes, please.' The happy look on his face gave her a warm glow, but her chest was still tight with worry.

Worry for the little boy, and worry about what she'd done coming out here. All of a sudden, her problems and life back in

Brisbane seemed to disappear; her focus totally on the situation out here. 'Come on, Petie, we'll go over to this side and look in all the nooks and crannies.'

'Nigel, where are you?' She jumped as Braden's voice boomed behind her, followed soon by Rory's equally loud voice calling the dog.

'Tweedle, dinnertime,' he yelled.

The search was fruitless. Half an hour later, they made their way back to the house after searching the machinery shed, the other buildings, and what Braden called the old cookhouse.

'He's gotta be in the house somewhere.' Braden's forehead creased with worry as he pushed open the back gate. 'Rory, you feed the pups and lock them into their run, and we'll go and start doing a room by room search inside.'

'I want to go with Rory and feed Cottie too,' Petie said.

Braden nodded. 'Okay, that would be a help.'

'He wouldn't have gone over to my donga, do you think?' Callie asked as she put the little boy down onto the one patch of green grass. 'I didn't see him on the way over.'

Petie bent down and picked up his puppy, and then followed Rory. 'Bedtime, Cottie.'

Callie looked over at Braden. A pulse was ticking in his cheek.

'Has Nigel ever done this before?' she asked quietly as the boys filled the dog bowls with kibble.

'No. He can be a handful but he's not usually sneaky.' He ran a hand through his hair again making it stick up more. 'I'm sorry the day has ended like this. When we find him, we'll sit down and I'll fill you in. Can you wait out here for the other two and bring them inside when the dogs are settled. If he doesn't turn up soon, I'll ring next door and get some help.'

'Okay.'

Braden turned to the steps and Callie froze as his body tensed and he jerked to a stop. She turned around and followed his gaze. A third puppy had pushed out of the kennels and joined the other two at the food bowls.

'What the hell?' Braden exclaimed as he ran past her to the dog enclosure. Ignoring Rory and Petie and the three pups, he hurried to the last kennel in the row of six—the one that the pup had come from. Callie watched as her employer dropped to his knees and peered through the low arched opening.

'Nigel Cartwright.' His voice was low and calm. 'Found you!
Are you going to come inside and have some dinner with us?'

Chapter 19

Callie's throat closed with emotion when she saw the look on Braden's face as he picked Nigel up and rested his head on his son's hair. His eyes glinted with moisture and she held out her hands to the other two boys. There was no sign of the cranky man of this afternoon.

'Come on, you pair. Let's go and get some tea sorted, and your dad and Nigel can lock the dogs in.' She assumed the dogs would be locked in.

'Thank you, Callie.' Braden lifted his head and his voice was husky. 'Nigel and I won't be long.'

The boys took her hand and they crossed the yard together and headed up the back steps into the kitchen. 'What do you usually have for tea?' she asked with a smile, as she wondered what Braden expected of her.

It was a crazy end to a crazy day, but she was sure she could manage to cook something for the boys' tea.

'Pizza?' Rory said hopefully. 'Can you make pizza?'

'Um, depends what's in the fridge,' she said. 'Let's go look.'

'I think Aunty Sophie left some pizzas in the fridge. She's a good pizza maker.'

Callie crossed to the fridge and opened the door of the combined upright fridge-freezer. 'We're in luck!'

As well as some pre-made pizzas there were several casserole dishes full of different meals.

The two boys waited while she took the pizzas from the fridge and put them on the bench. She tipped her head to the side. 'Ah . . . oven or microwave? And how many should I cook? I'm not used to feeding a houseful of men.'

That got a smile from Rory. 'We're not men yet. Daddy's the only man.'

'Silly Callie!' Petie piped up.

'Go and have a wash and I'll put them in one at a time, and then I'll ask Daddy how many when he comes in.'

By the time the microwave dinged three minutes later and the first pizza was cooling on the bench, she'd found the cupboard with plates in it. The table was almost set when the back door opened and Nigel walked in ahead of his father.

'Yum, pizza!'

'The other two have gone to wash their hands,' she said with a quick glance at Braden. His face was set but he did smile when Nigel looked up at him.

'Will I, Dad?'

'Yes. You can go and have a wash and hurry the other pair up. Smells like the pizza's ready. But before you do, don't you have something to do?'

Nigel came over to Callie and looked up at her. 'I'm really, really very sorry I said rude things to you, and I hope you aren't cross at me. And I really mean it—' his squeaky voice sped up '—and I'm not just saying that so you want to stay, because *we* want you to stay. We all do. A lot.'

Callie crouched down in front of the little boy. His eyes were red, and she knew he'd been crying. The look on his face broke her heart and she held out one hand. 'I accept your apology. Thank you, Nigel. I'm looking forward to settling in and getting to know you all.'

Nigel took off and Braden went to the fridge and took out a large container of juice. Callie went back to the cupboard and got out five glasses. They didn't speak.

Well, it looks like I've decided to stay, she thought.

Finally Braden came over to the benchtop where the pizza was cooling and his voice made her jump. 'Thanks, Callie. You were kind to the little demon, and I do appreciate what you've done.'

'It was pretty easy,' she said as he stared at her. Heat filled her cheeks as he kept looking. Finally he turned away and poured juice into each of the glasses.

'Should I put another pizza in the microwave?'

'Thanks, they'll eat the lot. The pizzas have been in the fridge since my sister brought the boys home a few days ago, and they're probably close to their use by date.'

'Aunty Sophie?'

'Yes, my sister, Sophie. She's responsible for all that food in the fridge. We were on our way to town to stock up the pantry when we came across you this afternoon.'

He handed her one of the glasses, and took a swig of his juice. Putting the glass down on the bench, his expression was rueful. 'I could really do with something stronger than this. It's been a day and a half, but we do need to sit and have a chat. The boys can have the pizzas and I'll put one of the casseroles in the big oven and we'll eat after they've gone to bed.' His eyes were dark as he looked over his glass at her. 'Is that alright with you?'

She nodded slowly, but she knew her voice was hesitant. 'We have to talk, and we have to eat, so it makes sense. Can I just ask one thing before the boys come back?'

'Yes?'

'Is it just you and the three boys here?'

'It is. Didn't the job agency fill you in on us?'

'I'm not sure. I might have been a bit stressed when she was telling me about the station and the trip out here.'

The conversation drew to a halt when there was yelling from the hallway and the three boys raced into the kitchen.

Callie lifted the plate with the pizza on it, and put it in the centre of the table, and then slid the second one into the microwave and set the timer. The whole time she was aware of Braden's eyes on her and she felt uncomfortable.

And she didn't even have a car if she had wanted to leave, or a lock on her door to make her feel secure through the night that loomed ahead. Not that she was intimidated by him, or even wary. She sensed he was a good man. A good man in a difficult situation that she hadn't worked out yet.

They were here with no mother or wife and the boys had been away with his sister.

She looked up and encountered his gaze still on her. Lifting her chin with a steadiness she didn't quite feel, she held his gaze. 'While the boys eat, and before we have our chat, could I please use the phone to let my . . . my family know I've arrived safely.'

He didn't need to know she had no family. And she wanted to tell Jen exactly where she was.

'Of course.' Braden finally looked away and gestured to the hall. 'The second door on the right is my study. The phone's on the desk.'

'Thank you.' Callie looked down and hurried out of the room. 'I won't be long.'

'Take your time.'

Chapter 20

By the time the microwave dinged that the third pizza was ready, the first two had been demolished. The boys were quiet as they shovelled ham and pineapple pizza into their mouths and Braden knew he was going to have to do something about their table manners. They'd gone downhill in the months they'd been with Sophie and Jock. But he wasn't going to say anything to them because he knew Nigel was still fragile.

After he and Callie worked out her duties, he'd give Sophie a call. Many of the things that Nigel told him had left Braden uneasy. He didn't like the thought of Sophie being in a relationship with Jock either. He'd never been terribly impressed with him, but he figured Sophie loved him and had seemed happy, so he didn't say anything. He was polite and welcoming to Jock when they visited, but it had been hard work when they'd lived in the donga for a few months.

Sophie had taken up with Jock a few weeks after Julia's accident. He'd arrived to help with the muster, and had flown the helicopter from *Lara Waters*. His mate, Kent, didn't have much time for Jock but Braden had always put that down to Kent still carrying a torch for Sophie.

'He's got an eye to the main chance, that one,' Kent said one afternoon as they watched Sophie and Jock ride in from the paddocks. 'Just watch him.'

As Braden stood to get some ice cream for the boys, he heard Callie's voice coming from the study, and he smiled when she laughed. She was probably telling her family about leaving her luggage in the irrigation channel.

'Daddy?' Petie's mouth was ringed by red sauce and Braden picked up the paper towel that was in the middle of the table.

'Yes, mate?'

'I like Silly Callie. Aw, don't rub so hard.'

'That's good. I like her too. But maybe she doesn't like being called Silly Callie.'

'I'll ask her,' Petie said importantly.

And Braden did like her, he wasn't just saying that. His first impression had been way off, but she'd been a trooper since they'd got home. Pitched in and helped search for Nigel without a murmur, and hadn't been precious like he'd first expected. He'd been too quick to judge her on the long red nails, the designer clothes, and the expensive luggage. And that sports car.

Despite what Callie had said about dealing with it herself, he'd call Anderson's garage in town tomorrow and get them to come and tow it there at his expense.

Braden served out three bowls of ice cream and then opened the fridge and looked at the neatly labelled containers. With a nod, he pulled out a chicken curry. As he opened the pantry to check if there was rice, Callie came back into the kitchen. Her cheeks were flushed and her hair was mussed as though she'd been running her fingers through it. She had beautiful hair and he wondered if the deep auburn glints under the light were natural.

'Wow, you guys. You must have been hungry,' she said with a grin. Her whole face lit up as she smiled at the boys and Braden found it hard to look away. 'Pizza's all gone and now ice cream!'

'We were,' Rory replied.

Braden was surprised at how quickly the three boys had accepted Callie into the household, and how easy they were with her. It was as though she'd been there for ages, and not just a few short hours. Nigel had apologised for being rude to her, and Petie obviously adored her already. His Sophie love had transferred already. Rory was slower to trust; he was the one most like Braden. He sat back and observed.

If she stayed—and he was hoping now she would—maybe things would be a lot easier.

'Okay, you lot, let's head for the shower, and then Callie and I are going to have a talk about your lessons.'

'Would you like me to do something in here?' she asked.

'I took out a curry and I was about to look for some rice. Does that suit you?'

'Sounds good. You go and deal with the boys and I'll poke around in the kitchen.'

Their eyes met and held and they shared a look of understanding as Nigel stood close to Braden.

'Say goodnight to Ms Young, guys.'

'Callie, please,' she said. 'If that's okay with you. Or Miss Callie.'

'Good night, Silly Callie,' Petie interrupted and they all chuckled.

'Goodnight, Miss Callie,' Rory said shyly, and Nigel repeated the same words.

'Night boys, sleep well. I'll see you in the morning.'

'I won't be long,' Braden said.

Callie was thoughtful as she opened the pantry looking for rice.
Maybe being here was going to be okay.

Chapter 21

'Come on in, Ms Callie. I thought we might make a totally new start.' Braden smiled and held the door of the study open for her.

Callie stepped through in front of him. 'Sounds like a good plan. It's been a strange start.'

She walked over to the desk and he stood and waited for her to sit down before he sat on the other side, the same chair she'd sat in when she'd chatted to Jen. She had shared many of the events of the trip, and the dust storm, with her friend; but about the job, she'd simply told her that she had arrived and the family were good. Jen had her laughing unexpectedly about a phone call from Greg, wanting to know where Callie and *his* car and *his* luggage were.

'Bastard,' Jen had said. 'So I told him you'd flown to Tahiti. He fell for it hook, line and sinker.'

'Oh, Jen. You're a shocker.'

Now Callie turned her attention back to Braden Cartwright as he held his hand out over the desk.

'Good evening, Ms Callie. I'm Braden Cartwright. Welcome to *Kilcoy Station*.'

'Thank you, Mr Cartwright. I'm very pleased to be here.'

'Braden, please.'

'Or Mr Braden?' Callie couldn't help saying with a smile.

'Braden is just fine, thank you, Callie.' Her boss leaned back in his chair and his shoulders relaxed. He'd gone in to check on the boys after they'd eaten while she'd loaded the dishwasher. Conversation over their quick dinner had been general, about the weather and the local district and the cattle that he ran on the station. Nothing personal or job wise had been discussed.

'Boys are all asleep?'

'Petie and Nigel are. I let Rory read for a while, but he's under a promise to turn the light out at eight o'clock. He's a good kid. He will.'

'They're all good kids,' Callie said slowly. 'You should be proud of them.'

'I am.' Braden reached up and ran his hand through his hair. She'd already noticed that he did that when he was stressed.

'Shall I tell you a bit about my background, and then you can tell me what you see as my role here?' She thought she'd ease into the conversation.

'I think I need to tell you about our situation first. You may decide it's not for you. I'm sorry the agency woman didn't explain it to you in Brisbane. You might have driven a long way for nothing.'

'So far I like what I see, and being out here, a long way from the city, suits me well,' she said carefully. 'For the time being.'

He nodded slowly and began. 'The three boys have been living with their aunt. My sister.' Braden steepled his fingers in front of him and looked at her. Really looked at her as though waiting for a reaction. As though she should judge him in some way.

She nodded. 'I picked that up. Aunt Sophie.'

And then waited while he stood and turned to a minibar fridge in the corner. 'I'm going to have one drink. Can I offer you one?'

She shrugged. 'Why not?'

'I have white wine or whisky.'

'Whisky on ice if you have ice.'

His eyebrows raised, her response obviously surprising him. 'Coming up.'

A moment later he sat again and placed two glasses with ice and a finger of whisky in each on the table.

He raised his glass and held it up. 'Cheers.'

'Cheers,' she replied, taking a sip as the fiery liquid warmed her throat.

Braden sipped at his and put the glass down. 'My wife and I went to Scotland for our honeymoon, and I discovered fine whisky.' He didn't draw breath and stared at the wall behind her as he continued talking. 'We came back to the station and worked together to build it into a successful concern. We had good seasons and Julia brought a lot of experience from her family cattle station in the Gulf Country. The boys came along, and then Julia was . . . was—' He picked up the glass and drained it.

Callie tensed. She dreaded what was coming.

Braden's voice was flat. 'Julia was killed in an accident. Just over two years ago. I didn't cope. Sophie and her partner took the boys for a while as I dealt with the fallout from the accident. When the coronial investigation was over, I fell in a heap and the boys stayed there. They came back last week and we're making do. I advertised for a nanny and here you are. And before you worry, the finding was accidental death. My wife was crushed by a horse in a storm.'

Coronial investigation? No wonder he had done it so hard. Callie's throat dried and she picked up her glass and sipped until a piece of ice stayed in her mouth. Finally she was able to speak. 'I'm very sorry to hear that.'

'Thank you. I've learned to cope, but I was worried about the boys coming back. I didn't know if I was capable of looking after them. Sophie and her partner decided to move away and she turned up here with the boys and a stack of food last week. Without warning. She figured that was the best way.' He finally looked at her. 'And you know what? I've surprised myself. I guess being a father and loving your kids helps you cope and you know instinctively what to do. It's been easy with them back. The caring part I mean. But not the dealing with their physical needs. Sophie gave me a list of what she said I needed, and I just shot off the nanny request to the agency.' He expelled a breath and she knew how hard it must have been to tell her all that. He sure wasn't holding back, and she appreciated his honesty.

'And you ended up with me. You probably could have done better. I'm just a teacher, but I haven't taught for three years.'

'Callie, so far, your interaction with the boys has been great. They have their problems. Nigel, well, Nigel, you've experienced firsthand. Rory is very wary, and Petie doesn't like to sleep by himself. As far as Rory and Nigel's schooling, Sophie lived closer to town, and they've been going to school in Augathella. It's too far for me to drive them in, so this week they've been home with me while I got sorted. I guess I must have told the agency woman that, and that's how she looked for someone with teaching experience.'

'So tell me what you need.' Callie bit her lip waiting for his response.

Braden did that hand through the hair thing again. 'There's too much for one person. I have to get back out with the cattle as soon as I can—there's a big muster coming up next month. It was Sophie's idea to hire help and she left me a list. You were the first one I asked the agency to fill. Someone for the boys. The rest can fall into place.'

'A list?'

Braden rummaged through the papers on the desk and picked up a piece of A4-sized paper with handwriting on it. He passed it over to her silently.

Callie took it and scanned down the list. 'This many staff would cost you a fortune.' He looked at her strangely and she shook her head. 'Unless you could get one person to do the lot. But this? A fulltime nanny to look after the boys,' she read aloud. 'A housekeeper to keep the house clean, do the washing and ironing. Three days a week. A gardener and a landscaper to keep the yard tidy for them to play in. Someone to drive them to school, and Petie to kindy, unless you find a teacher.' Callie lifted her head and looked at him. 'Well, you've found a teacher.'

'That's one thing ticked off the list, I guess.' He gestured to her glass. 'Would you like another drink?'

'Just a small one with lots of ice and some water, this time please.' A pleasant looseness had filled Callie's limbs and the tension of the day had eased. She was here at the cattle station, and even though it was a bit of a situation here, they were getting sorted and she was hopeful.

And not once in the past hour had she thought of *her* situation or Greg.

Braden rose and came back with their glasses refreshed. 'So, what do you think? Are you interested in taking on the teaching? Living out here? Putting up with us? It's isolated, but we do have some social things with the properties around occasionally if you wanted some entertainment.'

Callie shook her head. 'That's the last thing I want to do. I'm here for peace and quiet.'

He looked at her curiously when she didn't elaborate further. She had enough to think about and wasn't about to complicate matters by sharing her story.

'I'd like to have some time to think about it and then talk to the boys' teachers and see what they're up to. I don't have any doubts that I can take over their lessons, but that doesn't solve the rest of your problems.'

'How about you think about it over the next couple of days? We have to get your car sorted, and we have to go to town to get some groceries.'

'That sounds like a plan. It won't hurt the boys to have some time off. We can catch them up on their work. And I'm sure they need to spend some time with you and settle into being at home again.' Callie put her glass down and stood up. 'Thank you for being so honest with me, Braden. I've got a bit to think about. I'm tired and I'm going to head to bed now.'

'I'll walk you over.' As he stood, the phone on the desk rang.

Callie shook her head. 'I'm fine. You get that. I saw a torch in the laundry. Good night. I'll see you in the morning.'

Braden nodded and turned to the phone as she left the study. 'Soph,' she heard him say. 'I was going to call you later.'

Chapter 22

Braden leaned back in the desk chair. He was happy with the way the day had finally worked out and really hoped that Callie Young would decide to stay.

'Did the nanny arrive?' Sophie's voice dropped in and out as she spoke and Braden could only just hear some of her words.

'Yes, she did. A few dramas getting here, but all's well, I think. We were just winding up a meeting about her duties.'

'And? What's she like?'

Braden took his time answering. 'I think she should work out, if she decides to stay.'

'Why wouldn't she?'

'Ah, let me see, Soph. Maybe because we are hundreds of miles from anywhere. Maybe because I have three boys who have undergone some pretty serious psychological trauma, and maybe because the house is a mess and the pantry is bare. Is that enough to deter a young woman from the city?'

'How young?'

'I don't know, but she graduated her teaching degree about six years ago.'

'See that's why you need a housekeeper too. Someone to shop and cook for you.'

'Hang on a minute. I know I need help, but I don't want to fill my house with strangers. If anything happens up there and you ever want to come home you know you're always welcome.'

'What would happen?' his sister snapped back and that was so un-Sophie like, Braden knew straight away there was a problem.

'Are you okay, sis?'

There was a long silence and for a while Braden thought the call had dropped out.

'Wait,' she finally said. 'The service is patchy in here. Hang on, I'll go outside.'

Braden switched the speakerphone on and waited. He could hear Sophie telling Jock she was going outside. He frowned as raised voices came down the line and he heard Jock say 'your bloody family.'

If that guy did anything to hurt his little sister, he would have Braden to deal with. Finally he heard a door closing and then footsteps, and then some scuffling noises before Sophie came back on.

'I'm here again.'

'Where are you?'

The responding giggle was more like his little sister. 'I'm sitting up in a tree near the front gate.'

'Sounds like you. What's the place like?'

'Hot, wet, smelly.'

'Ah, just like home, plus the wet,' Braden quipped. 'Mind you, we were wet here today, but that's a story for when you come home.'

'What makes you think I'll be coming home?' Again the shrewish tone.

'Well, I was hoping that you would come back and visit one day.'

Braden tensed when a strangled sob sounded over the speaker. He bit back the question that was on his lips and waited. The way Sophie was tonight he didn't want to ask questions about Jock.

Finally the waiting paid off.

'I think I've made a mistake, Bray.'

'What sort of mistake, Soph?'

'I don't like it here, and Jock's being . . . being difficult.'

'Come home. And I'm not just saying that because of the boys. I worry about you. I worry that Jock's not right for you.'

'It's not that. He's just unsettled about the change, and he'll calm down.'

'Why would he need to calm down?' Braden decided to say his piece. 'I wasn't happy to hear that he'd been hitting Nigel.'

Another stifled sob.

'Has he hit *you*, Sophie?' Braden's voice was quiet.

'Only once. But it was because he was drunk.'

'I'll give the bastard drunk.'

'I shouldn't have told you. You've got enough to worry about.'

'You're my little sister, and of course I worry about you.'

'It's all good. I'll settle down. He'll settle down. The place is pretty, but it hasn't stopped raining since we unpacked. That's what's making us both moody.'

'Just remember I'm at the end of a phone call. I'll drive up and get you. All you have to do is ask.' Braden clenched his jaw and stared at the window. It was dark outside now, and he hoped that Callie had made her way back to the donga safely.

'I know you would and I love you for it. I'll keep in touch and let you know how I'm doing. I won't make any rash decisions. I'll give it a few weeks. And Bray?'

'Yes.'

'Give those three gorgeous little men a big kiss from Aunty Sophie. And promise you won't worry about me. You've got enough on your plate there. I'm okay. Probably PMT.'

'Too much information. I'll give you a call tomorrow night and let you know what we get sorted here. We're going into town tomorrow to do some shopping, and for Callie to call into the school.'

'Okay. If you need anything, give me a call. Love you, Bray.'

'Love you too, sis. Remember I'm here, won't you?'

'I will.'

Braden put the phone on the desk and walked over to the window. Flurries of dust hung in the faint light cast by the outside lights. It was going to be windy tomorrow according to the forecast, and the cattle were always skittish when it was windy. Not that he'd have time to get out there for a couple of days.

He rubbed his chin and was surprised at how rough it was. He must have looked like a hobo today.

The light was on inside the donga so it looked as though Callie had got back there safely.

Sitting talking to her had been easy, and it had been nice to have a chat and a drink with someone at the end of the day.

Although it mightn't be a good habit to get into. He was worried enough about having more strangers in the house, but Sophie was right. Hiring more help was the only solution if he wanted to keep the boys.

And he would not do anything that jeopardised that.

Before he reached the door of the study on his way to check on the boys, his phone trilled again.

'Soph?' he said quickly.

'No mate, it's Kent. I've got some great news. Jon Ingram's back in the district and he's looking for a job.'

'You bloody beauty,' Braden exclaimed. 'I've still got his number. I'll grab him before anyone else does. Thanks for the heads up, mate.'

Chapter 23
Monday

Braden's spirits were high as he backed the ute out of the big shed the following morning. Petie had slept in his own bed all night, the boys had been well behaved at breakfast and hadn't complained that they were out of cereal.

Jon Ingram had called him straight back and agreed to come and work for at least six months. The load that news took off Braden's shoulders contributed to his good mood and he grinned.

Nigel had gone out to feed the dogs without a complaint, and came back in whistling. When Callie Young had appeared at the back door as they were loading the dishwasher, Braden had been startled by the thump his heart gave when she'd walked into the kitchen, and he frowned now as he brought the ute around.

Don't know where that came from, he thought. And it wouldn't be doing it again. It was just his good mood and the novelty of seeing a woman. The blue skirt and colourful top were bright and cheery, and Callie's hair was pulled back from her face in a braid. The shadows had left her eyes and she looked fresh and attractive.

Petie was on one side holding her hand, and Nigel on the other. Rory was looking grown up with his hair slicked back, and standing a little way off to the side. He and Nigel were excited about going back to school to see their friends, and Braden had agreed if it was all right with their teacher they could stay at school while he did the groceries and went to the produce store, and Callie spoke to the their teachers. He'd called Kimberley Riordan—the deputy principal and long-time friend—at home to make an appointment for Callie.

'Come in any time, Braden. I'm off face-to-face teaching this morning, and I can fit her in whenever you get here. How are the boys?'

'They're good. Excited to have a nanny.'

'I'll look forward to chatting to her.'

Braden had smiled to himself. If Callie wasn't up to scratch, Kimberley would tell him.

Callie smiled at him tentatively as she stood in the doorway flanked by his sons. She looked like a teacher today, and her appearance was hard to reconcile with the woman striding away from her broken down sports car.

The trip into town was quiet. Callie took a great interest in the landscape, but he suspected it was so they didn't have to make small talk. Plus he'd been a bit brusque yesterday, but he thought he'd cleared the air last night.

A couple of times he went to speak to her but the first time, Nigel interrupted, and the second time she was intent on the view.

A harsh and rugged view that he knew every inch of, but the sky was clear again today and the light didn't seem as harsh as usual. The distant mountains had a misty blue glow and the irrigated paddocks beneath provided a rare green patch in the arid red dirt.

Fifteen minutes into the trip, they approached the section of the road where she'd left her car. As they approached, Callie stared ahead, and sat up straight and then turned to Braden.

'Isn't this where my car was?'

'It is. But the garage has already been out and put it on a truck and taken it back into town. I called them first thing. Old Jim Anderson opens up at seven.'

'Thank you,' she said quietly. 'I appreciate it.'

'Just have to wait and see what he says about it. Looked like a wheel bearing to me. Those low sports cars aren't built for our roads.'

'I know.' She pulled a rueful face. 'Something else I've learned. We city slickers are pretty naïve about the outback.'

'When it gets fixed, it might be better to leave it in storage in town. You can use Sophie's Camry wagon. She left it for whoever came out here to use. There's a seat in it for Petie too.'

'I'll see what they say at the school.'

So far, Callie hadn't given him any indication of whether she'd accept the job, and a little ripple of worry settled in his gut.

Hopefully by the time the day was over he'd have an answer. He really hoped it was a yes.

***

'Are you registered with QCT?' the deputy principal asked Callie after they had discussed the boys' progress.

'Yes, I have full registration.'

'And from what I understand, Braden doesn't have time to drive them into town to attend school.'

'That's correct. I believe that when his sister had the boys, she lived close to town and drove them in each day.'

'She did.' Kimberley sat back in the chair and picked up a pen and tapped it on the desk. 'Braden has given permission for me to share the boys' history and files with you.'

Both Nigel and Rory were achieving to the standard required, but Kimberley Riordan, the deputy, had concerns about them being taught at home. 'I'll be direct, Callie. I'm sure you're a suitable teacher, but the boys need to be at school. They need the contact with other children, they need to socialise and experience a normal school day. They've both had sessions with the school counsellor on various occasions over the past year, and Nigel in particular is carrying some unresolved issues.'

'I don't think the grief of losing a mother is ever resolved at any age, do you?' Although as a teacher, Callie could see the deputy's point and she understood where she was coming from.

'Of course it's not.' Kimberley looked at Callie and moisture sheened her eyes. 'Callie, we're a small town and a tight community. The circumstances of Julia's death were awful.' She removed a tissue from the box on the desk and dabbed at her eyes. 'As well as me going to school with Braden, Julia was my best friend, and I've known the two oldest boys since they were born. So as well as a professional interest, I also have a personal interest in seeing what's best for them. Nigel has been in my class this year, and I've seen his behaviour worsen as the terms passed.'

'Yes, in the two days since I arrived, I've seen some issues arise. He's a little boy who is hurting. I totally understand your concerns, and to allay them please know I've had a lot of experience with troubled children. Not recently, but in my three years at my school. If it reassures you, I'll send you a copy of my school references.'

'So you left the system and you've been working as a governess for a while?'

Callie had been so intent on listening to Kimberley and trying to find the best solution for the boys she'd forgotten all about her fear of being recognised. Guilt tugged at her. In the scheme of things, her worry was about a superficial situation. There were two little boys here, whose education—and happiness—depended on her honesty.

She drew a deep breath. 'No. This is the first position I applied for.'

'But you've been in education?'

'No.' Callie lifted her head and looked directly at Kimberley. 'I was working for a television network in Brisbane.' She waited for any recognition, but there appeared to be none. She swallowed. 'I'll be honest with you, Kimberley.'

'Please.'

'Leaving teaching was a wrong move. I wasn't in a good place. I'd just lost my parents—'

'You understand loss,' Kimberley said quietly.

'I do. Then I made some errors of judgment in a relationship, and in my career, and a recent event led to me quitting my job at the network, and thinking about my future and what I really want.' She shrugged and stared down at her hands, surprised to see them curled tightly in her lap. She forced herself to take a breath and relax. 'What I'd wanted was to get married and have a family, but that didn't work out. So all my energy now is going back into teaching. Let's just say I knew it was going to be easier out of the city. I applied for the job with the Cartwrights—not knowing the situation—but now that I do, I'm prepared to stay. I just wanted to see the boys' progress, before I made a final decision. I haven't told Braden yet.'

'Callie? I've got an idea. Give me ten minutes.' Kimberley gestured to the coffee machine on a round table near the office window. 'Make yourself a coffee and keep an open mind. I won't be too long.'

Callie nodded and walked over to the table and chose a coffee pod from the selection. Soon the aroma of brewing coffee filled the small office. Standing at the window, she looked out over the playground and smiled. It was morning break time and she could see Rory and Nigel playing handball. Kimberley was right; they needed to be at school but they lived too far out of town to be driven in every day.

Or did they?

But the problem was if she offered to drive them in, and they attended school she'd be out of a job. With a frown, she bit her lip.

Unless she agreed to take on one of the other positions that Braden's sister had listed. She didn't mind cooking, and once the house was tidied up, it wouldn't be hard to keep clean.

Her phone beeped in her pocket. She had given Braden her number so she knew when he was ready to pick them up.

I've been delayed at the rural produce store. Will be another hour. Sorry. We'll have lunch in town. That should keep Nigel happy ☺ **Braden.**

She quickly typed a reply. **No prob. Still in meeting with Kimberley. I have coffee** ☺

Callie waited at the window sipping her coffee as she watched the playground activities. Two teachers stood chatting as they did playground duty, and a group of girls with a skipping rope were counting out at the top of their voices. She felt more at home in this unfamiliar school than she ever had at Channel Eight. She'd missed the school environment; it was her happy place. Once she went back to Brisbane—eventually—she'd find a school close to home and settle back into teaching.

The door opened and Kimberley came back in followed by a young guy in a suit.

'Callie, this is Bob Hamblin, our principal.'

Bob held his hand out and Callie took it. 'Welcome to Augathella, Callie. Kimberley asked me to come in and meet you because she's had an idea that I see has merit.'

Kimberley looked intently at Callie. 'I didn't want to suggest this to you before I ran it by Bob, but he agrees that it's a good idea. I hope you do too.'

'I think I know what you're going to say and I agree. I was going to ask Braden what he thought about me driving the boys in every day, and taking on more of a nanny role at the house.'

Kimberley's smile was wide. 'You've got it half right, but what we'd like to do is offer you a casual teaching position. As you probably know, we have a shortage of teachers out here. All the new graduates want the coast or the city, and here you are dropped in our lap so to speak.'

Bob took over. 'We thought three days a week would suit both ways. You could drive the boys in, work at the school and then drive them home and then teach them at home on Thursdays and Fridays. I know it'll depend on your employer, plus you agreeing, but it would be good for the boys.'

'Also, Petie has been going to preschool three days a week and he could do that on the days that you teach. The kindy is affiliated with the school,' Kimberley added.

Callie didn't know what to say. Finally she found her voice. 'Wow. What can I say? It sounds like the ideal solution to me, but it's up to the boys' father.'

Kimberley reached over and put a hand on Callie's arm. 'I thought it might be easier for you if I spoke to Braden. After all, how long have you been here?'

'Um, not very long.'

Chapter 24
Three weeks later

'Bags, dogs, chooks, and wash,' Callie called as the boys tumbled from the Camry station wagon on Wednesday afternoon three weeks later. Braden had agreed and thought the school idea was great. The boys were happy to stay with their friends, and Callie had been at the school for three weeks and had settled into the school environment from the minute she walked in. She'd been given a Year Six class, and she wasn't teaching Rory or Nigel, but they still gained some street cred from their "nanny" being a teacher at their school.

'I'll do the dogs,' Rory called as Callie went around to the back seat and got Petie out of the booster seat.

'Aw, I don't want to feed the chooks,' Nigel whined. 'You always get to let the dogs out. Not fair.'

One look from Callie was enough to get him moving towards the chook pens.

'I'll go and get your afternoon tea on the table,' she called after them. 'Don't forget to have a really good wash in the laundry.'

'And change our school clothes,' Nigel called over his shoulder with a grin. 'And I bags feeding Bluey.'

'Can we have Milo, please, Mu …Silly Callie?' Petie asked as she swung him down to the ground.

'If you carry your bag inside,' she replied. Petie was the cutest and best behaved of the three of them, but she'd had to talk to him about him trying to call her Mummy. So far the talk had worked.

The past three weeks had been so good. The only flaw had been the disagreement with Braden about her salary. She'd told him that he was not to pay her for the three days she was teaching and he had insisted that he would.

'You can use that to hire a cleaner.'

'You're still looking after the boys on those days. You're driving in and out of town, and I'm going to pay you.'

If she'd told him that she hadn't taken the job for the money, he probably wouldn't have believed her. Callie had never got around to telling anyone here the real reason she'd left Brisbane, just that general first chat with Kimberley about wanting to get away. No one seemed to have recognised her, and her embarrassment had eased a lot.

But she still didn't want Braden to know about it. His opinion mattered to her, and she didn't want him to think less of her. The first impression she'd made had been bad enough, but she felt as though she'd redeemed herself a bit now.

It didn't really matter anymore. A flash in the pan, and surely something else would have taken over social media by now.

Maybe her reaction had been extreme—fleeing almost a thousand kilometres across the outback—but Callie was pleased she had. She was very happy with the way things had worked out.

There was only one thing that was unsettling her. Why did Braden's opinion of her matter so much?

She told herself it was because she wanted to be a good employee. It had nothing to do with the strong attraction that simmered every time she was with him. A couple of times their eyes had met and held and she had forced herself to look away.

Quickly.

That's how she had first noticed Greg. The eye contact and the long stares. And look where that had got her.

Callie shook herself from her thoughts as the back screen door slammed. 'Milo's ready,' she called.

Five minutes later, the three boys were sitting at the table eating everything she put in front of them.

'Then homework,' she said to Rory and Nigel. 'Petie, you can tell me what you learned at kindy today. You can all sit here at the kitchen table while I peel the vegetables for dinner.'

'Sh—I mean sugar, I forgot Bluey.' Nigel slid off his chair as the clatter of hooves came from the breezeway.

'Can you mix up the Denkavit by yourself?' Callie felt very knowledgeable knowing what a calf needed to drink.

'Yeah, Dad cut a two litre plastic container in half for me so I can fill the other one easier.'

'Okay, well don't be long, you've still got homework.'

Callie had never had much to do with animals but the red baby calf was the cutest little thing. The boys were hand feeding him, but the calf had taken a liking to Nigel.

Callie was cooking the evening meals and the household had settled into a routine. When she'd accepted the position at the school, she and Braden had sat down and worked out a schedule and her duties, and a salary that she had disagreed with.

'We'll see how this goes and then talk about it,' she'd said to Braden last night after the boys were in bed. Watching the way he listened to them, and interacted with them—his love and displays of affection—was heart-warming. He supervised their baths and teeth cleaning every night and then spent half an hour with the boys reading and talking. She wondered if he was trying to make up for the lost time they'd been away with their aunt and uncle. It didn't matter if the phone rang for him, or a worker came to the door, he would stay with the boys during that time. Callie had been surprised at the number of visitors over the past couple of weeks; the station wasn't as quiet as she'd first thought.

The callers were always to do with the cattle and the upcoming muster. Some were happy to leave a message, some waited the half hour until he was free.

She'd also added, 'If you only pay me for half the week, you can afford to get someone out to clean for that half the week and maybe do the yard.'

'I don't expect you to clean the house.'

'I know you don't, but your sister's right. You do need to get someone.'

'Okay, I'll work on it tomorrow.' Braden had put his head back and closed his eyes. They were sitting out on the veranda before she went back to her donga—that was part of the routine, and she'd catch him up with how the boys were doing at school.

The boys did their homework and Callie had cooked dinner by the time Braden came in and showered. Tonight she had no lessons to prepare so she was going to go back to the donga and send some emails. Braden had hooked her laptop up to the satellite network the first week she started at school, and she knew it was well past time to touch base with Jen again.

Chapter 25

As Callie was clearing the table and Braden was bathing the boys, a white ute came around the driveway and parked at the back of the house. She wiped her hands and went to the back door to greet the visitor.

A tall rangy guy carrying a small esky walked across from the ute and grinned at her as she stepped out onto the back veranda.

'G'day,' he said taking his Akubra off. 'You must be Callie. I'm Kent from next door.'

'Hello,' she replied closing the door behind her. 'Braden's just bathing the boys and then he'll read to them for a while. He'll probably be half an hour or so. Can I get you a cuppa or a drink?'

'I brought a six pack for Braden and I.' Kent held up the small esky and then headed for the outside table. 'Sit down with me and tell me about yourself while we wait for him. I've heard good reports from the school.'

Callie glanced into the kitchen and then shrugged. She was almost done in there. 'Okay, I'll just grab a soft drink.'

When she came back out with a glass of Coke and ice cubes, Kent had uncapped a beer and was looking out to the low mountain range to the west. The sky was a pale apricot and the low clouds were tinged with sunset gold. Callie sat on the chair opposite Kent, hoping that Braden wouldn't mind her socialising. 'Do you have kids at the school?' she asked.

'Hell no, I'm a confirmed bachelor,' was the laconic reply. 'My sister works there. Jacinta. Have you met her?'

'I have. She teaches kindy. Does she live out here too? I haven't had much time to chat to anyone yet.'

'No. She lives in town. She's got a year's contract at our school and then at Christmas she's heading north to Cairns. Her boyfriend works on the tugs in the harbour.'

'Did you grow up here?'

'We did.' He chuckled. 'And Jacinta's busting to get away. She'll soon learn there's no place like home. So a teacher, hey?' Kent lifted the bottle and drank deeply.

'Yep. And I love it.'

'And what about being out west? What do you think of our region?'

'It has its own beauty,' she said. Lifting her glass Callie pointed to the sunset. 'Look at that.'

The back door opened and Braden appeared.

'Hey, Kent. I was hoping you'd swing by. I want to run an idea by you.'

Callie stood and picked up her glass. 'I'll leave you two to chat.'

Braden put his hand out and touched Callie's arm. 'Please stay, Callie. No need to go. Kent and I will just talk work if you go. We'd appreciate your company.'

She hesitated for a few seconds and then sat back down on the chair she'd vacated.

***

Braden stayed standing. 'Can I top up your Coke?'

'Thank you. Just a quarter hour and then I've got work to do.'

Braden hurried to the kitchen and put fresh ice in her glass before he topped it up. The boys had gone straight to sleep. Three days back at school and kindy had worn them out. Petie had gone to sleep before he even started reading and he was pleased when the older two nodded off after fifteen minutes. It was usually "one more glass of water", or "one more story, please Dad" and bedtime could drag out.

But he loved it. Having the boys home was great. He should have woken up to himself and brought them home months ago.

Them going to sleep quickly tonight had suited him. He'd been anxious to get out onto the veranda with Callie before she went over to her donga. He told himself he was keen to sort out her salary and talk about the best days to get a cleaner in, and what those duties would be, but deep down Braden knew he just wanted to spend more time in Callie's company.

He hadn't heard a car or her talking to someone until he came back into the kitchen. Kent was sitting across the table from her and watching her as she spoke to him. The feeling that hit Braden was unfamiliar. Callie was wearing the dress she'd worn to school today, and her hair was still pulled back in a ponytail, showing off her pretty face and high cheekbones. The red nails and the red lipstick had gone, and he felt as though the real Callie had emerged. He didn't know what made her tick and why she had come out west, but he knew he was spending way too much time thinking about her.

The feeling that surged through him when he saw her talking to Kent wasn't exactly jealousy, but it was an unfamiliar feeling and he put it aside to examine later.

He sat on the chair on the other side of Callie and the conversation turned to the upcoming muster.

'Have you ever seen a helicopter muster, Callie?' Kent asked.

Her attractive laugh tinkled in the evening air. 'Kent, I've never been out of the suburbs of Brisbane so that would be a definite no.'

'Have you got a new pilot yet?' Braden asked. He couldn't believe Jock's timing in leaving the district. He would have known how hard it would be to get a replacement pilot. He wondered if Jock had deliberately chosen the time, and Kent's comments echoed his thoughts.

'Don't get me bloody started on Jock Evans.' Kent flicked an apologetic glance to Callie. 'Sorry, Callie.'

She lifted one hand. 'It's fine. I'm enjoying the quiet of the evening. I'm the extra here, don't let me stop you talking about work. I'm sure that's why you're here.'

Braden chuckled. 'Kent and I have been doing this for a long time , and we've solved many of the problems of the world on this veranda.'

Not to mention a few huge nights when they had both gotten rip roaring drunk after Julia's accident. Kent had been a mainstay for him. He was a good mate and Braden was still pissed off that Sophie had dumped him.

Callie sat there quietly as Kent quizzed Braden about the extra staff they'd hire between the two properties next week.

Kent reached for a third beer. 'I'm stoked that Jon Ingram is keen to come back here.'

'You and me both, mate,' Braden said, putting his empty bottle on the table. One beer would do him. He kept his ears open for the boys through the night. 'If he's keen on hanging around, I'll even give him a managerial role.'

Callie finally contributed with a cheeky smile. 'Can this guy clean houses and weed gardens?'

Kent rolled his eyes. 'Probably, he's a champion at everything he does and a really nice guy to boot.'

Braden nodded. 'He's a great cattleman and we're lucky Jon's decided to come back to our area.' He pulled a face when Kent winked at Callie.

'You'd better watch out though, Callie. Jon's a ladies' man through and through. He leaves a trail of broken hearts wherever he goes. After the last B&S ball there was even a cat fight over him at the bush breakfast,' Kent warned.

'No fear of that with me,' Callie replied as she stared over the veranda railing and focused on the sunset.

Braden wondered what had made her so independent. He had noticed she was averse to being told what to do, even if she came around and did it in the end. Someone had done a number on her and he wondered if that was why she had fled from Brisbane to a job she knew nothing about before she arrived.

Maybe one day when he earned her trust, he'd ask her why.

Or maybe not. It was none of his business, he told himself. Callie was an employee. Nothing more, and she was entitled to her privacy.

'Earth to Braden. You can't go to sleep after one beer, mate. You're losing your man status.'

'What?' He looked at Kent who was shaking his head.

'I asked you what you thought about old man Anderson's son's latest.'

'What's Billy doing this time?'

Poor Jim Anderson had hoped his son would take over the garage one day but Billy Anderson had never been interested. He flitted in and out of town every few months, always with a different scheme going.

'He's bought the produce store.'

'Fair dinkum!'

'And the bakery and the IGA store, so the grapevine says. We've missed you at the pub the past few weeks and you've missed all the local goss.'

'Where did he get the money for that?' Braden asked.

'Story is he won the lottery. But I'm not so sure about it.'

'He's always been a shonky one. A bit of a worry to know that he's running those businesses. The town depends on them. If it's true.'

'Apparently it is, but he's put managers in, Jeff at the pub said.'

'And Jeff would know.' Braden and Kent clinked bottles and chuckled.

'I have been out of the loop,' Braden said. 'We've been pretty busy here since the boys came home, haven't we, Callie?' He looked across the table and was surprised to find her eyes on him. Her cheeks went pink and she looked away.

'Don't let him make you work too hard,' Kent said with a wide smile at Callie. 'You're not on duty twenty-four seven. You can leave the station.'

'I'm happy with the way things are. I'm a bit of a loner, I don't need to go out.'

'We'll see about that. At the end of the muster we have a big bush dance. You'll have to come to that.'

'It's a long time since I've been to one of them,' Braden said.

Kent's smile faded and his voice was gentle. 'Might be time to get back out in the real world, mate.'

'Could be.' Braden kept his tone noncommittal. He knew well that Kent could be like a dog with a bone. He glanced at Callie as the legs of her chair scraped on the timber boards.

'I'm going to leave you guys to chat. I've got some work to do tonight.'

'Don't work too hard,' Braden said. 'You've been looking after us so well, plus you've been working two jobs for three weeks. Maybe you could take a day off tomorrow.'

Callie's eyes widened and she put her hands on her hips. 'No way. The boys will have lessons tomorrow and Friday, and then if we get everything done early on Saturday I might think about taking some time off then.'

Braden had been told off—again. 'Rightio. We'll go for a drive around the property and we'll show you all the sights. We'll take a picnic. The boys would like that. There's a swimming hole over near the mountains. How would you like that?'

'We'll see what Saturday brings,' Callie said. 'Goodnight, Kent. It was a pleasure to meet you. Good night, Braden. I might not see you in the morning, but I'll get the boys' breakfast and we'll be in the school room by eight o'clock so we can finish by two.'

He moved his chair back as Callie waited to move past him.

As she walked in front of him, he reached out and lightly touched her hand, ignoring the spark that ran up his arm. 'Goodnight, Callie, and thank you.'

She walked down the steps and headed for her donga. Braden stared after her until she had disappeared in the darkness.

Kent put his beer bottle on the table. 'What's going on there, mate?'

'What do you mean?'

'I haven't seen you look at a woman like that for a long time.'

'Don't be stupid. Callie's an employee. I'm just trying to make her welcome.'

It was hard to see Kent's expression in the dark. 'Be careful, Braden. You don't know her. Seems strange she turned up out of the blue from Brisbane. Why would someone like her come out here?'

'She answered my ad.'

'Whatever you say. But be careful. Don't leave yourself open, and for God's sake, don't look at her with those big cow eyes when there's other people around. You'll be the talk of the district.'

Braden reached up and flicked the light on as he glared at Kent. 'I think you've had too much to drink, mate. You're dreaming.'

'Am I? Do you know what she did before she came out here?'

'She was a teacher.'

'Maybe she was, but for the past few years she's been a television personality.'

'Bullshit.'

'No, it's true. Jacinta recognised her, but no one at school has told her that it's common knowledge now, because apparently she went through a tough time. Her bloke made a fool of her on television.'

'Her bloke?' Braden's hand stilled as he went to lift the beer bottle to his lips.

'Yeah, apparently they were engaged and he did the dirty on her. So she hasn't been honest with you. Be careful, mate.'

***

Callie lay in the single bed in the donga and watched the fan going round and round like her thoughts. Kent was a nice guy, but she'd had to force herself to pay attention to what he was saying a lot of the time. She had been too aware of Braden near to her and when he'd touched her hand when she was leaving, she'd jumped. She'd been on *Kilcoy Station* for less than a month and she'd been pulled head first into this family. She didn't know what to do.

The crazy thing was that she loved being out here. She loved teaching at the school, she was getting to know the parents and the community, and she loved living at the station.

Well, maybe not so much being in the donga—it was very different to her beautiful house—but she only slept and showered here; she spent most of the days and evenings in the house. And therein lay her dilemma.

She was getting too involved with the family, and too quickly. She loved the boys, she loved the house, she loved the work and she loved . . . no, it was just that her heart went out to Braden. Sometimes he looked so sad, she just wanted to put her arms around him and hold him and comfort him.

His grief and the boys' issues made her silly *#wrongforecast* experience and Greg seem so superficial. The three years she'd spent at the network had been a stupid choice; she should never have left teaching.

Callie rolled over and thumped the pillow. Her heart was telling her to stay and deal with the issues here. Not to run away again.

Logic told her to leave now, because her heart was getting way too involved on too many levels.

It was a long time before she went to sleep.

Chapter 26

Despite a restless night, and crazy dreams, Callie was up bright and early the next morning, but she waited until she heard Braden's ute leave before she headed over to the house. The boys would be fine; Braden would have checked on them before he left and he knew she was always over there before seven-thirty. Often she'd go over before Braden left, and have a cuppa with him, but this past week, she'd been trying to spend less time alone with him. They had their routine down pat, and the boys' well-being was the top priority for both of them.

Callie filled in an hour before Braden headed out, writing an email to Jen to reassure her, and tell her how much she was enjoying her time in the outback.

Getting the job at the school was a fabulous outcome, she wrote. *Best of both worlds. Braden is really happy with the arrangement and it's good for the boys and good for me. Braden is going to hire a house cleaner to come in on those days. He suggested that he gets someone who can do some cooking on those days to stock the fridge so I don't have to cook.*

He's a great employer.

It's really different out here, Jen. But beautiful. The sunsets are spectacular and my donga (don't you love that word) and the house and school are air conditioned so it's easy to put up with the heat.

My car is still getting repaired, but I am driving Braden's sister's car. She's the one who had the boys for two years. Braden's taking care of getting my car repaired.

I met his mate, Kent, last night. He came over to have drinks with us on the veranda. He owns the property next door. I've made some friends at the school. They are all young teachers. I think Bob, the principal, is under thirty!

Braden says... '

Callie bit her lip and read over what she'd typed. Braden this and Braden that. It was like when she and Jen were teenagers and all they wanted to do was talk about the current guy they were interested in. That worried her; she knew she spent way too much time thinking about Braden. She really liked him, and knew that she had to stop herself getting in any deeper. She reminded herself of what had happened with Greg. She wasn't ever going to trust a man again. But she knew Braden was different; he was a good man and she knew she could trust him. It was only because they were in close quarters that she was thinking about him so much.

And how did that explain the faster heart beat when she saw the ute come home, or when she turned into the gates of the property?

She hit the delete key and removed all, except one, mention of Braden.

Hope all is well there. Give the kids a kiss from me. Talk soon. Miss you heaps, Love Callie.

Pressing send, she logged out and snapped her laptop closed. She wouldn't need it over at the house because there was a computer set up for the boys to use in the schoolroom. As she made her way over to the main house, she could see the dust hanging over the road where the ute had driven out. Braden was heading away from town, and she guessed he was going over to Kent's place as they'd discussed last night.

Braden had given her the number of the sat phone so she could call him in case of any emergency, but she'd never had to use it.

Humming beneath her breath, she made her way across to the house.

All was quiet. Flicking the kettle on for a second cup of coffee, she took out three bowls as well as the packet of Weetbix, and checked the toaster was on.

The boys were good sleepers and the three days they drove into town, Callie always made sure she came across to the house earlier to wake them up so they'd have plenty of time for the drive into Augathella. It didn't matter so much on Thursdays and Fridays when they worked from home, but she still liked to keep to a routine.

The kettle flicked off and Callie reached for the instant coffee, and put two slices of bread in the toaster before she headed up the hall to the boys' room. As she was walking up the hall, she heard a muffled noise coming from the family room where the boys watched their DVD movies. As she stood at the door, her eyes settled on the large television screen.

How could she have let herself get so stressed by what happened at the network? With hindsight, she now knew that Greg had done her a huge favour. As she turned away from the door, another muffled noise came from the sofa in front of the TV. With a frown she walked quietly into the room and looked over the back of the sofa.

Nigel was curled up at the far end hugging a pillow, his little cheeks flushed and his nose red.

'Oh sweetheart, are you sick?'

As Callie hurried around the sofa, Nigel gave a great shuddering sigh and she realised he was crying. Without thinking, she sat beside him and held her arms open. She'd been careful with hugs and cuddles over the past weeks, staying as distant as she could; not wanting the boys to get too dependent on her for affection.

Nigel shook his head and turned his head away from her. 'No. Not sick.'

'Did you see your dad this morning?' Maybe he'd got into trouble, but Callie couldn't imagine Braden leaving with Nigel so upset.

'No.' Another sniff. 'But I fed Bluey after he left and then I came in here.'

'Did Bluey stamp on your foot again.'

'No.' Nigel nestled into her, and she placed a hand on his forehead to check he wasn't running a fever.

'What's wrong then, sweetie?' Did you have a bad dream?'

Two little hands crept around her waist and Nigel rested his head on her shoulder. 'No. Rory made me cry.'

'Do I need to speak to him?'

'No! Don't listen to him. It might give you the idea.'

'The idea?' Callie frowned as Nigel began to cry again. His hands held onto her T-shirt, bunching the cotton in his fists. 'What idea, Nigel?'

'Rory said you're not going to be our new mummy. That you're only our teacher. Forever and ever.' He lifted his head back and sniffed. 'I told him he was wrong because I have Mrs Riordan at school and Rory has Mr McIntyre. They're our teachers. Not you. You were here first before you went to school to help the other kids. So you're ours. I told Rory you're here to be our new mummy and he laughed and told me I was a big sook. He said that when it's school holidays you'll probably leave and we won't have you after Christmas. And he said'—another sniff—'we have to be big boys then and look after ourselves because Daddy has to go out and work with the cattle.' Nigel's chest heaved in another shuddering sigh. 'Mummy went away, and then Aunty Sophie left us here, and now Rory said you'll leave too. What's wrong with me, Callie? Is it because I'm the naughty one?'

'Oh, sweetie. No, of course not. You've been so good. At school and at home. And your school work is excellent.'

'So why will you leave us? Why can't you be our new mummy? I'm the only boy in Year One without a mummy.'

Callie's heart broke and she held him close rubbing his back through his PJs as she tried to think of the right thing to say. She was going to have to talk this out with Braden. She doubted if he knew how deep Nigel's issues were.

'I'm your nanny, and your teacher on the days we're not at school, Nigel. One day I probably will go back to my house in Brisbane. I live on a big wide river and I have lots of trees for treehouses and making swings. When I live back there, and you're a bit older, you could all come and visit me.'

'But why can't you be our mummy? You like it here, don't you?''

'I do.'

'So I don't get it. You like Daddy, don't you?'

I do, Callie thought. *Way too much.*

'I do. And your daddy is my employer.' She kept her voice brisk. 'And I like the three of you very much, and I love being your teacher here, and I love being your nanny and helping Daddy look after you. I love *Kilcoy Station*, and I love your puppies. So I think I'll be here for quite a while yet, so you can stop worrying. One day, you might have another mummy, but what you have to remember is that your daddy loves you very much.'

'Will you promise not to leave without telling us? Mummy did and she was yelling at Daddy before she left.'

Callie kept her face blank as her heart broke for the burden Nigel was carrying.

'When it's time for me to leave one day, I *promise* I'll tell you all with plenty of notice. We'll even have a party with cake and—'

'Coke?' Nigel said hopefully.

Callie ruffled his hair. 'We could maybe even have Coke just once.'

Nigel sat up and smiled at her. 'I really hope you keep *all* your promises.

Chapter 27

It was a difficult day in the schoolroom. The two older boys had been impossible to keep on task, and Petie had refused to leave the room and had been clingy. Despite the air conditioning, the heat had built all day, and a headache formed behind Callie's temples. She'd been worrying about Nigel and his insistence on her being their new mummy. She knew no matter how much she loved the job, and the family, she would have to set strict guidelines for her continued stay. Her presence would contribute to Nigel's hopes.

And hers. She forced that thought away.

At two o'clock, Callie wiped the perspiration from the back of her neck and called end of day. 'Let's have an early mark, guys. And maybe a swim?'

Braden had filled the pool a couple of weeks ago and Callie had been pleased to see that all three boys were strong swimmers.

'So many dams out here, the boys were taught as soon as they could walk,' Braden said when she'd commented.

Rory looked at her as though she'd suggested they walk to Augathella to the council pool. 'I don't think that's a very good idea.'

'What? What's wrong? Don't you want to swim?' Callie asked as she turned off the electronic whiteboard.

'Miss Callie,' Rory, always aloof, said politely. 'Look out the window.'

She walked across to the window at the other side of the room and stared.

And then frowned.

'What is it? Another dust storm?' The one she'd experienced in Mitchell a few weeks ago had been awful.

'No, it's a thunderstorm. When the sky goes that yukky yellow brown, it means we're gonna get thunder and lightning.'

'Going to, not gonna,' she corrected automatically as she stared at the eerie light outside.

'And lots of rain. Can the dogs and Bluey come inside?' Nigel asked screwing his face up.

'I'm scared of thunder,' Petie said holding onto her leg.

'How about we go in the middle of the house to the family room, and put a movie on, and we'll turn it up real loud so we can't hear the storm?'

Even as Callie spoke a loud clap of thunder shook the house.

'Quick, you guys go and choose a DVD and I'll bring the pups in. Then we'll have popcorn with the movie,' she said as three scared little faces looked up at her.

Quickly she ushered them down the hallway, and got the DVD going. When they were settled, she hurried to the door. 'Stay here, I won't be long.'

Another loud clap of thunder hit as she reached the back door. Two shivering pups and a determined red calf stared through the screen door, but there was no sign of Petie's pup, Cottie.

Opening the door a little, Callie pushed herself through so the calf couldn't get past her. Bluey had got in one afternoon last week and created havoc in the kitchen until they'd chased him up the hall and out the door into the breezeway. It had been wonderful to hear Nigel laugh as they'd all chased the calf.

She put her head down as a strong gust of dry hot wind preceded another clap of thunder. She'd never seen a storm like this before. The wind tore at her clothes as it swirled around her, gritty dust stinging her eyes and coating her lips. She bent down and picked up the two pups and carried them to the breezeway where she could shut the roller door, and lock them in. 'Come on, Bluey. You can go in there too.'

He followed as she knew he would. Any mess he made she'd clean up later. She got the two dogs and the calf in there safely, shut the roller door from the inside, and then went back through the screen door, into the house, down the hall and back out the kitchen door to look for Cottie.

The wind was even more ferocious now and as she looked to the west, a solid curtain of rain approached from the now-boiling clouds. As she scanned the yard looking for the missing pup, a cloud of dust swirled on the main drive into the property.

Thank goodness, it was Braden's ute.

'Cottie,' she yelled as she pushed against the wind. As she fought her way towards the dog enclosure a strong gust ripped a sheet of iron from the shed roof and lifted it into the air.

Callie screamed and ducked as the iron hit the ground only a metre in front of her. As she stopped, she spied movement behind

the dog run. Cottie was cowering between the back fence and a tree.
She put her head down to stop the dust getting in her eyes and
hurried over to pick him up.

'Look out, Callie!' Braden's yell reached her over the howling
wind.

***

Braden planted the accelerator when he saw Callie in the back
yard. The wind was buffeting the ute, and debris was flying around
the property. He jumped out of the ute and opened the main gate to
the house yard. The storm was as bad as the one the night Julia had
gone out in to rescue Taffee.

As he drove through the gate a sheet of iron lifted from the roof
and speared into the backyard, barely missing Callie. Braden didn't
stop to close the gate behind him. There'd be no cattle on the move
in this storm.

What the hell was she doing outside? He thought she'd have
more sense. All the memories of that dreadful afternoon two years
ago came rushing back as the ute sped past the shed to the house.

'You're not going out in this storm, Julia,' he'd yelled. 'Don't be
so bloody stupid.'

'Taffee's down at the dam. She'll be scared stiff.'

'I don't care. You're not going. It's a horse.'

'Stop me.' Her eyes had challenged him and he'd held her arm,
aware of Rory and Nigel listening.

'No. I'll rely on your common sense. Taffee will be fine.'

'She'll be scared, Braden.'

'She'll be fine. Listen, I can hear Petie crying. You go and get
him out of the cot, and I'll put the kettle on. I'll take you down in the
ute when the wind eases.'

Rory and Nigel had followed him into the kitchen, and a couple
of minutes later, Braden heard Petie crying again. At the same time,
the sound of the quad bike reached him and Braden had raced to the
back door in time to see Julia and the quad bike disappear into the
teeming rain.

He would never forget that moment as long as he lived.

Gritting his teeth he flung the ute door open as another sheet of
iron lifted from the side of the shed and twisted in the air towards
Callie.

'Look out, Callie,' he yelled.

He watched in horror as the edge of the iron sliced down her arm and she pitched forward to the ground just as the rain hit.

Chapter 28

Callie heard the sheet of iron flex in the wind as it flew above her and from the corner of her eye she knew it was coming down. She dived to the left, and as the heavy sheet hit her left arm, she tripped over the pup who had come running to her.

Gathering the pup into her arms, she lay on her side with eyes closed, winded and fighting for breath, her arm stinging.

'Callie, oh God, Callie.' Braden kneeled beside her and he pulled both her and the pup into his arms. 'Please Callie, open your eyes. Look at me, sweetheart.'

As the rain lashed them, Braden's lips brushed her forehead and she opened her eyes and took a deep gasping breath.

'I'm all right. I'm just winded.' She looked up and the intensity of his gaze made her heart thunder in her chest.'

'I thought I'd lost you too.' His arms held her tightly, and no matter how much she wanted to, Callie resisted the urge to sink into his embrace.

She opened her mouth to speak, but before she could Braden's warm lips covered hers. Callie closed her eyes again, caught between heaven and hell. This is what she'd dreamed of, but it wasn't right. She stiffened in his arms and the pup squirmed between them. But she couldn't resist and as she relaxed into his hold, her lips opened beneath his. The rain teemed down and finally Braden lifted his head away. His fingers were wet as he cupped her chin. 'We'd better go inside. Your arm's bleeding.'

She nodded mutely and sat up. The pup scampered off her chest towards the house.

'We need to talk about this later, Callie.' Braden's face was closed.

They made their way to the back door, and opened the door. A very wet pup left muddy footprints on the kitchen floor.

'Cottie,' Petie squealed and Callie's heart sank as she looked at the three boys at the window.

'Are you hurt, Miss Callie?' Rory's voice held concern.

'I'm fine, guys, thank you. Just a little scratch on my arm.'

'We saw the shed flying around the yard and we saw Daddy save you.' Nigel's smile was wide and Callie held back a groan. 'And he kissed you too.'

'Well,' she said brisky, without looking at Braden. 'I'm going to my place to have a shower and get some clean clothes on and then I have some popcorn to make.'

'And I'll put some betadine and a plaster on your arm. Is your tetanus vaccination up to date? And I'll walk you over.'

'Yes. It is, and I'm fine. I'd rather walk over myself, please.' Her heart was pounding and she needed some space. 'You need to be here with the boys.' Callie quickly opened the kitchen door and headed outside. Her thoughts were in such turmoil, she wasn't aware of the rain until she stepped into a huge puddle halfway to the donga.

Oh, shit, What the hell am I going to do?

She stood at the bottom of the steps and lifted her face to the rain, and the drops running down her face mingled with her tears.

***

Braden quickly changed out of his wet clothes, his heart thumping and his hands shaking.

'Bloody idiot,' he muttered under his breath, calling himself all kinds of a fool.

Why the hell did I do that?

Because he hadn't been able to stop himself. The relief when he had seen that Callie was not hurt had overwhelmed him and he'd lost the careful control he always kept in place. Although maybe not so careful if Kent had noticed him watching her last night.

'Who's a bloody idiot, Dad?'

His head flew up and his gaze settled on Nigel standing in the doorway.

'I am. I should have come home earlier before the storm hit. I should have made sure I was here to check that everyone was safe.'

'Miss Callie, looked after us, Dad.' Nigel's face screwed up in a frown. 'Will we still call her Miss Callie when she's our new mum, or will we call her Mummy?'

Braden froze as he pulled the dry T-shirt over his head. 'What?'

'She is going to be our new mum, isn't she? We need a new one, and Miss Callie is just right. You like her too because you kissed her.'

Braden swallowed and pulled his T-shirt down before he crouched in front of Nigel.

'Mate, Miss Callie is here to look after you, and to teach you. She is a lovely lady, and a good teacher and she is working very hard. She wants to keep you safe and happy, like I do, but we're not ready for a new mum yet.'

'But why not?' Nigel's bottom lip trembled and Braden reached out and pulled his son close as a surge of love hit him square in the chest. How could he have left his boys for so long? His selfish action as he'd wallowed in his grief had contributed to Nigel's unhappiness and it was up to him to dispel any hope of a new mum—yet—and not upset Nigel.

'Because we're just getting used to being us. You've only been back at home with me for a few weeks.' He smoothed back Nigel's hair and held his son's eyes with his as he searched for the right words.

'I do like Miss Callie very much, and we want to keep her here while she gets used to us. She's not used to the outback and cattle and puppies, so while she looks after us, we have to look after her too. While we do that I'm sure she'll be happy to stay and get used to us. Do you know what it means to try and make someone do something they don't want to do?'

'I do.' Nigel nodded slowly. 'I have to sit next to Amanda Brimble at school and I don't like that. I don't like her and she has a silly name.'

Braden's lips tugged in a smile. 'Okay. If we try to make Miss Callie do something she doesn't want, she'll feel the same way and she might want to go back to her house.'

Braden hoped his kiss hadn't done exactly that to her.

'So what do we do, Dad?'

'We all learn to live here together. We help Miss Callie and we don't say anything about new mums. What do you think about that?'

'I guess it's okay.'

'I love you, Nige, and your Mummy would be very proud of you too.'

'Why did she go away, Daddy?'

'It was a very sad accident, and it was her time to go.' Braden hated those platitudes; he'd heard the same phrases so many times at Julia's funeral and in the weeks afterward, but at six, Nigel wasn't old enough to hear of Braden's guilt.

'Can we have pizza now?'

Braden ruffled his son's hair. Strangely he felt calmer. Nigel had taken his thoughts away from his foolish behaviour. 'I think Miss Callie was going to make popcorn. Let's go see if she's back yet.'

Chapter 29

Callie left the big house before dinner and went back to her donga. She'd let Braden look at her arm, and held herself rigid while his warm fingers touched her bare skin.

'No need. It's just a minor cut,' she said. What she didn't tell him was that she was sure to be bruised as the iron had hit her hard, and her arm was aching.

'You were lucky. Just a nick that bled a little.' His voice held tension too; he was obviously embarrassed that he'd kissed her.

She wanted to cause the least fuss possible and just get out of there. Popping the corn had been tense; the silences in the kitchen had been long and heavy. A couple of times he had gone to speak, but she had shaken her head, and gone into the pantry, or up the hall to check on the boys.

'I'm not hungry. Are you right to get the boys something? There's some sausages thawed out in the fridge.'

'Yeah, sure,' he said. 'What about your dinner?'

'I'm not hungry,' she said again.

'Oh. Okay.' Braden's hand lifted towards her and then it dropped. 'Sleep well. And Callie?'

She froze and turned from the door. 'Yes?'

'We'll still do that drive tomorrow out to the river at the back of the property and take the boys for a picnic.'

She nodded and shut the door behind her.

No, *she* wouldn't be going on any picnic tomorrow. It was her day off and no man was telling her what to do. Anyway, Callie intended doing some very serious thinking tonight, and she wasn't even sure she would still be here tomorrow.

You promised Nigel, a little voice in her head interrupted.

Callie opened the door of her donga and sat down on the hard sofa. The room was quiet, the only sound was the whirring of her small refrigerator. No sounds of DVDs, little boys giggling or puppies playing. No sound of Braden telling the boys stories as they went to bed. No Silly Callie as Petie put his soft little hand in hers.

Leaning forward, Callie put her face in her hands. She should never have fled Brisbane and come here. Her arm throbbed painfully and her mind spun.

What should she do? Staying here would be awkward. Not because Braden had kissed her; she knew it was only a knee jerk reaction, his relief that she wasn't hurt. Pulling out her phone, she checked she had connection to the farm satellite and was pleased to see the connected icon.

She quickly dialled Jen's number, not even taking notice of what time it was.

'Cal, I'm so pleased you called. It's like you've dropped off the face off the planet.'

'Hi, Jen.'

'What's wrong. I can hear the tone of your voice. Are you okay?'

'Not really, I need some advice.'

'Fire away.' Jen's voice rose. 'Okay, I'll be five minutes. I'm on the phone. It's Callie.'

'Sorry, bad time?'

'Hon, every time is a bad time lately. The kids have been demanding. Damien is working lots of overtime and I'm going stir crazy.'

'Do you need a nanny?' Callie said quietly.

'Why? Are you offering? Hasn't it worked out?'

'Yes. No. Sort of?'

'What happened.'

'Braden kissed me.'

'The low life jerk. Where was his wife?'

'I didn't tell you the details, Jen. His wife died a couple of years ago and the three boys have been living with their aunty. It's just Braden and me and the three boys now. The boys are wonderful. And the problem is not really him. He's a really good guy.'

'I don't get it. He kissed you against your will, but he's a good guy.'

'Yes. I mean no. It wasn't against my will. It was unexpected.'

'Do you like him?'

'I do.'

'So what's the problem? Okay, I'm coming, Damien! Two minutes.'

'It's okay, Jen. You go.'

'No, he's fine. It's just that the kids are a bit of a handful at the moment and Damien's tired. Tell me what advice you want.'

'I don't know what to do. Should I stay or go?'

There was a long silence. 'I don't know what to tell you. I can only suggest one thing. Do what you feel is best for you. Okay? I'll call you tomorrow. Love you, Cal. And remember whatever happens we'll be here for you.'

Callie pressed end and stared at the phone.

What do I want?

I don't want to go through another Greg situation. I want to be happy.

Moving briskly, she went into the small bedroom at the back of the donga and pulled out her suitcase. A month ago she hadn't known this little family. Rory's and Nigel's and Petie's faces filled her mind, but she pushed them away. They were *not* her children. She was not family to them.

Opening the wardrobe, she pulled out her clothes and then cleared the bathroom cabinet with one sweep of her hand, and dropped it all into another small bag.

Insects chirped in the dark as Callie took one last look around the donga she had stayed in for the last month.

No regrets, she said to herself as a wave of nostalgia hit her in the chest. *Don't be stupid, it's a horrid donga.* Small, cramped and hot; think of your beautiful home on the river.

Strangely that didn't work.

Pulling the door closed quietly, she held the keys to Sophie's Camry wagon in her hand. She would leave it in town, and pick up her own car and drive back to Brisbane.

She would call Braden from wherever she was in the morning. She pulled a face; it would be Augathella because she wouldn't be able to get her car until eight a.m. She threw her one suitcase in the car. She'd sort out the jumpers and stuff that were still in the utility room cupboard down the track. She wouldn't need them at home anyway.

The Camry's engine purred to life and she drove slowly down the driveway keeping one eye on the main house, but there was no sign of life. As Callie got out and opened the gate, she felt like a thief in the night, but drew a deep breath and drove through and quickly got out and locked the gate behind her.

She hadn't driven in the dark on this road before, and she felt around the dashboard for the high beam switch. Eventually she found it, and then another switch below turned on the LED driving lights above the bumper bar, lighting up the road ahead.

Her thoughts swirled around and she took another deep breath.

Am I doing the right thing?

Am I leaving the boys—and Braden—in the lurch?

What was her problem anyway?

So Braden had kissed her. What was wrong with that?

Did you enjoy it?

Yes. I did.

Did your reaction frighten you?

Yes it did.

Why would that be, Calista Young?

Because I care about him. A lot. Too much. And those gorgeous boys.

Do you think this will hurt him?

As her conscience asked her that question, the bright lights of the Camry lit up the section of the road where she had first encountered Braden and the boys.

He had been so kind and thoughtful, and accepting of her. He'd fallen in the irrigation channel, and he'd retrieved her luggage. He was a good man. And she cared about him. A lot.

And what was she doing?

Running away like a coward.

Braden was not Greg.

Her foot hit the brake and she swung the steering wheel around so hard, for a moment she worried the car was going to roll.

But it settled on its four wheels and headed back down the road the way she had come.

A few minutes later she was through the gate, and had parked the Camry next to Braden's ute.

Chapter 30

Braden lifted his head and frowned as a car pulled up in the yard. He glanced up at the kitchen clock; it was heading for eight o'clock.

Kent?

He walked to the door and peered through the screen, surprised to see Sophie's Camry parked there. For a stupid moment, he forgot she was away and her car was garaged here now; he expected her to step out of the driver's side.

His frown deepened when Callie climbed out and he wondered why she was in the car.

God, she was leaving. Because he hadn't been able to control himself.

He held the screen door open as she walked quickly up the two steps.

Her cheeks were flushed and for a moment he worried that she was running a fever. Her eyes were bright as they held his.

'Where are the boys?'

'In the family room. I let them stay up because there's no school tomorrow. What's wrong?'

'I need to talk to you. Can we sit in the kitchen or out on the veranda?'

Braden's gut clenched. Callie *was* going to leave. She was here to say goodbye. He looked out at the car and the back veranda light lit up the interior. Sure enough her suitcase was on the back seat.

He lifted his hand and ran it through his hair.

'How about in the kitchen? I could do with a cuppa,' he said.

I could do with a strong drink.

Her eyes hadn't left him.

'Sit down and I'll make you a coffee.'

She nodded and did as he asked. As the jug boiled Braden crossed to the fridge and rummaged in the back.

'I hid these from the boys.' He held up a packet of Tim Tams.

'They must have been well hidden,' she said with a smile and his gut relaxed a bit.

'Behind the pumpkin.'

She smiled and Braden's hopes rose a little. If she was leaving she wouldn't look so damn relaxed . . . and beautiful.

Finally the jug boiled, the coffees were poured, and the biscuits were on the table.

Braden sat down and looked at Callie. Her eyes were still on his, but she was starting to look nervous.

He clenched his hands on the table. 'You're leaving, aren't you?'

'I was,' she said quietly. 'I got as far as the irrigation channel.'

'Then you remembered you'd signed a contract at the school.'

Her mouth opened to an O, and her eyes widened. 'Oh dear, I'd totally forgotten about that.'

'So, you said you *were* leaving?'

Callie nodded. 'I was. I got to where you rescued my luggage and I woke up to myself. You need me here,' she said simply.

'We do. And we want you here. There's a difference there, Callie.'

'I know there is.'

'I'm sorry I kissed you.'

'Are you?'

Her eyes were intent on his.

'I'm sorry I kissed you when I did. I'm not sorry I kissed you.' It was hard to look away from her, and his heart jumped when she smiled.

'I didn't mind you kissing me. I'm going to be honest, Braden. It's time for honesty. I came here because I was running away from a situation. I trusted a man and he let me down very publicly. I ran away.'

'I know. On a television broadcast.'

'You knew? You knew all the time?'

'Not all the time. Kent told me the other night. Jacinta told him. She recognised you.'

'Oh God, the school knows.' She put her hand over her eyes and then quickly dropped it away. 'But it doesn't matter, does it? It's not important.'

Braden reached over and took her hand and smiled when her fingers curled in his. 'Keep being honest with me, Callie. Why did you come back. Only because we need you?'

She shook her head and held his eyes. 'No. I came back because I care about the four of you. I couldn't leave. And I made a promise to Nigel. I can't let him down.'

He caressed the top of her hand with his thumb. 'It's been too fast and you've been thrown in at the deep end. With the work, the boys, and with me.'

'With you?'

'With the way I feel about you. I've got a suggestion. How about we start all over again, and get to know each other properly. Take our time. No rush. No expectations. Just so we both feel comfortable.'

'I think that's a good idea,' she said softly.

'So you'll stay?'

'Yes, I will.'

'Without rushing things and just this once, may I kiss you to show you how much I like that "yes"?'

Callie shook her head, and disappointment trickled into his heart. He'd blown it already.

'Sorr—' he began. But Callie stood and held one finger up. She came around to his side of the table and put her hands on each side of his face.

'No, I'll kiss you to show you I mean it.'

She stood beside him and he lifted his face to meet her lips. As her soft sweet lips met his, footsteps thundered down the hall and Rory came bursting into the kitchen, holding Braden's phone.

'Dad! It's Aunty Sophie and she really needs to talk to you.' He shoved the phone into Braden's hand.

Braden lifted his other hand and reached for Callie. She squeezed his fingers.

'Stay where you are, Miss Callie. We'll finish this later.'

'Dad!' Rory was hopping from foot to foot. 'Talk to Aunty Sophie. She's crying really bad. Quick, Dad!'

Braden frowned and took the phone, lifting it to his ear. 'Soph? It's me. Are you okay?'

A long shuddering sob drowned out Rory's incessant talking. 'No.'

'Sophie?'

'Bray? Can I come home please. To stay? I want to come home. I have to come home.' Braden's gaze met Callie's as his little sister sobbed into the phone.

'Of course you can come home, Soph. Do you want me to come and get you?'

Callie reached out and held his hand. 'Whatever you need me to do, I can help,' she said.

'Thank you,' he said, pulling her close as he continued to listen to Sophie.

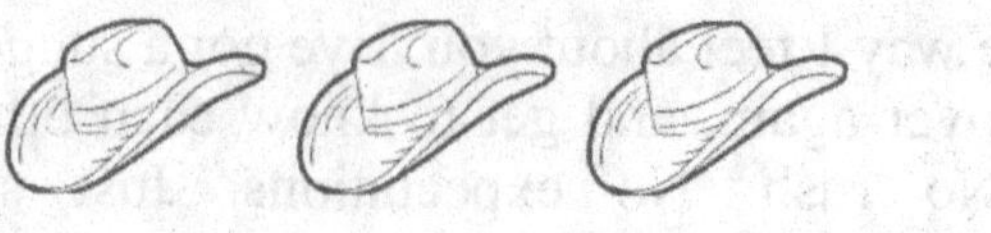

Outback Sky: The Pilot

ANNIE SEATON

The Augathella Girls: Book 2

Dedication

For my armchair travelling readers.

Augathella Characters-Book 2

Fallon Malone	Contract Pilot
Jon Ingram	Station Manager
George Malone	Fallon's great-uncle
Callie Young	Schoolteacher/ nanny
Braden Cartwright	Owner of Kilcoy Station
Rory, Nigel and Petie	Braden's sons
Sophie Cartwright	Braden's sister
Kent Mason	Owner of Lara Waters
Kimberley Riordan	School deputy principal
Bob Hamblin	School principal
Cheryl Hamblin	His wife
Jim Anderson	Local garage owner
Jennifer Shaw	School Counsellor

Chapter 1

The red, vintage F100 ute creaked when Fallon Malone leaned back and rested her elbows against the dusty bull bar. It was going to be a while before Jason arrived in the company helicopter so she put her head back, enjoying the morning sun on her face. There hadn't been much time for relaxation since she'd left Kununurra three weeks ago. The upcoming muster in an unfamiliar area and the state of Great-Uncle George's house had taken over her waking thoughts.

'It's only a little tidy-up, sweetie,' Mum had said when Fallon had mentioned she was going out Augathella way for a muster. 'Seeing you're going there, there's no point your father taking time off work and us driving all that way. Plus, you've got your ute if there's anything worth salvaging.'

Fallon shook her head as she thought back to that comment. That should have sent warning bells ringing. Anyway, her ute had gone in for a service when she'd hit town and needed major work done, so here she was, driving Uncle George's 1962 F100 ute. The ute was probably worth more than his house and its entire contents.

'And while you're there you can check poor Uncle George is eating properly. You're a good girl, Fallon. You appreciate the importance of family.'

After a restless night listening to creatures scurrying in the dark, Fallon had had enough of the house. She'd made herself a coffee in the grimy kitchen this morning dismissing the idea of a takeaway from the café; she didn't want to interact with people.

Yet.

Simply being away from the north and the black feeling that came with being up there was a relief, and she was determined to make the most of the time being away from memories.

The early morning sun bathed her face; it was nice out here at the Augathella Aerodrome. Soon, it would be too hot in the outback sun and she'd move into the shade. Hopefully, she wouldn't be at the airfield too long, although the alternative—sorting out a houseful of junk—was not appealing. The mountains in the distance held a pretty blue tinge as the sun climbed higher. The fresh air and the sunshine improved her mood and there was no one pressuring her. No one watching her every move. Fallon closed her eyes and tried to push away the thoughts of the north, but the image that replaced her memories was no better. She had to get that damn house out of her mind. Why the hell she'd ever agreed to sort it out was beyond her. Her focus out here should be the muster, not huge piles of junk in a ramshackle old house.

'You never know, Uncle George might even leave it to you,' Mum had said when she'd called her parents from the garage to let them know she'd arrived safely.

Almost thirty and she still felt as though she had to do that. But ever since *the incident*, Mum had insisted.

The incident. These days she looked at her life as before and after. Maybe she should change careers but Fallon knew—and wanted to do— nothing else.

'A house out in the sticks?' she'd quickly answered. 'No, thanks, Mum. I don't want it and I certainly don't want the multitude of "treasures" inside.'

Despite working in the outback, Fallon spent most of her time up in North Queensland on the water when she wasn't flying. Last long break, she'd gone sailing in a hire yacht out of Cairns. Being in the air and on the water were her two favourite activities.

For the fifth time since she'd woken up this morning, she'd wondered how she'd got roped into this family chore.

'Why don't you and Dad come out and visit while I'm here? If Dad's busy, you could catch a bus, I'm sure there'd be one from Brisbane.'

'I'd love to, Fal, but I've got the Red Cross fete to organise, and then we've got the cake stall. I couldn't possibly get away . . . maybe if Augathella was closer . . .'

'Stop thinking about it,' Fallon told herself. 'You cannot afford to get stressed out here.' She'd had her fair share of stress, and she rolled her eyes as she picked at a piece of skin at the side of her thumbnail.

Her stress indicator: chewed fingernails and ragged skin. She shoved her hands into her jeans pockets and vowed she'd leave them alone from now on.

'It's only just a little tidy up, love, before he sells the place and goes into the aged care home. We have to remember he's getting on.'

'How old is Uncle George anyway? I thought he was ancient when we came out here when I was a kid.'

'He's fifteen years older than my mum, so he must be about ninety now. But don't worry, he's as sharp as a tack. I just worry that

no one checks on his physical well-being. So, seeing you're out there
. . .'

Fallon sighed. 'So, what sort of a "little" tidy up?' she asked,
reluctantly giving in.

'Apparently, he's sold most of the land, and his little house on
the edge of town just needs to be cleaned up. You know, just sort the
house for him, mow the lawn, tidy the gardens up ready to put it on
the market. Maybe you could live there while you're doing the
contract work.'

'And when does he want to move out?'

'He told me a couple of weeks ago he's got an independent
living unit reserved at the aged care home in town. He's keen to sell
the house so he can move across to it. The poor dear sounds more
than ready.'

So, Fallon had rolled into town with a troubled gearbox,
deposited her car at the local garage to have it looked at, called her
parents, and then asked for directions to George Mason's house,
hoping there was a spare bed there for her.

'It's on the edge of town, isn't it?' she'd asked the man at
Andersen's garage.

'Don't tell me you're looking to buy that house?' He'd
scratched his head and frowned at her. 'Needs a bit of work.'

'No, I'm going to visit George,' she replied.

'He's not there,' came the quick reply.

For one moment, she worried that Great-Uncle George had gone
on to a better place. 'He's not there?' she repeated slowly.

'No, love. The council threatened to condemn his house, so he
chucked a wobbly, and moved into the aged care home up the road
there.'

'Chucked a wobbly?'

'Yeah, you know. Had a dummy spit. George is renowned for
that. Sorry, if you're a rellie, I shouldn't be critical.'

Fallon waved her hand. 'Don't worry about that. I only met him
once a long time ago. Anyway, how long do you think my ute will
take to get fixed?'

'Love, by the sound of that gearbox, I think it'll be in here at
least ten days. I have to get parts sent down from the Isa. But I'm
sure George will let you drive his ute if you need to get around.'

'Okay. So, where's this home he lives in now?'

She should have known by the sympathetic smile that things were very different to what Mum had said.

'Walk down to the shops and take the second street on the left. The newsagent's on the corner. Turn left and you'll see the driveway about fifty metres down.' He nodded. 'And tell the old codger, Jack Anderson said to say hello.'

'I will, thank you.' Fallon reached into her pocket and pulled out a tattered business card. 'My mobile's on there. Give me a call when my ute's ready, or if you need me to pay for parts.'

'Ah, I know that name,' he said glancing at her card.

Fallon froze. Surely not down here?

'You're the new pilot. Heard Jon had hired a woman as well this time.'

Fallon pulled herself up straight. 'Jon? I was hired by Kent Mason. And is being a woman a problem?'

'Nuh, should it be?'

'Sorry, I cop a bit of flack sometimes.'

'Well, wait until you meet my mechanic. *She'll* tell you what the issue is with your gearbox. I'm too old to get under a car these days. I run the business, order the parts, and my daughter-in-law does the work.'

Fallon grinned. 'Good to hear it. Anyway, Jack, give me a call when she checks it out. I'll be bunking at George's house, I think. What you said about it being condemned is a bit of a worry, though.'

'It's structurally sound. It was under threat of being condemned because he's a bit of a hoarder. Always has been. I think there was a bit of finagling going on, so keep an eye out.'

'Fingaling? In what way?' This visit was getting more complicated by the minute.

'You'll see,' he said cryptically. 'Good to see family here looking out for him at last.'

'You have a visitor, George.' The aide took Fallon out to the garden where her great-uncle was sitting in the shade.

'Who are you?' The grey-stubbled cheeks were creased in deep lines.

'I'm Fallon, Sally's daughter. Your *niece*, Sally.'

'I know who Sally is. What do *you* want?'

Great start.

'I came out to see if I could give you a hand in the house to get it ready to sell, but it looks like you're all sorted. You're here already!'

A wide smile lit up his face and a memory flashed for Fallon.

'Did you show me how to pull carrots out of your veggie garden when I was a little girl?' she asked slowly.

'I did. Did I turn you into a gardener?'

Fallon sat on the bench beside him and the aide smiled before she left them alone and went back inside.

'I'd like to be one day when I settle. I don't have a home at the moment.'

'Why don't you have a home?' His eyes were alive with interest.

'Because I'm a pilot and I work all around Australia. I'm a contract pilot with a Western Australian company. Mustering, crop spraying, and rural firework. Keeps me busy. And when I'm not there, I like to be on a boat out to sea.'

'Ah, I get it. I'm not stupid. I read the papers.'

'Huh?' Her heart sank as she looked at him. *Did it make the papers out here too?*

'You came out here for the muster, not to see me.'

'Two birds with the one stone,' she replied.

'Have you got somewhere to bunk down?'

'Not yet. You offering?' She knew her grin was cheeky but she was enjoying the banter with Great-Uncle George.

He dug in his pocket and held up a set of keys. 'You clean my place up for me, and you can stay there. I've still gotta sell it. They let me in here on a bond, but they're waiting for their money.'

'I'm only here for three weeks so I can give you three weekends and maybe the afternoons when I knock off from the muster. Or if there's any days I don't work.' She knew there wouldn't be much chance of that unless the weather turned.

'Done deal. That's the front door key, they're the keys to the sheds, and the silver one is to my ute. I suppose you flew your plane in?'

'No, I'm a helicopter pilot. The company is sending the chopper down tomorrow.' She reached out and took the keys. 'And thank you, my ute's in the garage getting a new gearbox.'

'You take bloody good care of mine then, but like Sally said, you're cleaning up the house, so you're gonna need it.'

'So, you knew I was coming. Why didn't you tell Mum you'd moved?'

'I did, but if she knew I'd moved already, there was no need for anyone to come out. But I can't stay and chin wag. I've got a game of cards to go to. Pick any bed you want.' His wheezy laugh turned into a cough.

'Fair enough. And when I'm tidying up, is there anything I need to put aside?'

He shook his head. 'No, send it all over to your mother. She's a good stick, your mum is. She's the only one in the bloody family who rings me. Shame she couldn't come out. Would've been nice to see her before I shuffle off.'

'I'll tell her. I'm sure they'll come for a drive next time Dad's got holidays.'

With a wave of a wrinkled hand, Great-Uncle George turned his back on her and shot off after an elderly man on a walker.

'Jack Anderson said to say hello,' she called after him.

'Don't you take my chair, you old bugger,' he yelled after the man on the walker.

Fallon had left the aged care home jiggling the keys he gave her, walked down to the house and let herself in.

And now as she thought about the mess she'd stumbled into, as she leaned back on the old red ute, she ignored the compulsion to chew what was left of her nails. She'd sort something and wouldn't stress.

She scanned the sky for any sign of the helicopter. Jason was late.

A cloud of red dust lifted in the distance and as she watched, two white vehicles gradually came into view. The Landcruiser tray-back ute parked beside the hangar, and the twin cab parked at the end of the track. The driver of the tray-back rolled open the door of the hangar and jogged across to where she was leaning on Uncle George's ute.

He was a tall guy with dark hair and a wide smile, and he held his hand out to her. 'Hi, you must be Fallon. I'm Kent Mason.'

She took his hand and his grip was firm. 'Good to meet you, Kent. I was going to come over and see you at *Lara Waters* this afternoon to find out the drill. I'm just waiting for my bird to arrive.'

'You drove in?'

'Yeah, I came a little bit early, I'm helping clean out my uncle's house in town. I'm waiting for my bird now.'

He nodded as he looked at the red vintage ute.

'Ah, Mason. I didn't twig. You're related to George?'

'That's right.'

Sympathy crossed his face. 'If you need a hand . . .'

Fallon chuckled. 'I'm right for the time being, but I'll keep that in mind. So, okay to call over to see you this afternoon?'

Kent shook his head. 'We've had some changes. Don't worry, your contract's still good. Braden and I are flying to North Queensland now, but Braden's new manager at *Kilcoy Station*, Jon Ingram, is in charge of the muster. I was going to call you tomorrow. I didn't think you'd be here yet. There's a meeting out at the station tomorrow afternoon. Braden and I will be back late tonight. Come out and meet everyone tomorrow. I'll introduce you to Braden now.'

Jon Ingram? If Fallon had known he was in charge, she would have declined the contract. She'd never met him, but she'd heard his reputation around the traps.

Didn't like women on his team, was pedantic, and was difficult to talk to.

As they walked over towards the vehicle, three small boys climbed out of the twin cab ute. Their mother walked around the front of the twin cab and took the smallest boy's hand.

The other guy came out of the hangar and put his arms around the woman. Their voices carried across as she followed Kent.

'I'll see you tonight, love.'

'I'm looking forward to meeting Sophie. I hope she's okay.'

'She will be, when we get her home.'

Kent stepped forward. 'Braden, Callie, this is Fallon. Fallon, Braden owns *Kilcoy Station*.'

'Good to have you onboard, Fallon.' Again, her hand was taken in a firm grip, by Braden this time, and the woman with the curly dark hair smiled at her.

'Welcome, Fallon. Good to meet you,' Callie said. Her smile was kind and Fallon felt untidy and weather-beaten beside her. She brushed her hands down her jeans. Uncle George's ute was as dusty as the house, and that was saying something.

Kent looked at his watch. 'Braden, we'd better get going. We've got a big day ahead.'

'Yes, the sooner we get there, the happier I'll be.' Braden leaned over and kissed Callie again before he ruffled the little boy's hair. 'You be a good boy for Callie today, won't you, Petie?'

'I will.'

'Rory, Nigel, we're going now. Come and give me a hug.'

In a flurry of dust and flailing limbs, the two older boys ran over, hugged their father, and took off to the pile of dirt beside the hangar where they'd already made a track for a couple of toy cars.

'Leave the helicopter on the left-hand side of the apron. How's your pilot getting back to base?' Kent asked.

'He's getting picked up in town in a company vehicle. They're heading to Brisbane for a meeting. It saved me a big drive.'

'Okay. We'll catch up at the meeting tomorrow. You'll be flying tandem with me. My chopper's out at my place. Oh, I almost forgot. Jon asked me to text you his number, but I can give you his card. Maybe give him a call and let him know you're here?'

'Sure. I'll call him after I drop Jason off in town.' She slid the card into her jeans pocket. Might as well get it over with and suss the new boss out in person.

Fallon stood beside Callie and Braden as Kent taxied the small Cessna out of the hangar. When it was on the tarmac, Braden jumped in and with a final wave, the plane was soon at the end of the runway lifting off into the air.

'Are you from around here, Fallon?' Callie let go of the little boy's hand and he ran across to the other two.

'No. I'm only here for the contract. I'm based in the Top End, but I was originally from Brisbane.'

'Me too. I can't get over how busy it is out here. I imagined country life would be quiet.'

'You and Braden and the boys haven't been here long?'

Callie's face flushed a deep pink. 'I haven't been here long. Just a few weeks. I came out to look after the boys.'

'But you knew them before?'

She shook her head, and her cheeks stayed pink. 'No. Braden and I—God, it's complicated, sort of. Ours is a new relationship. It just happened. Don't get me wrong. I haven't stepped in as a—'

Fallon put her tanned hand on Callie's arm. 'Hey, you don't have to justify yourself to me. If you guys have hit it off, and you're happy, that's great.'

'Thank you. I feel a bit self-conscious.'

'No need to. Life's taught me not to worry about what anyone thinks.'

'You said you were going into town to drop someone off?'

'Yes.' Fallon pulled out her phone and checked the time. 'He's a bit late. His lift will be waiting for him.' As she spoke, the familiar throb of a helicopter came from the north. 'Ah, here he is now.'

'I'm taking the boys into town for a milkshake. It'd be nice to have some grown-up company. Fancy a coffee?'

Fallon smiled. 'Sounds good to me.'

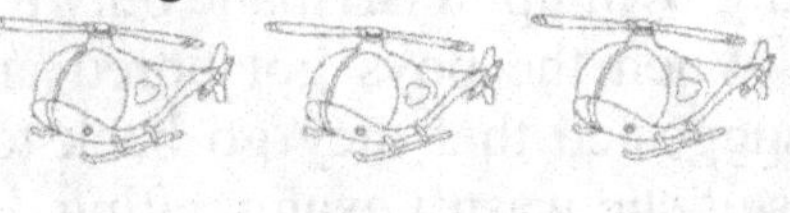

Chapter 2
Augathella
Callie

Callie and Fallon sat in the park with coffee and cake as the boys played and climbed up the pole that held the giant Meat Ant sculpture.

They'd hit it off, and when they'd discovered they were the same age and had grown up in Brisbane only a suburb apart, they felt like old friends. When the boys got bored and they finished their coffees, Fallon suggested that they go back to the house, so Callie could see for herself she wasn't exaggerating.

'Oh my goodness!' Callie knew her eyes were like saucers as Fallon led her down the hallway of her uncle's house The boys were in the backyard playing on a tyre swing hanging from a tree after Fallon insisted on checking it for spiders before the boys took turns swinging. Callie followed Fallon through the front door and her eyes widened.

'Oh heck, I see what you mean,' she said.

'Mum told me to mow and tidy up the yard to make it look presentable.' She couldn't help the chuckle. 'I wonder which shed the mower's in.'

They walked down the hall through piles of junk until they reached the back door and Fallon gestured across the untidy grass where the boys were playing.

'So yeah, Uncle George has sold off a couple of thousand acres, but . . .' She stood with her hands on her slim hips. Even with her dusty jeans and battered Akubra, Callie thought what an elegant woman she was. She'd have never picked her for an outback pilot.

'But?' Callie prompted.

'Well, he sold the biggest section, but there are still ten acres full of junk. I think outside is worse than the house, and I haven't even looked in the sheds.'

'Worse than the house?' Callie looked around. 'It's a fire hazard.'

'Not to mention vermin.'

Callie shivered and looked down half-expecting to see a rat's nest at her feet.

Fallon rolled her eyes. 'I don't think Mum had any idea how bad he'd let it get. He's lived here since he was born. Never married, no family, but look at what he's collected.' She pointed to an old fashioned cane pram in the hallway behind them. 'Uncle George never had kids so I'm guessing that's the cane pram *he* slept in ninety years ago.'

'That's incredible.' Callie walked over and looked at the dust-covered pram. 'It's an antique, you know. It's probably valuable. You'll never know what's in the house until every room and every cupboard is checked. Thoroughly. There could be some valuable items in here.'

'And lots of junk. But, you're right. I think I need to have a sort out, and then Mum needs to send an appraiser out.' Fallon pulled a face. 'It's kind of sad though. This was his life and he had no one to share it with. Now he's gone into aged care and no one cares about what he's left behind.'

Callie stared at Fallon as a strange, sad expression crossed her new friend's face. 'You do. And your mum does. He has family who cares.'

Fallon nodded and after a moment seemed to shake off whatever was bothering her. 'Anyway, this isn't my first priority. I've got a contract to fulfil and three adjoining stations southwest of Augathella to fly over for the next couple of weeks.' She tapped a finger against her cheek, and Callie noticed her bitten-down nails.

'I haven't worked with Kent before. I usually fly tandem with pilots from our company. Would I be out of line if I asked you what he was like?'

'He seemed like a nice guy the couple of times I've met him. Braden and he are best mates, so that's enough for me. They grew up together. And when Braden asked him to fly to Ravenshoe, he didn't hesitate.' Callie shrugged. 'I haven't really been in town long enough to get to know many of the locals. Just some of the teachers at the school where I'm working part-time.'

'Best not to know in small towns in my experience,' Fallon said. 'I keep to myself and put my head down.'

'Let's have another coffee one day before you start working full days. Your life sounds really interesting, Fallon.'

'And you too. I'd love to hear how another Brisbane girl ended up out here.'

Callie shook her head and was pleased when the usual red cheeks stayed away. 'It's a wonder you didn't know. Most of the world does! That's a story for over a wine one night. It's a shame you have to stay in town, Fallon. There's a spare room in my accommodation.' This time her cheeks did heat as Fallon looked at her curiously. 'If you ever get sick of being in this . . . um . . . this—'

'Junkheap?' Fallon grinned. 'If it gets too bad, I might take you up on that. I thought the boys were yours, you know,' she said. 'Teaches me not to make assumptions about people, doesn't it?'

***

Fallon

Callie's comment came to mind as Fallon sat at a table at the Drover's Hotel later that afternoon waiting to meet with Jon Ingram. He'd sounded okay on the phone and she wondered if she'd taken too much heed of what might have been gossip from the ringer at Barkly Homestead who'd told her what a difficult boss he was.

When Jason had flown in and she'd driven him to his lift in town, she'd gone back to George's house, called Jon Ingram and organised the meeting at the pub and then worked in the house for a while.

Fallon figured she might as well start in the room she was sleeping in, and if there were any nests of anything in there, she'd get rid of them. Last night she'd slept on top of the bed and left her jeans and boots on.

This morning when she got back, she stripped the bed, and then found an old washing machine in the laundry. When she'd gone to put the grey sheets in the hot water, she took a second look, shook her head and added them to the piles of rubbish.

A foray into the cupboards lining the hall at the back of the house resulted in the discovery of half a dozen sets of new single sheets still in their wrapping. Two sheets and new pillowcases had gone into the washing machine and were now drying on the old-fashioned pole clothesline in the backyard.

She'd put two hours into that room, and when she'd discovered a vacuum cleaner—still in the box and unused—in the bottom of the same cupboard, the room had had a top-notch clean. It now held a bed, a dressing table, the walls had been wiped over, and the window sparkled. Unfortunately, the lace curtain had disintegrated in her hand when she'd taken it down to wash. The rest of the "stuff" that had filled the room, she'd dragged out to the back hallway, leaving a narrow path between the assortment of goods, so she could get to the back door.

A hot shower, clean clothes and the feeling that she had achieved something—in one room anyway—put a spring in Fallon's step as she'd walked down to the pub for her meeting.

Once she knew the work schedule, she could plan her days at the house, and hopefully make some progress.

The glass holding her lemon squash was cool against her fingers as she sat back and surveyed the pub. She could have been anywhere in outback Australia. The old chipped wooden countertop, the pool table in the corner with a dartboard on the far wall, and the pub smell. The familiar mix of sweat, spilt beer, dust, and stale cigarette smoke absorbed for years by the threadbare carpet met her when she walked in. The sour smell mixed with the lingering aroma from the loaded cattle truck that had turned to the highway at the roundabout outside as she'd walked along the wide footpath and left no doubt she was in an outback cattle town.

A beer would have gone down well after her busy afternoon, but she wanted to make a good impression on the boss.

When he arrived. She glanced down at her watch. He was already ten minutes late.

She leaned back in her chair and put her glass down as a tall man with dark hair came in the side entrance, walked across to the bar and stopped adjacent to the table she was sitting at.

A pair of piercing blue eyes in a tanned and rugged face scanned the room and settled on her for a mere second before he turned to the bar.

'Two schooners, please, mate,' he said to the barman.

Fallon turned away; for a moment she'd been sure it was Jon Ingram, but it appeared it wasn't.

Her phone buzzed in her pocket and she reached down and pulled it out and checked her messages.

I can come out the weekend after next. Cleared my schedule, so leave it free. Luv, Mum.

Fallon rolled her eyes.

Leave it free?

By then the muster would be in full swing, and she'd be working long days, weekends and all.

Didn't matter anyway. Mum could sort it out while she was at work, and she could load the ute whenever she finished.

Can you leave it free? Her phone buzzed again. **Please?**

No guarantee. Fallon quickly texted back.

Okay, I won't come.

'Shit,' she muttered sliding the phone back into her pocket. Anger simmered as she thought of all the times she'd bowed to Mum's demands. Her mother had no idea of the fact that she had a job and her own commitments. Mum could stay in Brisbane because of a bloody cake stall, but Fallon was expected to drop everything and be available to clean out the house of a man who she'd met once in her life. No wonder she didn't go home to visit much. Mum didn't put herself out, and they'd never come north to visit her. Dad had holidays every year; they could make an effort.

Why the hell she'd ever agreed to help out showed what a short memory she had. Mum was a manipulator of the first order.

'Double shit,' she muttered again.

She jumped as the chair opposite her was pulled out, and a schooner of beer appeared in front of her.

Looking up, she encountered the steady gaze of those blue eyes she'd noted and dismissed a moment ago.

The owner of them leaned over and held out a tanned hand. 'Fallon Malone, I assume?'

She nodded, took his hand and shook it, noting the calloused palms. 'Jon Ingram, I guess?'

He let go of her hand but his gaze stayed on her as he lifted the schooner and took a sip, before putting the glass down on the table.

'You're expecting someone else?' She gestured to the beer.

'It's for you. You don't look like a Chardonnay sort of girl.'

'I don't drink anything when I'm working.' She eyed the ale frothing in the schooner glass.

'You're not working now. We're just going to have a casual chat out of hours.' His voice held a husky tone, and Fallon nodded and reached for the beer.

'Thank you. That will hit the spot then I guess.'

'Are you always this edgy?'

'What?' She put the beer down and stared at him. He hadn't taken his eyes off her for a second and she felt uncomfortable, and that annoyed her.

'Your stiff shoulders, and your mannerisms. You look tense.'

Fallon forced herself to stay in the position she was in; her stance or the way she was sitting was no different to the way she always held herself. 'No. I'm not tense. I'm sitting here waiting with interest to hear about the muster, and what your expectations are.' She knew her shoulders were stiff and was surprised to see her hand clench on the table as annoyance took hold. 'Perhaps you're more used to your Chardonnay girls, Jon. Would you make that same comment to a male pilot?'

She lifted her chin as the gauntlet was thrown down. The laconic chuckle really peed her off.

'Ah, I thought that would be the case,' he said.

'The case?' The words were short and clipped.

'That's why I prefer not to have women on the job.'

'I beg your pardon? Did I hear you correctly?'

He lifted his beer and took another drink, his eyes still on her. 'You did.'

'Are you trying to deliberately piss me off with your sexist attitude?'

'I think you were already pissed off when I sat down, weren't you?'

'Whether you were right or not has nothing to do with our conversation. Tell me why you prefer not to have women on the job?'

'Because, *babe*, you all think you have to prove something, and you all have this attitude that men differentiate your ability to do the job simply because of your sex.'

'Isn't that what you were just saying?' She picked up the schooner glass, tempted to throw the beer over him, but *that* would be the sort of thing he would expect a woman to do.

He shook his head slowly from side to side. 'No. Not at all. You're the one who asked would I make the same comment to a male pilot. So you obviously have a chip on your shoulder about being looked at as a female pilot. I don't care whether you're a man or a woman. If you can fly, and follow instructions, it's irrelevant.'

Fallon drained her glass as she tried to keep calm. 'Good. I can fly.'

'And can you follow instructions?'

'If they're reasonable.'

'That's not what I asked.'

'I gave you my answer. For example, if you told me to take my chopper up, and I thought the conditions were unsafe, then, no, I wouldn't follow your instructions.'

'And why would we disagree about the conditions? You would have to give me credit for knowing my job and the conditions. I'd say I've been working with cattle since you were in nappies.'

Fallon put her glass on the table and leaned forward. 'Are you always this difficult, Mr Ingram?'

'No, but I'm always bloody thorough in choosing the right staff for the job. Lives and livelihoods depend on it.'

'I was under the impression that I had been employed by Kent Mason and that my contract was watertight. Is this a job interview, or like I said, are you just trying to piss me off?'

'Temper, temper, Fallon.' His words dripped like honey, and she stared at him wondering how such a sexy voice could come from such an obnoxious person.

At least the "babe" had taken a hike.

She went to stand. At least if she walked out of this job, she could get out of sorting Uncle George's house.

His hand shot out and grabbed her hand as her fingers gripped the edge of the table. 'We haven't finished talking yet.'

'Oh, I think we have. Let go of me. Now.'

'If you sit down and listen to me, we'll—'

'I don't particularly want to,' she said staring down at his hand on hers. Despite being callused, his fingers were long and elegant, his nails clean and clipped short, and strangely it made her dislike him even more.

His grip tightened and her temper rose.

'You've signed a contract, Fallon, and we'll sit down together and discuss your conditions of employment in a civilised fashion.' He let go of her hand and Fallon sat back down reluctantly, taking a deep breath as she held his gaze.

His eyes were intense and she found it hard not to look away. It was as though he could read her thoughts.

She'd met some hard characters in the outback, but there was something different about Jon Ingram, and she didn't know what it was.

And she didn't think she wanted to find out, she decided as a tingle headed south.

Oh, no, she wasn't going there.

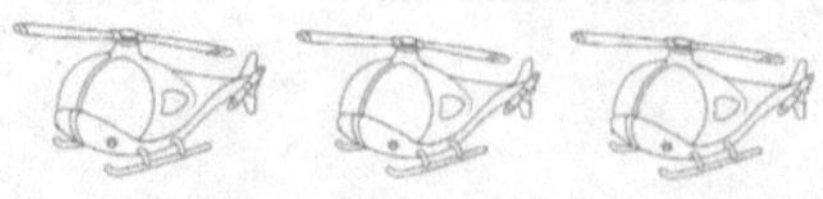

Chapter 3

Fallon Malone was nothing like Jon Ingram had expected. She had a good reputation and for some reason, he'd expected her to be older, but the woman who sat so reluctantly across the table looked as though she was just out of high school. Her olive skin was flawless and huge dark brown eyes framed by long dark lashes stared back at him. For a moment he wondered if they were cosmetically enhanced, but she wore no other makeup, no lipstick and no jewellery. When she'd stood to walk out before, he'd taken note of her dress: khaki cargo shorts, an elbow-length work shirt with a white T-shirt underneath that showed off a slim build. Her straw-blonde hair was just above shoulder length and despite the no-frills, she was altogether a very feminine and attractive package. Not the sort of pilot he wanted around the ringers and stockmen who were pretty rough around the edges. Somehow he couldn't see her fitting in as one of the boys; he had a rougher than usual crew this muster. It was getting harder each year to get a team together.

'You're such a sexist pig, Jon.' He could hear Mandy's voice and he pushed it away. It had nothing to do with being sexist; it was all about making sure his team were suitable and a good fit. There was a job to be done and the dynamics of the team was his first consideration.

Okay, so he was pushing Fallon's buttons to see what sort of reaction he'd get, and he got one.

A point in her favour. She could stand up for herself. Now it was time to stop pushing and get down to business before he overstepped the mark. There was a shortage of pilots, and if she wasn't suitable, he'd have to find another one bloody quickly.

He put his glass down and leaned back in his chair. Her large brown eyes were wary as she held his gaze steadily.

'So tell me about your experience, Fallon.'

Those pretty eyes widened at the switch in his demeanour.

'My experience? I'm assuming you're talking about my flying experience?'

'I am.' He nodded and kept his eyes on her. She was a very attractive woman, and the doubts about having her in the camp wouldn't go away.

She sat straight, but the clenched hands relaxed. 'I've been flying for ten years, and I've got over six thousand hours of flying time up.'

This time it was Jon who widened his eyes as she continued.

'I got my plane license the year I left school, and my helicopter license two years after that.'

He quickly did the maths in his head; that made her close to thirty, if not past it. Close to his age. He hid a smile as he recalled his comment about her being in nappies, but it had achieved the desired effect.

'I've been working for *Wyndham Birds* for eight years now. I'm very experienced in mustering all over. Most of my work has been up in the Kimberley in Western Australia. I've done some jobs in the Gulf but this is my first time here in Southwest Queensland.'

'Okay, so we'll need to go up and have a bit of a reconnoitre seeing you're not familiar with any of these properties, and the topography. The mountains to the west of Braden's spread can prove a bit difficult if the cattle head that way.'

'The cattle will head the way I send them.'

'Will they? I'm impressed. You must have some special skills, Fallon Malone. I'm yet to see that happen one hundred percent of the time.'

'I know my job,' she said simply.

Jon was impressed by her quiet confidence. Now if she could deliver what she said, he'd worry about the guys on the ground later.

'Did you fly in?'

'No, I drove in because—' She cut the words off and he was curious, but he didn't engage.

'No matter. Where's your company R22?'

'It arrived at the aerodrome this morning.'

'So how long is it here for, if you're in a vehicle?'

'As long as we need it.'

'And what's your time frame?' he asked. 'The contract is three weeks; if we go over, can you give us extra time?'

'Yes, the company always builds in a week at the end of each contract. The weather in the north can add a week or two to a muster. I'm not sure if that's the case here.'

'Good,' he said briskly. 'I'll meet you at the aerodrome in the morning.'

Her delicate eyebrows rose. 'So I am still employed by you?'

'And why would you think you weren't?'

She stared at him, her gaze cold and the fingers he'd noticed clenched on the table earlier clenched again.

'I just assumed you'd changed your mind.'

'I'm happy with what I've heard here but I want to see you fly tomorrow. This muster is huge and the way things have been out here lately, our three property owners need a damn good job done and a fast job.'

'I don't call three weeks a fast job.'

'No, but it's a big job and we'll be doing it properly. Okay?' He pushed his glass away and stood. 'I'll meet you at the airfield at 6.30 a.m.'

He grinned at the muttered, 'Aye, aye, captain,' behind him as he walked away.

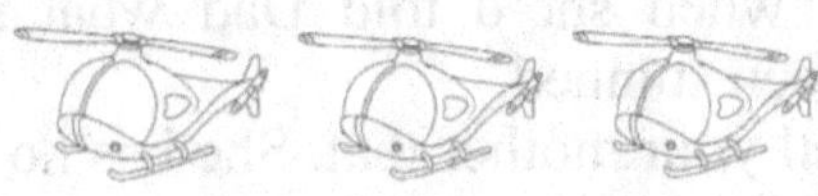

Chapter 4

Fallon ordered a takeaway burger and chips from the pub before she headed back to George's house. She planned to make a start on the kitchen having been instructed to not be late, so she'd have an early night.

She'd go out to the aerodrome early. It would be light enough by then to do the safety checks, and be ready to go when the "boss" arrived. It really irked her that she had to prove herself; her references were top notch, she was the pilot in most demand up north, and the company had recently paid her a great bonus for her work last year. She'd used it to increase her life and medical insurance cover; when she'd told Dad what she was paying for insurance, he'd been stunned.

'Don't you tell your mother that. She has no idea how dangerous your job is.'

'I'm careful, Dad. But if anything happened, I've still got a mortgage to worry about. And it never hurts to have income protection insurance.'

'I know you're careful, but I still worry.'

And this—*this cowboy*—wanted to see her in action before he'd commit. She'd show him action. With a bit of luck, he'd get airsick.

And what a cowboy; with his slicked-back dark hair, neatly pressed clothes, and manicured fingernails, he looked more like a cowboy from the movies than one of the rugged cattlemen she was used to working with.

But she thought with a shrug as she waited for her food order, he seemed to be a good operator, apart from his attitude.

A strange guy. The ringer she'd spoken to at Barkly Homestead had picked him right.

'Number six takeaway,' the woman behind the pub bistro counter called and Fallon walked over to collect her order.

'Here you go, lovey,' the woman said, handing over the white bag. She looked at Fallon with a smile. 'New in town?'

'Working here for a few weeks.'

'You know Jon, do you?'

'No, that was a work meeting.'

'Ah. You're the lady pilot we heard about.'

Fallon nodded.

Small towns.

'A word of warning. Watch him. He's a lady-killer.'

'Oh?' Fallon tilted her head to the side. 'A lady-killer?'

'Yep, Jon boy leaves a trail of broken hearts in every town. If you're after a fling, well and good, but if you're after anything more, like a ring on the finger, run a mile when he makes the move.'

'Makes the move? I'm an employee.'

'Doesn't matter, love. You're female and you're a looker. He'll make a move; he can't help himself. Jon left a few broken hearts in town when he was working here last time.'

Fallon forced a laugh. 'I don't mix work with pleasure.'

'That's what they all say. Trust me, he won't give up.'

'Thanks for the warning,' Fallon said politely. 'And thanks for dinner.' She turned and headed out to the street.

George's ute was in the shed. Cleaning that up was another thing on her to-do list. It was too beautiful a vehicle to let go of. As she strolled down the main street from the pub, she passed a huge black RAM ute with shiny bull bars. Shaking her head, she grinned. The JI numberplates were a dead giveaway.

Just what she'd expect from such a cool dude. Or a guy who thought he was a cool dude.

Hmm. A lady-killer, hey? He was a good-looking man, but she was not one bit attracted. Okay, so he was a looker, but his personality? Nuh. If she chose to sleep with anyone, she was picky, and his attitude had put her right off from the outset. She crossed the road and turned the corner and put her head down as she spotted the owner of the flash ute himself standing outside the pub.

A pretty young woman leaned against the wall, smiling up at him, and Jon leaned forward one arm outstretched and his palm against the wall beside her head. As Fallon hurried past, his words reached her.

'It's good to see you, Soph. And don't worry, he's not worth it. I'll look out for you.'

Typical, she thought. Obviously stepping into someone else's territory. She kept walking without a backward glance.

##

Fallon was in a deep sleep dreaming of a roller-coaster ride in her bird with Jon Ingram white-faced beside her, begging her to land.

'Not until you leave that poor, young girl alone,' she said as she dived the machine nose down.

She reached for the controls as an alarm rang stridently in the cockpit. Fallon looked around trying to see where it was coming from but the sound was overpowering. She'd never heard an alarm like that before. She flicked switch after switch on and off, but the alarm still blared. She looked at Jon's white face and, even though she wondered what was happening to her helicopter, she felt satisfaction at the fear in his eyes.

God, I'm a bitch, she thought in her dream. But he deserved it.

The alarm kept ringing and ringing, and gradually she surfaced out of her deep sleep.

Bloody hell, it was a telephone. She hadn't even known there was one in the house.

Fallon jumped out of bed, stubbing her toe on the cast-iron base of the bed.

'Shit, shit, shit.' She grabbed her foot, certain she'd broken something. Limping out of her room, she followed the sound of the ringing down the hall and into the dining room, past piles of newspapers and cardboard boxes full of tarnished trophies. She hadn't noticed them before and wondered what he had trophies for.

Making her way through the mess in the passageway that had been left between the piles of junk, she spotted the phone over on an old sideboard against the far wall. She grabbed the receiver and picked it up; the phone was a 1970s vintage with the circular dial pad, but it obviously still worked. She picked it up from the cradle, her eyes roaming over the beautiful piece of furniture she hadn't noticed behind the piles of junk. The sideboard was a genuine antique and with a good dust and polish, it would be beautiful.

'Hello,' she said quickly.

'Hello. Is that George's niece?' an unfamiliar woman's voice asked.

'Yes, it's Fallon Malone here. I'm George's great-niece. Who is calling, please?

'Sorry to ring you so late, love. It's Mary from the Quiet Whispers Nursing Home.'

Fallon glanced down at her watch she'd worn to bed because she had the alarm set for four-thirty. She squinted. It was just past midnight. Dread pooled in her stomach as she realised the only reason the home would be ringing would be to tell her there was a problem with George. 'What's wrong? Is he ... is he ... has he. . .?'

'No, George is fine,' the woman said. 'Well, he's not exactly fine. He's very distressed and we've tried to calm him as best we could but he won't settle unless you come to see him.'

'What? Now? It's the middle of the night,' Fallon replied.

'I know.' The words were followed by a sigh. 'I wouldn't have called if there'd been any other solution. He's usually one of our best-behaved residents. He's got a bee in his bonnet about you being in the house, and that you've taken off and stolen his ute and something from his bedroom.'

'What! He gave me the keys to his ute! Stolen exactly what from his bedroom?' Fallon said nursing her still throbbing foot. The worst she could be accused of was throwing out a pair of ancient mildewed sheets. 'I haven't even been in there. In fact, I don't even know which is his bedroom in this house. Have you been here? Do you know what I'm saying? Have you seen this house?' Her voice was shrill as she woke fully.

'Yes, dear, I know. I was part of the team that did his aged care assessment. The state of the house was one of the reasons he was fast-tracked. It was obvious he was incapable of caring for himself.'

Fallon shook her head and rubbed her eyes with the back of her spare hand. When did this become her problem? Mum could get the next bus out here, pronto. Before she could speak, the aide continued.

'He's got himself in a real state. Is there any chance you could just slip on some clothes and pop over? I know you're not far away from us. Come down and bring what George wants to see and just reassure him that you're still here and that you haven't got any bad intentions. Please?'

Fallon sighed and ran a hand over her hair. 'What exactly does he want and where do I find it?' she said more patiently than she felt.

'Apparently in his bedroom, under the end of the bed, there's a box with a pink lid and inside is all his precious stuff.'

'Stuff?'

'Look, it's probably not precious in terms of value. Just some memento he's attached to. He wants to be reassured that it's still there. We tried to get him to bring some possessions when he came to us, but the ambulance brought him here one night when he had a turn. All he had was the PJs he was wearing. We've asked several times if he wants one of us to go to the house and get some of his things. We find that usually settles our residents, but he refused point-blank. So with his aged care package, he had new clothes and toiletries purchased for him. He's never seemed interested in the house, but something on TV tonight set him off after dinner. He started yelling about this dreadful niece who was in his house. To clean him out of his fortune, he said.'

'Oh, for God's sake,' Fallon said. 'And you want me to come and see him while he's abusing me?'

'Yes please.' The voice was timid.

'All right. I'll come down now. I'll leave this box at—if I find it—at reception.'

'Um, no he wants to see you too. Just to be reassured that you're still here. I'm so sorry, Fallon, but he's keeping most of the floor awake with his yelling and his abuse.'

'What brought it on? He was fine when I saw him yesterday.'

'It's dementia. We've had to restrain him tonight. It's very sad but there's just no stopping him. You'll be okay. We've given him a little bit of a sedative but he's still carrying on, so if you can just grab that box and wander down, it'll only take fifteen minutes or so and then you can go home and get tucked up into bed again. I'm really sorry.'

'I'm on my way.' Fallon knew her voice wasn't over-friendly, but she was awake now. She might as well help them out. She walked along the hall and opened each door as she went. There were five other bedrooms and each room was filled with piles of junk, boxes and old newspapers just like the dining room.

Finally, she reached the one at the far end that seemed to have a bit more space in it.

'Gah.' She knew she was in the right room by the glass of clear liquid with a pair of false teeth on the side table next to the bed.

Poor guy. He didn't even have his teeth with him, she thought. She hadn't noticed his lack of teeth yesterday.

Dropping to her knees at the side of the bed released a cloud of dust. Leaning over, she lifted the faded chenille bedspread, unsure of what she would see under there. A pair of golden eyes looked back from the depths and Fallon jumped to her feet with a scream.

'Holy shit, what's that?' she yelled to an empty house.

A plaintive meow reassured her it wasn't a rat about to launch itself at her.

'Here, puss, puss, puss,' she called softly.

A thin black cat with a gleaming coat sidled out from under the bed and rubbed itself against her bare feet with another soft meow. Fallon dropped to her knees again and looked underneath the bed. Sure enough, there was a box with a pink lid. She slid it out. Although she was curious about his life, she had no intention of looking inside. She'd deposit it at the aged care home, and let Uncle George see she hadn't absconded with his worldly goods. She was learning enough about him from the contents of the house.

As she walked down the hall back to her clean room the cat followed her.

'How long have you been under there, puss?' All the doors and windows were locked, so the cat had obviously been locked inside unless it had a secret exit. She wrinkled her nose, wondering where the cat had been doing its business. Maybe that was part of the gross smell in the house. Then again, maybe not. Quickly pulling her cargo pants and work shirt over her PJs, she slipped into a pair of boots, put the box under one arm and opened the front door. The cat shot out obviously in dire need or looking for food.

'I'll feed you when I get back,' she said as she marched down the road to the aged care home.

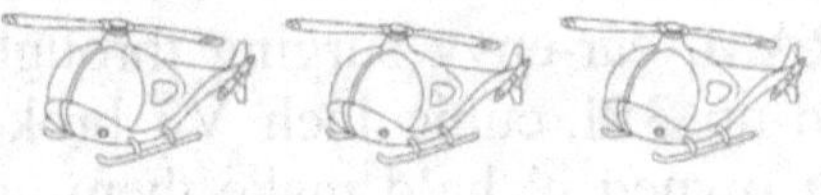

Chapter 5
The next morning

Jon Ingram waited in his car as the sun cleared the flat horizon, golden rays fanning the dawn sky. He'd suspected Fallon would get to the aerodrome early to impress him, so he'd arrived about five-forty-five a.m. Now as he looked at his watch for the fifteenth time in as many minutes and there was still no sign of her, he was unimpressed. She was almost fifteen minutes late.

He'd read her wrong. He thought she'd be here at sparrow fart. But she was obviously playing games by being deliberately late. He'd give her another fifteen and she was out. Contract or not, he wouldn't put up with someone unreliable.

Fourteen minutes later, at one minute to seven, when he'd been sitting there for an hour and a half, Jon sat up straight as a classic car tore along the road next to the aerodrome.

Low to the ground, the red, vintage F100 ute was in perfect condition, albeit a little dusty. It veered into the aerodrome, almost on two wheels—whoever was driving it was skilled—and kicked up dust as it approached the hangar where the helicopter was sitting. He got out of his RAM, car-envy surging through him as the throaty roar of a souped-up 351 cubic inch V8 broke the early morning silence. Whoever owned it, he'd make them an offer they couldn't refuse.

He *had* to have it.

His eyes widened with surprise when Fallon almost fell out of the driver's seat and ran barefooted over to the chopper. Long bare legs ending at a minuscule pair of pink—*pink*—shorts flashed past him as she ran bare-footed towards the machine. She glanced at him and didn't speak as she leaned against the side of the machine and pulled on the pair of work boots she carried. As he walked over he saw the look of horror that crossed her face as she looked down at the pink shorts.

As he got closer, he realised they weren't shorts, but looked like PJs.

Rather than balling her out as he'd intended over the past half hour, he couldn't help the belly laugh that rose from his gut.

'Love the look, Fallon. I've never had a pilot take me up in their PJs before. Goes nicely with the work boots.'

'Don't. Just don't,' she said. 'I apologise for my appearance, and I apologise for my lateness, so just leave it there, okay?' She stood straight and he couldn't help his eyes dropping to that gorgeous pair of legs that seemed to go forever. His lips twitched as he saw the cute little teddy bears on her pink PJ shorts.

'Okay. I will. Next time, just set an alarm.'

'I did.'

'Well, next time, wake up.'

If looks could kill, he would have sizzled on the spot.

'I just have to do the safety check and probably top up with fuel.'

'How about I go to the bakery and get us both a coffee while you do that?' He turned to the car. 'Love your wheels. 1962? Can I take it for a spin into the bakery?'

She hesitated and looked at him.

He glanced at the ute and grinned at her. 'Coffee *and* Danish pastries?'

'All right. Don't prang it. It's not mine.'

'Way to go.' He grinned at her. 'How long do you need?'

'It all depends. How much of a hurry are you in? What time do we have to be back?'

'We've got all morning. Or I have. We're meeting with the team at two this afternoon out at Braden's station.'

'In that case, can we delay our departure a little? I'll let you drive the ute and get the coffee if you drop me off back in town and I can get dressed properly.' Her face was as pink as her PJ pants.

With a chuckle, he nodded. 'Jump in and tell me where to go.' He shot a sideways look at her. 'Literally, that is. Not what you're thinking. Where you're staying.'

Fallon opened the passenger door and climbed up, and Jon walked around to the driver's side. He smoothed his hand over the beautiful paintwork before he got in.

'What a bloody beauty,' he said.

'Yeah, my ute's in dock. Needs a new gearbox, so I've been driving this one.'

He started the engine and closed his eyes as the V8 burbled. 'Who owns it?'

There was no reply and he looked over at her. 'Does it matter?'

'Yep. I want to buy it.'

'Ha, good luck with that. If you do, it's got nothing to do with me. After the night I've had, I'm not going there.'

'So who owns it?'

'My great-uncle.'

He nodded. 'Okay, so where am I taking you?'

'Go past the pub where we met yesterday, and then take the second left. The last house in the street on the edge of town.'

Jon did as he was instructed, checked the bakery was open as he drove past, and then took the second left. It was a long street and the last house was set back from the road, surrounded by half a dozen sheds.

'A farm once?'

'Apparently ten thousand acres. Still on ten acres now.' Her voice held something that showed she was unhappy about that.

'Okay, I'll drop you off and go and grab us some breakfast. Do you need the car keys or is there someone to let you in?'

'No, thank you. I put the front door key under the mat.'

'Is that safe?'

'In this town? I think so. I was walking through town at two a.m. and didn't see a soul. And no, I hadn't been out having a good time.'

'You can tell me that story later. I'll be back in ten or so. What sort of coffee?' Fallon Malone was turning into an interesting person.

'Cappuccino, please. Double shot. Thank you.' It must have been hard, but she lifted her head and looked at him once she was out of the car. 'I mean it. Thank you, and I promise I won't let you down again.'

'Babe.' He couldn't help himself and then felt mean when she visibly cringed. 'You're forgiven. Letting me drive this gorgeous beast has put me in your debt. Not to mention the PJs.'

'Good.' Finally a smile tilted her pretty lips, and Jon found it hard to look away as attraction tugged.

'I'll go and get some work clothes on,' she said as he pushed the unwanted attraction away.

He didn't get involved with anyone he worked with, contrary to his reputation. He'd knocked back a couple of offers of a night out— or in—and the gossip mill had started.

'If you must. I didn't see a problem with your teddy bear PJs,' he teased.

She pulled a face at him and slammed the door before she hurried along the path, bending down and scooping up a black cat when she reached the front porch.

Jon did the gentlemanly thing and looked away because it was obvious she was wearing nothing beneath the teddy bear pyjama pants.

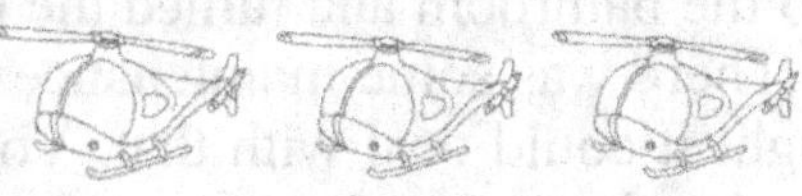

Chapter 6

Waves of embarrassment rolled over Fallon as she stood under the shower. Jon had said ten minutes until he came back and she headed straight to the bathroom and turned the tap to be greeted with lukewarm water. There was some maintenance needed on the house, but whoever bought it could deal with that. You pretty much had to run around under the showerhead to get wet in both the showers in George's house.

As soon as her great-uncle had seen her last night and she'd handed over the pink-lidded box, he'd smiled.

Poor George.

'Sally! Thank you,' he'd said, mistaking her for Mum. 'That daughter of yours didn't take them. Thank heavens!' He hugged the box to his chest and a single tear ran down his face. 'I don't want to lose my Josie's letters. I don't care if that girl's stolen my ute.'

'No, Uncle George. Everything is in your house. And the ute is in the shed,' Fallon said quietly as she exchanged a sad smile with the aide, and wondered who Josie was. When she'd come here to see him earlier, he'd been lucid. It was sad to see a huge strapping man like Great-Uncle George with his mind deteriorating.

'What's your cat's name?' she asked softly as he stared at her.

'Sooty. You know that, Sally, I've always had a Sooty,' he said with a nod. 'She won't eat fish. Just chicken. Ask Reg at the butcher. He'll get the right ones for you, all chopped up and then put the chicken meat through the cast-iron mincer on the edge of the kitchen bench.'

'I will,' Fallon promised. And made a mental note she'd also need to find a new home for Sooty before she headed north again.

Mary walked her to the door. 'I'm sorry I had to call you. That's the first bad episode he's had. He's a lovely old guy and usually pretty good. He had a fall at the dinner table last night, and we're worried he's had a TIA. He was a bit confused for a while and came good. Then he had his big panic when he woke up a couple of hours ago. The doctor will see him in the morning.'

'TIA?' Fallon queried.

'A little brain bleed. It can be the precursor of a stroke.'

Fallon had walked slowly back to the house and lay there awake for a long time before she'd drifted into a deep sleep.

And then she damn well slept through her watch alarm and woke up at 6.45. In a panic, she'd grabbed her shirt and boots and

George's car keys, and it wasn't until she was standing by the bird that she'd looked down and mortification flooded through her when she realised she was still wearing her pyjama pants. It had been the night *before* she'd slept in her jeans, *not* last night.

In her half-asleep mad panic, she hadn't even looked down as she'd grabbed her boots and run out to the shed. As she'd driven through the quiet town, her attention had been totally on the road, as she broke every speed limit, and she hadn't even noticed her bare legs.

Her face burned now as she quickly dried herself. She would never live that down, and she really hoped Jon would keep that to himself. Not the sort of story to be shared around a muster campfire.

She ran a comb through her wet hair, pulled on her cargos, a clean black T-shirt and work shirt, and then put the key back under the mat. The cat—Sooty—had disappeared in the house somewhere. She'd pick up some cat food—the chicken from Reg the butcher— and sort her out when they got back.

Seven minutes after Jon dropped her off she was waiting on the grass outside the rusted front gate when he pulled up.

'I'm impressed,' he said with a smile as she opened the door and then lifted the cardboard holder with two coffees in it.

'With?' Fallon forced confidence and sass into her voice and body language.

'Your speed. And you've had a shower too. Most impressive.'

'I'll be even more on the ball when I have a coffee. Which one's mine?'

'Both the same.'

'Thank you.'

'Just as well you had to go home. I wouldn't fancy going up in the air with you if you weren't on the ball.'

'Don't worry. I would have been. The coffee just gives me more energy. I wouldn't fly if I didn't feel up to it.'

She sipped her coffee and looked through the window as they passed the Big Meat Ant on the pole, crossed the wide sandy river bed of the almost-dry river, and then headed up the Old Tambo Road towards the aerodrome.

Jon turned the ute along the red dirt road into the aerodrome, came to a slow stop and cut the engine. His smile was wide. Fallon smiled back as he patted the steering wheel with a reverence that she understood.

'That's how she deserves to be driven,' he said.

'She's a beauty, isn't she?' she said. 'I'll be sorry to leave her here.'

'Absolutely original condition. Except I think the motor's been hotted up.'

Fallon shrugged. 'Don't know her history.' Maybe she'd talk to Mum and see what would be involved with her buying it. She knew Mum and Dad were the executors of Uncle George's will.

She frowned. Was that what Mum had been hinting at about the house? Gawd, that was the last thing she wanted to be lumbered with; inheriting that house would be a nightmare. Hopefully, Uncle George had a few years in him yet, although that TIA thing sounded a bit of a worry.

'Any chance of it being for sale?'

'What, the house?'

Jon shook his head. 'Are you sure you're awake? Is there any chance of this gorgeous vehicle being for sale?'

'Sorry. I was thinking about the house. If the ute's for sale, I'll be first in line,' she said. Fallon tossed him a glance, hoping that answer didn't put him into a bad mood again; she was still wary.

'Shame. I'd be happy to take it if you change your mind.' He was still smiling. Certainly a different mood to the one he'd been in at the pub yesterday. Maybe he'd got lucky, last night. He was in a damn fine mood this morning.

'I'll note that.'

'Good.' He reached between the seats and retrieved a bakery brown paper bag. 'I bought two sorts of Danish because I didn't pick you as an apple girl.'

'Is that the same failing as a Chardonnay girl?' Fallon couldn't help asking. If he could be pleasant so could she.

He grinned back. 'I thought the apricot one was a bit sweeter.'

'So I needed sweetening up, did I?' Fallon took the bag he passed over.

'No comment.' His grin widened and the tanned skin around his eyes crinkled.

'You weren't Mr Personality yourself at the pub yesterday.'

'I'm the boss.'

'Yeah and I'm the employee. Two-way respect is what I'm used to getting.' She looked across at him as he sipped his coffee. 'Aren't you eating?'

He reached over and she froze as his thumb wiped the side of her mouth. An exquisite tingle fired in her nerve endings, and they weren't the nerves around her mouth.

'You're covered in icing sugar. And no, I'll leave my *apple* Danish in the car until we come down.'

Fallon nodded slowly as understanding dawned. She ignored the increased heartbeat; that was the sugary Danish causing it to race. Nothing else. 'You don't get airsick, do you?'

'Depends on how good the pilot is.'

'Oh, I'm good,' she said. 'Don't you worry about that. But I'll be gentle with you.'

'Thank you. I like a woman who's gentle.' Their eyes met and held and she was the first to look away.

'Anyway, that's good to hear in regard to your *flying*, but I'll still leave breakfast until we get back.' He drained his coffee cup and she looked at him curiously, wondering if he really did get airsick.

He'd been nice this morning, so maybe she would give him an easy ride, and not the roller coaster one she'd dreamed about last night. That must have been her self-protective subconscious kicking in.

'Okay.' Fallon picked up her coffee and drained the last of it. 'Thanks for breakfast and again, I'm sorry I was late.'

'Come on, let's get this show on the road. We've got quite a bit of ground to cover.'

'Which direction are we heading?' Fallon looked across at the windsock at the side of the aerodrome, but it barely moved as the occasional desultory puff of breeze drifted in. 'It's a good morning, wind wise. The sky's clear but I want to check the wind forecast on my phone. I haven't had a chance to look this morning. Just give me a minute. I'll have a look before I do the safety check.' She reached for the phone in her pocket. 'No need if the wind's not right.'

'Clear skies. Wind from the south-south-west at five kilometres. No forecast of rain or storm and no change is expected for the rest of the week. There's a high sitting smack bang above us. Can you trust me?'

'I can.' She put her phone away. 'I'm impressed you've checked.'

'I have because I need to keep a close eye on the weather too. The last thing we want over the next three weeks is rain. First week is looking good.'

'How many cattle are we bringing in?'

'1500 head on Braden's place, 2000 on Kent's and I'm still waiting to hear from Craig Wilson. He'll be at the meeting at *Kilcoy Station* this afternoon.'

'There'll be a few trucks in.'

'Yep, we use a local company.'

'Do they export from Darwin?'

'No, Port Alma near Rocky. A third of the distance. Only seven hundred ks.'

'Much better.' She nodded. 'And which direction are we going in this morning?'

'South-south-west,' he said as he went to pass her the ute keys and open the driver's door. 'Or do I need them to lock from the driver's side?'

'Yes. I think so.'

Jon took the keys back and once she'd put her window up, climbed out and closed the door, he used the key to lock the driver's door.

Fallon tested her door, and it was locked. Last thing she wanted after George's rant was to have the vintage ute stolen. She'd take more care locking the shed at night from now on too.

They walked over to the helicopter together.

'The three properties cover about a hundred kilometres to the west and another seventy-five to the south. We'll do the boundary run first and I'll show you where the stockyards and muster camps are. We'll be mustering towards three stockyards. One for each property on their shared boundaries.'

'Okay.'

'Have you met Kent yet or did he call you?'

'I met both Braden and Kent yesterday morning when I was out here waiting for the chopper to come in. They were flying north apparently. I assume they're back. I had coffee with Callie afterwards. She was friendly.'

'Yes, they're back. They went to pick up Braden's sister. That was Sophie I was talking to when you passed us outside the pub last night. And yeah, Callie's the best thing that could have happened to Braden,' he said, but didn't elaborate.

'Good.' She nodded, not quite sure if she should respond. She was here to work. Not to get to know everyone's issues, even though she and Callie had clicked instantly.

'Hey, you don't know anyone looking for a job out here, do you?'

'What sort of job?'

'Braden's looking for a housekeeper and a governess. It's hard to get staff out here and keep them.'

'I'll keep an ear out, but I don't really meet many people on the properties. Just the muster camps. But sometimes you hear stuff.'

'No friends looking for a job?'

Fallon shook her head. 'I don't socialise much. I'm usually too busy.'

He looked at her curiously but agreed. 'Yeah, I know what that feels like.'

Fallon walked around the machine and carried out the safety checks. Jason had filled the tank for her before he'd left so it was all good. She walked around the bird, lifted the cowl and checked the fuel lines.

***

Jon stood back waiting while Fallon did the safety check. He swallowed back the nausea that threatened and made sure his stance was confident and his expression bland. He held the greatest admiration for the muster pilots, but she didn't need to know that yet. Fallon also didn't need to know how much he hated being up in the air. Give him a horse any day.

So far he was impressed with how she was handling her job. Economy of movement and a keen eye as she looked around the chopper. Her concern with the weather, plus her sense of humour, combined into a bit of a mystery package. Shame she was an employee; he would have enjoyed getting to know her better and spending some time with her.

Yesterday in the pub he knew he'd pushed her buttons, and his first impression hadn't been favourable, but when Fallon had dropped the sass and shown some vulnerability this morning, his opinion had changed. He'd actually felt sorry for her. He'd love to know what she was doing wandering around town at two o'clock this morning, but he guessed he'd never know.

And it's none of your business. As long as it didn't impact her ability to do her work.

But even yesterday in the pub he'd sensed something underneath and he wanted to get to the bottom of it, so he'd taken the sexist line to get a reaction. Maybe it had been the wrong thing to do, but, God, women, he thought, why can't they just be like blokes? With blokes, what you see is what you get.

But to be fair, Jock Evans, Sophie Cartwright's ex, had pulled the wool over everyone's eyes.

After he'd caught up with Sophie briefly at the pub last night, he'd had a quick beer with Braden and Kent. They'd driven into town because Sophie had wanted to stay with a friend and not go out to the property. When he'd been talking to her, Fallon had scurried past with her head down, all adding to today's perception that she was a private person who kept to herself.

Sophie was the opposite. He'd had to excuse himself because she'd wanted his sympathy, and wanted to tell him all about what had happened between her and Jock. Braden had told him enough for him to know that Sophie was pretty fragile, so he'd untangled himself gently from the conversation, with a promise to catch up later. They'd been good mates when he'd worked out at *Kilcoy Station* before, and Jock had just come on the scene. A good bloke, sociable, and a hard worker. He'd muscled in and broken up Kent and Sophie, that was the one negative in Jon's book. But Sophie was grown up, and it was for her to choose.

But she'd chosen the wrong man, well and truly. Braden didn't go into detail, but it sounded as though she'd been through a pretty hard time.

'Okay, Mr Boss. A bit late, but looks like we're ready to go. Climb in.'

Jon pushed Sophie to the back of his mind. At least he'd stopped thinking about flying for a while. 'Not *too* late.'

Fallon obviously had a reason for being late, and he respected that circumstances could change plans. He was reassured now; it wasn't disorganisation. She'd obviously had some sort of drama through the night. He stifled a grin. As long as everything was fine, it didn't matter. Fallon turning up in cute, brief pyjama pants had been a bonus.

Her demeanour this morning had been pleasant and efficient and he'd seen a glimmer of that sense of humour a couple of times.

Jon strapped himself in and took the headset she passed over, chastising himself mentally. It didn't matter whether he liked her or not. She was an employee. He needed to get his head back on the muster and away from the attractive woman who was about to take his life in her hands. He ignored the prickle of cold sweat that formed on the back of his neck and closed his eyes as she pushed the starter.

Not that he didn't think she was a top operator. Fallon Malone had come with excellent references and a top-notch verbal reputation. He'd heard of her and her flying skills a few times when he'd been up in the Gulf but they'd never crossed paths. When *Wyndham Birds* had put her name forward for this muster, he'd accepted readily.

Jon focused on his breathing as the engine started and he knew she'd be checking the instruments and getting all the systems working.

Give me a bloody rogue horse over a manmade hunk of metal.

Pretend it's Kent, he told himself as the helicopter lifted off the ground. Jon opened his eyes and glanced across at her, but Fallon was focused on the controls and didn't look his way.

Her fingers flicked efficiently over the dials and he watched closely as she gripped the single T-bar cyclic between them. He went to lift his hands from his lap to grip the side of the seat, but he managed to resist.

'Right to go?' Her voice crackled through the headset

He nodded, and mouthed, 'Right to go' as she glanced at him.

The helicopter lifted and tilted forward as she set a bearing. Neither of them spoke until they'd gained height and headed southwest across the red dirt below.

Jon managed to get himself under control and pointed down.

'There's a couple of properties in between town and the border to Braden's place, but he's got the biggest property around so we'll hit the eastern boundary of it soon.'

Fallon's voice came through the headset again. 'The river's low.'

'Yeah, they've been in drought again over the last eighteen months. There's some water in the river, enough for them to irrigate, plus they pump from the artesian basin. There's enough water to keep the pasture up and the cattle watered. They're in good nick out here most of the time.'

'What's that down there?' She pointed ahead to a green patch that covered around a thousand hectares in front of them. 'Not often you see that much green in the outback.'

'It's an organic wheat crop. A young couple came to town a few years back just before I left the area. They decided to have a go at it. Apparently, they're going okay, lots of orders from organic stockfeed suppliers and organic chicken farmers and the like. It's their third season and they've survived.'

'Good to see some diversification,' she said.

He nodded and gestured out of his side. 'Okay, if you look across to the west you can just see a set of cattle yards. That's the northeast corner of Braden's property, and those yards are the ones where the trucks will pick his beasts up. You'll bring the cattle out furthest to another set of yards to start with, and then bring them in to here a couple of days later. The same goes for Kent and Craig's places. A temporary holding yard to start with and then they'll all come back here over seven to ten days.'

'Not good access for the cattle trucks further out where you hold them?'

He lifted his thumb. 'You got it. There's a road that comes in from the back of Charleville the cattle trucks and road trains use. If you look west you might see them on the road as we fly. A couple of the other stations are already mustering.'

Fallon nodded. 'From the air?'

'No, horseback.'

All was quiet for another ten minutes as they approached the green and red variegated landscape ahead. The ground had held the moisture of last season's rains by the look of things. As he looked at the landscape below, his focus moved from his churning stomach.

He'd conquered his nerves and looked down at the familiar channel country of south-western Queensland. It was good to be back; it was sad that he was no longer needed in Normanton, the two years had been tough. The Gulf was different, but he was grateful his employer there had been so understanding He'd missed this landscape, he felt at home here, and Jon had been pleased when he'd heard Braden was looking for a manager. When he'd called, there'd been no hesitation on either side, and he figured he'd stay as long as Braden needed him this time. He had no commitments anymore.

'It's different to the north,' Fallon said. 'Not as much vegetation and no trees and only low scrub. That's fabulous for us.'

'Fabulous? How? For who?' He frowned.

'"Dead man's zone" we call it. Flying low and flying slow when mustering, you don't have time to react if a tree suddenly appears in front of you. And if there are trees, that's where the cattle like to get.' Her voice was tight and he noticed her hand tensed.

'I honestly don't know how you do it. I apologise for being flippant yesterday. It's not a career for the faint-hearted. I have the utmost respect for what you do.'

'And I respect you guys on horseback. I'm terrified of the bloody things.'

Before he could reply, the chopper shuddered as they hit an air pocket. Jon tried to remain calm and not grab hold of his seat, pleased he hadn't given in to the temptation of the Danish.

The coffee he could hold down but the last thing he wanted was to spew in front of Fallon Malone.

'Sorry,' she said. 'A bit of a bump there.' She glanced at him and frowned. 'All good?'

'I'm fine.' He tried to disguise his deep breath as he inhaled, covered his mouth and coughed. 'Just ahead to the east you'll see a shed about a kilometre away. And another set of cattle yards. That's Kent's place.'

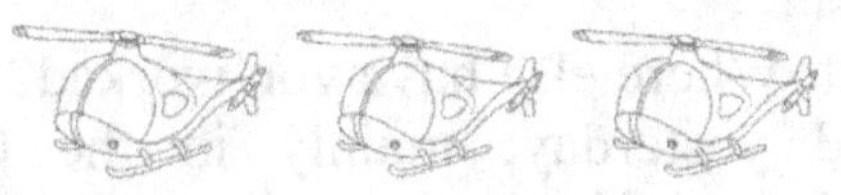

Chapter 7

Fallon looked ahead to where Jon indicated. She was feeling sorry for him. It was obvious he wasn't a good passenger, no matter how much he tried to disguise it. He was quiet as she approached the yards.

'I see them. Will we keep going to the third station or shall we go back? I've got the lie of the land now.'

'Yeah. He lifted his arm and looked at his watch, and once again, Fallon noticed the long, fine fingers. They looked like they belonged to a concert pianist rather than a cattleman.

'And you manage Brayden's place?'

'Yeah. I've just come down from Normanton where I was looking after a couple of big spreads. I managed his property a couple of years back when he lost his wife. When he was back on deck, I had to go north, but the channel country out here is like home to me.'

'So, here to stay?'

'Looks like it. Where else have you worked?'

'Like I said yesterday, mainly in the Gulf and the East Kimberley, but it is different down here. Should be a pretty easy muster with little vegetation.

'Strange we haven't crossed paths before. The station might cover a lot of land but it's a small cattle world. I have worked with *Wyndham Birds*.'

'Yeah.' She didn't say she had heard of him.

'If the cattle get spooked down there, nothing stops them. There's not many tracks and they scatter to the winds, so be aware of that.'

'How many ringers and stockmen on horseback?' she asked as she turned the bird back towards Augathella.

'We've got a team of about twenty and they'll rotate around the properties. Quad bikes and horseback.'

'Contract guys?'

'Yep, contract guys plus Braden and Kent and me.' He grinned. 'I'd say Sophie will be out there too, now that she's home. She's a natural on horseback. She can outride most of the guys.'

'Sounds like a good team. Always good to have the bosses out with the contract workers.'

'Will they camp out or is it close enough to the accommodation? I'm just trying to get a feel for the days and the times.'

'They'll camp out. Once the workers lived in their accommodation on the stations, but these days you tend to find they're seasonal. Plus we have a cook out there.'

'And do you find it hard to get them when you need them? The guys up north are finding it tougher each year.'

'Yes, there's a bloody shortage of good stockmen everywhere. They're all older blokes, these days. The young ones don't want to take it on.'

'Same in the north,' she said. 'Not to mention muster pilots,' she said raising her eyebrows.

'Yeah, your company assured me you had good references.'

'And I'm flying to your satisfaction.' She bit back a smile. The closer they got to the aerodrome, the more his hands relaxed.

'You are.'

'I've proved I can lift a bird off the ground and put it in the direction you told me. You still have to see ifr I can handle a cattle muster.'

Jon chuckled. 'Yep, you'll do, Miss Chardonnay.'

As they approached the aerodrome, Fallon nodded. 'I'm pleased. Thanks for showing me the land and the stations. It's given me a good idea of what to expect.'

They sat quietly once they'd landed, waiting for the rotors to slow.

Fallon made a note to refuel tomorrow. It would give her an excuse to leave Uncle George's house.

***

Jon climbed out as Fallon checked the instruments.

'Where's the meeting this afternoon?' she called as she followed him.

'It's out at Braden's.' He turned to her with a smile. Maybe you'd like to drive my work ute out and I can take the F100.'

'The RAM?'

'No, that's my good car. No one drives that.'

She chuckled. 'In that case, not a chance. I might follow you out though. I don't know this area well. I'd hate to get lost and be late twice in one day.

'Not a problem,' he said. 'Actually, I have to come back into town after the meeting. We could travel together if you like.'

Her deep belly laugh surprised him. 'You really want to drive the F100 that much?'

He grinned back at her. 'I do. And I still want to buy it.'

'I'll swap it for your RAM,' she said.

'Not a chance,' he said with a grin. 'Not that I'd go behind your back. Or swap it for my RAM.'

'It's not mine anyway That's why I was walking through town in the early hours. And why I slept through my alarm. Don't worry. It won't happen once the muster starts. It was a one-off.'

'A problem?'

'I'm staying at a rellie's place while I'm in town. Supposed to be cleaning it up to sell, but I think it's beyond me. It needs a skip bin out the front and a few brawny blokes to carry out the entire contents. Sad, isn't it, how life ends?'

Jon lifted his head and stared past her. His mouth was set; he knew all about that. 'You collect all this stuff in your life and even though it might be important to you, no one knows when you go. And you're the only one it's important to. I feel for you. It's not a nice thing to do.'

'Poor Uncle George. I had to look for a box under a bed last night and take it to him, so the nursing home could get some peace and quiet. He thought I was my Mum.'

'Sad,' he said, his voice clipped. 'Anyway, if the ute doesn't work out for you let me know. No matter when. My mobile's on my card.'

'I will. Where's home for you,' she asked curiously.

'Wherever I'm working.'

'No base? No home?'

He shook his head. 'No.'

Fallon nodded. They had more in common than she'd realised. 'Same for me. No base. I mean I've got a room in my family home in Brisbane, but I haven't been back for a while. Plus an investment property in Cairns. I usually bunk in the accommodation on the properties, but I agreed to stay here in town and help out.'

'If you need a hand,' Jon said, wondering what the hell he was doing. The prospect of spending more time with Fallon was appealing, but he pulled himself up fast.

Don't get involved with staff.

He frowned and shook his head. 'Sorry, on second thought I'll take that back. I won't have time.'

'I don't expect anyone to help. That's not why I mentioned it.' Her voice was cold. 'I'm sorry I dumped my issues on you.'

The mood between them changed after that, the lightness and the levity disappeared.

Jon regretted it, but it was necessary. He'd let himself be too attracted and let down his guard.

'Thanks for taking me up today. You did well.' He knew by the look on her face he sounded patronising. 'I'll come to your uncle's place about two and you can follow me out.'

As much as he'd love to drive that ute again, he wouldn't be tempted. Spending more time alone with an attractive employee was not a good move.

She shrugged. 'Whatever. I'll be ready.'

Jon strode off to his ute without a backward glance. He jumped in and took off back towards town, kicking himself.

When would he ever learn?

***

Fallon lifted her hand and wiped her forehead. She looked down at it; it came away black and grimy. Once she'd got back to the house, she'd worked off her cross mood by making a start on the kitchen.

On the way, she'd called into the nursing home and checked on Uncle George, but the doctor hadn't called in yet.

'You can go and see him if you want,' the lady in reception said.

'No, I won't upset him.'

She'd left the home and gone to the butcher in town to get the chicken meat for the cat. When she'd asked for Reg, the young guy behind the counter stared at her.

'Reg? There's no Reg here.' He frowned. 'Hang on. My grandfather used to own the shop. His name was Reg.'

She'd waved a hand. 'Sorry. Someone got their wires crossed. I just want some chicken meat so I can mince it for George Mason's cat.'

'Sooty won't each chicken. Has to have veal. I'll get you some. I'll mince it for you too.'

'Thank you.' Most things about this town were good. Everyone was friendly and she'd had a warm welcome wherever she went.

Fallon fed Sooty in the kitchen, and he'd scoffed the mince and then he'd wound himself around her ankles as she opened the cupboards. Every one she peered into was full of junk. It was a daunting prospect.

Now she was head down in the kitchen and so far had found nothing worth keeping. She stood at the window over the old sink and stared out over the dead back lawn.

What was she doing here and why was she focusing on the house? Since Jon had shut down at the end of the conversation, she even wondered what she was doing out here at all.

Fallon ignored her maudlin thoughts and pulled out the Gumption and a sponge and put her cross mood into scrubbing the sink as she tried to forget how much she'd liked Jon Ingram for a short while.

After a shower and a change of clothes, she backed the F100 out of the locked shed and was waiting outside the house on the road when Jon pulled up in a dust-covered work ute

He pulled up on her driver's-side, lowered the passenger window and called out, 'You right to go?'

The friendly expression was still missing; the man from the pub yesterday was back. Fallon nodded and gave him a thumbs up and put her window up, and went to press the air conditioning button.

'Damn,' she muttered as she remembered she wasn't in her ute; she was in Uncle George's.

'Double damn,' she muttered more loudly as she followed Jon's ute down the road. She'd forgotten to check the fuel.

Nothing had gone right since she'd hit this town.

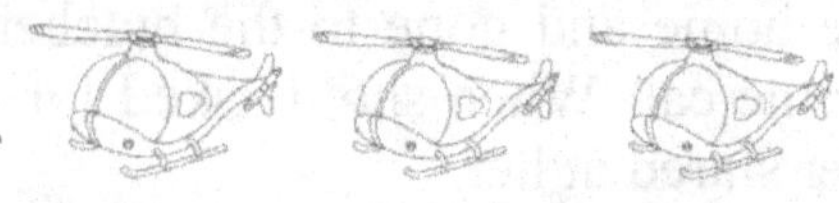

Chapter 8

Fallon glanced down at the old-fashioned semi-circular dial and was pleased to see it was three-quarters full. According to her information, the property was about forty kilometres out of town by road even though it seemed a lot less in the air this morning.

She had plenty of fuel to get out and back, so she relaxed into the drive, tagging him through town and out to the Charleville road.

It was a pleasant afternoon. The wind had come up slightly despite his forecast of no wind. She grinned at that and was cross that she was trying to get one up on him. The sky was a cloudless blue and the mountains in the distance glowed in the mid-afternoon sun.

The drive out was uneventful and after forty minutes she followed him through the gates of *Kilcoy Station.*

A dozen utes were parked along the back of a big shed down behind a large house. As she eased the ute to the end of the row, heads turned and mouths dropped. Uncle George's ute sure was a head-turner. Fallon grinned as she parked it in a sea of white work utes.

She climbed out, locked the door manually and walked over to Jon's ute as he pulled a carton of beer off the back of the tray.

'Thank you, that made it a lot easier to find the place,' she said.

'Come on, I'll introduce you to the team.' He nodded briskly.

Fallon had no choice but to follow him as they crossed the wide driveway. As she hurried to match his stride a voice called her name.

' Fallon!'

She turned around with a smile as she recognised the voice. 'Hi Callie, I'm just going to the meeting. I'll talk to you later.'

''All good. I just wanted to let you know in case Jon didn't tell you.'

'Tell me what?' Fallon raised her eyebrows.

'Braden's putting on a barbecue after the meeting. I was hoping you were going to stay.'

'I didn't know, but yes, that would be nice.'

'It won't be too late. But if you wanted to have a drink, stay over. You can have the spare room in my donga.'

Fallon waved a hand as Jon stood at the door of a big shed staring at her.

'I'll talk to you later, Callie.' She hurried towards the big corrugated iron shed.

The hum of many conversations reached her as she caught up to where Jon waited.

'So you're ready to start work finally?'

The unfairness of his comment rankled, but she ignored him. A dozen or so men in dusty work clothes stood around in a couple of groups. Most held a can of beer. She followed Jon over to the side of the shed where there were two large fridges.

'Can you open the one on the left, please?' he said with a nod at the fridge.

Fallon obliged, and after he'd slid the carton into the fridge where the shelves had been removed, he turned back and held out a stubby.

'No, thank you. I don't drink on the job.'

This time it was Jon who raised his eyebrows. He pulled the cap off his beer.

'Whatever. Find somewhere to sit.'

As she made her way over to a hay bale in the middle of the open shed close to where the men had gathered, she drew some curious looks, a few nods and a couple of hands raised in greeting.

Normally, when she was mustering up in the Gulf or Western Australia she'd know some of the ringers and stockmen, but being so far from her usual stamping ground all the faces were unfamiliar, although most of them held a welcoming smile.

'Grab a chair, grab a patch of ground or a hay bale,' Jon called over the noise as Braden and Kent walked in. 'Make yourself comfortable, guys,' he glanced at Fallon, 'and we'll let you know what's happening.'

Over the next fifteen minutes, he outlined the plan that he had given her a short version of this morning. As he spoke, Fallon was pleased that she'd done a flight over the stations with him because what he was saying made a lot more sense than it would have if she hadn't had the aerial reconnaissance of the two properties. The third one, well at least she knew where it was and what the setup was.

'So Wednesday morning,' Jon said as he wound up the talk. 'Six a.m. start. The quad bikes will head out to Braden's boundary, and those on horseback will head out to the main camp. We've got a truck arriving mid-morning with swags and supplies.' He glanced at Fallon. 'Kent and Fallon, up in the air about noon.

Fallon nodded.

Kent called out. 'Where do you want us to base ourselves with the choppers, Jon. In town at the Aerodrome where Fallon's bird is, or out at my place or here at *Kilcoy Station*?'

Jon frowned and rubbed his jaw. 'I think if you come out here to *Kilcoy* it'll be more central. Does that suit you, Fallon?'

He knew very well she had a bed in the house in town, but she'd taken notice of how long it had taken to drive out here; it just meant if the chopper was here she'd have an earlier start in the mornings.

Then she'd have to drive back into town in the afternoons if she'd planned on working on the house at night.

She lifted her hand in a casual wave. 'Not a problem.'

This was why she'd come to southwest Queensland. Uncle George's house would just have to wait. She made a mental note to call her mother later tonight. They were going to have to come and take charge.

'Okay guys, I think we're pretty organised. Bright and early Wednesday morning. Now come on over and join the barbie Braden's put on for us. I can smell the meat cooking and the beer's cold.'

Fallon wrinkled her nose as the enticing aroma of barbequing meat and onions greeted them as she walked over to the house with Kent. Jon was talking to a couple of guys, and one stared at her as she walked past with Kent. She met his gaze steadily and he looked away.

'You've settled in okay to town?' Kent asked as they walked to the house yard. 'Not working too hard in that old place of George's?'

Fallon chuckled. 'I could work there every day for a year, I think, and I wouldn't get anywhere near the bottom of what's in that place. I'm going to call my mum and tell her she and Dad are going to have to drive out and take over. From Wednesday, my priority is the muster. That's what I came here for.'

'I was just thinking about that while Jon was outlining the program. George is a well-known and well-respected citizen of our area, and I know I could get a work crew together to help out. If you stay around for a while after the muster we can give you a hand if that helps.'

'That's a very kind offer, Kent. I'll give it some thought.'

'Like I said, the offer stands. He's a good old bloke. He was always the first one to help out anyone who needed a hand. I can still see him back in the 2012 floods. He wasn't a young man then, but he filled sandbags for days. And then when we were cut off for two weeks, he found an old tinnie in one of his sheds and organised food drops to the houses that were cut off.'

'It's so interesting to hear about him. I'm afraid I lost touch when I grew up, but I have memories of being out here when I was a kid.'

Fallon looked around as they entered the small yard at the back of the wide house surrounded by long shady verandas. The barbeque area was in a breezeway between two identically-sized sections and the young woman that she'd seen John speaking to at the pub the other night was standing with two of the small boys who were with Callie at the aerodrome.

Kent led her over to the young woman.

'Sophie this is Fallon Malone. She's our other helicopter pilot for the muster.'

'Hi, Fallon, good to meet you.' Her smile was sweet, but Sophie frowned as she flicked a glance at Kent.

Fallon looked over at him. His face was set and the friendly expression in his eyes had gone.

'Right, I'll go and see if I can help with the cooking.'

'It's all under control, Kent,' Sophie said.

'I'll go and get some beer then.' He started to walk away and then stopped.

Fallon noticed the tension in Sophie's stance.

'Fallon, don't leave before we have a chat. I want to talk about how we'll work things out on Wednesday.'

'Rightio,' she said.

Sophie rolled her eyes as Kent turned on his heel and headed back to the shed. 'Kent's a nice guy, but he overdoes it sometimes. He always makes me feel inadequate.'

Fallon shrugged. 'Always good to have someone who's willing to help out.' She wondered what their history was; there was obviously some tension between them. She looked up as Callie came out of the house carrying a tray.

'Hi again. I see you two have met. Soph, can you go and get your potato bake out of the oven, please? Nigel and Petie, go and find your brother and then the three of you can feed the pups and lock them away. Otherwise, the guys will feed them too many leftovers.'

The two boys ran off, and Sophie went inside.

'I haven't had potato bake for ages. Not since I left home. Mum used to make it,' Fallon said.

'Goes down a treat,' Callie said. 'Sophie is an amazing cook. She's going to move home now that she's back in the district, and I'm going to pick up another couple of days at the school.'

'At the school?'

'Yeah, I came out here as a nanny for the boys, but I've picked up some casual teaching. I told Braden now that Sophie's come back, he doesn't really need me here.'

Her face flushed pink.

'And?' Fallon asked with a grin.

'He wasn't impressed. We sat down and worked out a new salary. I refuse to be paid for helping out, now that we're together. He's going to try and hire a housekeeper. I said it wasn't fair that Sophie came back in and took all the responsibility.'

'You said Sophie is his sister?'

'Yeah. She had the boys for a couple of years after their mum was killed.' Callie lowered her voice. 'She's had a pretty tough time. Between you and me, I don't think she's happy with me being here. That's one of the reasons that I've tried to pull back a bit. I think she resents me being here. It's made things a bit awkward. But don't get me wrong. I'm really happy Kent and Braden went and got her.'

'I'm sure it'll all work out for you. People can be hard work. That's why I'm a loner.' One of the reasons anyway, Fallon thought.

'Anyway, I'm yakking too much,' Callie said. 'It's just good to have another pair of ears. So, how have you been going?'

Fallon filled Callie in on her progress and ignored Jon as he walked past them and headed over to the temporary bar.

'He's another really nice guy. They seem to breed them out here.' Callie's grin was wide.

'He's okay. Seems like a good boss.'

'But?' Callie asked.

'We had a bit of a shaky start.'

'We definitely need a coffee date. I'm working in town tomorrow, and the boys have footie training. Do you want to catch up?'

'Sounds good to me.' Fallon pointed to the bar. 'I think Kent needs you.'

'Okay, go and grab a plate. Some of the meat's already cooked and here's Sophie with the potato bake.'

Kent came over to where Fallon was sitting alone on the edge of the group. A couple of the stockmen had come up and introduced themselves, but Jon had stayed away.

Not that she expected him to babysit her, just because she'd followed him out here. But she couldn't help the little bit of disappointment that sat in her chest.

'So let's have a chat.' Kent held out a can of beer.

'Okay then. One won't hurt. I'm going to head off soon. I don't want to risk driving back in the dark. Too many roos out there and I'd be horrified if I hit one in Uncle George's car.'

'Bit late. They'll be on the move already.' Kent glanced across to where Callie and Sophie were manning the food table. 'Callie said she hoped you'd bunk down here for the night. This will turn into a bit of a do, and Jed has his guitar and his mate, Bobby, is a bit of a bush poet. Worth staying. They put on a good show.'

Fallon bit her lip. 'God, I'd never forgive myself if I hit a roo in his ute.'

'Think about it. Now I just want to get sorted with the way you operate. It's the first time I've done such a big muster out here. I usually just do my own.'

'I'm used to—' Fallon broke off as she encountered the hostile gaze of one of the stockmen who hadn't spoken to her yet. At the back of the area to the right of the large barbeque, a small bar had been set up. Half a dozen of the men sat there, beer cans in their hands. The man stared at her with a strange look on his face and when she held his eye for a moment, he frowned but didn't look away. It was the same guy who'd stared at her before when he'd been talking to Jon. He looked familiar but she couldn't put a name to his face or place him.

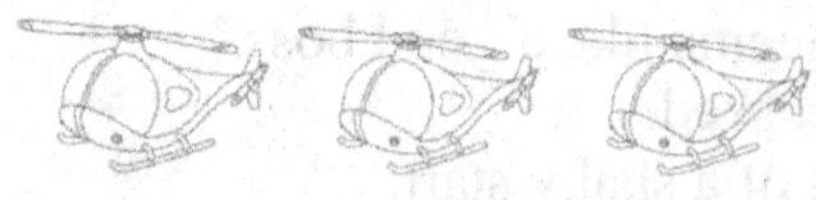

Chapter 9

'Will you camp out?'

Fallon turned her attention back to Kent as he asked her a few more questions.

'No, I'll drive back into town at night. I'm used to long distances. The only thing that worries me is driving George's vintage ute.'

'I'm sure Braden would lend you a farm ute.'

'I could take the chopper back to the aerodrome. I hope my ute'll be fixed in a few days.'

'Don't hold your breath. Jack Anderson's not known for his speed.'

'I'll have a think about it.' As she answered, Fallon was aware of the guy still staring. He watched her for a while longer and then turned to the man next to him and said something. The second man frowned and stared.

Fallon shrugged, just someone else who didn't want a female on the team. She'd encountered it before and didn't let it bother her as long as they stayed away from her and didn't cause trouble.

She gave her full attention to Kent as he continued. 'I'm sure I'll get used to working in a pair. I'm a bit of a worrier. I need to know exactly what's going to happen. It used to drive Sophie crazy.'

Fallon ignored the Sophie reference and chuckled. 'That's one thing we don't know when we're mustering from the air. And that's the thing I love about the job.'

'Mate, can you grab another carton from the shed?' Braden called out to Kent.

'Big drinkers, these guys,' Kent said as he stood. 'But Jon'll make sure they don't drink much out on the mustering camp. That's why he and Braden decided to put tonight on, plus there'll be another wind-up barbie after we're done.' Kent put his hand on her shoulder before he walked away. 'Thanks, Fallon. I'm looking forward to working with you. Now grab something to eat, before it all disappears.'

Along the middle of the breezeway, a table was loaded with paper plates, bread rolls, Sophie's potato bake, a big bowl of coleslaw, and a huge platter of meat.

'I wonder what the problem is,' Callie said as she came over to Fallon. Did something happen while I was inside?' She looked over at Jon and Braden who were heads-down talking outside the breezeway. They were both frowning

'No. I don't think so. I've been talking to Kent,' Fallon said.

'I'll be back in a minute. Get some dinner and I'll come and sit with you.'

Fallon picked up a bread roll and a small piece of steak, squirted tomato sauce on it and added a spoonful of coleslaw and potato bake. There were a couple of empty stools at the edge of the breezeway and she moved over and sat down—out of sight of the two guys who kept looking at her—staring out to the yard as she ate her bread roll. Braden's boys were playing on a structure at the back of the yard with three small pups running around them.

Everyone here seemed tense this afternoon, and she was keen to go back to town to the peace and quiet of the empty house. She'd drive slowly, put the lights on high beam and watch out for roos.

Even Callie wasn't her usual carefree self, and there was no sign of Sophie. Fallon put the second half of her bread roll down on the plate and dabbed at her mouth with the serviette. That was why she didn't have much to do with people. She didn't have time for all of this.

Doing her job, keeping to herself suited her just fine. Then when she was ready for a break, she'd head back to Cairns where she could go out on the water. One day when she'd saved enough, she'd move into her house there, and maybe do some flying over the reef with a tourist company.

Mum was always nagging her about being a loner but Fallon had never told her why. She'd never mentioned the incident eight years ago. Mum never read the news so she didn't know.

No matter what you did, people were judgemental and it was easier to stay away from them. Being alone was hard sometimes, and when she saw couples out together, looking happy, a small part of her wondered if she would ever find someone who understood her.

Suck it up, princess, she told herself.

She'd cry off the coffee date with Callie, and spend the time sorting George's house.

Her appetite gone, Fallon decided to head back to town. She stood and took the half-empty plate over to the large bin in the corner and dropped it in.

Jon was walking across to the bin as she turned. His face was set with deep lines grooved at each side of his mouth. 'Can I have a word, please?'

Fallon nodded. 'Is something wrong?'

He jerked his head rudely. 'Outside.'

***

Fallon's confidence and seeming self-sufficiency pissed Jon off. He was starting to regret that he'd listened to all the talk of how good she was and that he'd contracted her without an interview.

Now, he had more reason to worry about her suitability for the job.

He strode over to the shed and turned to gesture for her to follow.

That'd be right. She was lagging about twenty metres away behind him, and his temper fired. He stood, holding onto the door of the shed as he waited for her to walk over—at her pace—and when she stepped inside, he closed the door and flipped the lock over.

Her eyes widened and her lips were set in a straight line. 'Is that necessary?'

'I don't want to be interrupted. You have some explaining to do.'

She leaned back against the door and folded her arms.

God, she was annoyingly cool.

Ice Queen, not Chardonnay Girl.

He waited for her to speak, but not a word. Only a cool, hard stare.

'Why didn't you tell me you'd crashed a helicopter?'

Her face lost its colour and then a red spot appeared on each cheek. If it was possible, her lips tightened even more.

He waited her out, but she just stared at him.

'Well?' he said.

Still silence and his temper built.

'Look, Fallon, we need to sort this out. If I'd known you had a blemished record, I wouldn't have offered you the contract.'

She unfolded her arms and stood straight. 'And if I'd known it was *you* offering the contract, I wouldn't have signed it.'

'Why?'

'Because *you're* the one with the blemished record. Consider the contract rescinded, and may I suggest that next time you check your facts before you go making unfounded accusations. I'm sure there'll be some sort of clause in it that you can save face if you sack me but be prepared for a compensation claim from *Wyndham Birds*. There

191

were plenty of other jobs that they knocked back to send me down here. Plus, I'm not prepared to work with a manager who treats me like you've treated me.'

As she stared at him with fire in her eyes, he saw the moment she realised who'd accused her.

'Ah, I knew I recognised his face. He was the ringer up at Barkly Roadhouse. So memorable I can't even remember his name.' Her laugh was bitter. 'He seems to like spreading his opinion far and wide. That was the same night I heard what a shit boss you were. I thought it was just nasty gossip or sour grapes but he got that bit right, didn't he? You're a bully and a smart arse.'

She pushed away from the door and turned to flick the lock over, but Jon stepped forward and put his hand on her arm.

'Wait. Don't go tearing off with the shits.'

'What? How dare you speak to me like that? And take your hand off me. I'm leaving here now, and I'm leaving town tomorrow. I don't have to take this from anyone.'

Jon dropped his hand. 'Wait, please. Are you telling me you didn't have an accident? He knew all about it.' He ran a hand through his hair in frustration. Braden had told him to simply ask Fallon what had happened; he hadn't jumped to a wild conclusion. He should have got Kent to talk to her. He always seemed to be able to keep the peace.

'Listen carefully. I have never crashed a bird. If I had I would have been up front with you this morning, especially knowing you were shit scared about being up in the air.'

'I wasn't.' He lied, but he hated the thought of his weakness being recognised.

'Whatever you say. You might be loose with the truth, but *I'm* not. I have *been* in a helicopter crash. Perhaps your informer needs to get his facts straight.' Her eyes were glacial, but he could see her hand shaking. She wasn't as cool as she was making out.

'Tell me about it.'

'Why?'

Because if I have been lied to, I'll apologise to you, and I'll deal with the person who lied to me.'

'How will you deal with him? Drag him over here and lock him in a shed while you tear strips off him? Or is that only something you do to women?'

'I wanted to give you privacy.'

'Bullshit, Jon. You wanted to give *you* power.'

'Talk to me, Fallon.'

'Why should I?'

'Because I want to know what happened. I'll put a stop to any misinformation that's being bandied about.'

***

Fallon cleared her throat and put a hand to her mouth as she coughed. Her mouth was dry from the shock of Jon's unfair accusation. Her temper had cooled. She was disappointed in him, but to be fair she could see where he was coming from.

'Maybe you'd better change the way you work, or you won't be here for very long,' she said. 'Get me a drink, and I'll tell you what you want to know.' No please, no pleasant tone.

Fallon had meant water, but when Jon came back from the fridge with a can of beer and popped the top open, she took it and drank deeply.

She walked away from him and crossed to the small table beside the fridge. She put the beer on the table, pulled the chair out and sat down. He followed her over and his expression was wary.

'Sit down, and don't look at me like that. I'm the one who's been treated badly here. What I'll tell you is the truth. I have no reason to lie. I'm not staying and you can Google it and check what I tell you anyway. Your source could have done that, but he obviously just wants to cause trouble.'

She sat straight and clenched her hands on her lap as Jon sat opposite her. 'I don't talk about this. It took me a long time to get over it. I had a year when I didn't fly. Yes, I was in a crash. The pilot died and I survived, and if you're wondering why I am so pedantic when I fly, now you know.'

'Even though I already had my licence and I asked my instructor to take me up one afternoon to show me something, I guess it was technically my fault.' She was determined not to break. Even though it had been Ken's role, the guilt of making the request to go up that afternoon had stayed with Fallon a long time, and she had shed many tears.

'Ken, my instructor, was a good man. He was married, his kids were grown up, and his first grandchild was on the way. He was the one who always told us over and over again about autorotation and not to go too low and to keep our speed up. I had been up with him a few times when he did it, and I'd had one go myself, but I wasn't confident enough to try it again without another lesson. I wanted to be sure.'

'What's autorotation mean?' Jon's voice held a note that hadn't been there before.

'If you're flying at five hundred feet or higher, and you have engine problems you've got a good chance of being able to auto-rotate out of any difficulty. If you have an airspeed of seventy nautical miles, you've also got a fairly good chance of a controlled crash.'

'What happened?'

She picked up the beer and drank again, and began to feel a little calmer, but her voice was flat. It was like being back in that investigation after the crash when she had to explain the technical side of the crash. 'During autorotation, the main rotor blades are driven by forces caused by the air coming from underneath as the machine descends. It's a misconception that choppers just fall from the sky. When we muster, we fly under three hundred feet and can go down to thirty miles per hour when we're after a beast or a stray herd. If your engine fails or you stall, you don't have any time to react, and you're too low to do it anyway. You just fall to the ground. Ken misjudged and we hit the ground.'

'Were you hurt?'

Fallon closed her eyes.

The noise and the smoke . . . she knew she had to get out. The sound and the impact of the machine hitting the ground thudded through her chest and her head. Something wet ran across her left eye and she blinked, and it hurt like hell. Like saltwater when she dived into the ocean.

'Ken!' she screamed. 'Get out. Get out.' The bird was on its side and she had to undo her belt and climb up and over the side. She jumped to the ground and ran around to the front, her head pounding. The windscreen was smashed and she could see her instructor and friend. As the darkness began to take over her vision and her knees collapsed, she knew it was too late. Sobs shook her body and the last thing she remembered was putting her fist against her teeth to stop the pain.

'Physically? No. A bit of a scratch here and there, and a mother of a headache and earache for a week or two. But hurt? Not really.'

'Emotionally?' he asked softly.

Fallon opened her eyes. *When did he get up?*

Jon was crouched in front of her and his hands were holding hers. She hadn't heard him move or felt his touch.

'What—' Her voice cracked and she swallowed. 'What do you think? I couldn't help him. When I came to, I'd been dragged away from the wreck but then I watched it burn. And my friend was inside.'

His hands tightened on hers, and he shook his head slowly from side to side. 'How the hell do you get back in and fly?'

'You heal. But you keep yourself safe. Safe from everything.' She pulled her hands from his. 'I need to go.'

Jon was still in front of her and he blocked her escape. 'I'm sorry, Fallon. I was out of line and I shouldn't have spoken to you like that because of what I was told.'

'You can check my story.'

'I won't be checking anything, and I sincerely hope that you'll accept my apology and reconsider.'

'Reconsider what?'

'Staying.'

She lifted her head and held that piercing blue gaze. 'Why should I?'

'Because I want you to.' She looked down as he took her hand again, and smoothed his thumb over the back of her hand. 'It's no excuse, but my inappropriate behaviour was a reaction to me fighting myself. And this will probably be enough to make you run, but I'm going to be honest. Ever since I walked into the pub yesterday and saw you sitting there, something happened.'

'Something like what?' The gentle pressure of his thumb soothed her, but a wave of tiredness washed over her.

'I never mix business with pleasure. But I haven't been able to get you out of my head. And that made me angry. Not with you, with myself, and I seized on what Rod said. Without thinking about it, and I was out of line, and for that, I'm truly sorry.'

Fallon put a hand to her head. 'I don't know. I'm too stressed to think about it right now.'

'And you're not in any fit state to drive.'

'I'm not.' She was with it enough to admit that. 'Will you go and get Callie, please? She said I could stay the night.'

'Good.' His voice was brisk and he pushed up to his feet. 'We'll talk in the morning when you're feeling better.'

'Maybe. I'll see how I feel.'

Chapter 10

Fallon rolled over and stretched her legs. The sheets were a lot softer than what she'd been sleeping in for the past few nights at Uncle George's, and the pillow was heaven. She lay on her back, opened her eyes and watched the ceiling fan spinning slowly above her.

Callie had been super kind last night. She'd taken her out of the back door of the shed and around the other side of the house and then walked her down to the donga. Once she'd checked Fallon was okay, she put a bottle of water beside the bed, and told her to sleep well.

The sun was streaming in through the sheer curtains. Fallon rolled over and picked up her phone, and sat up quickly when she saw it was past eight. Her clothes and boots were on the floor, and there was a towel and a pack of toiletries on the table near the bed.

Embarrassment flooded through her as she sat up and swung her legs to the floor. At least only Jon and Callie had seen her lose her shit last night. Callie didn't even know what had happened between them in the shed, but she'd looked after Fallon, and made sure she was comfortable in the spare room of her donga.

Fallon didn't know what to do. The thought of facing Jon Ingram this morning—who she'd finally admitted to herself in the early hours, she was attracted to—was daunting. And *she* didn't mix business with pleasure either. She didn't even like him, so what was this feeling that consumed her?

Grabbing the towel, she headed for the tiny ensuite, vowing to put her embarrassment aside before she went outside. With a bit of luck, there'd be no one around and she could head back to town and decide what to do.

She stood under the hot water and quickly soaped her body, and then washed her hair, unsure of the water situation out here. She dried off, pulled her clothes on quickly, and finger-combed her hair. Then she pulled up the bed, picked up the water bottle and drank what was left. She dug in her pocket for the ute keys and was pleased to feel them beneath her fingers.

As she headed for the door, there was a tap on the other side. Expecting Callie, she put a smile on her face and pulled it open. Her smile faded and she took a quick step back as her gaze settled on Jon.

'Good morning,' he said. 'I was a bit worried you'd wake up early and head back to town, so I waited by your ute. Then I got worried when you *didn't* appear.'

'I don't run away,' she replied. 'I did that for too long.'

'Have you got any coffee in here? I've been waiting out by your ute since sun-up.'

'I don't know. I didn't look.'

'Will you? I'd kill for a coffee. And we can sit on your veranda and talk. There's no one around here. Callie's taken the kids to school, and I think Sophie must have gone with her. Braden and Kent have headed out to the camp with the stockmen ready for Wednesday.'

Fallon looked at him for a moment, ignoring the little jump of her heart, before she turned back into the donga and opened the cupboards in the small kitchenette.

To his credit, Jon waited outside.

'Come in, ' she said. 'You're in luck. There's some instant coffee and tea bags and long-life milk.' She lifted out the small plastic kettle and filled it at the tap. 'It won't compare with yesterday's coffee and Danish, but it's coffee.'

'Thank you.' Jon took his Akubra off and left it on the table on the veranda before he came in. 'Like you say, it's coffee. Did you sleep okay?'

'I did, thank you. Did you camp out?' Her voice was extremely polite.

'Slept in my swag next to my ute. I'm still staying at the pub in town. There's a manager's house at the back of the property I'll be moving into. Braden's getting it rewired. I lived there when I was here before, but it nearly burnt down, the power points were always catching fire, and the lights would work some nights and not others.'

Fallon put the coffee and milk into two cups and turned on the jug. She opened the fridge to put the opened carton of milk away and looked up at Jon.

'Would you like some toast? Callie's left some bread and butter and jam in here.'

'Only if you're having some.' His tone was as polite as hers, and Fallon was tempted to giggle.

She took the bread out and put two slices in the toaster on the bench. Although the atmosphere was so very civilised and tension-free, her hands were shaky and her heart was thudding.

When the jug boiled, she poured the water into the cups. The toast popped up, but Jon beat her to the cupboard and took out two plates. He quickly buttered the toast and added jam.

'One slice do you?' he asked.

'Is one enough for you?' she countered.

'Yes, one's fine.'

Fallon couldn't help the smile that tugged at her lips. 'We're being very polite. No Miss Chardonnay today.'

'I'm too scared to open my mouth apart from my pleases and thank yous,' he said. I'm scared of getting my head chopped off.'

His cute grin sent her heartbeat up to the next level, and she tried to feel cross at the effect he was having on her. Jon admitting last night that he was attracted to her had seemed to open something inside Fallon. She never had this reaction to a man.

Or if she had, it hadn't been for a very long time. It felt strange, but it wasn't scaring her.

Not too much.

'I'm pleased to hear that. Nice to see a bit of respect and manners.' Her tone was light and took any sting out of her words.

'Did you notice there's a veranda through that door?'

She looked at the door at the back of the donga he was pointing at. 'No. I didn't have time to explore.'

'Let's take our breakfast out there and sit. There's another table and chairs and a nice view over the dam.

When she nodded, Jon walked over and opened the door and then came back for his coffee and the plate of toast. He stood back and let her go outside first, and Fallon drew in a breath at the pretty sight.

A large dam shone blue under the clear sky, and in the distance, the western mountains picked up the morning sunlight.

'I feel at home out here,' he said. 'There's just something about the air and the landscape that's special.'

'Were you born out here? I mean is it your geographic home?'

'No, I was born on a station up on the Gulf. I grew up around cattle. My dad was the manager. When he died, Mum and I moved into Normanton, and I worked on a few different spreads up there. That's where I've worked most of my life.'

'How did you end up out here?'

So far their conversation was easy and tension free. It was as though they were two different people to the pair who'd gone head to head in the shed last night.

'I met Braden and Julia at a cattleman's conference in Longreach. He was looking for a manager and he offered me a good package.'

'And how long were you here for?'

'A couple of years. I was here when Nigel and Petie were born, but I'd gone before Julia's accident.'

'Is it okay to ask what happened? A car accident? I don't want to pry.'

'It's not prying. It's common knowledge. Julia was killed in a storm. The finding was accidental death. She was crushed by a horse.'

'Oh, how sad.'

'It was awful. I came down for the funeral. Sophie was incredible. She stepped in and took over looking after the boys. She grew up almost overnight.'

'You said you'd already gone by then. Did you decide to move on?'

For the first time, Jon seemed tense. 'No, family duty called.' He didn't elaborate, but she assumed it was to do with his mother.

Jon put his cup down and looked at her. 'Shall we talk about the elephant in the room?'

Fallon nodded. 'I accept your apology. I'm also sorry how I flared up too. I haven't talked about the crash for a long time, and it upset me.'

'That's fine. I was way out of line. I spoke to Rod last night and told him to pull his head in, and not gossip.'

'He wouldn't have taken that well.'

'He didn't. If he won't play by the rules, he can go.'

'Thank you. Now to put you out of your worry, I've decided to stay. I committed and I signed a contract.'

Fallon hid her smile as Jon's shoulders visibly relaxed.

'Thank you, Fallon. I really appreciate that. And I promise to be on my best behaviour for the whole muster.'

'It would leave you shorthanded if I went.'

He shook his head. 'We would have managed. But I'm really happy you're staying. I'd like to get to know you better. I meant what I said last night.'

'What about not mixing business and pleasure?' she asked as a little tug of happiness pulled inside her.

'Being friends isn't mixing business and pleasure.'

She nodded.

'And there's always weekends, and between musters to explore more.'

She looked at him, and something passed between them as she nodded again, and Jon smiled.

'You'll have to be very patient with me. I'm not good at friendship or anything else,' Fallon said.

'You and me both. I think we're both loners. We can learn together.'

Fallon leaned back and held his gaze. 'Can I trust you or is that a lady-killer pickup line? "We can learn together?" Learn what exactly?'

Jon put his head back and laughed. 'You've been listening to the town gossip, I'd say?'

'I have been warned. On several occasions.' She couldn't help smiling. 'So what's the go?'

'Apparently, it's because I break hearts when I refuse the offers of the local ladies.'

'It must be hard being a heartthrob.'

'Show a bit of respect, Fallon.' His grin was still wide. 'Okay, so what's your plan for today? You've got a day and a bit before the muster.'

'More house sorting out. And I might go and visit Uncle George.'

'Want some company?'

Surprise filled her. 'You don't have to. I thought you'd be busy out here?'

'I don't start officially until Wednesday. I just came out early to get things organised. So I've got some time up my sleeve. After seeing the outside of that house, I'd say you could do with a hand? Someone to help lift and carry?'

'I'm not going to knock back an offer like that. Thank you. Some company would be good, but I'll warn you. Poor old Uncle George's house is a bit depressing.'

'Well then, let's get to town,' he said. 'I'll give you the day on a promise.'

'Oh?' Her eyebrows rose. 'On a promise? What sort of promise would that be?'

'If you ask me out to the pub for dinner, and feed me, I won't say no.'

'I can do that.'

'Well, Miss Chardonnay. Let's go to town.'

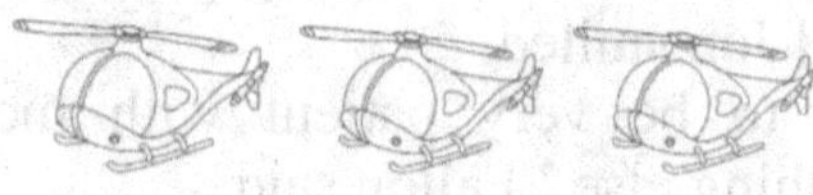

Chapter 11
Fallon

'How many casserole dishes does one man need?' Fallon sat on the kitchen floor and passed the last of two dozen casserole dishes up to Jon who was wrapping them and placing them in boxes on the countertop.

'Maybe they were wedding presents?' he offered.

'He never married.'

'Maybe they were his mother's?'

'Nope. They're seventies vintage. My mother has the same Corningware set. She just doesn't have dozens of them!' Fallon tapped her finger to her lips and then grimaced as she saw how dirty her hands were. She wiped her mouth with the back of her hand. 'Maybe he lived in sin? I had to take a box of stuff that had Josie's stuff in it to the aged care home in the middle of the night. I wondered who Josie was.'

'Maybe you could ask him when you visit him? He might like to talk about her if she was the love of his life.'

'He doesn't even know who I am. He's got dementia.'

'People with dementia will often respond if they're reminded of familiar things.'

'You sound as though you know about it.'

'Sadly, I do. That's why I had to leave here. To be close to my mum. It's a shocking disease.'

'I'm sorry to hear that. It makes me feel guilty that I get cross with my mum. I guess she only wants the best for me. I'm a pretty awful daughter.'

'I can't imagine that.' Jon held his hand out. 'Come on, I think you've done enough down there.'

She reached up and took his hand and looked down at his fingers before she stood. 'You have piano player's fingers.'

His cheeks flushed and Fallon pushed herself to her feet. Jon didn't let go and he tugged her hand so she was up against him as he leaned back on the kitchen bench. 'Don't you dare tell anyone, but Mum made me take piano lessons for that reason.'

Her smile spread wide. 'And do you still play?'

'I do, but I don't share that around. It doesn't go with the image.'

'What the lady-killer?'

'No.' He pulled her a little closer and she could feel his breath on her face as she looked up at him. 'The tough cattleman.'

'Well, I think—'

But Jon didn't wait to hear what she thought as his lips sought and found Fallon's.

Jon tangled his fingers in her short hair and his mouth was hard against hers. She opened her lips to him and he fell into the kiss, not wanting it to end. Kissing Fallon Malone reminded Jon of the time he'd been trampled on by a steer. When he came up for air, his chest hurt and he felt as though he couldn't breathe. His thoughts wouldn't settle and all he wanted to do was keep hold of her, and kiss her again, but Fallon pulled back.

'Whoa, boy,' she said, fanning herself with one dirty hand as something flickered in her eyes. 'I can see where your nickname came from. Lady-killer hits the mark.'

'Uh uh,' he said quietly. 'I haven't kissed anyone in this town.'

'As opposed to other towns?' she asked cheekily. He liked this Fallon.

Very much.

Way too much.

He didn't want to break her heart. A heart that he knew was already damaged.

But he couldn't help himself.

Her skin was warm against him and he lowered his mouth to her neck, caressing her skin with his lips. The sigh that warmed his skin spoke volumes and he knew exactly what she was feeling.

Finally, she pulled back and stepped away from him, but he could see the rate her chest was rising and falling. Her eyes were huge as she stared at him. 'If that's friendship, I don't know if I could cope with more.'

'We'll just have to take it as it comes. Unless you'd rather I left?'

He was pleased with her instant head shake and smiled at her words.

'No, you're too handy in the kitchen.'

'It's getting late. Are you going to visit your uncle? Then you have to take me for that promised pub meal.'

Her back was to him and her voice was hesitant as she crossed to the sink and washed her hands. 'Would you like to come with me? He might talk to a man?'

Jon hesitated. He wasn't going to admit to his weakness. 'You go. I've got a few calls to make, and then I'll have a shower and walk back and pick you up.'

'Walk back? So you can drive the ute again?'

'No. I thought we might have a bottle of wine with dinner. Make it a real date while we're off duty.'

'Okay. I'll go and clean up and visit him. What time will you come back?'

'Six okay?'

She nodded but stayed over the other side of the kitchen. 'Okay, just pull the door shut on your way out.' She disappeared up the hall before he could answer and Jon wondered if he'd upset her.

***

'Hello, young Sally. About time you came to see me.' Great-Uncle George's eyes were bright and lucid, and his smile was wide. He was clean-shaven and his hair was neatly combed.

'Hello, Uncle George You're looking very dapper today.'

He leaned forward and whispered, 'I got them to clean me up. Josie's coming to see me.'

'Is she?' Fallon widened her eyes. *The mysterious Josie.* 'Does she live in town?'

'Of course, she does. She lives in our house. Where else would she be?' His voice began to get agitated. 'She's late. Did you tell her to stay at home?'

'No, of course not.' Fallon searched desperately for something to say. 'Um, I went to the butcher and got that meat for Sooty yesterday.'

'What butcher? Who's Sooty? What are you talking about you stupid girl? You're the one who took my pink box. I want it. Go and get it. It's under the bed.' His voice turned into a full-blown roar. 'Now!'

The aide came hurrying into the TV room where they were sitting, and stood in front of George. 'Now what's the problem here? Have you had your cup of tea, George?'

'I don't want a bloody cup of tea. I want Josie to come. She can take me home, away from all you bitches.' He stood up and his chair tipped over as he lunged for Fallon. As she took a step back, two male aides came hurrying and each took one of George's arms.

'Come on, mate, we'll go for a walk in the garden.'

'Is Josie out there?' Suddenly his voice was docile. Fallon blinked back tears as a hard lump formed in her throat.

'Let's go and see.'

'Sorry, love, but you seem to set him off. Maybe it's best to stay away until we get his medication sorted out.'

'Medication?'

'The doctor has prescribed some anti-psychotic drugs and we're trying to get the dose sorted.'

'Why would he be on anti-psychotic drugs?'

'Don't be upset, love. We called your mother. She's the only contact we have. People with some forms of dementia can get aggressive and disruptive. They believe things that aren't true. And the more confused they are, the worse it can be. They can be a risk to themselves, and to other residents and staff, so the medication is pretty much essential.'

'That's sad.'

'Life's cruel. And we see it all in here. I'll give your mum a call and let her know what's going on. I'll call her when it's okay for you to come back for a visit.'

'Thank you.' Fallon's light and happy mood after spending the day with Jon plummeted. 'What was the point of cleaning out George's house? He'd never go back there, and it didn't matter what happened to everything in it.

As Fallon walked through town back to the house, she pulled out her phone and dialled home. It answered straight away.

'Fallon. Where are you? Have you started work yet? How's the house going?'

'Hi, Mum. I'm still at Augathella and that would be a no, and a yes. I've just been to see Uncle George. He's not good, Mum.'

'I know, sweetie. We're going to try and get out there, but there's always so much happening here. I'm on so many committees, I'm always needed.'

'You're needed here, Mum. *I* need you, too.'

There was silence at the other end of the phone for a while. 'That's lovely to hear you say that. I thought you didn't need us these days.'

'Well, I do, and it's probably a long time since I told you and Dad I love you. It would be good to see you. If you don't come out here, I'll come home after this contract is done.'

'That would be really good.' Her mother's voice was thick with emotion. 'And you know how much Dad and I love you too. We miss you so much, Fallon.'

Fallon cleared her throat. 'I have to go. I'm going out for dinner at the pub soon, but I just wanted to ask you if you had ever heard of a Josie? Uncle George is fixated on her visiting him.'

'Oh no, the poor dear. He must be losing it.'

'Why? Who was she?'

'Apparently, they got engaged before he went to Vietnam. She was a local girl, and she was killed in a road accident while he was overseas. I think it was after that he let the house go. He lost interest in everything.'

'That is sad. Anyway, Mum, I've done a couple of rooms, and I've got one more day left before I start work on Wednesday. I'll probably be out of touch if you're trying to call me, but you can leave a message at *Kilcoy Station* if you need me. I'll text you the number.'

'Thanks, love. Now you be careful up there. Don't go taking any risks, will you?'

'No, Mum. I never do.'

'Okay, we'll talk soon, and don't get yourself upset about George. It's sad, but he's a very old man. Love you, darling.'

'Love you too, Mum. Bye.'

Fallon blinked back tears as she walked along the footpaths. George might be an old man, but once he'd been young like she was. He'd had hopes and dreams, and his dreams had been dashed and he'd obviously never recovered.

It's a wake-up call for me, she thought. *I've buried myself away alone for too long. It's time to start living my life before it's too late.*

Fallon took a deep breath and quickened her pace, her lips lifting in a smile as a plan formed in her head.

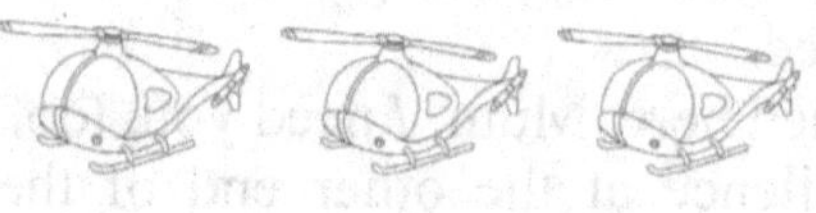

Chapter 12

Jon whistled as he did the buttons up on his dress shirt. He'd even got the ironing board out of the cupboard in his hotel room and pressed his shirt and jeans. A quick shower, a flick of the comb and a splash of the aftershave he'd bought at the local pharmacy, and he was ready to walk to the house and pick Fallon up for dinner. Guilt had stayed with him for a while; he'd sensed that Fallon would have liked company at the aged care home when she'd visited George, but he couldn't do it. The memories of those last few months with Mum in the home at Normanton were deeply buried and that's where he wanted them to stay. He knew if he had gone there with her, the smells, the vacant stares, and the cheery staff would have brought it all back.

The months she had been in there had been awful. Mum had been too young; she hadn't even reached seventy.

Jon pushed away the sad thoughts and took one final look in the mirror.

'You'll do, mate,' he said to his reflection. He couldn't believe he was going on a date, and with one of his team, but he'd fallen under Fallon's spell. She fascinated him; she was tough and sassy, but she was also gentle and vulnerable.

On the way down through the main part of the pub, he stopped at the bistro to book a table. Being a Monday night, he didn't think it would be busy, but he'd hate to have to take Fallon to the local fish and chip shop instead. To his surprise, Sophie was behind the counter.

'Soph? What are you doing here?'

Sophie's eyes were shadowed as she looked up from the napkins she was folding, but she gave Jon a smile. 'I'm working. Took a part-time job in town to get out of Braden and Callie's hair. They don't need me there every night. What are you doing? You're all dressed up.'

'I wanted to book a table. Although it doesn't look too busy.'

'It's going to be. We've got a busload of tourists arriving in half an hour. The bistro is full.'

'Damn.' Jon pulled a face.

'It's okay. Sean's opened the dining room tonight because the Rotary committee wanted dinner before their meeting, and we've got some other locals coming in.' She picked up a pen. 'How many and what time?'

'Two and in about half an hour. Maybe a corner table? Private?'

Her grin was cheeky. 'On a date, hey? Not like you to be out with the locals, Mr Lady-killer. Now you're a local again, you'll change your tune?'

Jon's face heated. 'She's not a local.'

'Hmm. interesting. I'm in the bistro tonight, but I'll make sure you get looked after.'

'Thanks, Soph. You're a sweetheart. How are you, anyway?'

'I'm okay. I've settled back in at *Kilcoy Station*, although it's funny being back at home. I know I made a wrong choice with Jock, and it was silly to move so far away, but it's all over now and I'll get over it.'

'Good. If you ever need a big brother's ear, just call me.'

She chuckled. 'Yeah, Braden's busy. Having the boys back and then hooking up with Callie, and the muster coming up, he doesn't have much spare time.'

'Callie seems nice. Do you reckon she'll stay?'

'I'd be shocked if she left. They're really good for each other. She's fitted in really well for a city chick. And the boys love her already.'

'I'm happy for them. Okay, be back soon.'

'I'm looking forward to seeing your date.'

'Be good.' He lifted his hand in a wave as he headed out.

***

Fallon glanced at her watch as she added a few drops of water to the mascara tube. It had been so long since she'd worn makeup it was dry and hard. She'd been pleased when she found lipstick and mascara in the bottom of her toiletries bag. The long floral dress she always carried in her bag was wrinkle-free and with a squirt of perfume had lost the musty smell from being packed away for a long time. The only problem was shoes, but once she'd given her boots a lick of polish, they sort of looked trendy with the calf-length dress. She'd washed her hair, and finger-dried it after searching for a hairdryer with no luck.

Butterflies danced in Fallon's stomach as she sat at the kitchen table—the clean kitchen table—and pulled out her phone. She was ready way too early. She flicked through her emails, read a couple of newsletters and managed to get her nerves under control.

God, that kiss. She hadn't been kissed so thoroughly for a long time.

If ever.

Had she made a mistake responding to him? Not that she'd done it consciously. Plus, was she too ready to trust Jon after he'd thought the worst of her yesterday?

Logic told her she was making a mistake. Her emotions, hormones, and heart told her she wasn't.

What would be, would be. And she'd be gone from here in three weeks or so, and there was nothing wrong with enjoying herself while she was here. It would be a first to let go and spend some time with someone else.

She sat up straight in the chair. Or was she making too much of an assumption?

God, why were relationships so hard? She pulled herself up. No. it wasn't a relationship. A friendship.

Tingles ran through her nerve endings as she thought of Jon's mouth exploring hers. Friendship didn't feel like that.

God, maybe she should just cancel. She tensed as footsteps came up the back path and a shadow fell across the back door.

'Come in,' she called as she stood and waited.

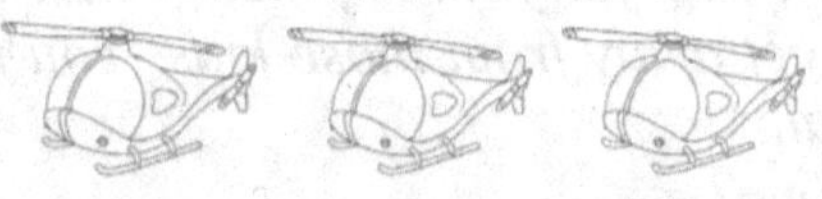

Chapter 13
Sophie

Sophie reached for the next pile of napkins waiting to be folded. What she'd told Jon about taking a job in town to give Braden and Callie some space, well, it hadn't been the exact truth. The problem was, she couldn't stand the sympathetic looks and the quiet that fell when she walked into the room.

She felt like standing there and screaming, 'I made a mistake, but I'm all right!'

But of course, she didn't. She went to her old room; the room that Julia had always insisted was hers, and lay on the bed thinking of the mistakes she'd made.

Okay, so she'd been the one who'd made the wrong choice, and the stupid mistake, and taken everything Jock had said as the truth.

We'll move away and we'll have a fresh start together, Soph.

Your brother doesn't like me. He wants to control you.

Yeah sure, Jock. Who had been the control freak? And she had fallen for it, thinking it was love.

I only want the best for you, Sophie, so that's not a good idea.

You need to get away from those kids. You're too young to be at their beck and call.

And the big one?

Once we get settled in the north, we'll start our own family.

But once Jock had her away from her familiar surroundings, and Braden's support, he'd changed. He'd shown his true colours, and she knew she had been an absolute fool.

The first time he'd hit her after a few beers had been an accident, he'd said.

The second time brought her to her senses and she called Braden. There wasn't going to be a third time. She'd driven to the small town of Ravenshoe and waited for Braden to arrive.

The worst thing of all was the embarrassment about Kent being involved with her "rescue". He'd been kind, but aloof, and she knew he was the one who judged her for her poor choice, and the stupid mistake she'd made.

The times the boys had said that Uncle Jock had been cruel to them, she'd taken it as being strict. She hadn't realised it had been physical cruelty, and she had been sick to the stomach when she'd discovered that.

'Sophie?'

Her head flew up and the napkins scattered on the floor as she met the gaze of one of the men she'd been thinking about. Heat flooded her cheeks as she met Kent Mason's steady gaze, and she knew he'd notice. He knew her well. Too well.

'Kent. I didn't hear you come in. How can I help you?'

'I assume you're working here?' he said, looking at the unfolded napkins on the counter next to her.

'No. I was just walking past and saw the napkins needed folding.' Sarcasm laced her words.

'Sweet of you.' His voice was clipped. 'Are you taking the reservations?'

'I am. When for?'

'Tonight. I heard the bistro is closed so I thought I'd better book the dining room.'

'Why? Has everyone heard I'm working tonight and wants to have a gander?'

Kent's eyes were cold. 'Actually no. My friends and I would like to have a meal. It's not all—' He cut off his words.

'It's not all about you, Sophie,' she finished for him sweetly. She knew Kent well enough to know what he'd been going to say.

'If it fits.' He raised his broad shoulders in a shrug.

'Oh, it fits. You're such an expert on me. You know exactly what a selfish bitch I am.'

The sigh that came from him hurt more than his words. All she was to Kent these days was nuisance value. An exasperation. Someone who'd created a situation so he'd had to fly her brother almost a thousand kilometres to rescue her from a situation of her making.

'How many and what time?' She just wanted him to go away.

'Four of us for seven o'clock please.'

'Do you have a table preference?'

'No.'

'Done.' She picked up the next napkin and started folding it.

Sean, the chef, came out of the kitchen and stood a little too close to her for comfort. Sophie stepped away from him a little.

'Did I hear some more bookings come in?' he asked.

'Yes, another six. It's going to be a busy night. That's ten tables in the dining room now.'

'Who's waitressing in the dining room.'

Sean frowned. 'You are.'

'So who's in the bistro?'

He looked at her. 'You are.'

'What by myself? Both? A busload of oldies in here, and ten tables in the dining room. I can't do that.'

'You'll have to. We've got no other staff. It's Maggie's night off and she's out of town.'

'I'd better go and set the tables then. I thought I was in here.'

'Get your skates on.'

Sophie started to panic. She'd had a couple of nights in the bistro, but she had no idea how the dining room worked. She'd never even waitressed before.

Take a deep breath. How hard can it be to ask someone what they want to eat? Take it to the kitchen and bring it back out.

Not rocket science.

She raced into the dining room, pleased to see that the tables already had clean tablecloths on them. And the cutlery was in an obvious place on the antique sideboard. She and Braden had come here for Sunday lunch when they were kids with Mum and Dad when they were still alive.

All she had to do was remember to set the table properly.

An hour later, Sophie was feeling a lot calmer. The bus passengers in the bistro had a set menu and all she had to do was carry the meals out and they swapped the meals around the table to whoever wanted chicken or steak. Once they were all served she smoothed her hair back and picked up a pen and the order pad.

Three of the tables in the dining room were full, and the customers had bought their drinks at the bar. Kent's party hadn't arrived yet, and she was surprised to see Jon already sitting at the table in the corner with Fallon, the new helicopter pilot. They must have come in when she was in the kitchen. She picked up two menus and walked over to them.

Well, well, well. Sophie hid her surprise when she noticed Jon holding Fallon's hand on top of the table. As she approached, Fallon moved her hand and put it in her lap.

Sophie looked down at the menus pretending she hadn't noticed.

'Hi, Jon. Hi, Fallon. Looks like you guys are right for drinks?'

A wine bottle sat in a cooler bucket on the table and their glasses were filled with white wine.

'Hello, Sophie,' Fallon said.

Sophie almost did a double-take. The new helicopter pilot looked drop-dead gorgeous. A pretty colourful floral dress with a sweetheart neckline, a touch of makeup and a pretty pink lipstick; Fallon looked totally different to the woman in the high vis shirt Sophie had met the other day at the station.

She handed Fallon a menu and reached for the napkin to put in her lap, but Fallon shook her head. 'No need to do all that.'

Sophie smiled and repeated what Sean had told her. 'There's only the menu tonight. No specials board, because the bistro is full.'

'That's fine,' Jon said. 'Don't worry about us too much. We'll be right.' The look in his eyes as he looked at Fallon surprised Sophie. Looked like the fancy dress and the makeup had woven a spell on Jon. As long as Fallon didn't hurt him, Sophie thought. Jon was a decent guy.

She looked from one to the other and was surprised to see a similar expression on Fallon's face.

Even more interesting.

'I'll be back to get your order in a little while.'

Sophie smiled when Jon reached up and squeezed her hand. 'You're doing great, Soph. Good to see you home again.'

She turned to go to the next table and froze when she noticed Kent, Bob Hamblin, the state school principal and his wife, and another woman—drop-dead gorgeous, of course—waiting at the door.

She plastered a smile on her face, picked up four menus off the sideboard and greeted them.

'Hello, Kent. Hi Bob, Cheryl. Please follow me, and I'll get you seated.' As they sat she waited for Kent to introduce the woman she didn't know, and then realised she was the waitress and didn't warrant an introduction.

She stood behind the unfamiliar woman and a cloud of musky perfume hit her nostrils as she flicked the napkin onto her lap.

Not even a thank you or a nod. She shoved the four menus in the middle of the table and said, 'I'll be back in fifteen minutes to take your order.'

'We'd like some drinks while we choose,' the perfumed woman said.

Sophie couldn't help herself. 'Bar's that way.' She gestured with her head and moved on to the small Rotary group at the next table.

'Would you like another drink while you wait for your entrées, Dan?' she almost whispered.

'Thanks, Sophie.' Dan, the president winked at her. 'We'll go to the bar too. You've got the Probus Club out there to deal with.'

'The what?'

'Your bus group.'

'Ah. Okay. I didn't know what they were.'

Sophie headed for the kitchen and ignored Kent's table. She frowned. Why was she letting them bother her?'

***

A little shiver ran down Fallon's back as Jon took her hand and they stepped out onto the street. Dinner had been wonderful. The food, the wine, the service, and most of all, the company. They'd both opened up to each other and Jon had told her about the rough few years looking after his mum.

Fallon felt as though they'd been friends for a long time. They were quiet, each lost in their own thoughts as they walked down past the shops to the corner that led to George's house. She wondered what sort of day George had had after she left.

'I wonder how George is going?' Jon commented as they passed the aged care home.

'Mind reader,' she said. 'I was just thinking that.'

'I'm sorry I didn't go with you today.'

She shook her head. 'After hearing what you and your mum went through, I don't expect you to. I probably won't go back again. It just upsets him. Besides, we'll be busy soon.'

They were quiet again as they walked through the silent streets, and it wasn't long before they were at the back door of George's house. Sooty was sitting outside meowing.

'Does he want to go inside?'

'He's got a secret entry that I haven't found yet. But no, he wants food. I swear he hadn't eaten before I found him in there. It's all he does.'

Jon held out his hand for the key when Fallon took it out of her bag. She hesitated when he opened the door, and then came to the decision that she'd been stewing over all night. Life was too short to wait for what you wanted. She took a deep breath and met his gaze.

'Would you like to come in?' she asked.

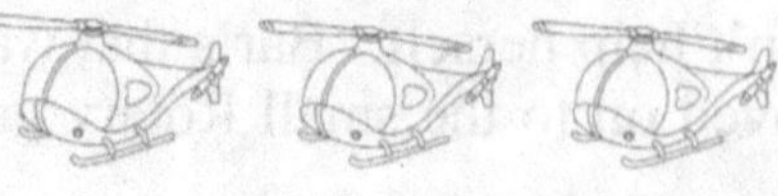

Chapter 14

'Get outa there,' Jon yelled as the lumbering black beast headed for a small stand of trees between the stockmen and the boundary fence. The noise of Fallon's helicopter above filled the air, and he didn't want her to have to come down lower. He'd been worried about that ever since she'd explained that auto stuff to him last week.

To his relief, the beast turned as Rod and his offsider galloped in behind it and got it back on track. The taciturn stockman had been even quieter since Jon had had a word to him, but the gossip had stopped. Less than six days after they'd started the muster on Braden's place, the last of the cattle were heading for the yards.

His headset crackled and Kent's words were loud.

'We'll head back to my place. Okay with that?'

'All good. Ask Fallon to ring me if she wants me to pick her up.' Fallon had left George's ute in town, and hers was still at the garage.

'You're hopeless, mate. I've never seen a man fall so hard and fast. Then again, Braden was nearly as quick when Callie turned up.'

Jon grinned and looked up as the two choppers banked to the east back to Kent's property where Fallon's machine had spent the past week or so. 'Your turn next,' he said.

'Nope. Confirmed bachelor here, mate.'

'I'll catch you for a beer somewhere later,' Jon said.

'Over and out.'

The speed at which his relationship with Fallon had developed made Jon very happy. He had no doubt that moving in together was right. They'd been inseparable since the first night he'd stayed at her place. After a couple of nights together in her single bed, they'd headed out to stay at the manager's residence at the back of Braden's property. The house came with Job's contract and had been recently renovated. The rewiring had been completed, so he had no fear of them being burned in their bed. Sooty had moved out with them and was proving to be a champion mouser. A couple of days ago Callie brought the boys and their puppies out, and Sooty had kept them all in line.

Jon hadn't felt this contented for a long time, and he knew he had a goofy grin on his face as he cantered after the stockmen. He pushed away the thought of Fallon leaving after the muster; he'd do everything he could to convince her to stay.

The noise of the helicopters receded and the only noise was the occasional snort of a beast and thudding hooves as the stragglers were herded into the yard.

Jon caught up to Braden as they went back to camp. The horses would stay out here, and he'd take Braden back to the house.

'A successful week,' his boss said as they headed along the road. 'Let's hope Kent's and Craig's go as well. Who's next?'

'Craig's place,' Jon said. 'Thought we'd get the furthest one out of the way. Kent's should be easier too. We're going to keep going and start tomorrow seeing we're ahead.'

'Do you need me?'

'No, we'll be right. They're a good team.'

'And so are Fallon and Kent. What're the chances of getting her to stay out this way or am I asking too soon?'

'If I had my way, it would be a given. I'll be doing my best to convince her.'

'Won't take much. I've seen the way you pair are together. You might be a fast mover, Jon, but I think she's as smitten as you are.'

Jon grinned. 'I hope so.'

'And if she goes, will you follow?'

'To be honest, mate? I'd have to think about it. I know it might seem fast, but I'll do whatever it takes—' Jon shrugged. 'I'm not going to let her get away.'

'Good on you. She's a good person. She and Callie have really hit it off too. Plus it'd be good to have two helicopter pilots out here.'

'I'll see what I can do.'

***

Fallon waited for Jon to come and get her at Kent's big shed.

They both leaned back on the fence and sipped on the cold bottled water that Kent had brought out.

'Thanks, I needed that.' Fallon wiped the back of her hand over her mouth. 'It was hot out there today.'

'Good job, though. You're an excellent pilot, Fallon. Made me feel rusty. I should do more flying, but there's always so much to do at my place.' He shot her a sideways glance. 'We need a pilot out this way.'

'Do you?' She stared at him. 'Is there a hidden meaning there?'

'Take it how you want. I know someone who'd be very happy if you stayed.'

'Do you?'

Fallon's stomach was unsettled. The more she thought about leaving here when the last muster was done, the more she wondered what she wanted.

No, she knew what she wanted—she wanted to stay with Jon. But she couldn't very well say to him, *I'm leaving my job and moving in.*

It was just the first excitement of a new romance.

And regular sex. She couldn't hold back the grin that tugged at her mouth.

'And by the grin on your face, you do too.'

'Do what?'

'Know who wants you to stay.'

'Because he needs a pilot?'

'That too.'

Fallon shrugged. 'I've got a job, and I've got commitments. But the time it's taking to fix my ute I could still be here at Christmas!'

'No one would mind.'

Jon was quiet when he picked her up and they took the back road home.

Home. Had a nice ring to it, but it was too soon.

Wasn't it?

'A big day for you. Tired?' she said finally. 'You're quiet.'

'Yeah, a bit, but it's great to be done ahead of schedule.' He reached over and squeezed her hand. 'And you and Kent did good. You work well together. It certainly sped up the process. You got those cattle moving well. Best I've seen.'

'I enjoyed it.'

'I've been thinking about Craig's place. We didn't fly over it last week, and now he wants to use the other yards, I think I should go up with you tomorrow morning. I want to be sure you know the route. Kent's busy in the morning and I'd like you to see how close the cattle are to the channels. If they get spooked we'd be in all sorts of trouble. And once we lose them, you know how hard it is to get them back on track.'

'Okay. Sounds like a plan. Would you like me to cook tonight?'

'How about we do it together? I'll barbeque and you can do some veggies.'

'I can do that.'

'I'd like to have a drink first though. There's something I want to run by you.'

Fallon's stomach sank at the same time a ripple of excitement began. She wondered what he was going to talk about, and what she would say if he asked what Kent had suggested.

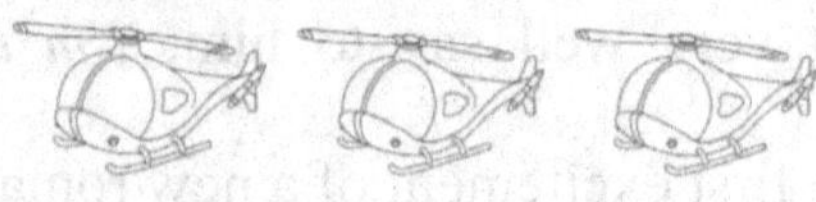

Chapter 15

Jon poured a white wine for Fallon and grabbed a beer for himself. They'd kept their drinks to only one a night as they were both aware of the big days they'd had ahead of them over the past ten days. They sat on the small porch that faced west and watched the sun sink behind the low mountain range.

'It's really pretty here,' Fallon murmured. Jon glanced over at her; she sounded half asleep. Maybe this wasn't the time to bring up his idea. Or was it a proposition? Or a proposal? He sat up straight and almost spilled his beer. A proposal, now that was an idea.

'Did you know this is where Braden and Sophie grew up?'

'I wondered. It was the original house on the station?'

'Yeah. Apparently, their parents were in their forties when they had the kids, and they've both been gone for a few years. Braden moved the location and built the big house when he got married.'

'Life goes so quickly, doesn't it? Seeing George and his house of old stuff really bothered me. Made me think.'

Jon moved his chair closer to Fallon's and took her hand in his. 'I've been thinking too. You might think I'm crazy, and I don't know how to say this, so I'll come right out and say it.'

His heart sank when Fallon pulled her hand away from his.

'Please don't. Please don't spoil it.'

'Hear me out? Please?'

Fallon sighed and waited.

'I don't want you to go, Fallon. I know everyone would say it's way too soon for any sort of commitment. Hell, other people who've known each other the short two weeks we have, would probably only be on their second date. I know it's too soon for the L-word, but honestly, I just want you to stay. The thought of you leaving and going so far away is awful.'

He waited while she put her head back and closed her eyes. Her face was pale and looked tired and he worried about the pressure he was putting on her.

'I love being here, and I really care about you, Jon, but it's too soon to be talking about leaving everything I know.'

'Can I cut to the chase? How important is "everything you know" to you?'

She shrugged. 'I don't know. It's familiar and it's safe.'

'I can be safe for you.'

'What if this flame dies down? What if I gave up my life and came here and then you realised it was the wrong thing. You wouldn't be able to tell me because I'd be here. I know I'm not making sense, but you want me to give up my life on a two-week fling?'

'It's more than a fling to me,' he said quietly. 'I've never felt like this before, and if I have to pull out the L-word, I'll use it.'

'Don't "pull" it out. Just let me go home, and we'll keep in touch and we'll see what happens.'

'I know what will happen. We'll both be busy with our lives with things that don't matter, and it'll be too hard. Fallon, I'm not prepared to risk that. Are you?'

When he finally found the courage to look at her, he saw the answer in her eyes, and his heart broke.

'Okay, I'll go and heat up the barbie. You put the veggies on.' Jon walked through the kitchen, took a second beer from the fridge and went out to the back deck. He stood, his hands grasping the railing as he realised he'd blown it.

****

Fallon barely slept, and when she and Jon drove to Kent's shed the following morning to take her helicopter up over Craig's station, her eyes were gritty and her stomach was roiling. She'd been sick every morning for the past week, and a horrible thought was niggling at her. She couldn't be pregnant surely? It was way too soon to get sick. Not that she knew much about it. She must have eaten something. Or it was the tank water? Or stress that was playing up with her? Her digestion was always the first thing to go when she was worried about something.

She'd gone as far as Googling early symptoms and it *was* possible. Strangely, the thought didn't spook her; she knew Jon well enough to know that he'd be happy too. He'd held her in his arms this morning, and for the first time, she doubted her decision to leave, but she told herself it was too soon. If it was meant to be— what a stupid term that was—they would keep seeing each other despite being three thousand kilometres apart.

Unless she *was* pregnant; then it would be a whole different ball game.

Yep, she'd looked on Google maps last night. Three thousand bloody kilometres. It might as well be to the moon and back.

Kent seemed to be in a bad mood too when they arrived at the shed.

'I'm in a bit of a rush. I have to go into town first up. Is there anything you need?' he asked, tapping his fingers on the side of his thigh.

'If you have time, and only if you do, could you call into Jack Anderson's garage and see if my ute is anywhere near ready?' Fallon asked. 'I haven't talked to him since before the muster.'

'I can do that.' He turned towards his ute. 'I'll give you a call later.'

'Thanks.' Fallon crossed to the helicopter and pulled her phone out. She hadn't even checked the forecast this morning. Too much on her mind.

'Damn,' she muttered.

'What's wrong?' Jon was staring past her towards the horizon, his face pale. His mood was no better than hers or Kent's, and she knew he wouldn't want to go up.

'No service here. I didn't check the weather.'

He pointed to the sky. 'No wind. No clouds and we won't be up long. Ten minutes out and then ten back.'

'Okay, jump in. I'll do the safety check and we'll be off.'

When she'd finished, and climbed in and passed him the headset. Jon had his head back and his eyes were closed.

'You okay?' she asked.

'I'll live. Let's get going.'

'North?' Fallon asked.

'North.' He nodded and slipped the headset on and closed his eyes again.

A small spurt of anger tugged at Fallon. *Men!* What was it about them that they had the right to be cross, but she didn't?

Okay, he was upset, but so was she. She wasn't sure if she was making the right choice, and she hadn't slept all night as she'd worried over the pros and cons of staying or leaving. She wondered how George was going, and she was worried about her ute and how much it was going to cost.

She checked that Jon was buckled up, and pressed the starter. As soon as the throb of the motor vibrated through the machine, she began to feel better, as flying took over her thoughts and not all those niggling worries.

Her nose was tickling, and she put her hand up as she sneezed.

Jon opened his eyes and glanced over. 'Not getting a cold are you?'

'No. It's the dry air.' She sneezed again and her eyes burned. God, that was all she needed today. A head cold.

'My throat's a bit scratchy too. I hope I haven't shared any germs with you,' came through her headset.

She flicked him a grin as her mood improved slightly. 'Bit late for that.'

At least she got a smile in return.

Jon leaned forward and pointed ahead. 'That's Craig's southern yards. Bear west about ten degrees and we'll get to his boundary where the main yards are.'

'There's a lot of cattle down there.'

'Yeah, he runs more than Braden and Kent. This is going to be the biggest muster of the three.'

Fallon changed direction as Jon indicated. Ahead to the northwest, the water of the channel country glinted in the morning sun.

'Ah, I see them. There's a few utes and swags down there already.'

'Yeah, some of the ringers came out and set up camp yesterday afternoon. Some went back to town too.'

'Okay, I've sussed it out enough now.' Fallon nodded.

'Most of the cattle are back the way we came so you'll be flying into the sun in the afternoons. Will that be safe?'

'Yes, Jon, it will be safe.'

Fallon moved the cyclic stick connected to the central column located between the two seats, to put the bird into a left roll to head back to Kent's station.

'Kent seemed a bit stressed this morning, did you think?' she said.

'Didn't notice. Probably worrying about the muster on his place.' He looked over at her. 'And Sophie.'

'Sophie?' She frowned as they began to turn back.

'Yeah, I didn't know but apparently they were a couple for a long time before her ex came on the scene. Kent was muttering to Braden about her the other day. Braden told me afterwards she was rude to the people Kent was having dinner with the night we were there for dinner.'

'I didn't notice.'

His voice was low. 'I don't think either of us noticed much that night.'

'True.'

The helicopter slewed sideways as a strong gust of wind came from nowhere. Fallon increased their airspeed and moved the nose up. She looked ahead with a frown. 'Jon, what's that ahead?'

He lifted his head and peered forward. 'How fast can we get back?'

'Why?'

'That's a mother of a dust storm coming.'

'And there'll be wind with it.' Fallon scanned the horizon. 'It's only a few kilometres wide. We're not going to outrun it, so I'm going to head north. I think we'll be able to avoid the worst of it that way. I should have checked the forecast.' She cursed herself for being slack and letting her worries overtake her usual safety procedures. 'I'm sorry, Jon. My fault. Tighten your belt.'

'I'm fine. I have every faith in your skill, Fallon.' His voice was calm.

'We're just going to have to go the long way home.' Fallon nodded. 'If it gets too close, we'll land and let it pass. Won't be pleasant if we have to sit it out.'

'You mean if the wind's strong?'

'Yes, I'd rather outrun it, because we won't have time or somewhere to tie it down.'

'What about Craig's place? The homestead I mean.'

'Which way is it.'

'Back towards the storm.'

'No, too much of a risk. We'll be fine. Look you can see the edge of it to the northwest.' Fallon didn't express her fear that the wind would be more widespread than the dust storm.

As they headed north, Fallon sneezed again. The sky darkened and she frowned. The storm was getting too close, too fast and they weren't going to outrun it. She looked down, but it was hard to see below the dust that was starting to swirl beneath them.

She kept her tone even as the wind began to buffet the chopper. 'I'm going to take her down. Do you know what's beneath us?'

'Channel country.'

'And that is?'

'Salt pans, salt lakes, lots of water, and some ground.' Jon grabbed for the side of his seat as another strong gust pushed the bird sideways and the first of the dust hit them. Almost immediately the auxiliary power cut as dust was sucked in through the intakes.

'Brace position, Jon. I'm going into autorotate.' Fallon focused on her breathing, drawing the air in deep and letting it out slowly. It was impossible to see the ground and the first rule of a safe landing was clear pilot vision.

Jon leaned forward. 'What about you?'

'I'm flying.' She barely heard him as she focused in the helicopter.

'I love you, Fallon.' He crossed his arms in front of his head.

Her heart lodged in her throat.

I can do this. After Ken had died eight years ago, she'd gone straight up and taken herself through an autorotation. Now, the dust shrouded them as the engine cut out completely. The whoosh of the air from the spinning rotors and the dust grinding on the windscreen were the only sounds. Fallon tensed, fighting to control the bird in the descent without an engine.

She pulled back on the cyclic and the main rotor blades picked up speed as she desperately tried to work out how high they were. Levelling off, she pulled up on the collective and stared through the side door. The windscreen was covered with brown dust. As she brought the chopper lower, a flash of water glinted through the dust briefly. They didn't want a water landing. She pulled back to slow her forward speed and glanced across past Jon. There was an expanse of green directly ahead of them; Drawing in another breath, she levelled the helicopter.

Five metres to go.

'Come on, Fallon,' she whispered as the grass loomed ahead. 'Do this for Ken.'

Her control held as the chopper got closer to the ground. 'We're almost there, Jon.'

The chopper flipped sideways in one swift movement as the skids sank into something soft on one side. The seatbelt held her pinned against the seat as water sprayed around them. Jon's head ricocheted off the metal door beside her as the machine tipped over to his side. His eyes were closed.

'Jon, are you okay?' she screamed.

There was no answer.

Chapter 16
Kent

Kent was having an early lunch at the coffee shop with Jennifer, the new school counsellor at the state school. She was working across Augathella, Tambo, and Charleville schools and had said it would be good to learn more about the district. He tried his best to get out of it at dinner the other night—saying not having kids at the school, he wasn't much help—but he hadn't been able to fob her off without sounding churlish. He'd somehow let her know today this was a one off. He wasn't available to drop everything and come to town for lunch.

He hadn't known that Bob and Cheryl were bringing Jennifer to dinner last week until Cheryl had rung up and asked him to book for four. It *had* been satisfying to see Sophie's reaction. It showed her he wasn't spending his life waiting for her to decide she was ready to pick up with him again.

Oh no. He'd had his heart broken by Sophie once, and he was in full self-protection mode now.

Jennifer was sitting at a table under the awning of The Hot Pot, the local coffee shop. She was dressed in a business suit, and heavily made-up, her perfume overpowering. Kent felt out of place, he'd headed off in his work clothes and he brushed the dust off his trousers as he walked over.

'Hello, Jennifer,' he said, trying to give her a friendly smile that didn't hold an invitation. To his horror, she grabbed his arm and planted a kiss on his cheek.

'Hello, Kent, it's *so* good to see you again.'

He nodded. 'Have you ordered?'

'No. I was hoping we might go to the pub again when I finish my coffee. I've had a really difficult morning, and I could do with a glass of wine.'

Kent resisted the inclination to raise his eyebrows. 'Sorry Jennifer, I've only got half an hour.'

She sighed. 'Okay, next time I'm doing an overnighter here we'll go out for dinner by ourselves.'

Will we? he thought. *I don't think so.* But he said, 'I can't stay long. We're in the middle of mustering and I have to get back to the station.'

She put a manicured hand to her head and patted her perfect hair. 'God, yes. This horrid child. Nigel Cartwright, he threw a chair at me.'

'Ah, isn't that confidential?'

She ignored him and her words rushed on. 'Okay. His mum might have died, and he might be upset, but how dare he do that?'

'It's understandable.' Kent was horrified at her lack of confidentiality and consideration for the poor kid, but he wasn't going to let on he knew the family.

'No, it's not.'

'Have you had grief training?' he couldn't resist asking.

'No. I'm a primary teacher and I've enrolled in a psychology degree under a training program because they can't get counsellors out west. Anyway, enough about me, Kent. Tell me about your station. Is it huge?'

Kent couldn't believe it when she literally fluttered her eyelashes. Before he could speak, a very familiar voice came from behind him.

'Hello, Kent. Unusual to see you in town at this time of day.'

He turned slowly, and sure enough, Sophie was standing behind him, dressed in her waitressing clothes.

'Hi, Soph. Working the lunchtime shift too, are you? I'm impressed.'

She nodded and waited, looking at Jennifer. Finally, she broke the awkward silence. 'Hello, I'm Sophie Cartwright.'

Jennifer flinched.

Kent's manners kicked back in. 'Sophie, this is Jennifer, she's the new counsellor at the school.'

'Ah.' Her eyes narrowed. 'My brother was telling me about you last night. You upset Nigel last time you were here.'

'And he upset *me* this morning!'

Sophie pursed her lips and Kent waited for it; he knew her well.

'Who's the grown-up?' she asked, putting her hands on her hips.

'I am.' Jennifer's voice was shrill. 'No child has the right to throw a chair at the teacher!'

'Even if that teacher told him Mummy was never coming back and he had to suck it up?'

Kent drew in a horrified breath. 'You didn't say that to Nigel, did you?'

'I'm afraid that's confidential.' Jennifer examined her perfect fingernails.

'And what were you doing seeing him today? You weren't supposed to see him again. Braden emailed a complaint to Bob.' Sophie had her hands on her hips now.

Jennifer shrugged, and Kent disliked her intensely at that moment. He stood and pushed his chair in. 'I'm sorry to be rude, Jenny, but I've got to go to the produce store and get back out to the station.'

'It's Jennifer.'

'Sorry, Jennifer. I hope your day improves.' He lifted his hand in a wave and turned to Sophie. 'Soph, I'll walk you to the pub.' He was surprised when Sophie nodded and slipped her hand through the crook of his elbow. The feel of her fingers even through his shirt brought back too many memories.

'What a cow,' she said loudly as they walked away. 'No one treats our boys like that and gets away with it. I'll be talking to Bob when I knock off at two.'

'Yeah, I agree,' he said as they approached the pub.

'I'm surprised to see you in town with that storm coming.' Once they turned the corner towards the pub, she removed her hand.

'Storm, what storm?' He looked up at the clear blue sky. There wasn't a breath of wind.

'There's a big dust storm rolling in. I rang Braden and told him I'd keep the boys in town at Aunty Rowena's place.'

'What about Callie?'

'She's off sick with a sore throat. I drove the boys in. Probably the dust.'

'Are you sure there's a storm?'

Sophie pulled a face and marched him across the road and up the slight hill behind the hotel. 'Look, I hope your girlfriend's not driving far this afternoon.'

'She's not my girlfriend and bloody hell, look at that. I'd better get home.' A huge, high rolling cloud of red and brown dust ran along the horizon as far as he could see north and south. It was the highest dust storm he'd seen for a long time and it was approaching fast. 'Shit, Jon and Fallon are flying in that.'

'What do you mean? In a helicopter?'

'Yes, they were heading out to Craig Wilson's place to look at the cattle yards.'

'When they saw that coming they would have turned around.' Sophie frowned and stared at the sky. Kent looked away; he found it hard to look at her since they'd broken up. It bought back too many memories.

'It's moving fast, so there must be a strong wind up high. I don't think they would have had time. I'll go to the SES and see if I can pick Fallon up on the radio. She might have put down out there.'

'Call Craig too, he might know. Maybe they stopped at the station.'

'Good idea. Thanks, Soph, I'll see you later.' His mind focused on Fallon and Jon, and out of years of habit, Kent leaned across and went to kiss her, but stopped when he realised what he was doing. He froze and cleared his throat. 'Okay. You take care.'

'You be careful too.' Her hand on his cheek as she lifted it almost brought him undone, and he moved back.

'I will. See you later.'

Kent didn't look back as he headed for his ute.

His head was full of Sophie as he climbed in and slammed the ute into gear, heading for the SES headquarters out near the aerodrome.

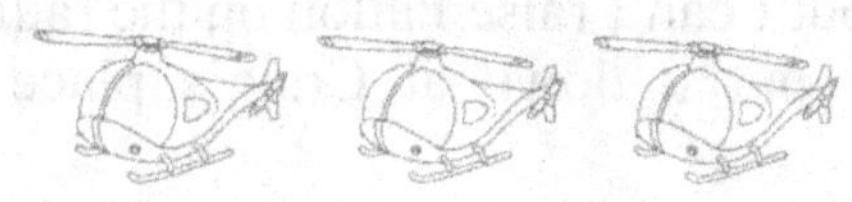

Chapter 17
Braden

Braden reached for his mobile as it rang for the fourth time in the last half hour. Sophie had rung to tell him about the storm heading to town and how she'd take the kids to Aunt Rowena's. That had made him feel guilty. Since Julia's death, he'd lost touch with their two aunts in town, but Sophie always kept in touch.

'Braden Cartwright,' he said, his attention on the spreadsheet on the computer.

'Bray, it's Kent. Would Jon and Fallon happen to be out there?'

Braden frowned. 'I don't think so. I haven't seen them since last night. What's wrong?'

'There's a huge dust storm rolling in and they flew out to Craig's place a couple of hours ago. I rang my place, but they haven't come back there and that's where Jon's ute is.'

'You think they're caught in it?'

'I hope not, but I can't raise Fallon on the radio.'

'Maybe they put it down at Craig's place when they saw it coming?'

'I got onto Craig and they're not there. He heard them go over a couple of hours ago.'

'What do you want me to do?'

'Not a lot we can do until this storm passes. It's just hit town. Won't be long before it reaches you. Just give me a buzz if they turn up. When the wind drops and it's clear, I'll take my chopper out.'

'Okay, keep me posted.'

'Will do.'

Braden saved his file, closed the laptop and headed to the kitchen. He'd told Callie to have an easy day seeing she'd felt too crook to go to school, but she said she was feeling better and headed to the kitchen to cook and freeze some meals, as well as make biscuits for the boys.

He stood in the doorway and watched her as she pulled a tray of biscuits from the oven and put them on the sink. Callie reached up and as she tucked a strand of stray hair back, she saw him. A sweet smile spread over her face as he walked over and put his arms around her.

'I thought you were working,' she said.

'I thought you were going to have a rest,' he countered.

'I feel fine now. My headache's gone, and my throat's back to normal.'

'It was probably the dust storm,' he said.

She leaned around him and looked out the window over the sink. 'What dust storm?'

'It's just hit town. Sophie rang, and then Kent. He's worried that Fallon and Jon are out that way in the helicopter.'

'I hope not. That one I was in at Mitchell was awful. Really scary, and I was inside a motel unit.'

'They are scary. Kent's going to keep an eye out for them. I think you should sleep in the house tonight.'

'Do you just?' she said with a cheeky grin.

'Well, I'll be lonely because the boys and Sophie are staying in town.'

'Hmm,' she said leaning into him. 'Not just because you want to have your wicked way with the nanny?'

'No, I'd like to have my wicked way with *my* woman,' he said brushing his lips over hers.

She chuckled. 'How about you help me clean up the kitchen and we'll have a—'

'A what?'

'A sleep?'

As Braden loaded the dishwasher and Callie covered the trays of biscuits, he kept his voice casual. 'I've been thinking.'

'Dangerous occupation, that,' she replied. 'Sorry.' She glanced at him as he came over to her. 'What have you been thinking?'

'I've been thinking it would be good if you moved into the house.'

She shook her head, and Braden put his hands on her shoulders. 'Hear me out, Callie?'

'Okay. What are you thinking?'

'Well, we're a couple now, aren't we?'

'I guess you could call us that.'

'The boys adore you and they hate you being over there at night in that small donga.'

'Do they?' She smiled.

'And so do I. It keeps me awake at nights.'

'Isn't it too soon? What would people say?'

'People like who?'

'Sophie?'

'No, my sister got stuck into me the other night and said it was about time you moved into the house. And although it's not the main reason, it's another reason. I think if Sophie could stay in the dongas, she'd come home more.'

'But this is her home.'

'It is to me. To us, but she lived at Jock's place for a couple of years before they moved north. I know she feels as though she's imposing. I even suggested that we open up the other side of the house.'

Callie lifted her hands and cupped his cheeks. 'That's a big step for you.'

'I need to take some big steps, Callie. I want to take a very big step.' He knew his voice was gruff. 'It's past time I cleaned out Julia's things, and we made full use of the house. Sophie said she'd help me but she won't move in there. So I want to suggest she has the donga. What do you think?'

His heart lightened when Callie finally nodded. 'Okay, I will, but on one condition.'

He raised his eyebrows. 'What condition?'

'As long as I have my own room. I'm not moving into your room. A small step first.'

'I can live with small steps.' Braden lowered his voice. 'As long as I can visit sometimes.'

Callie nodded, and he took her hand.

'Where are we going?'

'I thought we could take the opportunity to help you pick a bed? There's a few to choose from.'

'Lead the way,' she said with a sexy smile.

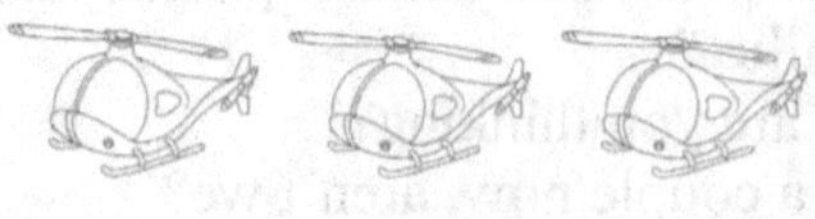

Chapter 18

Fallon wedged herself between Jon and the cockpit door on the other side of his seat and pushed as hard as she could but the door wouldn't budge. The chopper was on its side and the bottom of the door was buried in the soft mud.

Tendrils of panic wound their way through her limbs as she thought about fire. The tank had been almost full and she could smell aviation fuel. The chopper was on its side and as well as fire, she worried about it sinking, not knowing how deep the channels were out here.

Jon was out cold, but breathing normally, and his pulse was steady. There was no blood, but he had an egg-sized lump near his temple where his head had hit the metal when she'd brought the chopper down.

Frantic, she called his name trying to wake him up as she scrambled back over him and reached up to push her door open with both hands. It was hard at this angle, but finally, it moved and flipped over and hit the side of the machine.

'Jon, wake up. Please. we have to get out. We have to get out *now*.'

He muttered, and finally, his eyes fluttered open.

'Thank God.' Fallon tugged at his hands. 'I've undone your belt but you're going to have to help me. We have to get out fast.'

The chopper rocked as she managed to get him half to his feet, but he flopped back onto the seat. 'Can't. Dizzy.'

'You have to.'

Somehow, with a strength she didn't know she had, Fallon managed to push Jon up to her door. He leaned through it and she draped his arms over the top of the opening as he rested there with his eyes shut.

'I think I'm going to spew, Fallon.' At least he was talking and he knew who she was.

'That's okay, just do what you have to. But after we get you out.' She climbed over him and swung herself to the ground. She could just reach his hands and she tugged until he started to move with her.

After several long minutes of pulling and encouraging him, Jon was on the ground beside her. To her relief, this side of the machine was on solid ground. As the dust storm swirled around them, it was impossible to see more than a few metres ahead of them. She put her arm around Jon's waist and he leaned on her as they moved away from the chopper. The ground was soft beneath their feet and it wasn't long before their boots were sodden.

'Snakes,' he muttered. 'Bad out here.'

'Thanks for that,' she puffed out. 'Just what we need.' It wasn't long before they reached a piece of hard ground, far enough away from the chopper that if it did blow, they were safe.

Fallon helped Jon sit down, and she sat beside him. 'Lean on me, Jon. I'll look after you.'

He hadn't been sick, and he seemed to be waking more each minute. 'Should be looking after you,' he said.

Tears pricked at Fallon's eyes. They had come so close to death. It was a miracle that they had survived the crash from that height, but she'd be a lot happier once they got medical help. Jon had been out to it for too long.

She rested her cheek against his and closed her eyes. Even after knowing him for such a short time, she knew every inch of his face. The contours of his cheeks, his long eyelashes and the way he looked at her were familiar to her now, and she knew she couldn't walk away.

But this wasn't the time to tell him that.

'Jon,' she said as the wind roared around them, and dust stung their faces. 'Do you have your phone in your pocket?'

'In my hip pocket.'

Fallon reached down and he leaned over so she could get it out. As the screen lit up, relief surged through her as three bars of service showed at the top.

***

'I don't need to be admitted,' Jon complained. 'I just want to go home and sleep it off.'

Once the storm had settled it was only fifteen minutes until Kent's helicopter had hovered above them, and Fallon had directed him down to the wide expanse of solid ground about fifty metres from where she'd left Jon.

The doctor finally agreed to let Jon go on the condition that they stayed in town for the night, and he agreed begrudgingly.

'Just watch him through the night, Fallon. Keep waking him up and checking his eyes. If there are any problems, I'll send him to Charleville tomorrow for a scan.'

'I'm fine,' Jon insisted.

As they settled into the room that he'd had at the pub until a few weeks ago, Fallon sat on the bed beside him.

'If you're going to be a difficult patient, I might have to reconsider.' Her voice shook as the moments before the crash flashed through her mind.

'Reconsider? Reconsider what?'

'Staying out here. Not going back north.'

Jon's eyes crinkled and his lips tilted up in a huge smile. 'Really? You're really going to stay? Really and truly?'

'If you'll have me after I almost killed you.'

'It wasn't your fault.'

'It was. If I'd checked the forecast, we wouldn't have gone up.'

'Didn't you hear what Kent said?'

'No?' She shook her head.

'The storm only formed about a hundred ks west of Augathella and there was no mention of it on the forecast until it hit. So we would have still gone.'

Fallon's shoulders sagged in relief. 'That will stand me in good stead in the investigation. I'd hate to lose my licence.'

Jon sat up slowly and pulled Fallon into his arms. Her head rested on his shoulder and she absorbed the feel of his warm skin against hers.

'Do you know how happy you've made me?'

'I know. I haven't ever felt like this before either.'

'You know if you'd decided to go, I was going to follow you. I'd already discussed it with Braden.'

Fallon smiled as she lifted her head. 'There's a downside for you.'

'I can't think of one.'

'You get to help me clean out Uncle George's house.'

'Aha,' Jon said as his lips brushed the top of her head. 'But I also get to drive his ute too.'

'Maybe we could buy it off him? We might need it.'

' Need it?'

'Well, my ute's a single cab, and I have a little suspicion that I might need a bigger car, sooner rather than later.'

'You can drive the RAM anytime you need it, you know.' Jon leaned back and frowned. 'What for, moving stuff from the house?'

'Um no. Maybe for a baby seat. But only maybe. I *think* I could be pregnant.'

Fallon hadn't known that Jon's smile could get any wider.

Epilogue

'You've done an amazing job out here, love.'

Fallon smiled as she led her mother through Uncle George's house. Four weeks had passed since the crash, and those four weeks had been busy. Mum had arrived by plane earlier this afternoon, and Fallon had driven to Charleville to pick her up.

'Thanks, Mum. Jon and I spent a lot of time sorting out here after the musters were done.'

Fallon didn't see the need to tell her mother about the crash—after all, no one had been hurt, and there wasn't going to be an investigation. The dust storm had been accepted as the cause, and her boss from *Wyndham Birds* had flown down and told her how well she'd done to bring it down.

'I can't wait to meet your Jon. He must be pretty special if you're giving up your job to move down here.'

'He is. Very special.'

'Do you want to live here in George's house? I'm sure it would be fine.'

'No, we'll stay out on the station Jon's managing. Do you want to stay here while you're visiting? Or do you want to come out to our place? Or the rooms at the pub are nice. Whatever you want to do, we'll fit in.'

'I think I'd like to stay here,' her mother said. 'I can walk up and see George every day, potter around and sort out the things you've put aside, and maybe you could take me out to the station for a visit?'

'And how about I stay here with you for a few nights and we can have a really good catch up? I've got lots of news.'

'And a wedding to plan?'

Fallon held out her hand and her engagement ring sparkled in the late afternoon sunlight streaming through the now-clean kitchen window.

'Yes. And a wedding to plan. But a small one. Just our local friends here, and you and Dad, if you can get him out here.'

'He'll be here. I've given him the date already.'

Fallon smiled as her mother's eyes settled on the cane pram Fallon had spent the last two weeks cleaning and relining. 'Oh and I've got another date for you, Mum. I'd love it if you'd come out when the baby arrives.'

Jon was walking in the front door when he heard the happy scream from the kitchen, and he knew exactly what had happened. He'd been feeling that way ever since Fallon's pregnancy test had been positive. He followed the noise down the hall to the kitchen where Fallon and a woman he assumed was her mother were both crying and laughing at the same time.

Fallon caught his eye over her mother's head, as they both wiped their eyes.

'Jon, this is my Mum, Ruth. Mum, this is Jon.'

'Hello, Ruth, it's great to finally meet you.' He leaned forward and kissed her cheek before he put his arm around Fallon and kissed her soundly.

'I've booked a table in the dining room. Callie and Braden and the boys are coming into town, and Kent's going to meet us there.'

'And Sophie?'

'Sophie's waitressing tonight.'

Fallon and Jon exchanged a smile. The whole town was waiting for Kent and Sophie to get back together.

'Come on, ladies.' Jon crooked both arms. 'I'll be the talk of the town with a pretty woman on each arm.'

Mum looked at Fallon and nodded. 'He's a keeper, love.'

Fallon smiled. 'He's a lady-killer.'

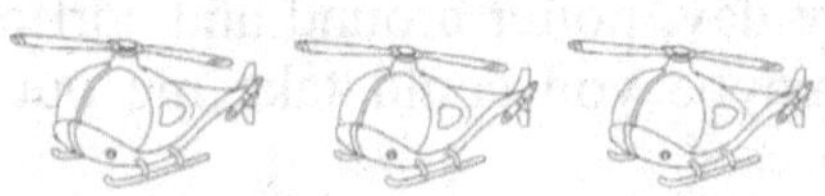

Outback Escape:
The Sister

ANNIE SEATON

The Augathella Girls: Book 3

Dedication

For the residents of Morweh Shire who gave me such a fabulous welcome!

Augathella Characters-Book 3

Sophie Cartwright	*Kilcoy Station*
Kent Mason	*Lara Waters*
Kimberley Riordan	Sophie's friend
Callie Young	Braden's partner
Fallon Malone	Helicopter pilot
Rory, Nigel and Petie	Sophie's nephews
Braden Cartwright	Sophie's brother
Jon Ingram	Station Manager
Amelia Foley	Jillaroo
Ben Riley	Shire Council Inspector
Jennifer Shaw	School Counsellor
Jim Anderson	Local garage owner

Chapter 1
Sophie

In the month since her brother, Braden, and her ex, Kent Mason, had brought her home from the cattle station at Innot Springs, Sophie Cartwright had picked up four to five shifts each week at the bistro in the local pub at Augathella. Much to Braden's disapproval, she'd also couch-surfed at several of her friends' places, ignoring his pleas for her to come home to *Kilcoy Station.*

As she wiped down the last table in the dining room, ready to knock off and head back to her friend Kim's house, Sean—the chef with wandering hands—poked his head into the dining room.

'Sophie, there's a bloke at the back door wanting to see you.'

Sophie stood stock still, her heart thumping hard. 'Who is it?'

'I dunno. I didn't ask. A big bruiser.' Sean came into the dining room and she took a quick step back. 'You okay? You look washed out all of a sudden.'

'He didn't say his name?'

Surely Jock wouldn't have the hide to come here looking for her?

'Nuh. Listen I'll hang around while you talk to him.' His grin was crafty. 'And then we can have a staffie drink when you're finished.'

'Thanks, but no. I have somewhere to go. I'm fine. I'll just stick my head outside and see who it is.'

Sean shrugged and went back to the kitchen while Sophie slipped the white waitressing apron over her head. Scrunching it up, she placed it in the linen bag with the tablecloths and napkins waiting for the laundry collection that came through from Charleville twice a week. Making her way over to the back of the bistro, she stood to the side of the open window, but it was too dark to see who was waiting out there for her. All she could see was the glowing tip of a cigarette.

Her heart thumped hard and she tried to breathe easily. Walking into the kitchen, she nodded at Sean. 'If you could just wait here for a sec, I'll see who it is.'

'It'll cost you a drink.'

'All right. One drink, then I have to go.' Sophie gave in; one drink wasn't a commitment. Sean was new in town, and he wasn't a bad guy. A bit touchy-feely but she'd coped. She knew his type; he'd stay here for a few weeks and then move on to the next small town. Maybe when he did, she could talk to the publican and offer to take over the cooking. She'd do a better job than Sean.

Sophie went to smooth her hair back and then stopped. If it was Jock outside—the man she'd shared a house with for two years and recently fled from—she'd be inside in a flash. The only others it might be would be Braden or Kent, but neither of them smoked.

'Are you gonna go out there or are you going to stand there biting your lip all night?' Sean flicked off the lights in the kitchen.

'All right, I'm going.' Sophie took a deep breath and slowly pushed open the screen door. It creaked as the figure of a man stepped towards her, a cigarette hanging in his hand.

'Sophie, you're late knocking off?'

She put her hand to her chest. 'Braden! What are you doing skulking around the back, and more to the point, what are you doing smoking? I thought you gave up years ago!'

'I did.'

'Hang on a minute.' Sophie called back into the kitchen 'It's okay, Sean. It's my brother. I'll see you Saturday night.'

'And don't forget, you owe me a drink,' Sean yelled back.

Sophie turned to her brother. 'Do we have to stand out here near the garbage bins? Come into the front bar.'

'No. I want to talk to you.'

'We can talk there.'

'No. I want to talk to you privately.' His voice was tense. 'That's why I'm smoking. It calms me. I have some things I want to say to you.'

'Maybe I don't want to hear them.'

'You probably don't, but it's time you listened to me. Come on, we'll walk up to the park. We can sit there.'

'Where's Callie?'

'She's home with the boys. I had to come to town for a meeting tonight so I figured I'd wait and see you. I didn't think you'd be so late finishing work.'

'There are a lot of tourists in town. Ready for Easter.'

'Where are you staying now?' her brother asked.

'At Kimberley's place.'

'I need you to come home, Soph.' He shook his head and dropped the cigarette butt and grinding it out with the heel of his boot. 'No, I *want* you to come home. There's a difference.'

'We can stay here and talk. It won't take long.'

'You reckon? You mightn't like it. I'm not going anywhere until I deliver some home truths.'

'So I'm not going to like it, hey?' Sophie folded her arms. 'And why should I listen to you?'

'Because it's about time you did.'

'Say whatever you have to, and then I need to go. Kim's waiting for me.' Her words were clipped. She knew exactly what Braden wanted to find out, but she had vowed to herself that Jock was in the past and she wasn't going to think or talk about it.

'Right.'

To Sophie's surprise, Braden's hand shook as he lit another cigarette.

'You're twenty-five years old, and it's time you took some responsibility,' he said.

Sophie's temper began a slow burn but she didn't speak and his next words shocked her.

'You broke off with Kent. A damn good man that you should be married to by now. You broke his bloody heart, and then you took off with that no-hoper. And then you moved away with him to that hovel we rescued you from. And now you're freeloading at any place in Augathella that'll put you up. What the hell is going on in your head, Sophie?'

Sophie took a step forward and poked her brother in the chest. Hard.

'Ouch.'

'Put that damn cigarette out and listen to me. As much as you're peeing me off, I don't want to see you die of lung cancer. For your boys' sakes. *I* don't care what you do.'

'You do, you know.'

'Okay, I do, but you have no right to speak to me like that. I didn't break up with Kent. *He* broke up with *me*.'

'That's not what he said.'

'So I'm a liar now too, am I?'

'No.' Braden ran a hand through his hair.

'Well, you ask Mr Perfect Mason what he did and why I broke it off. I'm not always in the wrong, Braden, although everyone seems to believe that. Mum and Dad always did, and now you're doing the same.'

'I want you to come home, Sophie. I'm worried about you, and you still haven't told me why you were so bloody scared of Jock. I'm not stupid. I saw the bruises on your wrists. You seem—I don't know—you seem lost.'

Sophie blinked tears away. 'All right. I am lost, and why shouldn't I be? Who has ever cared about me in this godforsaken place?' She focused on keeping her voice level and not crying. 'And how *dare* you tell me I have no responsibility? Who looked after your three little boys when Julia died? When you couldn't cope with them?'

Braden flinched. 'You did and I appreciate that more than you'll ever know.'

'So leave me alone now. Let me sort it out myself. I need to escape this town. I need to start somewhere new.'

'Doing what? And where?'

'I have some options.'

'No, I want you to come home.'

'Maybe for a short while. I'll think about it.'

'I'm not leaving until you agree.'

'All right. I'll come home if I can move into the donga.'

'They're both taken.' Braden shook his head. 'We've got new staff going in there. I'm building a new one too.'

This time Sophie knew she had the upper hand. Braden would never agree to what she was going to suggest, although it was way past time that he did.

'I'll move into the side of the house you closed down. Have you cleaned out Julia's stuff yet?' she asked bluntly.

'No.' His mouth set in a straight line.

'It's about time you did. It's not fair to Callie to have all Julia's stuff in that half of the house. I'll come home and help you clean it out and I'll move in there. It's not right that I live in that side of the house with you and Callie and the boys. What do you have to say to that?'

Braden looked at her for a long moment, and then he nodded. 'You're right. It's past time. I'll think about it.'

Sophie was lost for words for a minute. She hadn't expected Braden to agree so readily. She put her hand on his arm. 'It will be a step forward, Bray. And if you're as serious about Callie as I think you are, you need to do it. We'll always remember Julia, and I'll help you tell the boys about her as they grow.'

'That'll be a bit hard if you don't live here,' he said gruffly, but she knew it was now more emotion than temper that filled his voice.

'Wherever I end up, I hope they'll visit me.'

'Of course, they will.'

Chapter 2
Sophie

'Kim, have you got some spare shampoo, even one of those little motel ones? I forgot to bring mine.' Sophie poked her head around the bathroom door of Kimberley Riordan's house with a towel wrapped around her body.

'Sure, in the third drawer in the vanity and don't laugh. I'm a serial shampoo collector. Good to see one being used. Don't be long though. The bus comes at six.' Kim's laugh brought a smile to Sophie's face, something that had been a rare occurrence since Braden—and Kent—had flown north to bring her home. During the flight back from the north, she'd been so relieved to be going home, she'd managed to ignore the angst between her and Kent. Or more like the angst from Kent.

Talking to Braden last night had made her think about Kent way too much. Kent had barely spoken to her since she'd come home. So, they'd been an item when they were younger, move on, it was time he got over it. She had.

Liar, liar pants on fire, her conscience nagged at her.

'I have,' Sophie muttered crossly to herself as she rummaged through the array of shampoo in the drawer. Kim was right; there was a selection and a half, and the drawer was full. She took a tube each of shampoo and conditioner and turned the shower on.

She had more on her mind than worrying about Kent Mason. Besides, by the look of things he'd taken up with that new part-time teacher at the school. She'd seen them together twice this week.

Sophie had to decide what she was going to do about going home to *Kilcoy Station*. And she had to decide what to do tomorrow. She'd couch-surfed around half a dozen friends' places since she'd come back to the district. Kim's sisters were coming home to Augathella for Easter, so Sophie was moving on. It was a big weekend in town with the mystery fundraiser tonight, the billy cart races and rodeo on the weekend, and then the races on Monday.

Sophie pulled a face; she had no choice. She'd have to go back to the station. Braden had taken her stuff there when they'd flown home from up north, plus she'd need to get one of her good dresses and a fascinator if she was going to go to the races on Monday. Maybe she wouldn't go. Sometimes Sophie wondered if she was suffering from depression. Since she'd come home she found it hard to get enthusiastic about anything. She didn't want to be in Augathella, but she sure didn't want to be at Innot Springs with Jock. She didn't know where she wanted to be; this restlessness was not her usual mood.

Braden was sorted and Sophie was sure he didn't need her out at *Kilcoy Station*, no matter what he'd said last night.

Before he'd left to go home last night, he'd almost begged her.

'Soph, please come home. I need you. With Callie at school for three days a week, and the new jillaroo not here yet, things are hectic.'

'I thought you were going to hire a cook and a housekeeper? If I do come home, is that what you're after?'

'If you want to do that, I'll put you on the books.'

'Don't be stupid. You're not going to pay me.'

'It's not stupid. It's work. If you come, I'll pay you.'

'I've got a job at the pub.'

'Please, Soph.'

'I'll think about it.'

Sophie worried that it would be too awkward. Braden and Callie were in a new relationship, and now Callie had moved into the house. As a new couple they were good together and Sophie really liked her brother's new partner. Braden was happy and the boys had settled, especially poor little Nigel. She'd seen the boys in town a couple of times and they'd been ecstatic to see her.

If the dongas had been empty Sophie would have gone back home like a shot, but apparently, a new jillaroo was starting work at *Kilcoy Station* next week, and the other donga was being used by one of the contract station hands for a few months.

Braden, Callie, and the kids would be at the fundraiser tonight, so maybe she'd sit down with Callie and have a chat, see what she thought about it.

Maybe.

Going home would be the smartest thing to do, but there were the boys to consider too. She'd looked after Rory, Nigel, and Petie for so long, that they'd become reliant on her and she didn't want to put a spoke in Callie's wheel, so to speak.

'Hurry up, Soph,' Kim called. 'We've got fifteen minutes before the bus gets here. What are you wearing? I can't decide.'

'Jeans and a jumper.'

'Get a bit glammed up, though. It's going to be a big night.'

Sophie quickly dried off, wrapped her hair in a towel and headed for the spare bedroom to dig out her clothes. Two minutes to get dressed, two minutes to slap on some makeup, five minutes to dry her hair, and she knew she'd be ready before Kim was. Digging in her suitcase, she searched for the scoop-necked black bodysuit. She could wear it with her washed-out denim jeans and a vest; it would get cool out there tonight.

Her hair dried quickly and she scooped it up into a ponytail, grabbed her sparkly vest, put her boots on and hurried down the hall.

'You ready yet, Kimbo?'

'Almost. Be a love and grab my green ankle boots from the laundry. I'll meet you out the front. The bus is picking us up at the gate.'

Sophie did as she was asked and waited out on the front porch. Kimberley lived in her grandparent's house overlooking the river. The soft afternoon light filtered through the trees on the river bank and the breeze lifted the lacy fronds of the Moreton Bay Ash that stood sentinel near the bridge.

'Kim, three minutes,' she called.

Footsteps hurried up the hall, and Kim raced out, pulling the door shut behind her. She grabbed her boots and slipped them on over her socks. 'Thanks, you're a love. How is it that I can organise a class of twenty-five children with no problem, but can never be on time for any of my stuff!'

'You've always been the same,' Sophie teased. 'I remember when you used to go out in Braden's group, they always left you until last to be picked up.' She picked up the bag where she'd put a jumper and a bottle of water. 'Now tell me about this mystery outing. Why the secrecy?'

'I wanted it to be a surprise, but I guess we'll be there soon. It's a fundraiser for the school, and Craig has offered his property. You know that big camp kitchen area at his place where the grey nomies camp? Near the hot bore?'

'I love that bore. Has he still got the bathtubs alongside it?'

'Yeah, he's booked out for weeks ahead, now that the weather's cooling down. He said it was a good idea to have the function at his place because he'd have a captive clientele to spend money. Jim Anderson has let us have the three school buses to take everyone out there, and pick up at stations along the way.'

'Sounds super organised.' Sophie nudged Kim. 'Did Bob Hamblin organise it?'

'No, Jacinta Mason did.'

Kent's sister. That would mean he'd be there. One thing she'd always admire about Kent's family was their closeness and their ready affection. It had been so different to her and Braden's experience growing up. Their parents had been old school, with not a lot of overt affection displayed, but expectations clearly defined. Kent's parents had welcomed her to their station when she and Kent had started seeing each other in Year 12 after Sophie had begged to be allowed to leave boarding school and do her final year at the local high school.

'I suppose you've learned all you need by now, Dad had said. 'No need for university for you. You can help your mother around the station.'

Their father had old-fashioned values and old-fashioned views, and Sophie had seen a different world at *Lara Waters* when she and Kent had become an item. A world where her needs and hopes and dreams were respected. Kent's parents, Rhonda and Garth, had welcomed her with open arms, and as Sophie spent more time out there, she realised what a different household she and Braden had been brought up in. All that mattered at their home was the work ethic. Unfortunately that hard work had shortened the lives of both their parents.

There had been few family occasions and little time for celebrating life. Christmas had been celebrated with one gift each—a useful gift—and a baked dinner, and then back to work. Easter was a non-event, and when Kent gave Sophie an Easter egg the first year they had been together, he had been shocked to discover it was the first one she'd ever received.

They'd been lying on the grass out near the hot bore at the back of *Lara Waters*, watching the clouds above.

'So for real? No Easter bunny ever?' he said.

'Nope.'

'Santa Claus?'

'No, just a present from Mum and Dad. Always something we could use. The Christmas before my first year at boarding school I was given a pen and pencil set.'

Kent had rolled over and kissed her and there had been a lull in their conversation for quite a while.

'What about the tooth fairy?' he'd asked later that afternoon when they were soaking in the warm bore water.

'Nope. Hadn't heard of it until I was in late primary school. I had all my second teeth by then.'

She and Kent had split the week before the accident, but she pushed away the thoughts of that time. Jock had stepped in and cheered her up, and before she knew it, he'd asked her to move in with him. To his credit, he had been supportive when Julia had died, and he'd agreed to have the boys stay with them until Braden sorted himself out.

When she was looking after the boys after Julia's death, Sophie had ensured their lives were full of those special occasions; Santa Claus, the Easter Bunny, and the Tooth Fairy had been regular visitors in their household, much to Jock's disgust.

Sophie let out a regretful sigh now as she sat beside Kim.

'You okay?' Kim asked. 'Why the big sigh?'

'Yep. I was just thinking about Jacinta and Kent's parents. They're lovely people.'

'They are. Rhonda is an absolute hoot. You can always hear laughter when she comes to do the volunteer reading at the school. We miss her. Do you know how long they're away for?'

'No. I've just heard they've gone on a trip.'

'Yep, a cruise, Jacinta said.' Kim looked at her curiously. 'Doesn't Kent keep you up to speed? Do you see much of him these days?'

'No, but he was at the pub having dinner with the new school counsellor the other night.' No one else knew the acrimonious circumstances of their break-up. Not even Braden. If he'd known what Kent had done, he wouldn't have asked him to fly up to Innot Springs to bring her home. Kent should have said no.

'Oh, God, I'll have to warn him. Jennifer's latched on to every single man in town. The male teachers at school almost run when they see her coming. She's an absolute pain. From all accounts, she wants to find a husband and settle out here.'

'Kent's a big boy now.' Sophie was hoping he'd be busy and not at the fundraiser tonight. It was much easier not to spend time in his company. No matter what had happened, and what he'd done to her, he still made her heart race. Well, she'd be able to get lost in the crowd if there were that many coming from town and the surrounding district.

'Are you okay with Kent these days? You never told me why you broke up.'

'That was a long time ago.'

'But you were so good together, Soph. We all thought there'd be a wedding.'

And so did I, Sophie thought.

Kim looked at her, waiting for her to spill. 'Why did you break up?'

'Kent let me down.' Sophie was relieved to see the school bus come around the corner. 'Here's the bus,' she said.

'I bags the back seat if it's free.'

Sophie chuckled and shook her head, pushing away the thoughts of Kent. 'How old are you?

'Thirty-one. It's a long time since I played up in the back seat of the school bus.'

'Pease tell me not with my brother.'

'No, Braden only ever had eyes for Julia.'

Kim and Sophie exchanged a sad look. Kim had been part of the group of friends who had supported Braden when Julia died. That's when Sophie had become friends with Kim, even though she was six years younger than her.

'So what's tonight's function?' Sophie asked as the bus pulled up at the gate and they hurried down the front path.

Kim looked at her sideways. 'A fundraiser. You'll find out when we get there, but trust me, it's going to be a blast. Are you ready for Easter in Augathella?'

Chapter 3
The fundraiser.
Wilson Creek Station
Kent

'How the hell did you ever rope me into this, Ben?' Kent Mason sat in the small shed at the back of the makeshift stage and put his head in his hands. His stomach churned and he was worried he was going to throw up.

Ben Riley, his mate from high school days chuckled. 'There's no need to be nervous, mate. We've got this down pat. And it's for a good cause. The least we can do is contribute.'

'You always were a show pony at school.'

'Ha, thanks for that. Give me credit for a bit of talent. Once we get going you'll be fine. Trust me, you'll enjoy yourself.'

'I know I should have worn a mask. I still could. I think there's one in the glovebox of my ute from the New Year's Eve do. No one will know it's me then.'

'You mean a full mask? I thought you meant a COVID mask. How are you going to sing in a mask?'

'How am I going to sing when I'm shit-scared with nerves?

'Just follow my lead.'

'It sounds like there are thousands out there.'

'I think we're into the hundreds.' Ben opened the door of the shed a chink and peered through. 'The two front rows are filled with strangers. Must be the grey nomies camping at the bore.'

'I can cope with them. They don't know me. Jeez, Ben why I ever agreed to this, I'll never know. I'm sorry you ever came back to town.'

'That makes two of us, mate. Anyway, nerves are a sign of a good performer. If you weren't nervous I'd be worried. All you have to do is perform as well as you did when we practised at my place and you'll be fine.'

Kent took a deep shuddering breath and Ben frowned.

'You really are worked up, aren't you?'

'Duh, quick off the mark, mate.'

'Okay, what are you worried about exactly?'

'That I'll open my mouth and nothing comes out? That I'll forget the words? That I'll forget how to play my guitar? Is that enough? This is a big first for me. It's okay for you, you've been doing it in

Brisbane where no one knows you. Hell, man, I grew up with half the people out there!'

'So did I. And they're gonna love you. They're gonna love us! You said no one has a clue that you play and sing?'

'No. Up until you came back to town, it was something I always did at home by myself.'

'Well, that was a waste. You're going to be a huge hit with the locals tonight and they're going to dig deep and donate for the school.'

'And then it will be all over and I can enjoy the rest of the weekend.'

Ben shook his head.

'You know I'd rather be out in the yards facing a cranky bull than doing this.' He stared at Ben. 'What did you mean that makes two of us. I was thinking how lucky you were to get an engineering job on the council here.'

'Nope. I put down all of the major towns from Brisbane to Cairns on my application. The last thing I wanted was to come home to the outback.'

'And here was I thinking how lucky you were. Got a girl on the coast? Is that why you didn't want to come back?'

'No, I wanted to prove to myself somewhere I wasn't known. Here I'm Johnny Riley's son, and I'm accepted for that. Not for the job I do. Plus the old guys on the shire have been there forever and I'm getting all the shit jobs.'

'Can't be that bad.'

'Trust me, how many other shire engineers would have been roped in to do the council dog obedience classes?'

Kent felt a bit better as he laughed. 'Dog obedience classes? I didn't even know they had them.'

'Yep and yours truly is running the show, for frig's sake.'

'I—' Kent held his guitar tightly and widened his eyes as the noise outside quietened and the PA system crackled.

'G'day, folks. A special welcome to our campers who've joined us tonight and a big welcome to the locals who've come all this way from town. Thanks to Jim Anderson for lending us the buses. It's for a good cause, and tonight we're raising money for our local school.' Craig Wilson's voice boomed into the small shed. 'There's a great night planned, but before we introduce our special entertainment— and I know you're going to love these guys—Bob, our principal and

Jon Ingram are sitting over at the table to my left and taking entries for the hundred club. Five dollars a number. Come on over. Fallon and Cheryl are at the other table and they're selling tickets for the huge Easter raffle.'

Kent closed his eyes and took a deep breath. Maybe the crowd would be more interested in the winning tickets than the entertainment.

Craig's voice got louder. 'Sophie, can you help Kim carry the basket up so we can show the crowd the size of the raffle prize? Thanks, ladies A big thanks to the local pub who donated all the chocolate eggs.'

'Shit, that's all I need. Sophie's here.'

'Of course, she is. The whole town's turned up. It's the start of a big weekend. Now pull yourself together. Craig said ten minutes for ticket selling and then we're on.'

Kent hugged his guitar close and focused on his breathing.

Chapter 4

Sophie took one end of the giant basket, smiling as she and Kim negotiated the four steps up to the stage.

'There's enough chocolate in here to sink a boat,' Kim said with a grin.

The buzz of the crowd and the happy faces had put Sophie in a good mood. The sun was gone and now it was a clear still night; the wind had dropped and the stars sparkled in an indigo sky. The enticing aroma of frying onions and streak drifted over from the Lions van. Sophie caught Braden's eye and he grinned at her as she and Kimberley held the basket up. Her brother was standing at the back of the seated area with his arm around Callie. The three boys were running around the grass with most of the student population of the primary school. A buoyant mood filled the area and Kimberley smiled at her as she nodded towards the queue forming to buy raffle tickets.

'Looks like they're in the mood to buy.' Craig and his workers had set up a bar next to the hot food van. Some of the crowd had brought their own eskies, but there was a good queue at the bar too, a couple of kegs enticing thirsty patrons.

'Nothing like beer on tap,' Sophie said.

'And less mess,' Kim added. 'Come on. We'll leave this on the stage. If we put it to the left side at the front, it won't get in the way.'

'So what's this mystery entertainment tonight?' Sophie asked as they carried the basket to the side of the raised platform, placing it down carefully on the timber floor.

'Apparently a very good duo. I don't know much about it, Bob was pretty close-mouthed. Said it was to be a surprise.'

'Let's go grab a drink, and find a good seat where we can see what's happening.'

Kim nodded, following Sophie down the stairs. As they neared the grassy area, Braden called out to Sophie and beckoned her over.

'I'll catch up with you, Kim,' Sophie said. 'Can you grab me a beer please? I'll get the next one. I want to have a quick word with Braden.'

'Sure. I'll get us seats as close to the front as possible. Then we can get up and dance.'

'I can't see them having a mosh pit here. Or like that concert you took me to in Longreach when I was just legal!' Sophie rolled her eyes. 'No chance of that, these days, Kim. I hate drawing attention to myself.'

Kim grinned at her. 'Girlfriend in that bodysuit and jeans, you've already got the attention of every red-blooded male from here to Charleville.'

'Well. If they look at my face, they'll see a bit of *not interested*.'

'Famous last words, Sophie.'

Chapter 5
Sophie

'Hey, big brother.' Sophie made her way through the happy crowd and pecked Braden on the cheek. 'What are you looking so pleased about?'

'Nothing in particular. It's a great night, we had thirty ml of rain at the station yesterday and I'm taking Easter off.'

Sophie raised her eyebrows. 'That'll be a first.'

'Not really. It's just these past few months I've been working hard. Making up for all those months when I was a mess. Now life's settled, and there's only one thing that would make it better.'

'And what would that be?' she asked suspiciously, knowing exactly what he was going to say.

'I've thought about what you said. Will you come out and help me?'

'When?'

Braden put his hand up. 'As soon as possible?' He took her arm and they walked over near the fence where it was quieter. Sophie folded her arms. She really didn't have a decent argument.

'Ever since Kent and I brought you back, you've avoided coming home. You've only been out to visit once.'

'I'm coming out tomorrow to get something to wear to the races on Monday.'

'And then where are you going to stay? I know Celia is coming to stay with Kim for Easter.'

Sophie shrugged. 'I haven't decided yet.'

'I can't understand why you just won't say yes. You can stay in our side of the house. Is it because of Callie? Or have I done something to upset you?'

Sophie bit her lip as a myriad of feelings churned through her. How could she tell Braden what was wrong? *She* didn't even know what the matter was.

Okay, so she was embarrassed at getting sucked in by Jock and agreeing to move away from all she loved. She was doubly embarrassed that she had let Jock treat her the way he had for so long.

And it was doubly awkward that Kent had been one of her rescuers when she'd called Braden for help. The last thing she'd expected was to see his plane turn up, although to have Braden climb out and open his arms to her had made it bearable. She had felt safe.

'I like Callie. A lot. You're great together and I'm really pleased to see you both so happy. And the boys too.' She gestured over to the lawn where the three of them were playing with the other kids. 'Look how happy they are.'

'We're talking about you, Soph. I'm worried about you. Do you need to go and see someone?'

'See someone? Like who?'

'You know someone to talk to, After what you went through with Jock. Not that you've told me.' He looked her square in the eye. 'You need to talk to someone.'

'No. I *don't*. I handled it. And I got out. A lot of women don't. And you're a fine one to talk. You didn't go and talk to "*someone*" when everyone said you needed to.'

'Everyone?'

'Well, me. I did.'

'We're a fine pair, Soph. We've never been much good at knowing how to deal with *stuff*.' Braden moved closer to her. 'I'm just trying to help. I'm worried about you . . . please come home to *Kilcoy Station*. We all want you there. Me, and Callie, and the boys. I was serious about you taking the cooking on. If you do, I'll put you on the payroll. If you don't, I'll have to hire someone. I've got a team of new young ringers moving into the old sheds. We've got a busy winter season ahead.'

Sophie relaxed her shoulders and stared at her brother for a long moment. 'All right, but on one condition.'

'Anything you ask for!'

'Seeing the dongas are full, you and I will sort out the other side of the house. I'll stay in the closed-up section of the house to give you and Callie and the boys your privacy. And I'll do it for three months only.'

'And then what?'

'And then I'm escaping.'

'Escaping?' His eyebrows rose.

'Leaving, spot on three months. I feel trapped here, Bray. Everyone is looking at me and feeling sorry for me, but they don't say anything. Kim talked me into coming here tonight and to the races. I didn't want to.'

'And the rodeo and the billy cart race, I hope. Rory and Nigel have entered the under-nines. You should see the cart. Callie's done it in a rainbow theme.' Braden shook his head and stared at her. 'And where are you going if you leave? What are you going to do?' He ran a hand through his hair and she could see the worry etched on his face. Guilt tugged at her, but determination won.

'I don't know. I'll sort something. Look, the show's about to start. I'll come out early tomorrow and get organised. We'll talk more then.'

'Okay, Soph. Thank you. I owe you and . . .'

'And what?'

Braden cleared his throat and shuffled his feet. 'And . . . I love you, sis.'

Sophie swallowed and stared at him. She stood on her toes and brushed a kiss on her brother's cheek. 'I love you too, you big galoot.' She put her head down and walked away. For Braden to show her affection like that was a huge step. They'd not been a demonstrative family when their parents had been alive, and over the last few years, Sophie had come to realise what a sterile family life she and Braden had growing up.

Callie had been so good for Braden; tonight was the first time in their lives that he had shown Sophie spontaneous brotherly affection like that. She was still hesitant about moving to the station, but she knew Braden needed her; the more she thought about it, the more she realised it would be good to have her own space. She hadn't had that since they'd moved out of the original farmhouse that the station manager, Jon, and his partner, Fallon, lived in now.

As long as Braden could deal with her living in the side of the house where he and Julia and the boys had lived before Julia had been killed in the accident.

'Over here, Sophie.'

Sophie turned at Kim's call. Her friend was standing on a chair in the second row from the front of the stage and was waving at her.

'Quick, the show's about to start,' she said.

The mood of the crowd buzzed with anticipation as a spotlight lit up the centre of the stage where someone had placed two stools. A bank of amplifiers and sound gear sat behind a huge basket of Easter eggs at the side of the stage.

Sophie checked out the crowd as she hurried along the narrow walkway between the two sections of chairs; she was surprised to see that every chair was filled. To the left and right of each block of plastic chairs, families had spread picnic rugs and set up camp chairs on the grass. She smiled as she recognised some of her friends from school, not that she'd made many in the one year she went to the local high school. Once she'd met Kent they had pretty much been an item and hadn't spent a lot of time in the social group. It had been an idyllic year for her. For the first time in her eighteen years, she'd felt valued . . . and loved.

Now her current friendship group was made up of people Braden had become friends with over the years and they were all older than she was. Most of her friends were married now and already had kids. Some had moved away but she still kept in touch by email.

Maybe in the future she'd move to a town where she knew someone already. Sophie pulled a face as she reached the row where Kim was sitting. No, she would be independent and she'd find somewhere to move to where she could make a fresh start. No history, and no one who knew what poor choices she'd made. She'd escape this country town and the memories and she'd find a job in a totally new place.

But what sort of job?

Although Sophie had completed high school, she knew she had no special skills and little experience in the workforce. Even though she'd never finished her course, she could cook, so maybe she could move to a station in a different district. She made a note to start looking online for jobs.

Maybe she could move north.

No! She dismissed that idea immediately. Nope, nowhere near Jock. It would suit her if she never laid eyes on Jock Evans again. A shiver ran down her spine and she blocked the memories. She had been so naive.

'Sophie, hurry up! Stop daydreaming and come and sit down.' Kim was three seats along the row and had her bag minding the seat beside her.

'Okay, I'm coming I'm coming.' Sophie stood at the end of the row. 'Excuse me.'

The three people in the seats at the end of the row moved their legs sideways and held their drinks close to their chest as Sophie pushed through. In the front row in front, the mayor sat beside his wife but she didn't recognise the others with them.

'Quick, Soph. Sit down it's about to start. Here's your drink.'
Kim pointed to the stage where an attractive young woman in a red
dress and high heels stood holding the microphone. 'Look. Even a
proper MC. Jacinta has done a great job.'

'Who is that?' Sophie said. 'Someone I should know?'

'No. Apparently, she's the announcer at the new ABC radio
station. I haven't met her yet.'

'So Craig got her to do the honours to introduce this mystery
duo.' Sophie settled back in the chair and took a sip of her beer.
They had a fine view of the stage.

Kim looked at her. 'Um, Soph? I haven't been quite honest with
you. I actually do know who it is but I didn't want to tell you
because I didn't think you'd come.'

'Why not?' Sophie frowned. 'Why wouldn't I have come. I
know I'm not a big country and western music fan, but it's for a
good cause.'

'Um, you'll see soon.' Kim pulled a face.

The PA system hummed and the pretty woman spoke into the
microphone. 'Good evening, ladies and gentlemen. I'm Mel from
your local ABC station.'

A huge cheer went up.

'Thank you. It's fabulous to be here for the first function to kick
off the Augathella Easter events. A huge thank you to Craig and
Mandy Wilson for letting us use their station for the concert tonight.
I'm really looking forward to getting to know you all. It's a fabulous
fundraiser tonight, so dig deep and let's make a difference for the
local primary school. I'm sure we're going to see lots of students in
the billy cart races on Sunday. But without further ado, let's get this
music on the road. We've got a special duo for you and I'm sure
you're going to enjoy the music of "*The Augie Boys*". Please put
your hands together and settle back for some great music.'

Sophie rolled her eyes. '"*The Augie Boys*"? It's someone local?'

Kim nodded and took a swig of her beer in the plastic cup. 'Sure
is. It's Ben Riley and you'll see who else in a minute. So prepare
yourself.'

Sophie had no idea why she'd have to prepare herself. She didn't
know anyone local who sang or played music. The only semi-local
musicians she'd ever seen at the pub had come from Charleville,
plus there was a band from Tambo who had come through a few
times when she and Kent had still been at school. He'd loved his

music and was always playing something new for her. He'd introduced her to soft rock. Art rock, he'd called it back then. Kent had done music for his final exams, but she'd never seen him play an instrument.

Or sing.

Suspicion crept into her thoughts, and she shook her head.

Surely not?

The stage lights went out and the crowd quietened as the MC stepped off the stage. Plaintive guitar notes broke the silence, and the lights gradually began to come back on, until a spotlight now illuminated the two stools that had previously been empty.

Two guys in black jeans, black T-shirts and dark Akubras sat on the stools. The spotlight shone on them but they both had their heads down as the one on the right began to pluck the guitar strings. The music was beautiful and as she watched, spellbound, the guy on the left sat straight and lifted a harmonica to his lips. The music he made was magic.

Relief filled Sophie for a second, but it disappeared instantly as the second musician lifted his head and Kent Mason's eyes looked her way. For a moment she thought he was looking at her and then the woman sitting in front of her jumped up and waved madly.

'Go, Kent!' Jennifer Shaw screamed out.

Sophie let out a gasp and stared as Kent began to sing.

Kent?

It was his voice, but it was strong and true and perfectly in tune as he launched into her favourite Chris Isaac song. He had the most beautiful voice. Dismay filled her as he shared his hidden talent with most of Augathella.

'You okay, Soph? Bit of a surprise packet, hey?'

Sophie gave a brief nod, aware of Kim looking at her, but *she* was having trouble taking her eyes off Kent.

Chapter 6
Kent

Once they'd been introduced by the ABC announcer and they'd started their performance, Kent managed to switch off and ignore the crowd in front of the stage. He looked out over the faceless people and the velvet sky as pinpricks of stars began to appear above.

He and Ben were good together; he knew that. The sound system with the microphones and the amplifiers made them sound even better. Their voices harmonised well, and Ben was a gun on the harmonica. They played a set of six songs, back to back, and he didn't stumble on one word or one note. By the time they were singing the last chorus of the final song of the set, Kent was relaxed and enjoying himself.

As they wound it up, Ben gestured to Rusty Wilson, Craig's eighteen-year-old son, who was in charge of the lighting. Rusty was doing a great job, and on the last note of the song as their voices lowered to diminuendo, the stage plunged into darkness. As Ben and Kent exited through the back curtain and headed to the shed behind the stage for a break and a cold drink, the applause from the crowd and the calls for "more, more" was deafening.

Ben opened the door and Kent followed him into the small space. Ben held up his hand and they high-fived each other.

Euphoria flooded through Kent and the feeling was better than the high of soaring in the sky in his twin-engine Cessna.

'Told ya, mate. We blitzed it.' Ben paced around the small space as Kent went to the esky and grabbed two beers. He'd drunk three bottles of water on stage. He shook his head.

'Why was I so nervous? There wasn't any need to be, was there?'

'Because you take pride in your work. And are you for real? You've never performed live before? With a talent like yours!'

'Never. It's just something I've done for myself. Not even my sister knew I could sing until tonight.' Kent chuckled. 'I sing when I'm out in the paddocks. The cattle could tell some stories.'

'I'm mighty pleased that I heard you that night.'

Kent had been sitting at the back of his house strumming his guitar and singing one night a few weeks ago, not long after he'd flown Braden up to collect Sophie. He'd been feeling a bit unsettled, wondering why he hadn't been enough for her and how she'd ended up with that bastard, Jock Evans instead. He'd put his feelings into his strumming and singing, and hadn't heard Ben arrive, and the first he knew, Ben had pulled out his harmonica and was improvising beside him.

'We make a good team. I reckon we'll be asked to do some pub and club gigs after this. Are you up for it?' Ben swigged a can of beer in one hit.

'Really?'

'Yeah, once Mel interviews us, the word will spread. You on?'

'You're jumping the gun a bit, Ben, I'd say.' Kent was cautious in everything he did, but he couldn't help the grin pulling at his lips. 'If it does happen, I reckon I could find the time.'

'Let's go out and mingle with the crowd. You never know our luck. There are a lot of single women out there. A man might get lucky tonight.'

Kent grinned. 'You go mingle. I'm going to sit here and catch my breath for a while.'

***

'Another beer, Soph?'

'Huh?' Sophie came out of her daze. How come she hadn't known Kent could sing? He had the voice of an angel. And how hot did he look on that stage in his black outfit? She pushed away the feeling; she had no right to react like that, and she didn't want to anyway. Every woman from zero to ninety in the crowd would be salivating over Kent Mason tonight. He looked like a rock star, and more to the point he'd sounded like one too.

'Do you want another beer? We might as well, seeing as we're getting the bus home.' Kim yelled over the noise of the crowd.

Sophie jumped to her feet, finally gathering her wits. 'You stay there. My shout. Do you want some hot chips?'

'No, but I could go a steak sanga.'

Kim stayed on her feet. 'I'll grab the drinks and you get in the food queue. Steak sanga for you too?'

'Yes, I should eat.' Sophie wasn't very hungry but she knew she needed something to soak up the beer.

She made her way to the food tent and joined the food queue. A tap on her shoulder had her turning around.

'Hey, Sophie!' Callie held her arms open. 'I am so pleased you're coming home. Braden told me you'd agreed. I could barely sit still I was so happy. And you've made *his* night.'

Sophie wasn't sure what to say as she hugged Callie. Even though she'd agreed, she still wasn't sure it was the right decision. But since she'd sat there listening to Kent sing, her head wasn't in the right space to try and think about the next few months so she simply smiled at Callie.

Callie was on a high. 'And how good were Kent and Ben? Even with all the live outdoor concerts I went to in Brissie, I've never heard such a great performance.'

'Ben?' Sophie asked. 'I thought I recognised him. Was that Ben Riley?'

'Braden said it was a Ben he went to school with. I don't know his last name.'

Sophie nodded. 'It *was* Ben Riley. Fair dinkum, the night is full of surprises.'

'But what a great night. The boys are so excited. Are you coming to the billy cart races on Sunday?'

'Wouldn't miss it for the world.'

'And the races on Monday?'

'Yes, and the races.' Sophie couldn't help her smile. 'I have a reputation to uphold.'

'And the rodeo tomorrow? Braden's expecting the new jillaroo to arrive in town and he told her we'd be there. When do you think you'll come home?'

Sophie thought quickly. 'I haven't decided, but maybe I'll come out tomorrow. I've got the dinner shift at the pub. I'm not sure if it'll be busy after the rodeo or not.'

'There are a lot of tourists in town for Easter, so I'd say it might be. The two motels and the caravan park are full, and a lot of campers out here at Craig's.'

Sophie smiled at Callie. 'You sound like you've got to know the town very well. I know you're happy out at *Kilcoy Station,* but it must be very different to Brisbane.'

The queue moved forward a little.

Callie nodded slowly. 'When I came out here, I had no idea what I was coming to. Even the long drive out was a first for me. I encountered my first dust storm, and I had no idea about living on the land. I'm sure Braden thought I was a fool.'

'He got over that quickly if he did. So you've settled? No homesickness for the city?'

'No. I'm here to stay. I've contacted my friend Jen. She's going to property manage my house for me while I rent it out. Braden and I are going to go back to Brisbane before school goes back. I want to show him some of my furniture. It'll fill up some of the empty spaces in the house.'

Sophie hesitated. 'Has Braden showed you the other side of the house yet?'

'No. And I haven't pushed. We've been busy with me going into town to school. I know he finds it hard. Of course, he does. And that's why I'm not sharing his bedroom. You know, when I headed out here, I had no idea how life would turn out for me. I'm still not rushing into anything. I've only been out here six months.'

Sophie put her hands up. 'That's between you and Braden, Callie.'

'Sophie, you're family, and I'm very conscious of not pushing in. As much as I love Braden, I think we need to take things slow. Our relationship affects others, including you. I'm here to stay— if Braden wants me to.'

'I have no doubt of that, Callie. My brother has mellowed a lot since you arrived, and it's clear that he loves you too.'

Even in the dim light Sophie saw the blush rise into Callie's cheeks. Even though she came across as really confident, maybe Callie held the same fears and worries that she did too.

'One word of advice, Callie. Be careful. Don't risk your love by doubting, and not talking. Often there's no going back. I still don't know whether I'll hang around here. I'm thinking about moving away in a while.'

'I'm sorry to hear that, and I'm sorry about your relationship breaking up.'

'Which one?' Sophie frowned, wondering what Braden had told Callie.

'You and Jock.'

'God no. Don't be sorry about that. That was a mistake on the rebound. I was talking about the past. Way before Jock.'

The microphone crackled on the stage and Sophie looked up anxiously. She wanted to be back in her seat before Kent and Ben started singing again. 'Gosh, this food queue is slow. I feel like getting in the van and helping them!'

'We've got time. It's a thirty-minute break. Braden asked Craig what the program was,' Callie said, with a slight shake of her head. 'I think Craig's going to do the raffle ticket sales spiel now.'

Sure enough, Craig's voice boomed over the mike. 'Come and get your tickets. Don't miss out. Look at this fabulous prize. The biggest basket of chocolate you'll find anywhere in the Murweh Shire. I've also heard that there's a new second prize, young ladies. A mystery date with one of the fellas up here on stage. I wonder which one it is?' Craig grinned as there was a rush of young women to the raffle ticket table.

'You'll have to buy some tickets, Sophie,' Callie said.

'Nuh.' Sophie shook her head. 'I'm over dates, mystery or otherwise, for life.'

'Well, at least you can enjoy the music. Braden told me Ben's a local too.'

'Yeah, I went to school with Ben. His parents have a wheat property not far out of town, and his mum is a dog breeder. I was surprised when he came back. He always swore he was going to move away.'

'I'm glad he's here. They sing so well together, and Kent's a whizz on the guitar. They're so good! I'm having the best time.'

'They are.' Sophie didn't let on how surprised she was by Kent's presence up there; she didn't really want to talk about him. She reached over and looped her arm through Callie's. 'I know I've been a bit preoccupied since I got home, but I want you to know I'm really happy that you and Bray are together. And I do hope we can be good friends.'

'Thank you, Sophie. That means a lot. I hope we can be friends too. Fallon and I have already hit it off. I couldn't believe it when she and Jon crashed in that dust storm.'

'She must be a damn good pilot.'

'Braden said she's the best. Did you know she and Jon are having a baby now? It's great that they've moved into the house at the back of your station. Having Jon there gives Braden more time to spend with the boys.'

The man under discussion strode across the grass to stand with them. Sophie saw the minute Braden noticed that she had her arm looped through Callie's and his expression changed to one of deep satisfaction.

'What's the hold up with the food?' he asked. 'I'm starving and the boys are making noises about hot chips and icy poles.'

'It smells so good, even the families who brought a picnic have lined up for a steak. More money for the school,' Callie said. 'I've got a big order. I know the appetites of those three little men. But I didn't think of icy poles. They'll probably melt.'

'Grab three,' Braden said. 'I'll put them in the esky with the beer and the ice.'

Sophie met her brother's gaze and he smiled at her as he mouthed 'thank you' above Callie's head.

Chapter 7

Kent

Ten minutes before they were due to go back on stage, Kent decided he needed to find some food. Since they'd stopped playing, the adrenaline had dissipated and he knew he needed an energy hit if they were going to play for another two hours. The appetising aroma of steak and onions had drifted across and his stomach grumbled. He stood and put his guitar at the back of the stage.

Kent knew he was the opposite of Ben. The last thing he wanted to do was put on a performance as the star of the show. He was embarrassed enough about performing in front of people who knew him, but he knew they'd done good, and there was nothing to be embarrassed about. He grabbed his black Akubra and plonked it on firmly, putting his head down as he left the shed and headed for the Lions' van.

So far, so good. He moved through a crowd of unfamiliar faces, and no one called out to him. As he joined the back of the queue at the van, he looked up and encountered his first familiar face.

And of course, it had to be Sophie Cartwright.

She was walking towards him carrying a couple of steak burgers wrapped in white paper, and a bucket of hot chips. Uncertainty crossed her face and Kent knew she was weighing up whether to keep walking, or stop and acknowledge that she'd seen him. He took the choice away from her.

'Hey, Soph,' he called out. 'I didn't know you were here. Not working at the pub tonight?'

In fact, he had been hoping she wasn't here. But at least he hadn't made a fool of himself.

'*Act normal,*' he whispered under his breath.

'No.' Despite her one-word reply, Sophie did stop beside him. Her eyes held his and he ignored that kick to his heart that had never gone away.

The silence lengthened and became awkward. 'You sing very well,' she finally said. 'I didn't know you could, Kent.'

Okay, if she could play it normal, so could he.

'I'm sure there were a lot of things we didn't know about each other.' Hurt laced his words, but Kent refused to lash out. No matter how much Sophie had hurt him by her actions, and despite his resolution never to forget how much he'd been hurt—that kept his heart safe—he knew if he said what he was feeling, it would turn

273

into a blue. Kent had buried his hurt and kept his distance when Sophie had moved in with Jock.

When Jock had come to see him and told him that he and Sophie were in love with each other but she wouldn't go public because she didn't want to hurt Kent's feelings, Kent had laughed in his face.

'You're living in dreamland, mate,' he'd said. 'I'd advise you to stay away from my Soph if you want to keep out of trouble.'

Jock Evans was a show pony and had been out with most of the single women in the district in the six months since he'd hit town and started work at Jack Anderson's garage. He didn't settle with anyone; it was a well-known fact he was a user, and he'd got into a bit of trouble at the pub a few weeks back and had been banned for fighting.

Jock's eyes had been as hard as steel. 'Maybe you should ask Sophie.'

'I wouldn't insult her by doing that,' Kent had replied.

'You're in for a fall then, mate.' Jock had taken a step closer, but Kent had held his ground.

Kent and Sophie had been a couple since high school, but since his parents had semi-retired and left the management of *Lara Waters* to him, they had seen less of each other. His sister, Jacinta, wasn't interested in the station, and worked at the school in town. Sophie was at TAFE in Charleville through the week at her hospitality course, and for two months back then, Kent had been busy most weekends, mustering and supervising the ringers.

Sophie helped Julia out with her three small nephews when he was working weekends. Two weeks after Jock had bailed him up, Sophie had come to see Kent and told him she was breaking up with him, he'd been heartbroken. The fact that she wouldn't say why worried him, and he'd spent many sleepless hours trying to figure out what he'd done. *Why* she'd broken up with him, and *why* had she turned to Jock Evans of all people.

I loved her. And I thought she loved me.

Maybe he'd been too complacent and taken for granted that Sophie knew he'd fully intended they would marry in the future and run *Lara Waters* together. Maybe his communication skills had been lacking. Maybe he should have shown her how much he loved her. Maybe he had taken her for granted.

When Sophie moved in with Jock Evans only a couple of weeks later, Kent vowed never to trust a woman again. How could she have thrown away what they had? They'd spent so long together, enjoyed being together, and they'd been a couple. No reason, no explanation. A part of Kent died that day, and he'd vowed he would never give his heart again, even if it meant turning into a cranky old guy like Fallon's uncle, George Malone.

It had been so hard to stay away from Sophie when only a few days later Julia had died in a horse accident at *Kilcoy Station*, and the boys had soon moved to Jock and Sophie's place.

Now the woman he had once loved stood right in front of him, her voice cold, and her eyes almost shooting icicles at him.

Where had his warm and lovely Sophie gone?

Maybe she had just been a manifestation of his imagination. Maybe he'd only seen what he wanted to, and now she was showing what she was really like. 'Perhaps there was, Kent. And one of the things I didn't know was how mean you are when things don't go your way. Just remember you brought it all on yourself.'

'Mean?' He stared at her as she grabbed for the chips as they started to slip from her grip.

'Yes, mean,' she hissed. 'The look on your face now says it all. I don't think I can sit there any longer and hear you sing bloody love songs. You are such a fraud.'

Kent's mouth dropped open as Sophie turned on her heel and strode away. His appetite had vanished and he turned and walked back to the shed behind the stage. That was the most he and Sophie had ever talked about their breakup since the day she'd left him two years ago.

What had she meant by saying he'd brought it all on himself?

'You ready to go again?' Ben was inside holding a beer as Kent pushed the door open.

Stuff her, he'd sing all the love songs he wanted to, and he'd sing them bloody well.

'Let's go get 'em,' Kent said, determined to show Sophie that he could ignore her nasty words.

'I've created a monster.' Ben slapped him on the back as they headed for the stage.

Chapter 8

Two years earlier

It had taken less than a month before Sophie suspected she had made a mistake moving in with Jock. By that time, Julia's accident had rocked their world and they'd somehow survived the funeral and all that went with it; their lives had changed. Sophie had tried to support Braden as best she could. Kent had been amazing and had moved into the house with Braden to field phone calls and visitors while Sophie coped with three little boys who had lost their mother. They had managed to be civil to each other; the circumstances called for no less.

But the closeness they once shared was in the past. Jock had agreed for the boys to come and live at the station they were now managing—his job had only lasted six months at the local garage.

'Of course, they can come and stay with us. I love the little tykes. They might as well be here, otherwise, I'll never see you,' he'd said. 'But you know you'll have to give up your course at Charleville. You can't expect me to take up the slack for you.'

'Take up the slack for me?' Sophie had questioned him the night before she was going to collect the boys, her eyes wide. She'd come back to their place for one night because Jock had asked her to, but all she'd done was worry about Rory, Nigel and baby Petie.

'They're your rellies, and anyway, I'm sick of coming home to an empty house and having to cook my own meals after a day out in the paddocks. The accident happened at a good time. It's woken you up to yourself about doing this course. Waste of time. You can get a job anywhere around here without needing a certificate to say you can do it. Braden can put in a good word for you. I said I'd give you some time, but it's time for you to start pulling your weight around here. I'm not a charity.'

Sophie had stared at him, and too upset to talk, she'd disappeared into her bedroom. The manager's house on this station was a dump, and she sat on the side of the hard bed and squeezed her eyes shut to stop the tears coming.

The accident had happened at a good time! Had he really said that? How could he?

She hadn't told anyone about the letter that had arrived the morning of Julia's death. A letter offering her a scholarship to finish her Certificate IV in Commercial Cookery working in a restaurant on the Brisbane River with Damon Dean, one of Brisbane's top chefs. She had already known that living with Jock wasn't going to work out, and had decided to take the offer.

Before Sophie could think any more about what she'd given up, Jock had opened the door.

'I'm so sorry, Soph. That came out the wrong way. You know me. I'm not real good with words. I'm an insensitive bastard, not good enough for you. I'm sorry. I do care about you, Soph.'

His arms had gone around her, and she'd stood rigid in his grip. She wasn't ready for a relationship and he knew that. They were all on edge; grief did awful things to the way you thought and spoke. She had to stay now; the boys needed her, and she needed a home where she could look after them. Jock had agreed, and she had to make the best of the situation. If only Kent hadn't spoiled everything.

It could have been she and Kent helping Braden out. Sophie had pushed those thoughts away and the next morning she drove across to *Kilcoy Station*. Taking a deep breath, trying to be strong to talk to Braden, she stepped out of the car and made her way to the back door. Kent had been waiting there.

'The boys are in the living room, I've got the TV on. Petie's had a bottle and he's happy on the floor.'

'Where's Braden?'

'He's still asleep. He had a bit too much to drink last night.'

'Again?' Sophie moved around the kitchen tidying up. Anything not to meet Kent's eyes.

'Yes. It's a good thing you,'—he hesitated slightly—'and Jock are doing for Braden, Soph. Take the boys away for a couple of weeks; it'll give him a chance to get back on an even keel. Don't worry, I'll keep a close eye on him. You just look after the little ones. Nigel's been crying all morning and asking for Mummy.' The whole time he was speaking their eyes didn't meet.

'Poor baby.' For a moment, Sophie wanted to lean into Kent and have him hold her and comfort her, and then she remembered what he'd done. Her eyes welled as she realised she needed to thank him for helping Braden in the past week. She swallowed back the lump in her throat. 'Thanks, Kent. You've been a great help.'

He'd shrugged. 'Braden's my best mate. Of course I was here for him. He said last night for you to take the boys home with you and he'd come out and see them later in the week. He doesn't want to see you this morning. He's not in a good place. I'll stay here with him for the day.'

Tears ran down Sophie's face and when she'd looked up, Kent had been staring at her, his eyes full of sadness. Again, all she wanted to do was crawl into his arms and let him hold her until everything was better.

No matter what.

Life was too short; they should have talked about what had happened. Maybe she could have forgiven him.

But now she straightened her shoulders, reminding herself that what he had done had been *unforgivable*. Okay, so she'd loved him once, but Kent was here for Braden now, not for *her*.

Sophie knew she had to grow up, grow strong and learn to deal with things. She forced herself to remember that things had changed. She couldn't cling to the past.

She had to look to the future, and consider the welfare of her three nephews.

As she packed the car and drove out with the boys in the back, she had no idea it would be two years before they went home again.

Chapter 9
The fundraiser.
Wilson Creek Station
Sophie

Kim grinned up at Sophie as she made her way along the narrow row between the seats.

'Excuse me. Sorry, sorry.' Sophie apologised as she trod on booted feet, knocking one can of beer flying as she pushed along to the seat beside Kim. The smell of spilled beer mingled with frying onions and the appetising aroma of the hot chips she carried.

'I thought you must have been peeling the spuds,' Kim said reaching for the chips. 'I'm starving.'

'There was a queue a mile long. Listen, are you okay if I leave you here and go look after my nephews?'

'Sure. It's been non-stop chat here. Half the school staff are in these two rows.'

'It'll give Braden and Callie a chance to have a dance.'

'I just want you to have a good time, Soph. Are you going to eat first?'

Before Sophie could answer the stage lights came on, and Craig took the microphone.

'A big round of applause, the Augie Boys are back!'

A loud guitar riff filled the air and Sophie raised her voice to be heard. 'Nuh. I'm not hungry anymore.' She stood and reached for her bag. 'I'll go out this way. Fewer feet to tread on. I'll see you on the bus later.'

'Are you okay?' Kim's eyes narrowed.

'Yeah, why?'

'No reason. You don't seem very happy.'

'I'm fine. Just a bit preoccupied. I've had a chat with Braden, and I'm going to move out to *Kilcoy Station* tomorrow. It'll give you space for you and your sisters to have a good catch-up.'

'It's fine if you want to stay. We can make room.'

'No, it's time I went home. I'll strip my bed and wash the towels for you in the morning.'

'You don't have to do all that. We'll have a yak on the bus on the way home.'

'Okay. I'll see you in a while. I'll meet you out where the buses are when it's over. Enjoy the entertainment.'

Sophie put her head down and made her way along the row, aware of Kim's curious expression as she crossed to the grassed area where the boys were playing chase with a few kids from school.

There was already a crowd on the flat area in front of the stage, but Callie and Braden were sitting in the back row. Braden sat sideways in the plastic chair at the end of the row keeping a close eye on his three sons.

Sophie walked over and put her hand on her brother's shoulder. 'I'll watch the boys for you. You pair go and have a dance.'

'You sure?'

'Yeah. It was too noisy for me up the front.'

'Bit of a surprise to see Kent up there, hey sis? Did you know he could play and sing?'

'No, I didn't. Have the boys had their icy poles yet?'

'Yes, they've eaten and they'll play until the end. Then they'll sleep all the way home.'

'Off you go then. Go and show Callie your moves.' Sophie grinned. 'Does she know what a great boot scooter you are?'

Callie leaned over. 'What's boot scooting?'

Braden jumped up and took her hand. 'You don't know what boot scooting is, city girl? Come and I'll teach you. You're in for a treat.'

The look on her brother's face as he led Callie to the front of the stage brought a smile to Sophie's face. She could put up with hearing Kent's singing if it made Braden and Callie happy.

But she didn't have to look at the stage.

##

Sophie watched the boys for a while and then put her head back and looked up at the beautiful night sky. It was a crystal clear night and a myriad of stars sparkled above them in an indigo sky. As she looked, a star shot across the sky.

Sophie smiled. Her mum used to say that a shooting star meant something good was going to happen. Maybe she was going to get a great job as a chef in an exotic location and get away from all the unhappiness here.

Rory and Nigel raced over to her, with Petie not too far behind. 'We're hungry, Aunty Soph.'

'Again?' She dug in the basket that Callie had packed and found enough snacks to keep the boys happy as they sat beside her. Once they were settled, Sophie closed her eyes and listened to the music, and tried to block out that it was Kent singing. Ben was good too, she would focus on his voice.

If she'd known what the night was going to bring, she would have stayed home.

Home? She didn't even have one.

Sophie shook herself mentally. Having words with Kent had left her unsettled, and she was letting things get to her way too much.

An hour and a half later, Braden and Callie came back to where Sophie was sitting. Their cheeks were glowing, but they were both laughing. It was wonderful to see her brother happy, so she shook her morose mood off.

'I can now officially boot scoot, Sophie,' Callie told her with glee.

'And she's a natural,' Braden said.

Despite Braden's expectations that they would play with their friends until late, the three boys had crashed. Petie was curled up in the chair beside Sophie with his head in her lap, and Nigel was on the ground at her feet leaning back against her legs, his chin on his chest.

Rory was still awake in the chair on the other side of her, but his eyes were heavy.

'Time to take these boys home to bed,' Sophie said. 'The music's over, isn't it?'

'Yeah, Craig's just going to draw the raffles and then Jim will get his drivers to bring the buses around. But we might get these boys onto the bus now. There'll be a rush soon.' Braden bent down and scooped Nigel up into his arms. 'Cal, can you get Petie?'

'I can.'

'Rory, you okay to walk, buddy?'

'I'll walk with Auntie Sophie.' A little warm—and sticky—hand crept into hers.

'Did you have fun, Rory?' Sophie asked.

'I had the best time. Did you, Aunty Soph?'

Before she could answer, Craig's voice boomed across the crowd. 'We have raffle winners. Jennifer Shaw has won the Easter basket, and . . . drum roll'—Craig sounded a drum roll into the microphone but it simply sounded like static—'ta-da! The winner of the date with our lead singer, Mr Kent Augie Boy Mason is . . . Sophie Cartwright.'

Chapter 10
Sophie

The Rodeo

The morning had been busy with an early start, and after getting back to town late last night, Sophie was tired. Since Sophie had seen Kent on stage she'd been unsettled. Her sleep had been broken by dreams of Kent sitting up on the stage, singing and shaking his head and pointing at her every time she stood to leave.

After helping Kim with the washing, and tidying the large house, it was too early to go to the billy cart races so she decided to take her things out to *Kilcoy Station*. The closer she got to the property, the more unsettled she felt, even though she knew it was time to go home. She'd hidden away in town long enough. The only comments she'd had from locals when she'd been working at the pub had been a friendly welcome and no one seemed to be judging her about the Jock situation. Her coming home was her business, and no one needed to know why she had. Braden was a different matter, and even though he'd dropped everything and got Kent to fly up to get her as soon as she'd called him, they still hadn't talked about what had happened.

And she didn't want to. She wasn't going to.

Coming back home to Augathella had been the wrong decision, but when Jock had grabbed her and yelled at her, she had come to an instant decision. She had made it clear what their relationship was, but he'd started to touch her before that, and she'd become scared of being in the house with him.

She knew Braden and Kent had seen the bruises on her wrists when they'd come to get her, but they'd said nothing, and she hadn't been in any state to talk. She should have taken herself away from Jock without calling Braden, but when Jock had been violent towards her she had been terrified.

Even though she'd not been happy for a long time, in the past Jock had provided a home for her and the boys. The little ones had kept her busy, as had looking after Jock. He'd agreed to share his house with them and even though he had a short fuse, he'd never once raised a hand to her before. He had, however, isolated her from her family and friends. He always wanted to know where she was going when she went to town, and how long she'd be. She knew she had reason to be grateful to him, but when she'd been so busy with the boys, he had gradually taken control of her, and she hadn't really been aware of it.

Moving such a long way away from Augathella had obviously been a part of his ploy to get what he wanted. When he'd suggested it, she'd reluctantly agreed. She had no reason to stay in her hometown. But she'd also had no interest in a relationship with him, and he'd agreed that they were simply sharing a house.

No ties. No relationship.

She'd fallen for it when he'd told her it would help Braden, and let her brother establish a relationship with his sons without her in the background.

In hindsight, Sophie realised how manipulative Jock had been and how foolish she'd been to agree to move away with him under the guise of a platonic relationship. He'd never had any intention of that. He had been after a share in their station the whole time. She had believed him, but had learned her lesson.

First Kent had lied to her, and then Jock had conned her. Her weakness back then, and her agreeance to move away with Jock disgusted her.

She'd been so gullible. 'Why do we have to go so far? There's plenty of work around here,' she'd asked. Even though it had been time for the boys to go back to Braden, she'd worried about leaving them and not being on call.

'It's a fantastic offer, Sophie. A flash house, a new Landcruiser and a great salary package. And they want a cook too.' Jock had stepped forward to put his arms around her, but she'd moved away. 'A new start away from the past, the grief and sadness, plus it'll give your brother a chance to be a real father to those three little fellas. When he's settled, we can go back and you can take your share in *Kilcoy Station*. Then we can be a real couple.'

She'd pulled away from him. 'We're not a couple, Jock. That was never the deal.'

'But we will be. You know I'm in love with you. I wouldn't have taken those bloody kids on if I hadn't cared about you.'

Now she knew exactly what Jock had cared about.

Money and land.

In hindsight, she'd realised when they lived in Augathella, Jock had known her family home was close enough for her to go back home if he did the wrong thing. It hadn't been until they'd moved north, and Braden was a long way away, that Jock had shown his true colours for the first time.

He'd thought he had her where he wanted her, and she knew he would have been astounded that she was thinking of leaving.

Jock Evans had misread her. She hadn't been in a relationship with him and didn't intend to be. Sophie knew she had been stupid to move away with him, but she hadn't been thinking straight. Julia's death and Kent's betrayal had messed with her head, and she'd seen the move as a means to get away.

When they'd arrived at the property and the so-called fabulous job at Innot Springs, she had been dismayed. The house wasn't far off being a hovel, there was no car, and no job for her. Jock tried to bluff his way out of it, but she knew he'd been lying all along.

A month after they'd arrived Jock had come home from work early. Sophie had spent the day trying to clean up the house they were living in, and hadn't had a meal ready. He'd grabbed her so hard, she'd cried out in pain.

'It's time for you to move into my bed,' he snarled. 'I'm over this.'

'What?' Her eyes had been wide as he'd advanced on her.

'You bloody heard me. I've supported you and those little bastards for two years. And what do I get? Not a word of thanks from your bloody perfect brother, or one friggin' dollar. And what do I get from you, you frigid bitch?'

'I am *not* your partner, Jock. I share a house with you, and moving here was the biggest mistake I ever made.'

He shoved her so hard that she hit the wall and lost her balance, sliding down to the floor. As he moved towards her she cowered, his large frame looming over her as he grabbed her wrists and roughly pulled her to her feet.

'I'm going to the pub. You think about what I said.' He stormed out and slammed the door of the ramshackle house behind him.

She sobbed so much she'd found it hard to talk to Braden on the phone. Her words were jumbled, but she'd finally got it out. 'Bray? Can I come home, please? To stay? I want to come home. I have to come home.'

Locking herself in her bedroom she avoided Jock before he left for work the next morning. Braden and Kent had arrived in the afternoon. She hadn't seen or heard from Jock Evans since, and she didn't want to.

Chapter 11
Kilcoy Station – Sophie

Now, after three weeks in town, Sophie was finally going home. Just before she turned onto the last road that led to *Kilcoy Station*, a cloud of dust warned of an approaching vehicle. Braden and Callie and the boys passed her yellow Camry wagon with a toot of the horn. Callie waved madly and the boys grinned as they flashed past on their way to town. Sophie had left the Camry at *Kilcoy Station* when she headed up north with Jock. Braden had had it serviced a couple of times, and Callie had been driving it since she'd arrived to look after the boys.

Sophie knew she might as well have stayed in town and come out later after the billy cart races were over, but she probably would have been pressed for time, working at the pub tonight. She dumped her two bags in the breezeway and used her key to open the side of the house that hadn't been used since Julia's death.

She might as well get straight into it. Braden had tentatively agreed for her to live on this side. If there was too much to do to make it habitable, he would have to find someone else to work here as the cook, although if Sophie was honest, she was looking forward to getting back to what she loved doing. It had been a long time since she'd cooked.

During her sleepless periods throughout the night, she had come to the decision that from today, no one was going to tell her what to do. She had made poor choices twice over the past few years, and she knew why. If she'd been stronger, she wouldn't have gotten to the stage she had with Jock, and she wouldn't be feeling so depressed by last night's dream about Kent.

The door from the breezeway opened with a creak, and a blast of stale cool air greeted Sophie. Coming in here was going to be hard and she was pleased she was alone. She suspected Braden hadn't been in here since he'd locked this side of the house off two years ago.

Sophie wasn't sure what to expect; she'd lived out here with Braden and Julia when they were first married, and she knew going into this part of the house full of memories of Julia was going to be hard.

It had to be done.

She suspected there *would* be a fair bit to do before she even had a room ready to sleep in. A strange feeling overcame her and she held onto the doorknob tightly, reluctant to go any further. But she took a deep breath and forced herself to walk down the hall. She'd choose one of the guest rooms—not as many memories there—air it out, get some linen from her stuff she'd brought back from the north, make the bed and come here after her shift at the pub tonight. It would be a late night because the pub would be busy after the billy cart derby this afternoon. She'd brought her stuff that she'd taken from the house at Innot Springs. It had almost filled the small cargo hold in Kent's plane. There had been some stuff that she'd had to leave behind, but it wasn't important to her. Jock was welcome to it.

Sophie walked slowly down the hall, past Braden and Julia's bedroom, and the nursery where Petie's cot was still made up, a Disney mobile hanging motionless in the stale air.

Her eyes pricked as she paused in the doorway, and looked at the drawings that Julia had stencilled onto the wall before Rory was born. She had been so excited when their first child arrived.

'Oh, Julia.' Sophie sniffed as a tear spilled over. 'What a loss. What a waste.'

Julia had been like a big sister to her, and had been one of the few people—if not the only one—who had truly loved Sophie with no judgment, no criticism.

Julia had been there when she had found out what Kent had done. Julia had been the only one who knew. She had taught Sophie to be strong, and Sophie had used that same strength to put her grief aside and be strong for Braden after the accident.

Brushing the tears away, Sophie closed the door and walked down the dusty wooden-floored hall to the guest bedroom.

An hour later her new room was clean and fresh, the bed made up and the small ensuite wiped over. Her clothes were in the wardrobe, her treasured possessions on the shelves and her teddy bear on the chair next to the bed. Kent had won the purple teddy for her—a Tambo Teddy—at the Charleville show when they were in year twelve.

When they broke up, she couldn't bear to part with it, and Teddy had travelled with her. She'd shoved it in the bottom of a bag when Braden and Kent had picked her up so Kent didn't see it.

Her stomach grumbled and she looked at her watch. It was almost twelve. Sophie crossed to the wardrobe and took out her black skirt and white shirt for her shift at the pub, placing them into a plastic bag to take with her. She'd head to town now so she didn't miss the billy cart derby.

She'd make sure that Braden came in here tomorrow. It would be difficult for him but she'd be there for him. It wasn't fair to expect Callie to be involved. If Braden reneged, her brother would blow his chances of having her out here as the cook for the station staff.

They both needed closure. If Braden's relationship with Callie was to have any chance of succeeding, he had to let go of these physical reminders of the past. Memories would have to be enough.

With a determined head shake, Sophie backed out of the foyer and pulled the door shut behind her. She'd go to the billy cart derby and grab a late lunch there. She looked across at her car and pulled out her phone.

Braden picked up straight away.

'Bray it's me. Can I borrow one of the farm utes to come into town? I don't fancy driving home after the pub tonight in my car. Too many roos and emus about.'

'Home?' She could hear the satisfaction in his tone.

'Yes, home,' she said briskly. 'I've sorted out one of the guest rooms in your old wing.'

Silence.

'And I have a task for both of us,' she said. 'The rest of the rooms need sorting. It's time, Braden.'

'I know.'

'Can you get Callie to take the boys somewhere and you and I will get into it?'

'Not tomorrow. I've got a lot on at the rodeo.'

'Fair enough. But promise we'll get to it in the next few days?'

'Yes. I promise. And you don't have to ask about a ute. The keys are still hanging on the hook near the freezers in the breezeway.'

'Has the derby started?'

'Another hour. Rory went really well in the practice run. Try and get in here for the race.'

'I will. I'm leaving now.'

Sophie didn't look back as she drove one of the farm utes out and headed to town.

Chapter 12

Sophie's eyes widened as she searched for a parking spot around the corner from the pub. Normally quiet, Augathella was packed with cars, familiar and unfamiliar, all obviously in town for the billy cart races. The word about the good prizes on offer must have spread, and there were even a couple of cars with New South Wales number plates taking up some of the parks. Augathella hadn't been this busy for a long time.

Sophie locked her car and walked around the corner. Families lined both sides of the wide street, the smell of coffee and burgers came from the pub, and at least ten people said hello to her as she walked through the crowd looking for Braden, Callie, and the boys. She'd promised Rory and Nigel she would come and watch this afternoon. They'd been excited because they had helped Braden build a cart over the past few weeks.; it was good to see him taking such an interest in the boys now. She glanced at her watch; the nine years and under race was the first, and the races began at one o'clock. She had about half an hour to find them. The mood of the crowd was buoyant and she couldn't help smiling.

'Aunty Sophie. There's Aunty Sophie.' An excited squeal rang out above the noise of the crowd. Callie was holding Petie halfway up the hill.

Sophie waved to them and made her way through the crowd lining the footpath. A familiar voice made her pause as she almost reached Callie and Petie.

'You're full of it, love.' Old Reg, a well-known bushie from one of the outlying properties, his voice as distinctive as a saw cutting a rough piece of bloodwood wagged his finger at a young woman Sophie didn't recognise. 'I've never heard such a load of tripe in all my life.'

The woman grinned up at him and shook her head. 'Nope. I'm right. You can check.'

Sophie watched the exchange with interest. Reg was a true bushie; his face sported a long straggling grey beard, and an old tattered Akubra with more holes than brim sat on his head.

'And where, pray tell, would you suggest I check that ridiculous information?' Despite his appearance and his strange voice, Reg's words were always cultured.

'Google? The library?' The young woman's eyes danced with merriment.

"I still think you're pulling my leg.' Reg chuckled, and Sophie could tell he was enjoying the exchange. He doffed his battered hat and grinned at the woman. 'I will at that. The library it will be, first thing on Tuesday morning!' Reg turned and walked into the pub where Sophie knew he would spend the rest of the day. He'd been a regular there for as long as she could remember. He and a couple of other old locals would sit outside with a beer for the whole afternoon and watch the world go by.

The young woman turned with a wide smile and almost bumped into Sophie. 'Whoops, look out, Chilli,' she said apologetically.

For the first time, Sophie noticed the woman was holding a lead. A beautiful golden retriever looked up at Sophie as much as to say, 'Get me out of here.'

Please?

Sophie crouched down and smoothed her hands over the soft fur. 'Aren't you a beauty?'

The young woman replied. 'She is.'

'What's her name?'

'Chilli Girl, but I call her Chilli.''

'Hello, Chilli.'

The dog let out a satisfied groan as Sophie tickled her ears.

'She loves that.'

Sophie smiled at the dog's owner as she stood back up; she didn't recognise her. 'Are you visiting Augathella for Easter?'

'No, I've come here for work.' She held out her hand. 'I'm Amelia Foley.'

Sophie shook it. 'Welcome to Augathella. I'm Sophie Cartwright.'

'Cartwright? Are you Braden Cartwright's wife?'

Sophie chuckled. 'No, I'm his sister. You know Braden?'

'I haven't met him yet, but he interviewed me on the phone.'

Sophie's curiosity was piqued. 'Interviewed you?'

'Yes, I'm starting work at his station.'

Sophie stared and a strange feeling settled in the pit of her stomach. Maybe Braden had got sick of her stuffing around in town, avoiding going home.

'As the cook?' she asked.

'Heck, no!' Amelia shook her head. 'I'd poison anyone who was unlucky enough to eat what I cook. I have trouble opening a tin of baked beans, but I think it's because that's the last thing a person should have for a meal, don't you? I'm starting work as a ringer, but I prefer to be called a jillaroo. That has a much nicer ring to it, don't you think?'

Sophie nodded, as she tried to keep up with the conversation. 'I've never thought about it, but I suppose it does. So you're the one moving into the donga accommodation near the house?'

'Yes, that's me. But I'm on holiday until Tuesday. I'm meeting Mr Cartwright out there then. I heard there was an Easter festival in Augathella so I decided to come and suss out the town. I'm staying at the showground in my Landcruiser.'

'With your dog?'

'Yes, Chilli's a sweetie. Really well behaved. Loves people and she doesn't bark unless someone threatens me. Where I go, she goes. Dogs are wonderful companions, don't you think? No wonder they call them man's best friend. But they could say woman's best friend too. So many of those phrases that "they" come up with are sexist, don't you think?'

Sophie felt like she'd been hit with a volley of words, but she smiled. Amelia had a sweet personality, and she could see how she had become involved in a conversation with old Reg.

'Braden's here somewhere. The kids are going in the race. Does he know you have Chilli?'

'Oh yes, I checked I could bring a dog before I accepted the position. I have my own portable fence. Chilli will be fine and I won't let her go inside the donga. I assume it has a porch of sorts?'

'It does.' Sophie nodded. Curiosity took over. 'I'm moving back out there, to help Braden out, so I'll be cooking your meals. Tell me about yourself, Amelia. Where are you from?'

The more Amelia spoke, the less Sophie could imagine her working with the cattle on *Kilcoy Station*. Braden was in for a shock; he would have assumed a ringer would bring a working dog, not a golden Labrador.

And one with its own portable fence.

She grinned.

Amelia tilted her head to the side. 'I should have known you weren't Mrs Cartwright. I knew I'd heard your name. You won the date with the hot cowboy singer at the concert last night. So lucky.' She put her hand to her chest and fluttered her eyelids. 'I bought ten dollars' worth of tickets. A girl can always hope.'

Sophie drew in a deep breath and tried not to let it out in the sigh that threatened. She'd tried to forget about that, but Craig Wilson had caught up with her just before she and Kim had got on the bus to go back to town. He'd pressed a voucher into her hand.

'Here's your prize, Soph. There are a few noses out of joint that you won it.' To her horror, Craig had winked at her. 'Might be just what you need to bring you both to your senses, girl.'

She'd tried to hand it back to him. 'I don't think so, Craig. Give it to someone else.'

'No way. You won it fair and square.'

'No, I didn't. I didn't even buy a ticket.'

'Well, someone was looking after you. Enjoy your date.' With another grin, he'd turned and left her standing there holding the prize she didn't want. Sophie had shoved the voucher into her bag and tried to forget about it.

She let her breath out and looked at Amelia. 'Not lucky. Kent's just Kent to me. He's our neighbour. Not a hot cowboy singer. I tried to give the prize away, but apparently, I can't.'

Amelia straightened up and pointed up the hill. 'Look, they're lining up for the first race.'

'I'd better go. My nephews want me to see their rainbow billy cart. Do you want to come with me and meet Braden?'

'Sure.'

Amelia shortened Chilli's lead and walked beside Sophie as she walked up the hill to where Callie and Petie were waiting.

She lowered her voice and spoke quickly before they reached them.

'Amelia, just so you know. Braden is a widower, and Callie up here is his new partner. Just so you don't make the wrong assumption.'

'Thank you. Appreciate that. I'm always putting my foot in it. It drives my mother crazy. She tells me I should keep my mouth shut and think before I speak. You know she even wanted to send me to a finishing school in Switzerland to learn that sort of thing.'

Sophie stared. 'And did you?'

A finishing school graduate working as a ringer! Hell's bells, Braden. What have you hired? she wondered.

'No, I left home and worked on my first cattle station instead.'

Petie ran across to Sophie and hugged her legs. 'Aunty Soph, it's so exciting. Are you going to watch my big brother win the race?'

Sophie and Callie exchanged a smile.

'I hope so, Petie,' Sophie said. 'Callie, this is Amelia. She's coming out to work at *Kilcoy*. I'll leave her here with you, while I run up and see Rory and wish him luck.' She held Callie's eyes. 'And Petie, this is Chilli Girl. Give her a pat.'

Chapter 13
Kent

The Billy Cart Race

Kent crouched down behind the billy cart as Braden checked the front wheels were straight and tight. Nigel leaned over behind him and Kent grinned as the little boy tapped on Rory's helmet.

'Is your chin strap tight enough, Rory?' Nigel said loudly.

'It is. There's no need to yell.' Rory pushed his little brother's hand away.

Kent stood up and took Nigel's hand. 'Come on, mate. We have to go back behind the line so they can get ready to start the race. Your dad can stay there. You boys sure did a good job painting that billy cart.'

'Aunty Soph!' Nigel let go of his hand and took off.

Kent's attention honed in on the lithe figure in loose grey pants and a sleeveless shirt that clung to her body, her long brown hair loose on her shoulders. His stomach sank. He wasn't ready to face Sophie yet. He didn't care that she'd said he could sing well; it was calling him a fraud that had hurt, and then bloody Craig had drawn her name out and she'd won that stupid raffle Craig had created to raise funds for the local RFS.

I'm not a rock star, I'm a cattleman.

He saw the instant that Sophie noticed him standing there. She stopped walking up the hill and waited for Nigel to run to her.

Stuff it. He wasn't going to let her treat him rudely. Kent sauntered over and stood behind Nigel who was talking at nineteen to the dozen.

'Dad's told Rory *eggxactly* what to do. And I reckon he's going to win.' Nigel was jumping about, his words tumbling over one another. 'Did you see his helmet? Dad's going to buy me one for my new bike when I get it.'

'The cart looks pretty good. Love the paint job,' Sophie said. She looked up and her eyes snagged Kent's. No matter what had passed between them, no matter what he was supposed to have done, and no matter how rudely she treated him, Kent was damned if he could stop that bloody flutter in his belly every time he was with Sophie.

It was because they'd once been a couple.

That's all it is.

His body hadn't caught up with his heart yet. He didn't even particularly like her anymore. Her soft and happy personality had hardened; she wasn't the sweet girl he'd once fallen in love with.

But still, that was no reason for him to be rude back to her. Plus, he knew it really annoyed her when he spoke to her as though they were still mates.

'Morning, Sophie,' he said brightly. 'Ready for the action?'

Her lips tightened as she looked at him, and her eyes were hooded. 'Yes. It should be a fun day.'

'I hear you're coming back out to work at the station.'

'Perhaps.'

He stared at her. 'Braden told me you're cooking for the stockmen.'

'I might be.' She shrugged.

'I thought you'd agreed.'

'I said I *might* be. I won't be staying around so it depends what Braden needs and how long he needs me for.'

'Where are you going?' For the life of him, he couldn't hold back the question.

Another casual shrug. 'Don't know yet, but like I said I won't be staying here long.'

Before he could answer, Sophie gave him a dismissive glance and took Nigel's hand. 'Come on, Nigel, we've got to be down near the finish line when Rory comes down the hill.'

Kent refused to let Sophie's rudeness bother him and he turned to watch Rory as Braden leaned over and gave him some last-minute advice as the rainbow-painted billy cart sat on the ramp. On the other side of Annie Street outside the Evans' house, he could see Callie sitting in the shade with Petie on her lap. Fallon Malone and Jon Ingram were with her. They had a good vantage point about halfway down the track. Sending a swift look Sophie's way he checked she wasn't going over to them, and when he saw she was heading to the finish line across Main Street, he hurried over the row of tyres dividing the two lanes.

'Hey, Kent.' Jon held out his hand and shook it. 'I haven't seen you around for a couple of weeks.'

'Work's been full-on, mate. I know you guys are busy over at *Kilcoy Station* too.'

'We sure are. New staff ready to get sorted, and cattle to move. '

'Hi, Callie.' He smiled at Braden's partner and then turned to Fallon. 'You're looking well, Fallon.'

'Thank you, Kent. Now the morning sickness has passed, I'm feeling good. I'm ready to go back to work, but Jon talked me out of it.'

'Make the most of it. I hope you'll be back to work for the muster next year.'

'I will. My mum and dad are moving out to Augathella to live in Uncle George's house for a few months after the baby arrives.'

She was interrupted by Craig Wilson's booming voice as the PA came to life.

'Welcome everyone to the first heat of the Under Nines. All billy carts have passed the scrutineers' check and we're ready to go! Rory Cartwright and Evan Hudson are our first carts off the ramps. Just a reminder to everyone who is participating this afternoon in all age groups and opens, that no peddling, pushing, paddling or propulsion of any kind is permitted. We'll be watching! Now are you ready, boys?'

Kent grinned as Rory gave a thumbs up and Petie screamed out, 'Go Rory!' He turned to Fallon with a wide grin and said, 'That's my big brother.'

The race began and the screams around him cheered Rory on. At the bottom of the track, Sophie and Nigel were jumping and yelling and Kent forced himself to look away from her and focus on the end of the race. Her loose pants were cinched in by a wide black belt, and he thought how beautiful she was. As the two carts approached the finish line, the yells and screams got louder as Rory crossed the finish line a good metre ahead of his opposition. Braden ran down the hill and helped Rory out of the cart, sweeping him into a big bear hug.

Kent watched, feeling happy for the family. Life had certainly improved for them since Callie had come on the scene. Grief had etched wrinkles in Braden's face, but he smiled a lot more these days.

Braden ran up the hill with Rory on his back almost like the happy guy he'd been before Julia had died in that awful accident.

Kent stepped away and let them all make a fuss of Rory.

Jon and Fallon moved across to him.

'You going in the rodeo tomorrow, mate?' Jon asked.

'I'd like to,' Kent said. 'Depends on whether the cattle truck comes early enough. I've got some new steers coming. You going?'

'Wouldn't miss it. I'm one of the clowns.'

'Way to go. I forgot you did that when you were here before.'

'Bullride and bareback for you?'

'I've entered, but it depends on the truck.'

'You got all-round cowboy when I was here a couple of years ago from memory? I've never seen anyone ride like that. Either before or since.'

Kent nodded. 'Two years ago.' It had been the month after Julia's accident, and a few weeks after Sophie had broken up with him. He hadn't cared what risks he'd taken that year and had cleaned up on most of the events.

'Jeez, time flies,' Jon said.

'It does. Anyway, I've gotta go. Might see you there tomorrow.' Kent turned quickly and headed towards his truck. Sophie and Nigel were coming up the hill, and he didn't want to talk to her again.

It bloody hurt too much.

Chapter 14
Kent

Kent glanced at the clock on the kitchen wall and grabbed his Akubra and keys. He'd have to get a move on if he wanted to get his entry in for the steer riding. He'd had no intention of going to the rodeo; he had enough to do out on the station with the new steers arriving. The truck had arrived early, and he needed something to get his mind off Sophie Cartwright.

Work wasn't enough. He'd been on a high on stage on Thursday night but had come down with a thud after his words with Sophie at the billy cart derby yesterday. He'd convinced himself that he was over her, but since she'd come back to the district he couldn't get her out of his head.

Even though every interaction had been unpleasant, he didn't want to care about her anymore.

His head told him one thing, but every day his heart told him different. The day they flew up to that property at Innot Springs and collected her had been one of the happiest in his life. It seemed as if she had finally woken up to herself, and come home. Braden had silently pointed out the bruises on her wrists and if Jock Evans had appeared, he would have thumped him.

Self-disgust filled Kent. Even after she'd dumped him for that no-hoper and lived with Jock while they looked after Braden's boys, he should have known that Sophie didn't give two hoots for him. There was no way he'd try to rekindle their relationship.

Over and over he told himself, she wasn't to be trusted, but nothing worked. He'd even tried to get interested in Jennifer, but that was a disaster.

Sophie filled every waking thought. Maybe he needed to go and see someone. Perhaps he needed to call his mum and have her talk some sense into him.

As he pulled the back screen door shut, his mobile buzzed in his shirt pocket. A wry grin tilted his lips as he looked at his mother's face on Facetime call.

'Onya, Mum,' he thought. Not the first time he thought his mother had some sort of second sense where he was involved.

'Mum, hey there!'

'Hello, darling. How are you?'

'I'm great,' Kent lied. 'Just heading out to the rodeo.'

'I thought you might be.'

'Where are you and Dad?'

'We've just cruised into a place called Pioneer Bay in the Whitsundays. We're waiting our turn to get the launch to the town. Shopping, lunch and a swim in a huge lagoon pool. It looks divine from the photos.'

'How's Dad? Is he going okay?'

The joy in his mother's voice lessened a little bit. 'He's good. He had to go back down to the cabin. He forgot his wallet. Still forgetful.'

'But nothing worse?'

Kent had been worried about his father in the last few months on the station and had willingly taken over the management when his father admitted it was getting a bit too much for him.

'No. He gets cross because I keep a close eye on him. But he is fine. He's actually learned how to relax. He's read his way through half the library on the ship.'

'Good to hear.'

'He said to ask you how much rain you've had out there. He'd been watching the floods in the north-west. Jacinta never knows when we talk to her.'

'No floods here, but enough rain to give us a heap of feed, and fat and shiny cattle. I had a truck come in with more steers this morning.'

'He'll be pleased. He's proud of you, Kent. Now you tell me, how are you really?'

'I told you, I'm good. Why?'

'I was talking to Shirley Rogers on the phone last night and she told me Sophie Cartwright's back in town.' With her usual bluntness, his mother cut straight to the chase. 'So how are you coping with that?'

Kent leaned against the wooden boards of the old farmhouse and stared out over the paddocks. 'You're a mind reader, you know, Mother dear. I was just thinking about a chat with you when you called.'

'I knew you wouldn't be coping. Have you seen her yet?'

Kent let a small sigh of relief escape. He wasn't sure if anyone else knew the circumstances of Sophie coming home, and he didn't want to lie to his mother.

'Yeah, a couple of times. And she was at the billy cart races yesterday. Rory won his age division.'

'Good on him. So has she gone back home to *Kilcoy Station*? Shirley said that no-good fella she left with isn't with her.'

'I think she's going back to Braden's to cook for the contractors soon.'

'Good. I hope you don't intend to let her go again.'

'Whoa there, Mum!' Kent's fingers held the phone tightly. 'Sophie left of her own accord with another guy if you remember. She made it quite clear she didn't want me, so there's no chance of anything starting up between us.'

'Even though you'd like that?'

'Gawd, Mum. Give me a break.'

'I know you, son, and I know she's the woman for you.'

'Shame Sophie didn't think that.'

'Like I said, don't you let her go again.'

'That's not what I wanted to hear. Anyway, I'm seeing someone.'

'Who?'

'A new woman at the school.'

He didn't want his mother to focus on Sophie too much, but he lowered his voice and said honestly. 'Okay, I want you to tell me how to stop thinking about Sophie.'

'Well, there you go! I rest my case. If you still love her, give it your best shot.'

Kent was quiet for a minute.

'Are you still there?' his mother asked. 'And who are you seeing anyway? Do you think it may work out? That might help.'

'Yes, I was just processing what you said. I've been out a couple of times with the new counsellor at the school.'

'Do I know her?'

'No. She's only here part-time.'

'Listen, love. I have to go. The boat's here and your father's waving to me. I'll call you tonight, okay? Love you. And Kent?'

'Yes, Mum?'

'Follow your heart.'

'Love you too, Mum. Give Dad a hug for me.'

Kent was thoughtful as he made his way to his ute. His mood swung from hope to anger.

Follow his heart? Or trust logic?

There was no doubt that Sophie had betrayed him. Could he get over that and try to win her heart again? He pushed his phone into his shirt pocket. Even though it was good to talk to Mum—she was always good for advice—his mood had deteriorated.

Chapter 15
Sophie

Sophie rolled over in bed and glanced at the bedside clock she'd put on the side table. She was surprised to see it was heading for noon. Last night at the pub had been huge, and it was after one by the time she got back to the station. The wind was whistling outside; the first cold winds of autumn had arrived. She'd had to pull up a second blanket in the early hours.

For the first time, Sophie began to think that working out at the station would be better than being in town. Locals and tourists alike had crowded the dining room and bistro last night and Sean in his wisdom—because he had a second chef and a kitchenhand for the weekend—had decided to open for takeaway as well. It was all right at the kitchen end of things but Sophie had been in the front of house by herself.

Bistro, dining room, and takeaway. She was sure she'd run all night.

Literally. Taking orders, delivering meals and clearing tables from six until eleven. She was pleased she'd worn her joggers. At ten o'clock she'd hurried into the kitchen and seen the pile of plates waiting to be washed at the sink.

'Sean, if you think I'm loading the dishwasher you're wrong. Get the kitchenhand to do it.'

'But—' Young Kelly Leary pulled a face. 'I'm going out for drinks with my friends tonight. I'm already late.'

Sophie stared at Sean.

He pulled a face. 'If you want to keep getting shifts here, you can stay until eleven, Kelly,' he said.

'Not fair,' she grumbled.

Sophie had headed back out to deliver the last of the desserts and by the sound of the banging in the kitchen, she knew there was one unhappy young girl in there. But it had been a busy night and good for the town.

Now she lay in bed watching the autumn sunlight play across the ceiling. A vague sense of contentment crept over her. This was home, and she wondered if maybe she could be happy here.

Maybe—if the cooking job worked out—there'd be no need to take off for the city.

She shook her head. No, after Easter, she'd ring Damon Dean and see if there was any chance of taking up that scholarship. It wasn't fair on Braden and Callie for her to hang around, and it was too difficult with Kent nearby. The two stations worked closely together. A perfect example was yesterday, asking her questions about her job there. It was almost as though he was part of *Kilcoy Station* wanting to know the ins and outs. She'd call Brisbane tomorrow, and then she would have a definite time frame for Braden for the station cooking.

She climbed out of bed, took a shower and slipped on a warm and comfortable tracksuit. Making herself coffee and toast in the kitchen on the other side of the house, she picked up the *Southwest* newspaper that was on the kitchen table. The swinging chair on the verandah was a perfect spot once she manoeuvred it into the sun and settled in. The longer she sat out there, the happier she felt.

A short while later her mobile chirped and Sophie jumped, surprised to see the newspaper on the floor. Disoriented, she rubbed her eyes and reached for her phone

'Sophie, It's Braden. Are you coming into town for the rodeo?'

Sophie was surprised. 'Are you already there?'

'Yeah, we came in early. I'm part of the committee these days. Are you coming in?'

'I wasn't going to. I was late home last night.'

'Yeah, I heard you come in. I waited up until I heard you.'

A warm feeling suffused Sophie. It had been a long time since anyone had worried about her safety.

Or was it happiness she felt?

'Why do you want to know?'

Exasperation filled her brother's voice 'Hang on. Nigel! Last warning or you'll be going home.'

In the background, Sophie could hear Nigel crying at full volume. She instinctively reached out her hand as though she was there to comfort him. When Nigel was in a paddy he was inconsolable. 'What's wrong with Nigel?'

'He forgot his cowboy hat and all the other kids have theirs. I was hoping I'd catch you and you might bring it in.' Braden's voice held a wheedling tone. 'Please, Soph?'

Sophie held back a sigh. There went her relaxing day. 'Alright. But for Nigel. Not for you, big bro. And you'll owe me.'

'You're a—holy hell, gotta go.'

'What's wrong?'

'Kent's come off.'

Sophie put her hand to her mouth as Braden stopped talking. He mustn't have ended the call because she could hear him huffing as he obviously ran. In the background, she could hear the noise of the crowd. Her blood chilled as a siren overlaid the noise.

'Braden? Are you there? Is Kent okay?'

But there was no reply.

One of the reasons Sophie hadn't been fussed about going to the Easter rodeo was because she hated rodeos. When she and Kent had been together, she'd reluctantly gone along with him. She'd mainly gone to make sure he was all right, and she hated every minute of watching him in the ring. The year before his dad had handed the management of the property over to him, Kent had followed the season in western Queensland. That's where he and Braden had first met Jon Ingram. Jon had been one of the clowns at the Winton rodeo when Kent had won the bull ride. They'd hit it off and at that rodeo, Sophie learned that their actual job title was "protection athlete".

She'd hated the bull riding—it was known as the most dangerous sport in the world, but Kent had laughed.

'Nah, Soph. *Jon* has the most dangerous job. I'm *on* the bull, but he throws himself in the path of an 800-kilogram beast to keep me safe.'

Sophie had put her hand to her mouth and then grimaced as the red gritty dust settled on her lips. 'I hate the whole lot. Why on earth would you do that, Jon?'

At the time Jon had shaken his head and she leaned forward. It was hard to hear him speak over the noise of the crowd.

'Kent has more chance of getting hurt than we do. That's why we do it. For the guy on the bull, they're not in control. They're on the back of a beast—a cranky beast with an unwanted human on its back. A beast that weighs about 800 kilos. It's not a fair match. When the bull flings the rider down, they can't do much about it, and there's a chance of it turning into a nasty wreck. That's where we come in.'

Sophie shook her head. 'Well, I think you're all mad. One day it's *not* going to have a good ending.'

Kent had slipped his arm around her waist. 'We know what we're doing, Soph. I'd never put myself into danger.'

'Well, you just remember that, Kent Mason. You say you'd never put yourself in danger but look at what you do!'

'It's total focus, sweetheart.'

'I worry about you, Kent. It's bad enough when you're doing cattle work, this is unnecessary.'

That conversation stayed with her now as she shed her tracksuit, quickly pulled on jeans and a long-sleeved T-shirt, dragged her hair back and went looking for Nigel's hat.

Please, don't let today be that day. Ten minutes later, she was in the farm ute speeding towards Augathella.

Chapter 16
Sophie

Sickness roiled in Sophie's stomach as she turned onto Elmes Street where the rodeo grounds were. No matter what had happened or what Kent had done, she didn't wish him any harm. All the way to town as she bumped over the corrugations—she drove way too fast—she'd thought of the injuries she'd heard about at rodeos.

As she pulled up at the end of a long line of cars, an ambulance drove slowly from the ground and turned towards the main road.

No lights, no sirens.

The crowd was silent and panic built in her chest. That didn't look good.

As the ambulance passed the ute, Sophie caught sight of the sombre faces of two paramedics sitting in the front.

She grabbed Nigel's hat and her purse, slammed the door shut and ran towards the entrance. Once she'd paid her entry fee to a man she didn't recognise, she hurried through the crowd looking for Braden and Callie.

Finally, she spotted Braden with Jon—in full clown colours—at the chute where the broncos and bulls ran out. Trying to stay calm, she ran over to her brother, and not focusing on that last unpleasant conversation she'd had with Kent.

She had been a bitch, and it had been unnecessary.

What if he was . . .

No, he couldn't be. Braden and Jon were talking quietly together but looking calm. Even though Kent had let her down and broken her heart, she didn't want him to be hurt.

As she drew closer the crowd erupted in a roar as the gate to the ring opened. More cheers went up as two clowns ran into the ring and started a mock fight. They turned as the chute opened and half a dozen kids ran out holding ropes.

The noise of the crowd and the mood reassured Sophie a little but she still grabbed Braden's arm when she reached them. The smell of frying steak and onions reached her from the Lions' van, and she fought the nausea that rose.

'It's not bad, is it? If it was bad, they'd be quiet and going home, wouldn't they, Braden?'

'Is what bad?' Braden turned to her.

'Kent?' She swallowed. 'The ambulance?'

'No. He's fine, but they had to take him to Charleville.'

'If he's fine why would they take him to Charleville?

'You know we don't have X-ray facilities here. Kent's fine. Look here comes Rory.'

Sophie followed Braden's gaze to the ring and she couldn't believe what she was seeing.

'For God's sake, Braden? Are you mad? Letting Rory go out there?'

Braden stared at her, his face a picture. 'What's wrong now?'

Jon glanced her way and then jumped lithely over the rail and ran into the ring.

'Kent's just been taken to hospital and you're encouraging your son to participate in this awful sport?' Sophie's voice rose in pitch. 'How irresponsible are you?'

Braden put his hands on her shoulders, but she shook them off. 'Calm down, Soph. It's only dummy roping.'

'I don't care what it is. It introduces him to the sport. I suppose that's why Nigel wanted his hat.' She shoved the hat at Braden. 'Is he going in it too?'

'He is. And there's nothing wrong with it. They're country kids, Sophie. You of all people should know that. I remember you going in the dummy roping when you were a kid.'

She nodded, embarrassed by her attack on her brother. 'Yes, I'm sorry. You're their father. I was out of line.'

Braden put his arm around her shoulder. 'Don't worry. I know you would have been worried about Kent, but he's okay, so calm down. The other ambulance is on the way so we've brought the dummy roping event forward.'

'What's wrong with him exactly?'

'Busted arm and a nasty egg on his head where he hit the ground. Jon managed to distract the bull and Kent rolled over and got up by himself.'

'That's a relief. I was worried when you dropped out of the call.'

'I'm pleased to hear that. Shows you have a bit of kindness left in you.'

'What's that supposed to mean?' She put her hands on her hips 'If you don't want me around, I can soon head out.'

'Sophie, calm down. You're so bloody sensitive these days. I just meant that I've noticed how you and Kent dance around each other now. I was simply pleased to see that you were worried about him. I didn't mean anything by it and I wasn't having a go at you.'

'Of course I was worried. I'd worry about anyone. You know how much I hate rodeos.'

'You didn't always. After we watch Rory, we'll go grab a cold drink. There's something I want to ask you.'

She raised her eyebrows but smiled, trying to be a bit nicer. 'Hey, you owe me, brother. I brought the hat to town.'

'Good to see you smile, Soph. And you know, it's really good to have you back at home.'

Sophie shrugged. 'For a while. Where's Callie?'

Braden pointed to the grandstand. 'In the middle on the left with Petie. He wanted to go in it too, but he doesn't make the age cut.'

Before she knew it, Sophie was standing on the bottom rail of the fence cheering Rory on, as the local kids took turns to rope the dummy bull—a plastic head on a light metal frame on wheels.

She rolled her eyes as Rory got the rope around its head three times in a row, and took out first place. 'No stopping him now. I guess he's your son.'

Braden stood straight and grinned, pride evident in his expression as Rory ran over. 'Sure is.'

'What favour did you want to ask me? Spill, and then I'll go and get us all a cold drink and meet you in the grandstand.'

'I forgot I had a truck coming early tomorrow.'

'And, the favour is?' She knew what was coming.

'Can you go to Charleville and pick Kent up in the morning? I told him I'd get him, but I forgot about the cattle truck.'

'What about Jacinta?'

'She's working at the races.'

'Oh.'

'You can take the good four-wheel-drive tomorrow,' Braden said.

'Well, thank you for that, but *if* I go, I'll take Gladys.'

'Come on, Soph, it's the least you can do.'

'What's that supposed to mean?'

'Sheesh. Don't be so bloody touchy. Kent flew me up to get you with absolutely no hesitation.'

Sophie lowered her eyes, her voice quiet as she realised she was being really hard to get on with. She had to figure out why she was in such a contrary mood. 'Alright. I'll go and get him.'

'Good girl. He's going to ring me when he's ready. I'll send you a message if I'm out with the truck.' Braden slung his arm around her shoulders as they walked over to the grandstand.

'And we need to sit down and have more of a chat too,' he added.

'What another one?'

'I want to know what happened with Jock.'

'Uh uh.' Sophie shook her head.

'I saw the bruises, Soph. I can guess what happened and I think you need to report it.'

'No, it's in the past now.'

'Maybe it is. But what if he does it again to someone else? Or worse? Or did he do worse to you?'

'No. He only had to do it once. And I knew I was out of there. I rang you as soon as he left.'

'So will you at least get it on record that he hurt you? Or threatened you?'

'I'll think about it.'

Chapter 17
Kent - Charleville Hospital

Kent cursed himself as he lay in the back of the ambulance. He should have known better than to ride that damn bull. He'd given in and let his mood govern his actions.

His head was fuzzy and random thoughts flittered through. He closed his eyes and opened them with a jump.

Can't go to sleep. Cattle to move.

Kent opened his eyes and focused on the roof of the vehicle above him, but it was too hard to focus. He closed his eyes again and concentrated on what he had to do at the station.

Bloody stupid thing to do, coming off that damn bull. His mind hadn't been in the ring, and when he'd come off, he should have rolled but he'd put his hand out to break his fall.

And broken his arm, or his wrist or whatever the X-ray was going to show. All he knew was it was hurting like a bastard, even with the pain relief the paramedics had administered.

The only good thing about it was that Sophie hadn't been there to see him come off. She would have taken great delight in telling him how stupid he was.

And I am, he thought.

Sophie. Images of her stayed in his thoughts. Images from years gone by.

Her beautiful green eyes filled with love as she'd looked up at him as they lay by the creek the first time they'd made love.

That thought *hurt*. He filed it away where it lived in his heart. What had he done that made her stop loving him? Because she *had* loved him. They had been so happy, and then almost overnight, the closeness went and she's taken up with that loser.

Maybe it was because bad boys held an attraction. Maybe he hadn't paid enough attention, and worked too hard, but Dad had been winding down and he'd been spending a lot of time out on the station. In the early days of their relationship, Sophie had loved spending time with Mum, but suddenly she'd stopped coming to *Lara Waters*.

His eyes blurred again.

Forget Sophie.

Focus on work.

After the recent rains, he had a lot to do at the station. At least the new steers had arrived and were okay for a while in the paddock he'd put them in. He was going to have to swallow his pride and ask for help, or maybe he could hire someone like Jon Ingram? Maybe Jon had some contacts? Kent's mood lifted a little. The only thing he wanted to make sure of was that his parents didn't feel as though they had to come home from their extended trip.

Anyway, he was pretty sure that while they were in Brisbane, Mum would be looking for somewhere for them to retire. She had a lot of family there, and as hard as it was going to be, it was close to medical care *if* Dad's health declined.

It sounded as though the progress of the disease had slowed, but the future looked bleak.

Kent nodded to himself as he lay there and a sharp ache gripped his head. He'd find someone to help for a couple of weeks, and he'd fly to Brisbane and meet Mum and Dad when the cruise ship docked.

##

Kent woke to a bright light shining in his eyes.

'Sorry, Kent. No sleeping until the doc checks you out.'

'Where are we?'

'Halfway to Charleville. Just stopped to take your obs.' Mitch, the local ambo, and a mate from school turned the small torch off. 'How are you feeling?'

'Like shit. But I'll live. I hope.' Kent managed a grin.

'Hope so.'

'You know you'll be admitted. Doc won't let you go home with a concussion, and I'd say you'll have a cast on that arm.'

'Hope not. Maybe I've just wrenched it.'

'You were going well until you came off. Paul and I had a good view from where the ambulance was parked.'

'You'll have to get back there so they can start it up again.'

'Nah, we had a second ambulance in town in case there was another one needed, so the events weren't held up.'

'I'd have been popular if that had happened.'

'Don't stress, mate. It's all good. You always did worry about others.'

'As long as it didn't ruin the day.'

'It didn't. Look you'll be back home before you know it. An X-ray and some attention to that arm, and you'll be as good as new.'

Kent saw the glance the paramedics exchanged and he knew they were concerned about him. 'I will be.'

Mitch glanced at Paul, the other paramedic. ' Do you know if the X-ray girl stayed or do we have to get a locum in again?'

'Larissa stayed. I'm taking her out for dinner tonight, so I'll have another trip back to town when we knock off.'

'Excellent,' Mitch said. 'Another city gal falls in love with the west.'

'Come on, let's get back on the road. Not far to go now, Kent.'

'You're not feeling nauseous?'

'No, just a bit fuzzy.'

'Good. Just stay awake.'

It was almost dark by the time Kent had been poked and prodded by Doc Henry, X-rayed by the sweet Larissa, and then plastered from wrist to elbow.

The doc was happy with his head injury but insisted on him staying for the night.

'How long will I have this on for?' Kent lifted his left arm as the nurse took his obs after he'd eaten a light dinner.

'Probably around six to eight weeks. It could take longer if the break isn't clean but apparently, yours was pretty basic. You'll need to wear your plaster cast until that broken bone heals.'

'Damn. I wonder if I can ride while it's on.'

'See what Doc Henry advises when he discharges you in the morning.'

'What time does he usually come in?'

She grinned. 'I can guarantee it will be early. He'll be keen to get to the races at Augathella.'

'Damn, I forgot about the races. I'm supposed to be helping there.' His smile was rueful. 'And yeah, the doc likes a flutter, and he always picks a winner. Knows his horses.'

The nurse smiled sympathetically as she clipped the board on the end of the bed. 'Sleep well.'

When she'd gone, Kent reached for his phone. Luckily it had survived the fall; he'd zipped it into his front shirt pocket. He pressed speed dial for Braden.

'Hang on, mate. I'll just go outside.'

Kent could hear voices, loud music and kids yelling. He waited for a minute.

'We're at the pub.'

'Yeah, I could tell. Lucky you. Have a beer for me.'

'How are you? Gonna live?' Braden asked.

'A bloody broken wrist and a mother of a headache. Should be right to go in the morning. Listen don't worry about getting me. I forgot the races were on. I'll sort a lift home from here. Doc Henry might even give me a lift.'

'Don't worry about travelling with Doc. I've sorted a lift for you. Gotta go, mate. See you when you get home. I'll organise someone to help you with those steers too.'

Before Kent could respond, Braden disconnected. Probably having a great time at the pub with all the families and friends who would be there. If he'd been more focused he could be there too, instead of lying alone in an old hospital room a hundred kilometres from home.

With a sigh, Kent lay back on the pillow and closed his eyes.

Chapter 18
Sophie

Sophie was up at the crack of dawn and headed for the kitchen.

Might as well get it over and done with. The sooner she got to Charleville, collected Kent and dropped him at *Lara Waters*, the sooner she could stop worrying about it. Being in a car with him for an hour was going to test her willpower. With a bit of luck, she could drop him at his ute in town and he could drive to *Lara Waters* from there.

You could drive with a cast on, couldn't you?

They'd never really talked about what had happened between them and she didn't want to start now. The thought of the two of them in a car together terrified her; she knew that was why she was so unsettled. Kent had tried, but she'd clammed up. To verbalise what had happened would reduce her to a blubbering mess, and she hadn't wanted him to see her like that.

Now, she didn't want to see him at all, and she didn't want to talk to him.

I don't.

Really.

She wanted to take her car this morning because she had the car audio system connected to her phone and they could have music on, to save the need for a conversation on the way back. She'd take it slow and watch out for kangaroos.

To her surprise, Braden was in the kitchen when she went across, and the smell of fresh-brewed coffee greeted her.

'Morning, brother. That smells good.'

'Mm.' The sound was closer to a grunt.

'Sore head, hey?'

'A bit.'

'I'm not surprised. I could hear you from the bistro last night. I take it Callie drove home?'

A nod.

'Late?'

Another nod.

'What time's the truck coming?'

'Soon.'

She watched as Braden poured a mug of coffee for her and passed it over. 'Ta.'

'Bistro was busy again last night.' Finally a whole sentence from her brother.

'Yeah. You'll be pleased to know I gave Sean my notice last night. I can't cook here and work nights there too.'

'Good.

'You want me to start Monday of next week?'

'Yes, please. And I've already put you on the books. No arguments.'

'Okay, and I'll pay board.'

'You won't.'

'I will.'

Braden pulled out a kitchen chair and sat down. Sophie crossed to the coffeemaker and filled her travel mug.

'Look, Braden. The contract workers pay board. I can't freeload off you,' she said as she pulled out a chair and sat opposite him.

'For Christ's sake, Sophie. You're family.'

She stared at him.

'And not only that, how much do I owe you for taking the boys for all those months? And I don't mean money. I mean, I *owe* you. We won't discuss it again. You're not paying board.'

Sophie shrugged.

The only noise was the hum of the fridge as they drank their coffee. Finally, Braden broke the tense silence.

'The contract ringers and the two new permanents arrive on the weekend. So it's good that you're here now.'

'I met one of the new staff in town at the billy cart derby the other day.' Sophie closed her eyes as she sipped the strong brew. Somehow it always tasted better when Braden made it. 'Did you end up meeting her? Amelia was her name.'

'No. I was busy with Rory. My little champion.' Braden's grin was wide. 'But she's coming out here tomorrow to check out her digs.'

Sophie frowned wondering whether to say anything about her dog but decided against it. It was none of her business. 'She seemed really nice. Likes a chat. She had old Reg lined up. They were having quite an intense talk.'

'He does like a chat.'

Sophie stood and took her mug to the sink. 'I'd better go.'

'He hasn't called yet,' Braden said.

'I don't want to be back late. Sean's got me working with Kelly this afternoon to show her how to set the tables.'

'It's not rocket science, is it?' Braden frowned. 'So you won't be at the races?'

'No.'

'Me either. We've had a big enough Easter, and I need to catch up on some work. I'm surprised you're not going. Couldn't you have swapped a shift? I thought you'd want to keep your winning streak going for Fashion of the Field.'

'I'm not really interested in it anymore. Most of my friends have moved away and . . .'

'And it's something you and Kent used to do together.'

'No. I wasn't going to say that.' Sophie glared at him. 'Just let it go, okay?'

'Okay, okay.' Braden put his hands up. 'Listen, change of subject. Do you want me to hire someone to help you with the clean-up and stuff down in the cookhouse?'

'No, I can handle that. I mean I'm only cooking for how many? Eight? Ten?'

'Yep. Ten.'

'I'll be fine.'

Sophie picked up her travel mug and headed for the door.

'Sophie? Have you got any days off this week?'

'Tomorrow and Wednesday. Sean's going to see how Kelly goes by herself. Why?'

'I thought we might get in and . . . get in and sort out . . . Julia's stuff.'

Sophie walked back to the table and put her hand on her brother's shoulder. 'Sounds like a plan.'

'Callie'll be in town at school both those days, and Petie will be at kindy and the other two at school.'

'I'm in.'

Braden cleared his throat and met her gaze squarely. 'I want to tell you first, Soph. I'm going to ask Callie to marry me. What do you think of that?'

'I think that's wonderful news. I've seen the way you look at her. I know you love her, and that's all that matters.'

'No one will ever replace Julia, but she's gone.' Braden's voice broke. 'I have to move on. And like you said, clearing out the house is the first step. It needs doing. It's past time.'

Sophie shook her head. 'I was too harsh with you. No, not past time. You needed time to grieve. If you're ready to do it now, it's time. I'll help. And if it gets too hard, we'll soldier on together.'

'Thanks. I'll go over and see Kent this afternoon, and get his big trailer. I thought we might get new furniture for the house too. Give it a real turnout.'

'Leave it a while and include Callie in that.'

'That's a good idea. But I have to wait until she agrees to marry me. I worry I'm rushing her and that she'll say no. She's never lived in the outback. She'd not had anything to do with cattle work, and I've got the boys.'

Sophie nudged Braden with her shoulder. 'Three boys she loves and is fantastic with, and you've no need to worry. I've seen the way she looks at you.'

'It's a big ask, Soph.'

'There's only one thing I'd worry about. How would you feel about having more kids? Does she want children?'

'We've never talked about it.'

'Well, my advice is, talk to her. Communicate. Most relationship problems come from lack of honesty.'

'Is that what happened with you and Kent?'

'That subject's closed, Braden. So leave it.'

'If you ever need to talk . . .'

'I know. I have a big brother with a soft heart and a good ear. I'll keep you in mind.'

'Okay. Don't forget to ask Kent about the trailer. If it's okay. Tell him I'll go over after lunch.'

'Speaking of which I'd better get going.' She turned to leave again, but Braden grabbed her hand. His fingers were rough and callused against hers. 'Soph? Be kind to Kent. He's a good man.'

She raised her eyebrows. 'Is he?'

'You know he is. I'd love to see you two get back together. For the life of me, I don't know why you ever broke up. And neither does Kent.'

'Well, that's not going to happen, Braden. You need to accept that and butt out. Once you get a permanent cook, I'll be leaving.' Sophie's temper began to fire and she strode out of the kitchen before she said something she'd regret. She and Braden had made their peace, and she wanted it to stay that way.

Kent? A good man?

Pah! She'd thought that once too.

She'd loved him with her heart and soul before he let her down.

Chapter 19

Kent

'Thanks, Doc. One more question. Can I drive with this thing on?' Kent nodded down at his plastered arm, now supported in a sling.

'In a day or two, as soon as the headache and dizziness have been gone for twenty-four hours,' the old doctor replied.

'It's all gone now.'

'So if it stays away, you can drive tomorrow. But don't overdo it, Kent. I know what you cattlemen are like. You think you're invincible.'

'We are. Almost.' Kent grinned. 'A favour? Are you going to the races in Augathella today?'

'Sure am. Want a tip?'

'No, I'm hoping for a lift.'

Doc shook his head. 'You don't need one. Your driver's waiting for you in the waiting room.'

'Great, Braden's a good mate.'

Doc looked at him curiously. 'Okay, if you have any more headache issues or blurred vision, you get straight to the clinic. Anyway, come and see me in two weeks, and I'll see how that arm's going.'

'Thanks, Doc. I'll take it easy.'

The old doc's wrinkled face split into a grin and he tapped his nose. 'And just for the record, *Spyzain's* a sure thing in race three.'

Kent grinned back. 'Got it.' The old doc was legendary with his horse knowledge.

Once the discharge papers were signed, Kent went into the bathroom and dressed in the clothes he'd been wearing yesterday. They took a bit of dusting down. He went to cup his hands under the tap and wash his face, but the damn cast held him up. The next few weeks were going to be bloody difficult.

Five minutes later he'd managed to wash his face and slick back his hair. He put his phone in his pocket and headed out to the waiting room.

There was no sign of anyone there, and he wondered if the doc had been mistaken. He pulled out his phone to call Braden, but he was interrupted by a voice behind him. A voice he knew very well.

'Kent.'

He turned slowly, putting his phone back in his pocket, as he tried to control the increase in his heart rate.

'Sophie? What are you doing here? Did Braden send you in?'

'I don't know what you mean by *in*, but yes, Braden asked me to come to Charleville and get you. He's got a cattle truck in this morning.' Sophie stood there, dressed in a pair of jeans and a long-sleeved close-fitting T-shirt. It struck Kent how much weight she'd lost; he hadn't noticed before. Then again, he tried not to look at her. It hurt too much.

He had to bite his tongue not to comment, and when he spoke his words were garbled. 'You drove all the way to here, I mean to Charleville to get *me*?'

Her voice was matter-of-fact, and he was pleased it didn't hold any of the angst of the other night. 'Well, you went much further to collect me when I needed to get home. I owed you.'

'Well, it's very kind of you. But you didn't need to pay me back. I could have found my own way home today.'

'That may be the case, but I'm here now, so you might as well come with me. Do you need to do anything before we go? My car's in the car park.'

'No. I'm right to go. Doc Henry signed me out.'

'Good. Come on then. I have to get back quickly because I'm working this afternoon.'

Sophie strode off and Kent watched as she headed down the corridor ahead of him. Halfway along, she stopped and turned.

Her face was closed as she waited for him to catch up.

'I'm sorry,' she said when he caught up to her near the lift. 'I didn't ask how you were feeling. Do you need a wheelchair?'

'No. I certainly don't. I've got a broken wrist, not a leg.' Kent knew his tone was curt. He hated being at a disadvantage. Even though his head was still a bit achy, the last thing he wanted was Sophie pushing him along in a wheelchair. 'And I'm feeling fine.'

Nothing more was said until they reached the car park. Kent's eyes widened in surprise. 'You've still got Gladys?'

Their eyes met over the top of the yellow Camry wagon and the look they exchanged held lots of memories.

'Yes. I left her at Braden's when I moved away.'

Moved away? Kent thought. More like *ran* away.

Sophie waited beside the door as he climbed into the passenger seat. When he was in, she closed the door for him, walked around and got in the driver's side.

Kent felt totally useless, his left arm in a sling. He reached down and did his seatbelt up. At least he could do that by himself.

Being in a confined space with Sophie for over an hour was going to be hard. It would be a great opportunity to ask her all the questions that he'd had for her when she dumped him so suddenly, but he didn't want to get her offside yet.

They were both quiet as she started the engine and reversed out of the hospital carpark. He put his head back and closed his eyes.

Damn, she still wore that same floral perfume. He hadn't noticed it until they got in the car. All he could think of was how he used to nuzzle his nose into the soft skin of her neck and inhale the fragrance.

'Is your head aching?' she asked softly.

'A little bit,' he replied honestly.

'I was going to play some music on the way back,' she said.

So you didn't have to talk to me, he thought.

'Would it bother you?' she asked.

'Possibly.'

He noticed her fingers tense on the steering wheel as she waited to turn left onto Sturt Street.

'Okay. I'll leave it off and I'll keep quiet. Go to sleep if you want,' she said.

'No, it's fine. We can chat.'

This time her fingers were white from gripping the wheel.

'You're probably better to rest.'

'No, I'm supposed to stay awake.' It was only a little white lie. 'We can catch up on each other's news.'

How prosaic that sounded.

Catch up on each other's news?

Here he was sitting in a car with the woman he had once loved so much.

If he was truthful, she was the woman he still loved, even though she had treated him so callously.

What he'd like to do was be honest and tell her how she'd broken his heart and find out once and for all why all of a sudden he hadn't been enough for her.

Why she'd left him for that no-hoper.

This was going to be a very long trip home to Augathella.

Chapter 20
Sophie

This was going to be the longest trip she'd ever driven back to Augathella. Her car had never seemed so small as it did this morning. As she reached down to put it into drive, she had to keep her fingers to the right so she didn't accidentally brush Kent's jeans.

Three years ago, in this same car—Kent had called it Gladys because he said it reminded him of his mother's Aunt Gladys; she always wore yellow. In those days they'd even held hands as she'd driven.

Sophie swallowed when he said they could catch up on each other's news. That was the last thing she wanted to do.

'Not much news to tell here,' she said crisply. 'I'm only home for a while to help Braden out, and then I'm off.'

Kent didn't answer and she searched for something else to say, something that didn't relate to them. Then again, there was no them.

That was in the past.

She scouted around for a safe topic. 'So how's cattle prices been here?' She finally came up with something away from the personal. 'I haven't had a chance to ask Braden.'

'Not bad. Not good.'

'Fair enough. I heard that the big muster went well.'

'Yes. It did.'

Sophie tried to focus on her driving. Once they would have chatted nonstop, their words tumbling over the other's.

'How are your parents?' As soon as she asked that she regretted it.

No. Too personal. Way too personal.

'Mum's good. Dad's not well.'

'I'm sorry to hear that.'

'He's been diagnosed with early-onset Alzheimer's.'

Sophie drew a quick breath as shock filtered through her. For the first time her words were genuine. 'Oh no, Kent, that's awful news. Braden didn't tell me.'

'Braden doesn't know. I haven't been able to talk about it. I guessed I thought if I didn't tell anyone, it mightn't be real.'

'How's your mum handling it?'

He turned to look at her, and she took her attention off the road briefly. Their eyes met and a warm feeling uncurled low in her stomach.

'You know Mum. She's always positive and sees the good side to everything. That's why she took Dad off on this three-month cruise. She said they would have a good time, and it would be something they could remember together.'

He clenched the fingers of his right hand until his fingers were white, but didn't say anything more.

Sophie cleared her throat. 'I loved your mum. You know that. And I loved your dad too. I mean I still do. I feel for her, it's an awful thing. Maybe he won't deteriorate too quickly.'

'Maybe not. We can only hope. Mum and Dad love you too, Sophie.'

Shit. She didn't want the conversation to get so personal. They were barely on the road to Augathella. There was still an hour to go.

Kent half-turned in the passenger seat and she saw his wince as he readjusted his sling.

'Have you had some painkillers today?'

'No. I didn't want them. I need to have a clear head.'

Sophie sensed his eyes on her and discomfort settled in her stomach as warmth moved up her neck.

'It's good to talk about it, Sophie. Maybe I'm overreacting. Maybe it won't be as bad as my imagination plays out at night.'

'Well, I'm here and I'm listening, so talk as much as you want.'

Strangely she meant it. It broke her heart to hear what Mr Mason was going through. Even though she called Kent's mum by her first name, she'd never felt right calling Mr Mason anything else. He had teased her about it and always joked with her.

'One day, I hope you'll be calling me Dad, Sophie,' he'd said the last night she'd had dinner at their house.

And then her world had fallen to pieces.

'I'm pleased you're listening. I'm pleased we're actually talking. It's been a long time. I miss those days, Soph. Mum and I were talking about you yesterday morning.'

'Oh.' Her voice was quiet.

'Yes, she'd heard you were home. She was full of all sorts of advice.'

'For me?' Sophie frowned.

'No. For me.'

Neither of them spoke for a while. Sophie wondered what Rhonda Mason would have advised Kent, although if she was honest she had a fair idea. She also knew that Rhonda wouldn't have known what Kent had done. She doubted if anyone else did either. It must have burned out quickly.

Hold that thought, she told herself. Remember what he did. She could feel sorry for the family, and what they were going through, but that didn't mean automatic forgiveness for Kent.

'Do you want to hear what she said?'

Sophie shook her head. 'No. Try to rest. We'll be in town soon.'

'I'd like to try and talk to you, Sophie.'

'We're talking.'

'No, I'd like to talk about us. Mum's advice was clear.'

'No, Kent. You and I don't have anything to talk about.'

'Will you just answer one question for me? One question, with an honest answer. It's time I moved on.'

Chapter 21
Kent

Kent stared ahead, not game to look across at Sophie. He wondered what she'd do if he pressed the issue. Knowing how strong-willed she was, he wouldn't be surprised if she even pulled up and put him out at the side of the road.

But while they were together in this small car, and he had her attention he was going to push. They'd never talked when she'd broken it off. He'd been hurt, and then when she moved in with Jock Evans, anger had taken over. He'd vowed never to trust another woman as long as he lived.

'All right, one question, but if I don't want to answer, I won't.' She stared straight ahead and focused on the straight road.

'Right. But I'd appreciate honesty. Mum told me to follow my heart on the phone yesterday, and I can't do that until I have closure.'

'Closure from what?'

'Closure from us.'

'There is no us.'

'No, there isn't, but there was for a long time.'

'So what's your question?'

Kent took a deep breath and tried not to frown when pain ran up his arm into his shoulder.

'Why did you stop loving me? Was it something I said? Something I did that you decided you didn't like? Did I outgrow you? Was I going too fast?'

'One question, you said. Which one do you want me to answer?' Her lips were set in a straight line, but he could see the tension in her shoulders and heard the quiver in her voice.

He moved in the seat, and his arm throbbed again. Tension filled his body as he thought. 'The main one, I guess.'

'The main one? Which one would that be?'

'For God's sake, Sophie, don't be so bloody close-minded. Listen to me. I'm trying to find out why you stopped loving me. Maybe I shouldn't have said anything. It's so bloody hard. I've tried to move on. It's been over two years now, and you know what, I can't. How can I try to love someone else when I don't know what's wrong with me? How can I trust someone else to love me, and keep loving me?'

He finally found the courage to look at her. Two spots of deep pink coloured her cheeks, and as she turned to him briefly her eyes flashed with anger.

'You poor thing! You thought you could get away with what you did, and sweet little Sophie would be there waiting for you.' Her words were bitter and Kent widened his eyes.

'Get away with what I did? What did I do?'

'Don't, Kent. Just don't. I've moved on. I've forgotten about it. I don't want to rehash it all. You hurt me so badly, I had no choice.'

'I hurt *you*? You're the one who broke it off and moved in with another man, not even a month after I'd planned to ask you to marry me. I even had the ring. And what did I get? A phone call telling me we were done. You didn't even have the guts to come and tell me why, face-to-face!'

'Because I knew if I looked at you and you said you were sorry, I'd probably forgive you and regret it for the rest of my life. I know everyone wanted us to get married. Your parents, Braden, the whole bloody town, but *you're* the one who ruined it so don't you dare blame me.'

Confusion filled Kent. He shook his head and the movement bloody hurt. 'I have no idea what you're talking about.'

'Don't make it worse with a lie. You're the one who brought it up. You can't take the truth? So drop it.'

Kent reached over and put his good hand on her arm. His stomach sank when she flinched and he moved his hand back quickly. 'Talk to me, Sophie, please. Tell me what you mean.'

'No. There's no point. I told you two years ago, Kent, that we were through. It's time you accepted it.'

'Did you do the same thing to Jock? Is it that you just can't commit, Sophie?' He regretted his words as soon as they came out.

'That is none of your business.' Her voice broke and he knew it had been a low blow.

'I'm sorry. That was out of line. Can't you see—'

Anger hummed through the silence in the small car. She reached forward and turned the music up so loud it thumped through his aching head

Kent put his head back and closed his eyes.

Well, that went well. Thanks for the advice, Mum.

Not another word was spoken until they reached the outskirts of Augathella.

'My ute's at the rodeo ground. Drop me off there.' He couldn't even come up with "please".

He didn't care what the doc said about not driving until tomorrow. If he ran off the road, who would care?

As he unlocked the door of his ute, Kent regretted that thought. A lot of people would, and he wouldn't do that to his parents.

From this moment on, he wasn't going to give Sophie Cartwright another thought.

Maybe he'd call Jennifer and see if she'd like to come out for a visit. He was going to go stir crazy sitting out there by himself, and not being able to work.

He didn't let himself think of the emotions that Sophie Cartwright had brought screaming back.

Chapter 22
Sophie - that evening

Sophie stared back as Kelly dropped the knives and forks she was holding and gestured angrily at the half-set table.

'So what's wrong with that? And why are you so shitty?' the young girl demanded.

'I'm not "shitty" as you put it,' Sophie replied coldly. 'Have you never set a table before? Or at least had a meal at a properly set table? This is the dining room and it's more upmarket than just collecting your cutlery and packets of salt and pepper at the bistro. That's why the prices are higher in the dining room. And *that's* why we make it look good.'

Kelly's voice was scornful. 'What? You pay more for a meal in here because someone arranges the cutlery on the table. What a bloody rip-off.'

Sophie tried not to grit her teeth and counted to ten under her breath. 'That's correct and you are going to be the someone who sets the table correctly.'

'Well, I'm the waitress, and I don't see why I have to be the one to set the tables too.'

Sophie rolled her eyes. 'So who's going to set them? Will we get Sean to come out of the kitchen and do it? Or maybe Hilly can leave the bar and come and do it instead?'

'Don't be smart-mouthed, and you are shitty. And you're only a waitress too!' Kelly's hands went to her hips.

'Only for two more nights, thank God,' Sophie retorted. 'So, pay attention and we'll get these tables done.' She moved across to the next table. 'Now watch me. Fork on the left. Spoon and knife on the right. Bread and butter plate to the left of the fork.'

'For God's sake, does it really matter? If they want to eat, they'll find their cutlery.'

Sophie's temper finally boiled over. 'Look, Kelly, if you don't listen and do what I show you you'll likely be out of a job.'

'I don't really care. I'm more interested in what's wrong with you. Did you have a fight with your boyfriend or something?'

'Not that it's any of your business, but I don't have a boyfriend. Now you watch me do this table and you do that one.'

As Sophie pointed to the round table beside Kelly, her thoughts weren't focused on the table setting.

Instead her thoughts were on, *"or something"* as the young waitress had said.

An hour ago, Sophie had pulled up beside Kent's ute in the car park at the rodeo grounds. She'd sat there tight-lipped as he got out without a word.

Guilt ripped through her as she drove across from Riverside into town. She'd pulled up at Meat Ant Park and walked across the soft grass and sat on one of the seats trying to calm down.

Leaving Kent to fend for himself had been the wrong thing to do, but she couldn't take any more. If she hadn't promised to help Braden tomorrow, and if she hadn't committed to cook until he found someone permanent, she would have packed Gladys and just left.

And where would you go? that little nagging voice asked her. The same little voice that had told her she was doing the wrong thing moving away with Jock. But she hadn't been thinking straight back then. All she'd thought of was the boys needed to be with their father. Jock had tried for a relationship, but by that time she'd known what he was after, and it wasn't her.

She wasn't good at making decisions, so she'd stay and help Braden until she got her thoughts in order and her emotions back in check.

On her way to the pub to start her shift, she called into the police station and asked them to put on record what Jock had done. It was time to stand up for herself. She'd been a fool to go with him, and for the life of her she didn't know why she had.

'So?' Kelly's voice made her jump.

Sophie blinked and looked around the dining room. The tables were all set and as far as she could see, everything was in the right place.

'Good. Looks good. Thank you.'

'You were off with the pixies, so I copied the one you did. Are you okay, Sophie? You look really unhappy.'

Sophie cleared her throat. 'Yes, I'm fine.' She forced herself to smile. 'Just a bit on my mind, but thanks for asking. Are you right to help Sean with the cold larder now? I'm going to take a short break. I have to make a quick phone call. Lunch rush won't start for half an hour.'

Kelly nodded and headed for the kitchen.

Sophie went out to the small yard at the back of the pub where caravans often pulled up. Six caravans and two campervans filled the space, but they were all locked up and there was no one in sight. The tourists would all be at the races. She pulled out her phone and walked along the grassy footpath as she waited for Braden to pick up the call.

'Hey Soph, did you get him home okay?'

'I got him back to town and dropped him at his ute.'

'God, he's a stubborn bugger. I hope he was okay to drive home.'

'He should be out at *Lara* by now. You're going over there, aren't you? Maybe you could give him a call and check he got home safely.'

'I'll go over in a while. I've got a pump to move first. How was he feeling this morning?'

'He was okay.'

'Are you?'

'Why?'

'You sound funny.'

Sophie stared along the street as she reached the corner. Old Reg was sitting at a table at the front of the pub. A schooner of beer sat in front of him and he lifted a hand and waved when he spotted her. Sophie managed a smile and stayed on the corner as she spoke to her brother.

'I'm all right. Probably should have driven him all the way, but we sort of had words.'

'Sort of.'

She stayed quiet.

'Okay, he's a big boy. I'll be a couple of hours yet. Amelia should be here by the time I get back to the house.'

'Amelia? I thought she was coming out tomorrow.'

'Changed her mind. And it suits because you and I have plans for tomorrow. I think she's going to move in early, so I might need you to cook a couple of meals before the weekend.'

'I can do that. And if I'm cooking I can do some for Kent and maybe drop them over.' Sophie surprised herself when that came out.

'That'd be neighbourly.'

'I have to get back to work. See you tonight. Say hello to Amelia and Chilli for me.'

'Chilli? Does she have a partner?'

'You'll see.'

'Okay, I'm sure I will. Listen, did you ask Kent about the trailer?'

'Sorry, I forgot. Gotta go.'

Reg had finished his beer and gone into the bar to get another one, so Sophie hurried along past the front of the pub to the door of the dining room. As she was about to step inside, a car pulled up and a dark-haired woman got out and hurried around to the footpath.

Sophie froze and stared as the woman opened the back door and unstrapped a toddler from a baby seat. Hitching a bag over one shoulder, she held the child with one arm. She must have sensed Sophie staring because she turned and looked over at her. Her lip curled and Sophie braced herself.

'Come back to town with your tail between your legs, have you, Sophie?' Ros Evans, Jock's sister stared at her with dislike.

Sophie lifted her chin and held her gaze. Ros had been a couple of years below her at high school. Sophie hadn't liked her then, and she liked her a lot less now. In fact, she could barely look at her after what had happened.

'Too good for my brother, were you? Poor Jock's heartbroken.'

The events of the morning: Kent's persistence in trying to rehash the past, Kelly's incompetency and whining, and now seeing her nemesis, tipped Sophie over the edge. Her temper flared and she took a step toward Ros.

Her voice was cold. 'Your brother's lucky not to be up on a charge. The police were insistent that I press charges.'

'Oh, you poor diddums.' The malice fair dripped off Ros's words. 'It was probably only what you deserved.'

Sophie's mouth dropped open. 'Are you serious! You think it's all right for a man to hit a woman?'

'Like I said, you probably deserved it.'

Sophie shook her head slowly. 'No woman deserves that, and no woman should have to put up with it. I feel very sorry for you with that attitude.'

'Now you're back in town, are you going to cosy up with Kent baby, again?' Ros leaned forward, a sneer on her face. For the first time, Sophie noticed the fine wrinkles around her mouth and her lank hair. Ros lifted the toddler onto her hip. 'Just one word of advice. You be careful there, honey. Good old Kent might be the golden-haired boy around town, but he doesn't take responsibility for his actions.'

Sophie looked at her in horror as Ros gestured to the toddler on her hip. 'Doesn't want to know about you, does he, little man?'

Cold seeped into her chest as she took in the little boy's dark hair and olive skin.

Just like Kent's.

Chapter 23

'Morning, Sophie.' Callie called as she herded the boys across to the garage. 'Sorry can't stop to chat. There's a staff meeting this morning. Coffee's on.'

'Hi everyone. Have a top day.' Sophie smiled as Petie ran over to her and wrapped his arms around her legs.

'You have a topsy day too, Aunty Sophie.'

She bent down and hugged him. 'I will have a topsy day, Petie, now hurry up and follow Callie. You don't want to be late for kindy.'

Callie waited for Petie to run across to her as the other two boys raced into the shed.

'I'm in the front today,' Nigel called out.

'No, it's my turn.' Rory's voice echoed from the garage.

Callie rolled her eyes and then her gaze held Sophie's. 'You okay?'

'A bit tired. I didn't sleep very well.'

Callie put her briefcase down and walked across the path to stand beside her.

'Neither did Braden. It's going to be a tough day for you both. I wish I could help, but I know it's better to let you do it together.'

Sophie blinked, unsure of what Callie meant and then she remembered. Today was the first day she and Braden were cleaning out Julia's stuff.

'Yes, it will be,' Sophie said softly, feeling bad that she'd forgotten. She'd been so absorbed in her own worries through the night that she hadn't given today a thought.

Callie's eyes filled with tears as she reached out and squeezed Sophie's hand. 'Look after him, Soph. He's a bit strung out this morning.'

'I will. Thanks, Callie, we'll be fine.'

'Don't worry about cooking tonight either. I'll bring Chinese home. I'll get enough for Amelia too. I think she's moving into the donga today.'

'Thanks. Now hurry up or you'll be late. Watch out for roos.'

She watched as Callie hurried to the shed and soon the throaty roar of Braden's twin cab broke the still of the morning. A few minutes later, all she could see was the dust hanging over the road east.

The kitchen was empty so Sophie grabbed a quick coffee and then went looking for Braden. It took a while but finally she found him at the back of the breezeway making up cardboard boxes and putting them onto a trailer.

'Right to start?' she said briskly.

He looked up at her and nodded. 'You look like shit.'

'Thanks, my darling brother. I'm tired.'

'Do you want to leave it until tomorrow?'

'No, come on, we'll get started. Where did you get the boxes?'

'Kent had them in the shed with the trailer. Apparently his Mum had them ready for when she packs up in a few months. We'll empty them when we're done and I'll take them back with the trailer.'

'So he got home safely?'

'Yes. He looked like shit too.'

Sophie shrugged and didn't comment as she followed Braden around the side of the yard. She didn't want to think about Kent Mason, and she sure didn't want to talk about him.

'I went to the police station yesterday and filed a report,' she said.

Braden held the door open for her as they reached the side of the house. 'I'm pleased. A bit of closure for you too, then. Maybe you won't look so miserable all the time. We've been worried about you.'

Sophie pulled a face at him. 'I shouldn't have come back to Augathella. It would have been better to start somewhere new.'

'And where would you have gone? You don't know anywhere else.'

'I can learn. I'm thinking about moving to Brisbane and taking up a traineeship if I can get one.'

'Are you sure? We'd miss you.'

'I need to get away, Bray. Especially now.'

'Why especially now?'

'Because Ros Evan's back in town.'

Braden frowned. 'And that means Jock is too?'

'Not that I know of.'

'So what's Ros got to do with your decision?'

Sophie swallowed and lifted her head to meet her brother's concerned eyes.

'She just does. I don't want to talk about it. But I saw something yesterday that really helped me make the decision. I have to escape this place. I'll never have peace if I stay. You don't want to see me moping around for the rest of my life.'

'I just want you to be happy, little sis. You gave up those two years to look after the boys, and then that jerk let you down.'

Sophie put on a brilliant smile. 'It's a new me from today. I'm sick of being unhappy. We've had some tough years, so let's go get started because I have a call to make to a Brisbane restaurant.'

'That reminds me, Callie said she'd bring Chinese home,' Braden said as they entered the side of the house where Sophie had set up her room.

'Yeah, I saw her before they left.' This time Sophie's smile was genuine. 'So did you meet Amelia?'

'I did. Bloody hell, she can talk.'

'And what about Chilli?'

'Yes, I met Chilli too. I was expecting a working dog, but he's okay. I said he can stay. Would you believe she carried her own fence in the back of her Landcruiser?'

'She is unique. I'm looking forward to getting to know her a bit more.' Sophie put her hands on her hips. 'Okay, so where do we start?'

Chapter 24
Sophie

Thursday afternoon

Many tears had been shed, but Braden and Sophie had also smiled and laughed as they cleaned out the side of the house that had been locked up for two years. Precious mementoes and Julia's jewellery had been stored safely, and now Braden sat on the sofa in the family room as Sophie vacuumed the last room.

She turned the vacuum off, left it on the rug in front of them and flopped down beside him.

'A good job done,' she said, leaning her head back on the sofa. 'And about time.'

'Thanks, Soph. That was tough, but I feel better now it's over. You know, a few weeks ago I was even thinking about asking Jon and Fallon if they'd like to swap houses.'

'What? And move the kids and Callie to the old house?'

'Yeah, it was only a thought, but I was so stressed about going through Julia's stuff, I considered it for a while. Anyway, they wouldn't have moved. I was talking to Fallon at the billy cart day and she said they love it out there.'

'I was too. She looks well.'

'Strange how things work out. Callie arriving, and then Fallon not long after.'

'Good to see some new people in the district.'

'It is. Anyway, thanks again. I couldn't have done this without you.'

'It's all done now. Another step forward.'

'And what about you? You look a bit more settled now,' he said.

Sophie shrugged. 'I had something to focus on for the past two days.'

'I'll keep you busy down at the cookhouse. You can focus for as long as you like. You know, you could always stay as the permanent cook.'

'I might have to. I'm going to try to call Damon Dean before I make up my mind though.'

'You gave that traineeship up to look after the boys, didn't you?'

'It was the right thing to do at the time.'

'And I'll appreciate it for the rest of my life.' Braden grinned at her. 'They all love their Aunty Soph.'

She nudged him. 'And they love Callie too.'

'I think we'll be fine. Depends on whether Callie says yes or not.'

'Don't rush her.'

'I know. Now that we've cleared out all this, I'm ready. I'm impatient.'

'I know that well. Just bide your time. You'll know when it's right.'

Braden held her gaze. 'What about you, sis? How can I make sure you're happy?'

'I'll be fine. I'll stay out here at the station for a while and avoid town. I can order online and get the store to deliver bulk orders.'

'Why do you need to do that? Are you scared you'll see Jock?'

'No. It was seeing his sister that brought me undone. I'd prefer not to see her again.'

Braden frowned. 'Why? Because of Jock?'

She shook her head slowly. She lifted her eyes to meet her brother's. They'd grown closer again as they'd worked together over the past two days. Braden deserved to know the truth. Maybe sharing it would take a load off her.

'It's all a mess. I was a mess. I had the boys to look after and I was worried about you. But most of all, it was because of Kent.'

'Kent?' His frown deepened. 'What's she got to do with Kent?'

'Kent cheated on me with Ros Evans when we were still together. And if my gut feeling is right, he's the father of her toddler.'

'What!' Braden jumped up so quickly that the vacuum cleaner went flying.

Chapter 25
Kent

Thursday evening

Kent had suffered injuries before, but he'd never been in a situation where he only had one functioning arm. He'd always taken his health and fitness for granted, and hadn't been this incapacitated before. Sure, he'd had scrapes and bruises when he'd been a kid and he'd had a sore butt many times from rodeo falls, but he'd never known how hard it would be trying to do everything with one arm.

'Bloody hell,' he muttered on Thursday afternoon as he tried to fill the jug one-handed. He'd been updating his spreadsheet—at least his right hand was working—bringing the accounts and cattle weights up to date. Now, a man couldn't even make himself a simple cup of coffee. As Kent turned the tap off in disgust a car pulled up outside the front of the homestead and he crossed to the door.

His mood improved instantly when Braden got out of his twin cab, a six-pack of beer under his arm.

Kent used his good arm to push the screen door open and went out to the verandah.

'You're a lifesaver, mate!'

'How are you feeling?' Braden didn't look at him as he put the six-pack on the small table that sat beside the two easy chairs.

Kent manoeuvred himself carefully into the chair closest to the door. 'I'm going stir crazy. Stuck in the house. I'm finding the simplest things hard to do with one arm. Can't make a cuppa, can't cook a damn meal. I even considered inviting Jennifer out for the company.'

'Did you?'

'No, I thought better of it.' He looked curiously at Braden; he didn't seem himself tonight.

Braden pulled the top off one stubby and passed it over to him.

'Thanks, mate.' Kent leaned back in the chair and looked out to the west.

The sun was a brilliant ball of gold sitting above the horizon and the late afternoon sky was shot with shards of silver and pink. Kent's prime bull was silhouetted in the light and for the hundredth time today, Kent wished he could get outside and work. The chores were piling up; he was going to have to get help.

They sat there in silence as they drank their beers until Braden broke the silence.

'I called Jon this afternoon. He said he can give you three days a week.'

'Are you sure you can spare him?'

'I can.' Braden turned away and stared at the boundary fence.

'Are you okay, mate? Seems like something is bothering you? I can make other arrangements.'

'Sophie and I have been cleaning out the other side of the house the last couple of days.'

Kent nodded. 'That would have been hard. I can understand why you're a bit low.'

'No, I'm not low. You see, the thing is, Sophie and I had a heart-to-heart this afternoon, and she told me some pretty hard stuff.'

'About that bastard who conned her?'

Braden turned to him and his eyes were cold. 'Some of it, but most of it was about you, Kent.'

Kent put his beer down on the table and sat straight. 'About me?'

'Yeah, mate. I want you to be totally truthful with me. My sister's been pretty badly hurt and I'm looking out for her. I won't have anyone else hurt her. Her mental health is so fragile these days, she said she's going to hide out on the station. She saw something in town and she won't leave *Kilcoy* now. She's going to order the grocery supplies online and have it delivered, so she doesn't have to go to town.'

'Is Evans back in town?' Kent tried to clench his hand but the damn cast got in the way.

Braden's gaze was still square on his, and his mouth was tight. He put his beer down beside Kent's.

'No, but his sister is.' Braden didn't take his eyes off Kent's. He felt like he was under an inquisition.

'His sister? Why? Did she give Sophie a hard time too?'

'In a way, apparently. Maybe you'd like to tell me about it?'

Kent held Braden's gaze and frowned. 'Me?'

'Yep, you.'

'I don't even know his sister. Do I?'

'I don't know. Do you?' Braden's eyes narrowed. 'You telling me the truth, mate?'

'What the hell is going on, Braden? If I tell you I don't know his sister, I don't. What's her name and what's she got to do with me? Or Sophie?'

'For the last time, Kent. Are you being truthful with me?'

Kent picked up his beer and finished it on one deep draught. Not because he wasn't going to answer, but because he needed a minute to control his temper. He and Braden had been friends for a long time, but his mate was pissing him off big time with this inquisition.

He kept his voice controlled as he put the beer down on the table harder than he should have. 'I am being as truthful as I can. If you stop beating around the bloody bush and tell me exactly what you want to know, I can tell you. And I'll tell you once and once only. I don't lie. You tell me her name and I'll tell you if I know her.'

'Roslyn Evans.'

Kent frowned again and thought hard. 'I vaguely remember the name from school, I think.'

'And? Since then?'

'Since then I've never seen her, and I don't even remember what she looks like. Do you know her?'

'No. I think she left town after year ten. She came back to town when Jock did.'

'Okay. There's something you're not telling me. How about *you* be honest with me now? What the frig's going on, Braden? What's she done to Sophie, and where do I figure in all this?'

'Roslyn Evans has a child. A little boy about two years old, and Sophie suspects you're his father.'

Kent's mouth fell open as he stared at Braden. 'What the hell? Sophie thinks I have a kid? With this woman I don't even know?'

'Well, according to Sophie you know her very well. She finally admitted to me why she broke up with you. She said you slept with Ros Evans, and when she saw her little boy in town, she was really upset because he looks just like you. Maybe she's jumped to the wrong conclusion.'

'Sophie said what?' Kent pushed himself to his feet and stood over Braden. 'She reckons I slept with this Ros person—who trust me, I don't even know— and that's why she broke up with me? That's more than a bloody jumping to conclusion. It's a frigging outright lie.'

'That's what Sophie told me about an hour ago. And that's why I came straight over here.'

'Well, what I'm telling you now, is that's the biggest load of bullshit I've ever heard.'

'I hope so. I didn't believe it when Sophie first told me, but she said she knew she was right.'

'Well, I'd like to know how she's so damn sure of that. I hope you know me well enough to know that I am telling you the truth. I don't know this woman, and I've bloody well never slept with her. The only woman I've ever slept with is Sophie, and she bloody broke my heart when she left me for that jerk.' Kent's voice rose. His heart was pounding and his head began to thud again. He flopped back into the chair and put his good hand over his face. 'I'll kill the bastard. This has got Jock Evans written all over it. What a coincidence it's his sister making up this shit! Evans always wanted Sophie and he always was as jealous as hell of you and the station. After we split, I heard him mouthing off at the pub one night, and I told him to zip it. He was bragging that when he married Sophie he'd get a share in your station. He said some pretty awful things about your situation, and he was saying how he hated having your boys with them. He saw Sophie and your boys as a way to get hold of your place.'

Braden ran a hand through his hair. 'She told me he pressured her. I feel so bloody guilty. If I'd been stronger when Julia died, none of this would have happened.'

'You can't blame yourself. Sophie made her choice. But at least she showed some sense and didn't marry him. If that bastard ever shows his face around Augathella again, I'll go for him. And I'm going to go and find that damn woman and threaten her with legal action if she so much as hints that she knew me. Who else thinks that of me? Even you believed it, Braden.'

'I'm sorry, mate. I'm sorry I had to ask you if it was true. Sophie's convinced it's the truth.'

'And you know what? That hurts more than anything. That she would believe that and not come and talk to me about it. I thought she knew me better than that. I thought she loved me, but it was all on my side, obviously.'

'Hang on, mate. You don't know what he and his sister cooked up. Plus, it all happened that week, that . . . the week that Julia had her accident. None of us were thinking straight at the time.'

'The bastard. I'll bloody take him on,' Kent growled.

'Let it go. He's gone now.'

'I'll fly up there.'

'You've got a broken arm mate. Talk to Sophie. I know you still care about her, don't you?'

'Do I?' Bitterness surged into Kent's chest, and he felt physically ill. 'I don't even know if I *could* care about someone who didn't trust me. Not only did she break my heart by believing that crap, but she hurt my parents too.'

Kent hadn't noticed Braden get up, but he felt a warm hand on his shoulder. Kent looked up, surprised to find his eyes were blurred from tears.

'Mate, I think you and Sophie need to talk this out. You need to find out the truth from her. How they convinced her, and how bloody Jock Evans ever conned her into moving in with him.'

Kent shook his head. 'I don't think I want to talk to her. I don't want to know the details. It's bad enough for me that she was with him for almost two years. How can I ever forget that?'

'How about you come back with me and talk to her?'

'No way. I need to do some thinking.'

'Kent—'

'Thanks for coming over.' Kent turned away. He felt like he was going to vomit.

'Mate, I—'

'Take the rest of the beer with you.' Kent stood and went inside, closing the door behind him.

Chapter 26
Sophie

'He won't be long, Sophie. Can I make you another coffee? Get you a wine?'

Sophie shook her head and paced along the verandah again. She was waiting for Braden to come home. Callie knew what was going on and she'd come out a few times to check on her. Braden had been gone almost two hours and Sophie was stressed to the max. Braden had believed her but insisted he was going to confront Kent.

Sophie had begged him not to go, but he'd taken off.

How long did it take to ask a question and come back home?

Once the boys were in bed Callie had come out with two mugs of coffee and stayed with her. As they sat waiting, Sophie poured her heart out. Callie couldn't believe what she told her.

'Oh, love, I'm so sorry. I knew you and Kent had been together once, but I had no idea anything like that had happened. I can't believe he did that. Trust me, I know how soul-destroying it is.'

'Well, he did and I guess I can accept that he cheated on me, but I can't believe he doesn't even acknowledge his own child. He's not the man I always thought he was. Not the man I loved.'

'Are you sure the little boy is his?'

'She said Kent didn't take responsibility for his actions. She looked at the little boy and said, "Doesn't want to know about you, does he?" '

'And you really think he's Kent's child? What made you so sure?'

'He's got dark hair like Kent.'

'And?'

Sophie stared at Callie. 'I guess that's all.'

'Look, love, from what Braden said, Jock isn't a good person. I know you were with him for a couple of years, but Braden has no time for him.'

Sophie put her head down and spoke quietly.

'I wasn't with him like you think.'

Callie frowned. 'But you've only been home a couple of months?'

'It didn't take me long to realise what Jock was like. This is going to sound stupid, but we were never a couple. We had a couple of dinner dates, and a drink at the pub one night. I moved in with him to teach Kent a lesson. I was stupid. I wanted to show Kent that he wasn't the only one who could find someone else. The fact that it was Ros's brother seemed to make it better revenge.'

'Oh, Sophie. It must have been such a dreadful time for you.'

Sophie stared into the darkness. There was still no sign of any headlights on the road. 'When Braden went to pieces, I told Jock I didn't have time to see him again because I was going to look after the boys. He offered that we all move into his place. And I took up his offer. We shared his house until he wanted to move away and I brought the boys back. You probably know that because that's when Braden advertised for a nanny.'

'Look. Here he comes.' Callie's voice had Sophie's head turning to the road. Headlights lit up the road as Braden's ute came over the hill.

'I'll leave you two to talk.' Callie reached for Sophie's mug and squeezed her hand before she went inside. 'It'll be okay, Sophie. Just remember we all love you.'

Braden didn't even drive across to the shed. He pulled the ute up at the bottom of the steps and jumped out.

Sophie walked slowly down the steps to meet her brother.

He reached out and took her hands. 'It's all right, Soph. Everything's going to be all right.'

'What? How can it be all right?' A wave of despair rolled over her, despite the grin on Braden's face.

'It's not true. None of it's true.'

'Did he know about the child?' Her voice was bleak.

How could it be all right?

'I said none of it's true. Kent didn't even know who she was. He didn't sleep with her. It was all a setup.'

Sophie felt the blood leave her head and Braden grabbed for her.

'Come on, we'll get you inside.'

##

An hour later, Sophie didn't know how she felt. She didn't know what to do. Callie was sitting beside Braden, and Sophie could see she was keeping a close eye on her.

'You have to go and see him, Soph. If you're worried about going yourself, I'll take you over in the morning.'

Sophie pushed herself up from the soft sofa. 'No. I'm going to go over there now. I owe Kent a huge apology. I should never have doubted him. Back then, or when I saw her with the kid.'

'It's late,' Braden said.

'It's only eight-thirty. If it looks like he's asleep, I'll go back over in the morning.'

Braden went to speak, but Callie interrupted him. 'Leave it up to Sophie, love. She knows what she wants to do. What she needs to do.' Callie stood and came across to the door to where Sophie was standing. 'Just remember we're here for you. We always will be.' Callie looked up at Braden as she said that and a silent message passed between them.

'Okay. Be careful, there are a few roos about tonight.' Braden came over too, and put his arms around her. 'And what Callie said too.'

He dropped a kiss on the top of her head, and Sophie headed out to the ute.

She hadn't realised how much she was shaking until she tried to turn the key.

Chapter 27
Kent

Kent stood at the kitchen sink gripping the edge of the bench with his good hand for a long time after Braden left. Thoughts circled in his head, and he knew if his wrist hadn't been broken, he would have been in the air on the way to Innot Springs first thing in the morning to sort out Jock Evans.

But really, what good would that do?

The lie that had been told to Sophie had caused so much heartbreak. Maybe if it hadn't been told the week of Julia's accident, they would have sorted it and it wouldn't have been believed; there would have been time for questions. But that week had been horrendous, and Braden and Sophie had had too much else to deal with.

It was too late.

Kent leaned forward and rested his head on the counter, bracing himself with his good hand. It was hard to accept that Sophie had doubted him so easily.

After a few minutes, he stood, and tried to shake off the black feeling that was creeping into his heart. He'd survived the last two years, and this was what he'd needed to get over his love for her. He had more to worry about now than a woman who had doubted his love—Dad's dementia and looking after the station.

He had loved Sophie, but the person he had loved hadn't really been the woman he'd thought she was. Untrusting, and ready to drop him after believing one damn lie.

Kent turned the kitchen light off and walked into the living room. He'd lit the fire before Braden had turned up—luckily he'd had some kindling in the woodpile and hadn't had to fight with the axe one-handed. He put another log on the fire and half-closed the flue. It was going to be a cold night. He'd have to be up early in the morning; Jon was coming over to do some cattlework for him.

As he went to turn the living room light off and head for the shower, headlights played over the wall. Curious, Kent walked to the front door, and his heart stilled as Gladys, Sophie's yellow Camry pulled up outside the house.

For a minute he was tempted to turn the light off and ignore her. It was clear that Braden had told Sophie what he'd said, and she'd hot-footed it over here, thinking everything could be mended with a simple, 'here I am.'

Well, Sophie Cartwright could go take a flying leap. He didn't know if he'd ever forgive her for believing that about him. And he didn't particularly like the nasty person she'd turned into since she'd been living with Jock Evans. Braden had called it mental health, Kent called it downright bitchy.

Despite his anger, Kents's hands shook and his heart thumped as her light footsteps sounded on the steps and then along the verandah.

He walked slowly to the front door and as he opened it, her hand was raised about to knock.

For a moment their eyes met, and then Kent looked away.

'Sophie?' he said tersely. 'I was about to go to bed. What do you want?'

Her eyes widened at his rude greeting and a glimmer of guilt settled in him but he pushed it away.

'I need to talk to you,' she said.

'I've got an early start tomorrow.' He ignored the quivering of her bottom lip.

'Fair enough. Can I come in for just a moment? I really do need to talk to you.'

Reluctantly he opened the screen door and held it as she walked past him. Her familiar perfume washed over him, and his resolve weakened slightly. He gritted his teeth and made himself think of Jock Evans. The man who'd shared her bed for the past two years.

Kent turned and faced the woman he'd once loved.

Had. Remember *had.*

'So? What did you want to talk about that couldn't wait?' He folded his arms as best he could with a damn cast on and stared at her. 'Did you want to organise that date you won at the concert? I think it's expired.'

Sophie stood straight and bit her bottom lip, and her voice wavered.

He stared.

'I owe you an apology, Kent. Braden told me what you told him this afternoon. I want to tell you I'm sorry and that I do believe you.'

He shrugged. 'Good. Is that all?' His voice was harder than it had ever been in his life. But damn, how much had she hurt him? How much of his happiness and his life had she taken away by believing that lie?

Hurt crossed her face and he saw the instant that she pulled herself together. 'Yes, that's all. Thank you for your time.'

He crossed the room back to the door and held it open. 'If that's all . . .'

Her expression was blank. 'Yes, I guess that's all. Unless you want to talk?'

He raised an eyebrow. 'The time for talking is long gone. You made your choice, and I learned to live with it. Just because you know now that your choice was wrong, doesn't mean that everything should be rosy again. I've moved on, Sophie. I don't know what you expected or what you wanted, but there's nothing left for me.' The lie was bitter in his mouth, but the need to lash out and hurt her, as much as he'd hurt for the past two years, was impossible to ignore.

'Okay, I just wanted you to know I'm very sorry. I'll go and I'll leave you in peace.'

She walked past him but he couldn't let her have the last word. He reached out and put his hand on her arm. The feel of her soft skin beneath his rough fingers sent a shaft of unbearable memory rocketing though him.

'What did you think I'd do, Sophie? Welcome you with open arms? Forgive you for doubting me? Well, it's way too late for that. I know now you never loved me. If you had, there was no way you would have believed that shit.'

'I—'

'No, I don't want to hear anything more. We were over two years ago when you chose that path, so there's no point rehashing it now. Good night, Sophie. And goodbye.'

How the hell he managed to keep it together until she walked out and he shut the door behind her, Kent would never know. He'd gone so close to taking her into his arms and pretending that the past two years hadn't happened.

He still loved Sophie Cartwright and probably would for the rest of his life, but he wasn't going to risk his heart being broken again.

The sound of Gladys leaving his driveway broke his heart all over again.

Chapter 28
Sophie

All of Sophie's hopes and dreams sank like a stone as she drove towards the gate of *Lara Waters*. She shook her head from side to side and bit her lip as her throat ached. Regret sat in her chest like a stone.

No. How could she have ever doubted Kent? She had caused this whole mess.

All she wanted to do was keep driving. Leave this unhappiness behind her. Escape to somewhere where there was no deceit. No sadness. A place where she could find happiness again. Tears welled in her eyes and spilled over onto her cheeks. Kent hadn't even given her a chance to explain.

All she had seen was the glittering darkness of his eyes. The man who had once loved her, the man who had laughed with her. The man she had hoped to spend the rest of her life with, had looked at her with hate in his eyes. And she couldn't blame him.

But I loved him so much. I still do.

Sophie knew she'd never stopped loving Kent, even when she'd believed the worst of him.

Her heart ached as she gripped the steering wheel and turned for home.

Home?

Kilcoy Station, where Braden and Callie and the boys were about to make a happy future if Callie accepted her bother's proposal. And Sophie was sure she would. She could see the love she had for Braden and the boys in her every word and action.

Tears blurred Sophie's vision, and she flicked the headlights onto high beam as she approached the crossroads. The road to the left led to *Kilcoy Station,* and straight ahead led to Augathella and the highway to freedom.

A new future for me. A future where no one would know what a fool she'd been. Where no one knew how she'd been gullible, and thrown away true love.

She sighed, closed her eyes for a brief second, knowing she had to go home. In her hurry to get to Kent, she hadn't even brought her purse with her.

Opening her eyes, she approached the cross roads. Turning left towards Kilcoy Station she vowed she would leave in the morning.

Increasing her speed, Gladys juddered in the deep corrugations. Braden needed to get the road graded. Sophie hadn't even noticed them before in her hurry to get to Kent.

As the wheels hit a patch of bulldust, she slowed the car, and glanced to the right quickly as a shape shadowed the driver's window.

The car slewed as she slammed her foot on the brake pedal hard. *But too late*.

A huge kangaroo bounced off her door and flew up onto the windscreen. The glass shattered and as she pumped the brakes again, it bounced off the bonnet and landed in front of the car. She wrenched the steering wheel to the left but Gladys was already heading off the road as the front left tyre followed the corrugation. She hit the ditch and the car began to roll.

Sophie screamed, let go of the steering wheel and covered her head with her arms. It was too late to do anything else.

##

Drip. Drip. Drip.

Liquid dripping on the side of Sophie's face woke her. Confused, she opened her eyes, not knowing where she was for a few seconds and why there was water dripping on her face. She wrinkled her nose as the pungent smell of petrol burned her nostrils, and it all came slamming back.

She'd rolled Gladys after hitting a roo. Her limbs trembled with shock and cold in the total dark. She tried to sit up, fumbling for her phone but she couldn't find it. She couldn't see outside or where Gladys had ended up, and she could only hope she wasn't in the irrigation channel. Her face was wet, and when she lifted her hand it came away covered in something sticky. She put her fingers to her mouth and knew straight away it was the metallic taste of blood. Her heartbeat picked up and she panicked, not knowing what to do, or where the blood was coming from

Take a deep breath, calm down.

She had to find her phone. She had to call Braden. Trying to stay calm, she braced herself and undid the seat belt and fell, jarring her arm on the door catch as she landed on the inside of the door. She scrabbled around feeling for her phone but had no luck. As she moved, the smell of petrol got stronger and she knew she had to get out of the car.

Her head spun as she pushed the door handle, and to her great relief, the door opened and she fell out onto hard dirt, not into water.

Her hand pressed into a sharp rock, and Sophie cried out as it sliced her skin open.

Pushing herself to her feet she backed away just in time as a flash of flame was followed by a loud explosion that filled the night air.

Gladys was on fire.

Blocking the thought of snakes in the knee-deep grass, Sophie ran from the car, getting as far away as she could. The orange glow split the night sky and the irrigation ditch lit up in front of her. She pulled herself up onto the edge.

She looked at the channel that snaked ahead into the dark, and then back at Gladys. If she followed the channel, it would take her back to Kilcoy Station. There was no point staying on the road; there'd be no traffic out here at this time of night. The road only led to their station and it ended there. It would be more direct to follow the irrigation channel. Her eyes gradually adjusted in the faint starlight. Taking a deep breath, she set off slipping and sliding in the soft red dust.

After only a hundred metres or so, her head began to spin and she knew she couldn't risk falling into the channel. Her legs throbbed and a cold feeling rose in her chest.

Sophie sank to her knees and began to cry.

Chapter 29
Kent

Kent paced the living room. His first thoughts were that Sophie had got everything she deserved He ran his hand through his hair, going over their conversation. Remorse filled him. He'd gone out to the veranda and watched Gladys until the tail lights disappeared and then he realised there was no point standing out there any longer. She wouldn't come back; he knew he'd been too harsh on Sophie.

He tried to be fair and put himself in the same position as she'd been in, imagining what he would have done if he'd thought she'd cheated on him.

He would have been angry and probably shut down for a while. He had to admit he wouldn't have gone looking for her.

Pride was a terrible thing.

A destructive emotion.

But no matter how he tried to imagine it, he knew he could never imagine the circumstances of that week when Julia died.

He'd give it a few days, and go and see Sophie.

Too wired to go to bed, he headed to the kitchen and was trying to fill the kettle when the phone rang.

He crossed to the bench, glanced at the clock and picked up the handset. 'Kent Mason.'

'Kent. I'm sorry to bother you and I know it's probably the worst timing ever, but I just wanted to check that Sophie was still with you. Just tell me to butt out, once you reassure me.'

'Sophie? No, she only stayed a short time. She left here a couple of hours ago.'

'She left?' Braden's reply came quickly.

'Yes.'

'She's not home yet. I thought you two must have made your peace when she didn't come back.'

'She left here about nine. She only stayed ten minutes.'

'What? Did she say where she was going?'

'No. Are you sure she's not home?'

'Positive. I've been waiting for her and assumed she was still at your place.'

'Would she have gone into town?

'I doubt it. Jeez, I hope she hasn't broken down.'

Or worse, Kent thought.

'I'll go and look for her. I'll follow the road to your place,' Kent said.

'Thanks, mate. I'll start this end. Hopefully one of us will come across her.'

'We should do. If she's broken down, one of us will find her. She would have had the sense to stay in the car. It's cold out there.'

'Right. I'll see you in twenty.' Braden's voice was tight.

Kent grabbed his keys and raced out to his ute. He ignored the pain in his arm as he put it into gear and dropped the clutch. The wheels spun as he accelerated down the driveway. At the gate he turned the ute onto the back road that led to Charleville. The road was dry and there had been no wind. His headlights lit up the fresh tracks of Gladys's tyres in the soft red dirt. He kept his eyes dead ahead as he sped along the dirt road in the dark.

The lefthand turn off to Kilcoy Station wasn't far ahead. As he approached the intersection, he looked for her tyre tracks and relief filled him as they veered to the left. Kent swung the wheel to the left and stayed in top gear to save his arm. Ahead there was a faint glow above the road and his eyes narrowed.

Panic clenched his chest as he realised it was fire.

'Jesus, no!' he yelled as he accelerated down the corrugated road and then swerved to the side of the road before the fire ahead. Almost falling out of the vehicle, Kent found his balance and ran across to the still smoking wreck. In the middle of the road was the carcass of a huge roo, and he could see what had happened. Sophie had hit the roo, and the car had rolled onto the passenger side.

Frantic, he put his hand to his eyes and looked into the darkness, but there was no sign of Sophie. Panic closed his throat as he considered the worst. He knew he was responsible for this.

He'd refused to listen to the woman he still loved and he'd sent her out into the night.

The rumble of a vehicle came from ahead and in the distance, he saw the lights of Braden's twin cab approaching from *Kilcoy Station*. He took another step towards the smouldering vehicle, his whole body tense, praying she had got out.

As he walked around it, his spirits lifted as he noticed the dirt beside the car was disturbed. Relief filled him as he saw footsteps leading into the bush.

Thank God. She'd managed to get out; Braden must have picked her up and was coming to tell him she was okay.

Kent sat on the side of the road, his body still shaking from seeing her car burned out. He waited for Braden to reach him. A couple of minutes passed and he managed to get his breath back; the tension easing a little.

The instant he saw Sophie he would tell her how he felt. The thought of how close he had gone to losing her steeled his resolve. He stood as Braden's twin cab approached.

Kent's spirits plummeted when he saw that Braden was alone. Braden's twin cab slewed to a stop, and he jumped out, his face white.

'Holy hell. Is that Sophie's Camry?'

'Yes, it's Gladys, but look.' Kent grabbed his arm. 'It's all right, mate. She got out. Look here, you can see her footsteps. I thought you must have picked her up down the road.'

'No, I didn't see her and I was looking. Jesus, Kent, she must be hurt. She could be anywhere out there.' Braden hurried across to Sophie's Gladys. 'Fucking roos. She's hit a fucking roo and rolled.'

'Calm down, mate. We'll find her. You take my ute and go bush on the other side of the road. Put the headlights on high beam It's higher than yours. I'll go on foot on this side and see if I can see any tracks in the dirt.' Kent ran back and grabbed a flashlight from his ute, closely followed by Braden.

Braden jumped into Kent's ute and headed into the scrub on the other side of the road. Kent walked past the wreck lighting the way with the strong flashlight, keeping his eyes on footsteps in the red dirt. He called out when he spotted where she'd left the road.

'Sophie,' he yelled. 'Sophie, can you hear me?'

The only sound was the faint hum of his ute as Braden ploughed through the low bush on the other side. Ahead was an irrigation channel, half-full with brown water. He reached the edge and shone the light ahead, and sure enough her footsteps were along the edge.

'Good girl,' he muttered. Sophie would have known it was quicker to follow the channel home. He hurried back to the road and jumped into Braden's ute and drove back the way he'd walked.

There was still no sign of her. Every hundred metres or so, he leaned out the window and checked that he could still see her footsteps in the fine red dirt.

The last time he slowed to check, her footsteps had disappeared. Kent stopped the car and climbed out and ran back along the channel. About fifty metres back, the track stopped. He held his hand to his eyes and scanned the bush around him.

'Sophie, where are you?'

About a hundred metres towards the road, there was a stand of gidgee scrub silhouetted by the moonlight. Kent paused as a faint cry came from that direction.

A bird? Or a cry for help.

'Sophie,' he yelled again, flashing his light ahead as he ran towards the stand of low trees.

'Braden?'

He stumbled as her voice came from that direction.

'Sophie, where are you?'

As he got closer, there was a movement to his left and as he turned the light, Sophie pushed herself to her feet. 'Kent?'

He covered the distance quickly and took her in his arms, his eyes scanning her for injuries.

'Sophie, my love. Are you all right? Are you hurt?'

'What did you call me?'

'I'm so sorry. It was all my fault. I should never have spoken to you like that.'

She looked up at him. 'What did you call me, Kent?'

'What I should have told you before, instead of being a prize bastard. I love you, Sophie. I always have and I always will. I died a hundred deaths when I saw Gladys burning. I thought you were still inside her.'

Kent closed his eyes as Sophie's arms crept around his waist, and he barely noticed the throbbing of his wrist. He lowered his head and rested his cheek against hers. 'I'm never going to let you go again, Soph. I love you. Can you forgive me for the way I spoke to you?'

Her eyes were wide as she pulled back and stared at him. 'It was all my fault.

'No, it was mine. Are you hurt?'

'Just a bit of a sore head, and I cut my hand on a rock. I'm all right. Do you really mean what you said?'

'Of course I do. I've never stopped loving you.'

'And I love you, Kent. I always have. I'm so sorry.' Her voice was thick with tears.

'We've got a lot of talking to do, Soph, but first we need to let Braden know you're okay. If it wasn't for this blasted arm, I'd carry you to the ute.'

He put his good arm around her and kept his eyes on hers until they reached the twin cab. Her cheeks were flushed and she was smiling.

'Whatever happens, whatever we have to talk about, it's okay,' he said.

'Kent, I need you to know one thing right now.' Sophie put her hands on his shoulders. 'I never slept with Jock. It was just a share arrangement to start with and he was helping me out. I need you to know that right now. We can talk later.'

Joy burst through Kent as he held her close again. 'We can talk later. We have all the time in the world.'

Sophie lifted her arms around his neck and pulled Kent's head closer to hers.

'Kiss me?' She pressed her lips against his mouth. 'Please, kiss me, Kent. It's been such a long time.'

An unbelievable feeling ran through him as she closed her eyes and his lips claimed hers.

Sophie opened her eyes as he murmured against her lips. 'Way too long.'

Kent was still kissing Sophie when Braden drove up a few minutes later.

Epilogue
Two days later

Sophie stood beside Kent in the living room of *Lara Waters* when he called his parents. According to the itinerary on the fridge, their ship was docking in Brisbane this morning.

'Mum. Hi, it's me.' His arm was around her. 'I've got someone who'd like to say hello to you. And I have some news I know you'll be very excited about.'

Kent handed the phone to Sophie but kept his arm around her. She leaned into him, unable to believe the happiness of the past two days. She kept pinching herself, waiting to wake up, but it was true.

She and Kent were back together. And. . .

'Hello, Rhonda,' she said shyly. 'It's Sophie.'

'Sophie? How lovely. It sounds like my son actually listened to me for a change. How are you, sweetie? It's so lovely to hear your voice again.'

'I'm really good,' Sophie replied with a smile up at Kent. 'Really good. I'd love to see you. We were wondering what your plans were as we'd like you to . . . hang on, I'll put Kent back on. I want him to tell you the news.'

Sophie leaned into Kent as he took the phone from her.

'I know you were going to stay in Brisbane for a while, but we just wanted to know when you'll be home.'

Kent smiled at Sophie as his mother obviously wanted to know more.

'Well, we want to know because we want to set the date for our engagement party.'

Sophie grinned up at him as she heard Rhonda's delighted squeal through the phone.

'Next week? You're going to rush home, Mum? Yes, we'll be here. Sophie and I aren't going anywhere, are we?'

'No, we're not,' she said as she reached up to kiss her fiancé.

##

Later that afternoon, Sophie parked Kent's ute near the shed at *Kilcoy Station*. Braden had asked them to come over and babysit the boys. Since the night Kent had found her near the irrigation channel, they hadn't been apart. Sophie stayed at *Lara Waters,* and there had been many hours spent talking.

Kent swung his good arm around her shoulders as they walked to the house. It sounded like there was a battle going on inside, and sure enough Petie came racing out, closely followed by Nigel.

'Aunty Soph,' Nigel said urgently. 'Don't tell Rory where we're hiding.'

Two of the boys' dogs followed them into the dog kennels, and then all was quiet.

'You ready for a fun night?' Sophie asked Kent with a teasing grin.

'Will a broken wrist get me out of playing hide and seek?'

'Not a chance.'

Callie came out of the kitchen and hugged them both. 'Fabulous news, you pair. I'm so happy for you. Braden couldn't wait to get home and tell me the other night. The best news ever!'

'Where are you pair off to tonight?' Kent asked. 'Is there something on in Augathella?'

Callie shrugged. 'I have no idea. Braden said it's a surprise and told me to get dressed up.'

Sophie hid her smile. She knew exactly what her brother had planned for tonight. If all went to plan, the engagement party in two weeks would be a double celebration. She hadn't told Kent what was going on, but he'd soon know.

They waved a nervous-looking Braden and a bemused Callie off, just before Kent was roped into the game of hide and seek.

Sophie stood on her tiptoes and kissed him before he headed off with the three boys. 'I'll go and get some dinner sorted. Do you mind if I ask Amelia to come over? I feel a bit guilty that I haven't been here to cook. The whole crowd of contractors arrive tomorrow, so I'm going to have to start work for Braden.'

'As long as you come home to me every night.' Kent kissed her and the three boys made gagging noises.

'Not you too,' Rory exclaimed with disgust. 'Dad and Callie are always kissy-kissy too.'

'Love is grand,' Kent said with a laugh. 'You'll find out one day.'

'Rory's already got a girlfriend at school,' Nigel teased.

'I have not!'

'You have so!'

'Have fun.' Sophie threw Kent a smile as she headed up to the dongas to see Amelia.

As she walked to the accommodation area, an unfamiliar ute came along the road from the back of the property. She waited and was surprised to see Kent's singing partner, Ben Riley in the cab.

'Hey, Ben. Are you after Braden? He's not home.'

'No. I knew he was going out. I just have to check on the foundations of the new donga he's building. He asked me to check the concrete thickness. I had to come out and see Jon and Fallon, so I came across the back way.'

'Kent's here too,' she said looking down at the engagement ring on her left hand. They hadn't shared the news outside family yet. She'd let Kent tell his friend after they told Jacinta.

'Great, haven't seen him since the rodeo. I'll catch him on my way out. This won't take long. Is that the dongas over there?'

'Yes, there's only one of the two occupied at the moment. The new one's pegged out at the far end.'

'Thanks. I won't be long.'

Sophie detoured via the cookhouse. She'd placed an order online at Kent's place yesterday and Callie had asked them to deliver it to the cool room in the cookhouse.

All was well, and she closed the cookhouse door behind her, planning the meal to feed the group tomorrow night.

'It's a bloody danger!' Her head flew up as Ben's angry voice reached her as she approached the dongas. 'It needs to be in a kennel or in a muzzle.'

'Well, if you spoke to *him*—not *it*—properly and not just barged past, he—'

Sophie didn't hear the rest of what Amelia had to say because Ben's roar drowned out her words.

'So it's my fault your bloody dog bit me?'

'Oh no,' Sophie muttered under her breath as she hurried over.

Ben and Amelia stood glaring at each other, her hand at the scruff of her dog's neck. If dogs could glare, Chilli was glaring at Ben too.

'Hi Amelia,' Sophie said brightly, ignoring the tension filling the air. 'I just came down to ask you to the house for dinner tonight, but it looks like you guys need to chill out a bit. How about you both come with me now, and we can have a beer or a wine? Ben, you've knocked off now, haven't you?'

He nodded. 'I have.'

'Well, both of you come up to the house and I'll tell Kent you're on the way. I think he'll be pleased to have a break from the boys.'

Sophie turned and headed back to the house to tell Kent they had company.

It would be an interesting way to spend the time, while she waited for Braden and Callie to come back.

Hopefully engaged.

Sophie smiled as she lifted her hand and her engagement ring sparkled in the late afternoon sunlight.

Outback Winds:
The Jillaroo

ANNIE SEATON

The Augathella Girls: Book 4

Dedication

For our four beautiful grandchildren:

Benny, Charlotte, Charlie and Georgia.

Augathella Characters-Book 4

Amelia Foley	Jillaroo
Ben Riley	Shire Council Inspector
Sophie Cartwright	Station Cook
Kent Mason	Sophie's fiancé
Braden Cartwright	Sophie's brother
Callie Young	Braden's partner
Jon Ingram	Station Manager
Fallon Malone	Helicopter pilot
Jacinta Mason	Kent's sister
Harry Higgins	New doctor in town
Ruth Malone	Fallon's mother
Jenny Riley	Ben's mother

Chapter 1
Amelia

'That thing is a bloody danger!'

Amelia stared at the man who was glaring at Chilli Girl, her gentle golden retriever.

'It needs to be in a kennel or wear a muzzle.' His mouth was set in a straight line, and his tone was decidedly unfriendly. Normally Amelia wouldn't have flared up, but she'd just hung up on a call from her father and her mood had plummeted.

'Well, if you spoke to *him*—not *it*—properly and not just barged past, he—' she put her hands on her hips as Chilli crept behind her legs—'look, you've scared her.'

'So it's my fault your bloody dog bit me?' He frowned. 'He's a danger.'

'Chilli Girl's not a danger or a thing!' Amelia reached back and held onto Chilli Girl.

'Chilli Girl? I thought you said it was a he?'

'So if *it* was a he, or *she* was a he, she'd be more dangerous, and you'd be happy to yell at her?'

'What the—?'

The guy—who was starting to look familiar—and Amelia stood glaring at each other; her hand was on the scruff of Chilli's neck. If dogs could glare, Chilli was glaring at him too. Not that she'd hurt anyone, she was too gentle; she was just taking Amelia's side.

As she should.

Amelia lifted her chin, and Chilli gave a little whimper, sensing her mistress's mood. The mood that had more to do with her family than this guy. *He'd* just added to her day. She turned away from the cranky man and crouched down.

'It's okay, sweetie. Don't be sad. I'm fine. I'll be fine,' she murmured. 'No point letting two cranky men upset my day.' Amelia led Chilli to the gate of the new fence she'd put up, and gave her a gentle push. 'I put some treats in your bowl. Go and cheer up, I'll be fine.'

As she turned back to the man, he looked at her as though she was a complete ditz. That set a flame to the temper that had been simmering since Dad had demanded she come home this morning. He'd found her a job in Weipa, not far from their cattle station. A receptionist for the new solicitor who happened to be a friend of his.

'What?' she snapped. 'What are you looking at me like that for?'

He shook his head. 'I'm sorry. I don't mean to be rude, but you don't know if your dog is a dog or a bitch?'

'Don't call her a bitch. I hate that word. She's Chilli Girl, and she's a girl.'

'Okay, whatever she is, she needs controlling.'

'No, she doesn't. She didn't *bite* you, she was just being friendly. She liked you until you upset me and now if you want to get to know her, you'll have to win her back. She doesn't like people who speak to me like you just did.'

He pointed down to his work trousers. He looked totally out of place out here on the cattle station. Neatly creased trousers, a long-sleeved business shirt, a tie and a clipboard in his hand. '*She* ripped my trousers. Before I spoke to you.'

'I'll pay to replace them. She wasn't trying to hurt you; she wanted to play I've been on the phone and she was bored. Chilli's like a child. She needs stimulation, and she needs to play. I haven't had a chance to take her for a walk this morning. I'm sorry that she chose you as a potential playmate. You just happened to wander past at the wrong time. What are you doing anyway? It looks like you're working here, Mr—?' She widened her eyes as a thought came to her. 'You're not my new neighbour are, you? If you are, you'll have to make friends with Chilli Girl. I really hope you're not about to move in next door. You don't look like a ringer. No, you're not. You're a professional of some sort. The trousers, the long-sleeved shirt, the clipboard. Dead giveaway.' Amelia watched as his expression changed from disdain to mirth. 'Don't you dare laugh at me! It's disrespectful unless I've done something to amuse you.'

He chuckled again and her temper soared.

'I told you not to laugh at me.'

'I'm sorry. I'm not laughing at you. I'm laughing at the situation.' He smoothed his free hand down his perfectly pressed trousers—albeit with a *slight* tear—and then held it out to her. 'Let's start again. 'I'm Ben Riley and you're—?'

'I'm cross,' Amelia said, glancing to the left as she became aware of someone standing a short distance away from them

'Hi, Amelia,' Sophie said brightly, looking from one to the other with a quizzical expression on her face. 'I came down to ask you to the house for a drink, but it looks like you guys need to chill out a bit. How about you *both* come with me now, and we can have a beer or a wine? Ben, you've knocked off now, haven't you?'

He nodded. 'I have.'

'Well, both of you come up to the house and I'll tell Kent you're on the way. I think he'll be pleased to have a break from the boys. He's probably hiding from them.'

Sophie turned and headed back to the house.

Amelia looked at Ben for a long moment and took his outstretched hand. 'I guess you know my name now. I'm Amelia Foley and I won't say it's a pleasure to meet you. Yet.'

Chapter 2
Ben

Ben's cranky mood disappeared as quickly as the red dust from the willy willy that puffed along the fence behind them. 'I'm sorry you're still cross, and I'm sorry I was angry at your Chilli Girl. It's not been a good day for me. Let's take up Sophie's offer and start over.'

He was pleased when Amelia Foley reached over and shook his hand. And was surprised to feel the callouses on her small hand. She was petite and looked more suited to being at one of his mother's garden parties than bunking in a donga out in the bush. She was finely built and quite pretty. Dark hair, rosy cheeks—although they could be from the temper he'd caused. She didn't look like someone who would talk the leg off an iron pot, but once she started talking there was no stopping her.

Wide blue eyes held his. 'I'm Amelia Foley and now I know who you are. You played in the duo at that Easter concert.'

'I did.'

'So, what are you doing out here with a clipboard?' Her voice still held a slight tinge of anger, and her cheeks stayed that pretty rosy pink.

'Well, to answer your questions in order. No, I'm not your new neighbour. And I'm carrying a clipboard because I'm writing down the specs for the new dongas that Braden is going to build.'

'Why?'

'Because I'm an inspector at the local shire council, and I like what he's doing. I was interested to see them. I'm not inspecting or anything. There's no need to do that on a private station. He did ask me to check the concrete thickness, but that's a favour, not a council job.'

'Good.'

'Why good? That I'm not inspecting?'

'No. That you're not my neighbour.'

'No, I'm not. So, I guess you're still cross at me. I don't blame you.'

'Sort of. You wore my bad temper because I was already a bit out of sorts, but that's another story you don't want to hear. Okay, we'll start again. It *is* a pleasure to meet you, Ben Riley. I've forgiven you now, but you have to promise to be nice to Chilli Girl.'

'I can do that.' He nodded, but he wasn't going to let her get away with being rude to him 'And likewise, you're forgiven. Are you on a bush holiday? You're a long way from town. I didn't think Braden had started the holiday thing yet. He's been talking about it for a while.'

'No, I'm not on a holiday thing. I'm here for work.'

'Ah, you're the new nanny, now that Callie's working at the school.'

'No.'

'The cook?' He shook his head. He couldn't see her in the cookhouse. She looked like someone who should be sitting in a posh restaurant. Her voice was very cultured even when she was rabbiting on.

'No.'

'The housekeeper?'

'You're full of assumptions, aren't you, Ben Riley?'

'Sorry, you're hard to pick. I'm usually on the ball.'

'With women?'

He realised her hand was still in his and he let go. 'Hey, I'm not trying to come onto you or anything.'

'That's good because I wouldn't be interested if you were.'

His anger crept back in. 'Ditto. But I am going to ask you out for a coffee if you're in town, to apologise for my behaviour.'

He frowned.

Where the hell had that come from?

Her shoulders straightened and he was slightly offended when she laughed. 'No, thank you. I'm here to work, and besides, I don't know when I'll get to town again. It depends on what days Braden wants me to work.'

'Okay, what sort of work?'

'The cattle. I'm the new jillaroo.'

Surprise filled him again; that was the last thing he would have picked for her. It must have shown on his face as she put her hands on her hips.

'Sexist too, Ben Riley. Anyway, Sophie's waiting for us at the house. I'll meet you up there.' She turned away, but he reached out and held her arm, not wanting her to think he was a total arse, but the words that spilled out weren't what he'd intended. What was it about her that pushed his buttons? Delicate and dainty, but as strong as steel, she stared at him with her chin up.

'Hang on a minute. I haven't finished. In my role with the shire, I'm going to direct you to bring your dog, he, she or it, whatever, to the dog obedience classes in town.

'What? Why should I do that?'

'You don't want a dog bite complaint put in, do you?'

'You'd do that? You know, I really *don't* like you.'

'Yes, I'd do that.' He fought the grin that threatened as he looked at the determined expression on her face. 'For the safety of the Augathella community.' The grin tugged harder as he looked at the docile golden retriever sitting there with a smile on *her* face.

She wouldn't agree to have coffee with him, but she could damn well come to town and he'd see her again.

Whether *she* liked it or not. If he had to stay in Augathella, he might as well enjoy himself.

Chapter 3
Amelia

As she and Ben approached the house—despite her instruction he go without her, *he* had waited—Amelia was surprised to see Kent, the other half of the singing duo, standing close to Sophie. From what Amelia had gathered the other day at the billy cart races, Kent and Sophie didn't get on. She'd even tried to give away the prize, she'd won. A date with Kent, the singer.

Now that Amelia had met the other half of the duo, she was pleased there hadn't been a raffle with the guitarist as the prize. She grinned; maybe they'd known they wouldn't sell many tickets for a date with a cranky man.

Sophie and Kent exchanged a glance as she and Ben came up the steps. Amelia was on one side of the wide stairs; Ben was on the other. She'd left Chilli in the fenced enclosure at the donga and Ben hadn't commented. In fact, they hadn't exchanged a word as they'd walked the hundred metres across to the main homestead.

Amelia had looked around with a satisfied sigh as they'd walked up. She hadn't had a chance to see much of the place so far, but she really liked what she could see.

The property wasn't as big as her family property up in the Gulf Country, but it was nowhere near as neat and tidy around the homestead as Dad insisted theirs was kept.

All the time. Not a blade of grass out of place. Not a recalcitrant drooping flower to be seen.

Then again, it made a difference when you could afford to employ a gardener just to maintain the house yard. A house yard that was almost a thousand kilometres from the nearest city and decent shops. Not to mention two and a half thousand kilometres to the boarding schools she and her five brothers had attended.

Despite the untidiness of the house yard, the unkempt garden, the swing set, and the bikes and toys scattered on the unmown grass held an appeal that was lacking at her family home. When she and the boys had been growing up—when they'd not been shipped off to boarding school, they had to keep their bikes neatly in the shed. She certainly couldn't imagine one of Mum's garden parties being held here, but the station had a warm welcoming feel.

It was a real *home*. A happy home. Amelia was sure she was going to be very happy working here for Braden Cartwright.

In fact, she was happy with everything here so far—except for the shire inspector. Sophie and Callie had welcomed her warmly, and Braden seemed like a really nice guy.

'Hi, guys. Grab a seat.' Kent smiled down at Sophie. 'I've just got to make a quick call and I'll bring some drinks out. Are you in a hurry, Ben?'

'No, not at all. How's the wrist?'

'Getting there. I'm actually coping a lot better.'

Envy ran through Amelia as she saw the way that Kent looked down at Sophie before he headed inside. Looked like they'd made up.

Amelia sat on the double sofa opposite the table and immediately regretted it when Ben smiled and sat beside her.

What was it with this guy?

One minute he was cranky and bossing her around, the next he was smiling at her and asking her out.

No way.

Amelia moved as close to her end of the soft seat as she could.

'Looking forward to starting work, Amelia?' Sophie sat on the chair across from them.

'I am. I was hoping to catch up with Braden and see what the schedule is. Is he around this afternoon?'

Sophie smiled, an air of suppressed excitement about her. 'Not at the moment. He and Callie had some important business to attend to. They should be back in an hour or two.'

'No matter. I'll see him in the morning. I'm getting myself organised.'

'So, a jillaroo, hey?' Ben said. 'A trainee station hand.'

Amelia raised her eyebrows. 'What's with the tone, Mr Inspector?'

Sophie's eyes widened.

'My *tone*?'

Amelia fought her rising temper as he kept talking.

'I guess I'm surprised that Braden's happy with a trainee when he has so much work on. Is this your first stint out of the city?'

'This is my first job in the west,' she answered. He didn't have to know she called herself a jillaroo because it sounded better than a ringer.

Bloody assumption-making rudeness. She really didn't like him. And she'd been honest enough to tell him that. No wonder Chilli Girl had bitten his trousers; she was an excellent judge of character.

Sophie stood. 'Okay, guys. Kent and I are babysitting. The boys have been playing hide and seek with him. They love hiding inside and goodness knows what sort of a mess they've made in there. Petie loves to get in the linen cupboard, but he pulls everything off the shelves before he climbs in, not knowing he's leaving a big clue in the hallway. I'll hunt them outside for a while.' Sophie disappeared through the door, and there was an uncomfortable silence between Amelia and Ben when they were left alone.

She cleared her throat and tried to think of something to say. He leaned back against the soft cushion, looking very much at ease.

Finally, she resorted to the weather. 'Looks like it hasn't rained out here for a while?'

'No.' The one-word answer didn't encourage that conversation to continue.

Stuff him. She could wait him out. He didn't know that she was used to dealing with five brothers who delighted in pushing her buttons. Silence was always a good strategy to keep control.

Amelia fought the chuckle that bubbled up. Her other strategy to feel comfortable with strangers was to talk non-stop until the other person interrupted. Mum had tried to teach her that wasn't ladylike, and that had made her do it all the more.

The silence was finally broken by pounding footsteps and happy yells as Braden's three boys ran out onto the wooden veranda.

They pulled up quickly when they saw they had company. Amelia was impressed with their manners as the tallest boy walked over.

'Hello, we saw you at the billy carts. Where's your dog?'

Ben gave her a look and she glared back at him before she turned to the boys.

'Hi there. Chilli's over having a snooze at our donga. Now let me see if I get your names right.' She put one finger to her lips. 'Rory, Nigel and—'

'I'm Petie, and it's really nice to see you again.' The littlest boy held his hand out and she took it with a smile.

'It's good to see you again, too, Petie. You have lovely manners.'

It was so good to have that uncomfortable silence broken.

'Callie taught me how to say that. I think she's going to be our new mum. I really, really hope so.'

'Ssh, Petie. Dad said we had to keep it a secret.' Rory lowered his voice. 'We're not allowed to say, but he's taken Callie to the range for the sunset and—'

'And he's going to ask her to be our new mum.' Rory obviously didn't want to be left out.

'Looks like we'll have to keep a secret,' Ben said.

'Hi Ben,' Rory said. 'Did you know we all have new dogs too? Callie said we might have to take them to your puppy school in Augathella to teach them some manners.'

'That sounds like a plan. What are their names?'

'Bumper, Tweedle and Apricot,' Nigel said.

'Great names, Nigel.' Amelia couldn't help her smile despite the new knowledge that Ben had something to do with the puppy school in town. She turned to look at Ben. 'Would that be the same school as the dog obedience school?'

He held her gaze steadily. 'It is, but Nigel, it's not my puppy school.'

'Can you come and watch if we come into town?'

'I can. I help out sometimes.'

Amelia raised her eyebrows as he glanced over at her, that damn sexy grin on his face again.

Gosh, where did that thought come from? She didn't even like the man.

'Amelia—is it okay if I call you that? —is going to bring her dog in too.' Ben glanced across at her again. He'd been doing that a lot since he'd sat beside her.

'Oh cool,' Nigel said. 'Would Chilli like to come and play with our pups now?'

Normally Amelia wouldn't have hesitated, but she was aware of Ben watching her. 'Maybe later. She's having a sleep now.'

'Okay, maybe we'll see her at the doggie school in town,' Nigel called over his shoulder as the three boys took off down the steps leaving her alone with Ben again.

Before the silence could become uncomfortable, Kent walked out juggling a tray with six glasses. Sophie was behind him, carrying a bottle of champagne.

'We're both really pleased to have you here with us to celebrate.'

'Callie and Braden's news?' Ben asked.

'No, our news. I asked Sophie to marry me and she said yes.' Kent beamed as he put his arm around Sophie. 'You guys are the first to know outside the family. We were waiting for Jacinta—my sister—to come home from Brisbane before we told anyone, but I just called her. We're really hoping it might be a double celebration tonight.'

Ben jumped up and hugged Sophie and then held out his hand to Kent. 'About bloody time, you two. We've all been waiting.'

Amelia stood too and came across to where the three friends were standing and gave them both a quick hug. 'Congratulations. Look, you don't want a stranger here. I'll head back to my donga and spend some time with Chilli.'

'Don't be silly.' Sophie shook her head. 'You won't do any such thing. This is going to be a party, and we'd love you to stay.'

'If you're sure?' Amelia said hesitantly.

'Absolutely,' Kent chimed in. 'Now take a seat while I get Ben to pop this cork. There are only so many things a man can do one-handed.'

The cork was popped and the fine crystal flutes filled with the effervescent liquid. When Sophie and Kent were settled on the other sofa, Ben raised his glass.

'To Sophie and Kent, may your wishes all come true.'

Amelia leaned forward and clinked her glass with the others. She watched Kent and Sophie as their engagement was toasted. The look on Kent's face as he held his fiancée's gaze was one that she hadn't seen very often. The only other time she'd seen it before was when Josh, her younger brother looked at his wife, Marnie. Sadly, Dad hadn't approved of him proposing to a station hand, and he'd given Josh an ultimatum.

The girl *or* his share in the property.

Amelia had been so proud of Josh when he'd chosen Marnie and they'd left *Granite Springs* and moved to Darwin.

Amelia hadn't had to make the choice, because being the only girl, she wouldn't get a share in the property, unless she married someone that Dad approved of. Frustration burned in her gut. She could be home working with the cattle on their spread, but to Dad, that was not a woman's role.

The last face-to-face fight she'd had with her father had seen her storming out, yelling at him. 'It's the twenty-first century, Dad. I don't know how the hell Mum's put up with you for thirty-five years.'

Today when he'd called had been the first contact she'd had with home since she'd left three months ago. And Dad hadn't changed his stance at all.

Pulling herself back to the happy moment here, she shook the thoughts of home and Dad away, and raised her glass. 'Nicely put, Ben. And yes, may all your wishes come true, Sophie and Kent. I'm really honoured to be a part of your day. I'll never forget it.'

'Thank you, Amelia. It's a very special day. It's been a long time coming, but we finally sorted ourselves out, didn't we, Kent?' Sophie looked across the yard as a white twin cab ute came up the road, slowed and turned in the gate. Excitement filled her voice. 'Oh look, here's Braden and Callie now. Oh please, please, I so hope she said yes.'

They all watched as the boys ran across to the vehicle when it pulled up outside the shed.

Amelia blinked back happy tears as Braden and Callie climbed out and held hands as they walked across to the boys.

Callie crouched down when they reached them and held her arms open. Braden stood there smiling.

'I guess she said yes,' Sophie said with a catch in her voice.

Chapter 4
Ben

'Another beer, Ben?' Braden's smile hadn't left his face since he and Callie had joined them. There'd been another round of congratulations, and then Ben had had a couple of beers.

Ben got a shock when he looked at his watch 'Geez, it's almost nine. If I have one more, I'll have to bunk here in my swag if that's okay.'

'Sure is. Did you say nine? I didn't realise how late it was. I'll light the barbie and throw some steaks on.'

'It's a wonder the boys haven't been out looking for dinner. I've been slack.' Callie stood. 'I'll get them sorted and then throw a salad together.'

'Don't worry too much, love. Let's do burgers. Does that suit everyone?' Braden stood beside Callie and put his arm around her waist. 'Kent and Soph, you're welcome to stay the night.'

'We will,' Kent agreed.

Ben nodded as well. 'Thanks, mate, I will too. I'll give you a hand to cook.' He looked over at Amelia; she was curled up in the corner of the sofa, her legs tucked beneath her. Looking up, she caught his eyes on her, and a faint tinge of pink coloured her cheeks again. She uncurled her legs and sat up.

'Can I help you in the kitchen, Callie?' She looked away from Ben.

'Thanks, Amelia. I'll get you chopping some onions. Sophie hates doing that.'

'I sure do. I'll get some tomato, lettuce and beetroot going. Burgers sound good to me. Can we have eggs on them too? I'm starving.'

'You're always starving, Sophie,' Braden teased.

'Runs in the family, big brother, and those three boys are the same. You must miss me now that I've moved over to Kent's.'

'Callie and I manage, don't we, love?'

'We do.' Callie reached up and kissed Braden's cheek.

'Do you need some buns out of the freezer? Won't take long to thaw,' Sophie asked as she stood.

'Yes, please,' Callie said.

'Come and help me, Kent.' Sophie tugged him up by his good hand. 'You should be able to manage one bag.'

'I'm not that incapacitated,' he replied, nudging her shoulder.

By nine-thirty, the steaks and eggs had been cooked, the smell of frying onions filled the air, and a long table had been set up in the breezeway.

Ben sat opposite Amelia, as the two newly-engaged couples naturally paired up. Rory, Nigel and Petie had apparently taken care of their own dinner.

'I can't be cross. They've all crashed in their bean bags in front of the television.' Callie had come out of the kitchen with her hands on her hips. 'While we were out here drinking champagne, they raided the kitchen. It won't hurt them to have Tim Tams and potato chips for dinner one night, will it?'

Sophie laughed. 'No, it won't. They were celebrating too.'

Braden had gone inside and helped Callie put the boys to bed while Kent and Ben manned the barbeque.

'Bet you didn't do this in Charters Towers,' Kent said to him as Ben flipped the steaks over.

'Only because I didn't know many people there. But I will give you that. There's nothing like country hospitality. I did miss it when I was there.'

'Yet, you're breaking your neck to get out of here. Can't understand you, mate, but each to his own.'

'Yeah. I couldn't believe it when I got seconded back to Morweh Shire. They thought they were doing me a favour sending me home.'

'They were. Who'd want to live anywhere else?'

'Me,' Ben replied.

'If you had your own place and weren't living with your olds, you might find it better.'

'Maybe.' Ben shrugged. He'd had that thought himself but he didn't want to buy his own place until he was sure where he wanted to settle. At the moment, that place wasn't Augathella.

Kent sent him a sideways look. 'Is there someone special up north? Have you left your heart there?'

'Hell, no. I'm going to stay a free agent until I'm forty. I'll think about a wife and kids then. By that time, I'll know where I want to live.'

'Famous last words, mate. I saw the way you were sussing out the new ringer. She's a looker.'

'That may be, but she's not my type.'

'Why's that?'

'She's sassy and bossy and hang on . . . did you say ringer? I thought she was a trainee jillaroo.'

'No, she's really experienced. She comes from one of the biggest stations up in the Gulf.'

'Really? She looks more like a city girl.'

'I saw you checking her out a few times tonight.'

'She sure led me on. Don't you tell her I know where she's from. I'll hold that one up my sleeve. And don't go trying to set us up.' He wasn't going to tell Kent that he'd asked her out already, and been knocked back.

Amelia's rejection had stung, but to be fair they hadn't got off on the right foot. He had to admit she was a very attractive woman, and maybe they *could* spend some time together, but her expression had shown she wasn't interested.

More than once.

And if there was one thing Ben knew, he wouldn't be pushing.

He wouldn't.

Chapter 5
Amelia

Amelia woke just after dawn as she always did. Not because it was getting light, but because Chilli Girl was making the usual "time to wake up" noises to let her know it was time to go for a walk. Amelia slipped on a pair of jeans and a hoodie over the T-shirt she'd slept in. After gathering up a doggie-disposal bag out of habit, and her phone, she slipped on a warm pair of socks and her boots. By the time she opened the door, the first fingers of sunlight were shining on the hills to the west.

She'd go for a long walk, and with any luck, Ben Riley would be gone by the time she ventured down to the homestead to have the meeting she and Braden had organised last night.

It would be interesting checking out the paddocks, she'd noticed a few cattle not far from the house yard last night before it got dark. As she stepped onto the front porch, she caught a glint of sunlight in the distance. A large expanse of water sparkled in the early sunlight.

'Good morning, Chilli Girl. Were you warm enough out here last night?' Amelia crouched down and dropped a kiss on Chilli's nose, before clipping the lead to her collar 'I can see some water. We're going to go for a long walk, and then have some breakfast.'

Even though Braden had said it was okay for Chilli to go inside the donga, Amelia hadn't thought it was the right thing to do. He'd been good enough to let her bring Chilli to a working station. If it got too cold at night, Chilli could sleep in her van at night.

They set off across the first paddock, and Amelia admired the sleek and shiny cattle in the distance. It was a glorious morning, with the promise of warmth already. Even though she'd grown up in the Gulf Country, she was well used to the cold after her ten years of boarding school in Toowoomba.

The dam was further away than she'd thought and by the time they reached it, the sun was high in the sky and she'd removed her hoodie. The dam covered a couple of acres and the paddocks around were obviously irrigated. The grass was green and lush, so different from the dry tussocky grass of the Gulf. Contentment settled over Amelia; Braden had said that the contract here was a long one if they were both happy with her first week. This morning, they'd discuss her work.

'Oops, Chilli, we'd better get a move on. I can't be late to meet the boss!'

##

An hour later Amelia had fed Chilli, eaten a quick bowl of muesli and dressed neatly in good jeans and button-up collared shirt. She reached for her clean boots and gave them a quick wipe-over with her socks.

'Now you stay here and behave. I won't be long.' As Amelia gave the instructions to Chilli, she wondered whether she had made a mistake bringing her out to the station. When they'd been travelling, she'd been no trouble at all; she was a well-behaved dog who never barked or showed any aggression.

The incident yesterday afternoon with Ben Riley had rattled Amelia. Not that she thought Chilli would have hurt him—or anyone—but the fact that she'd be out working long days on the station would mean she'd be left in the small fenced area for hours at a time, and it wasn't really fair to leave Chilli unattended.

Biting her lip as she strode along the road towards the homestead, she worried about Chilli. Maybe she'd have to see if she could have her boarded in town the days she was working. She shook her head with a frown; she really hadn't thought this out well. The road out here had almost finished her two-wheel-drive van, and the thought of driving in and out of town every week didn't appeal. She could almost hear her dad talking to her. 'So typical of you, Amelia. Just plunge into things without thinking about it.'

That was unfair because she usually *did* think things through. She'd picked up Chilli, a rescue dog, on the spur of the moment a few months ago because she was lonely. Such a cute little pup, and she'd quickly grown into a lovely young dog. All the more reason to think about buying her own place and settling.

Maybe land close to Augathella wasn't too expensive. A small holding would do her, big enough to run a few cattle, have enough room for her horse, Brinny, and maybe grow some vegies and have some chooks. She didn't need a big flash house or shed. It would be fun to do an old place up, a home that would be hers and Chilli's.

Finance wasn't a problem, thanks to an inheritance from her beloved Grandma—her mother's mother who knew that Dad wasn't going to give his only daughter any share in the family property.

I don't care. Amelia was determined to make her own way in life, even if it was with a little help from Gran.

As she drew closer to the homestead her mood plummeted further as she saw Ben Riley walking out towards his ute. She'd hoped he'd be long gone by now.

'Good morning, Amelia.' His smile was wide and she forced one back. Last night, she'd warmed to him a bit, but she was still wary.

'You're looking very swish this morning,' he said.

Amelia scowled. 'Would you say the same thing to Braden or Kent?'

He frowned as he swung a swag onto the back of his ute. 'Get out of the wrong side of the bed this morning, did you? Or are you hungover?'

'No, to both.' Amelia glared at him. 'You're looking a little seedy yourself. You put away a few beers last night.'

'Were you counting?' he asked. 'I'm flattered that you take such an interest in my well-being.'

'No. I wasn't.' She wished she'd merely nodded at him and kept walking. Not even her brothers got her this cranky. She forced a sweet smile to her face. 'I have a meeting with Braden. You have a lovely day, Mr Riley.'

'Oh, I intend to. I hope you do too, Ms Foley.' He reached into his shirt pocket as he walked over to her. 'Here's the details for the puppy school.'

Her eyes widened. 'Puppy school?' She bit back the rude answer that sprang to her lips.

'Yes, remember? Before I knocked off last night and we became social acquaintances, I directed you to bring Chilli Girl to the dog obedience classes in town.'

'Are you for real?'

'Yes, I certainly am. To avoid any more dangerous confrontations with the public, I directed you to bring her to the classes. Take the card and call. My mother will fit you in.'

She took the card from him and put it carefully in her shirt pocket. 'I thought that would normally be a ranger role?'

He nodded. 'Yes, it is, however, we are a small shire and we share the load. I'll see you in town.'

Without another word—or direction—he climbed into the ute and drove out towards the gate.

Amelia was thoughtful as she approached the house. Was he serious, or was he having a lend of her? She could have sworn a smile was playing around his mouth as he'd been "directing" her.

Braden came out of the house as she walked up the steps. 'Morning, Amelia. I hope you slept well. We had a pretty late night, didn't we? Have you had breakfast?'

'I have, thank you. I've been for a walk out to the dam too.'

'Great. I ate with Ben. Kent and Sophie left early, and Callie's taken the three boys to school. Did you know she works in there as a teacher three days a week?'

'No, I didn't.'

'Come on, we'll go over to my office in the big shed. I'm looking forward to hearing more about what you prefer to do. We've got a few different areas that I need filled.'

'Great, I'm looking forward to working here.'

Amelia's mood lifted. Everything was going to be fine.

Chapter 6

Ben sang along with the radio as he drove back to town. He was heading home to have a quick shower and shave, and change into some clean work clothes before he headed into the shire office. Being Friday, there was a staff muster at nine-thirty to wrap up the week.

It was one of the newly-elected mayor's communication strategies, and the mayor drove out to both Augathella and Morven offices to attend the meetings each week. The communication in the shire was top notch and it was one of the happiest workplaces Ben had worked in over the past few years. Shame it was where he didn't want to be.

Although last night had been fun. It had been great catching up with friends and seeing them so happy.

It had been one of those off-the-cuff occasions that usually turned into the best nights. Seeing Kent and Sophie engaged and living together now, had been great. Kent had been bloody miserable at the fundraising gig they did at Craig Wilson's place at Easter.

Seeing Braden happy, and his boys back to their normal boisterous selves had been really good too. Ben had been living in Longreach when Julia had been killed, and when Kent and Sophie had broken up around the same time, but he had no doubt about the grief and unhappiness that had touched *Kilcoy Station* since then. Mum had kept him up to date, and she'd gone to Julia's funeral. Ben had made the effort to catch up with Braden as soon as he'd arrived back in town.

Callie seemed like a good person, and the boys loved her, from what he'd seen last night.

And then there was Amelia Foley. As much as he hated to admit it, Ben was very keen to see her again. Even this morning, when she'd been on the way to her meeting and was cold as ice to him, he'd not been able to stop looking at her. It wasn't just her looks; there was something about her that fascinated him.

Last night as they'd celebrated the two engagements, he'd caught himself watching her a few times.

He knew he'd been pushy about the dog obedience class, but he hoped that was a ruse that would get her to town. Either that, or it would turn her off him for life.

Either way, it didn't matter. He was on the lookout for a new job; a job far away from Augathella where he'd grown up. So, if she did agree to go out with him, it would only be a casual date.

No strings attached.

His mother's Audi was in the drive as he pulled up outside the sprawling weatherboard house where he'd spent his childhood. As Ben opened the front gate, a small silver bullet shot off the veranda and raced down the path.

'Hey, Albie boy, watcha doin'?' He bent down and gave in to the exuberant licks all over his face and neck from his mother's little dog.

'Hi, darling. Did you have a nice night?' His mother came around the side of the house, garden hose in hand.

'Morning, Mum. And yes, I did.'

He'd called from Braden's to let Mum know he wouldn't be home last night. Another black mark against living in Augathella. Christ, he was almost thirty-two years old, and he was ringing his parents to report in. Too bad if he'd wanted to bring someone home after a hot date. The only other alternative was a room at the pub, and if he did that it would spread around the town like wildfire.

Nope, he was out of here.

Which reminded him that he hadn't checked the online job site for a few days. That would be his first task this morning after the muster at the council office.

The other thing he'd maybe have a look at was the land for sale around the district. That was another alternative. He was starting to like this job on the shire; it was living at home and feeling like a teenager that was doing his head in.

'Let me cook you some bacon and eggs. Have you got time before you go to work?'

'Thanks, Mum. I had a feed with Braden.'

'Okay, I'll just make a pot of tea for us, then.'

'I really don't have time. I just came home for a quick shower and shave. I've got a meeting.'

'All right. You go and jump in the shower and I'll get your clothes out for you. I'll still make a cuppa in case you feel like one after your shower.'

Ben gritted his teeth and raced up the steps and into the bathroom. There was no point objecting. Even if he told Mum not to do it, his clothes would still be laid out on his bed. The same bed he'd had since he was ten years old.

No wonder Dad went away so much. He spent most of his time working on remote properties.

As Ben dried off and shaved after a quick shower, guilt trickled through him. Mum was lonely, and she'd always wanted to be needed. He walked into his room, and sure enough, a neatly pressed pair of clean trousers and his favourite shirt were laid out on the bed.

He dressed quickly and hurried into the kitchen where she was sitting at the table, a pot of tea and two mugs in front of her.

'Just a quick one, Mum,' he said, feeling sorry for her. 'I've got a meeting soon.' He dropped a kiss on the top of her head and she smiled up at him. 'What have you got planned for today?'

Kent poured a mug of tea, and Mum pushed over the sugar basin and a teaspoon.

'Not a lot, love. A bit of gardening, a load of washing, and I'll take Albie for a walk later. What would you like for dinner?'

'Don't bother, I'll sort something.' Ben hated committing to being home for dinner each night. 'Oh, and while I think of it, Mum, I gave out one of your cards today. If an Amelia rings, can you book her in as early as you can?'

'Amelia? Is she new in town?'

'She's working out at Kilcoy Station. She's got a lovely golden retriever, but she's a bit naughty.'

'Amelia is?'

Ben chuckled. 'No, her dog. Chilli Girl. I've got a tear in the trousers I chucked in the laundry basket. Anyway, I suggested that she brings her into puppy school.'

'Thanks, darling. It's been quiet these last couple of weeks. Everyone's been busy with Easter and the school holidays.'

'Dad still coming home next weekend?'

His mother's face lit up in a wide smile. 'Yes, and he'll be home for two whole weeks.'

Kent nodded. 'Sounds good. I'm heading up to Tambo the weekend after next, so you'll have some time to yourselves. Kent and I have a gig at the pub.'

'I'm so proud of you. You were both so good out at the Wilson's place. Aren't you pleased I made you take those guitar lessons after school?'

'I am, Mum. But I have to get going now. Not sure if I'll be in for dinner tonight, so please don't worry about cooking for me.'

He grabbed his keys and headed for the back door.

'I'll cook you something just in case and leave it in the fridge.'

Ben sighed as he headed out to the ute.

Mum meant well, but she was doing his head in.

Chapter 7
Amelia

After spending an hour with Braden, and discussing what he expected, Amelia was on top of the world. Jon Ingram, the station manager had arrived halfway through their meeting, and joined them for a coffee.

Braden needed her for cattle work, but he was mainly looking for someone who specialised in the health of the beasts. And that was right up her alley.

'You know,' he'd said. The sort of things you don't need to trouble the local vet for. And poor Jed McAdam is run off his feet. He can't get anyone to move out here and work his practice with him. We get to know our herd, and we know the problems we face, so if we can handle most of it out in the paddocks, that saves us time and money.'

Jon nodded. 'With the experience you've had, Amelia, that will save us heaps of time. I'll take you out on horseback next week to the steers that are close in and you can see what we mean. When we go way out, we'll camp out. I guess you've got a swag and a groundsheet?'

Amelia nodded, but she hesitated before she spoke.

Braden interrupted. 'I know exactly what you're worried about, but don't worry. When you're working out overnight, Chilli can go in the pen with the boys' three dogs. That is if you're happy with that?'

Amelia could have kissed him. 'Really? Are you sure that's not a huge inconvenience? I was going to try and get her boarded in town.'

Braden chuckled. 'I'm sure Ben would have looked after her for you. He puts on a tough front, but he's always been a softie when it comes to dogs. His mum used to work at the vet after she retired as a teacher, and now she has the puppy preschool.'

'No. I wouldn't trouble him, but if you're sure she'll be fine here. . .'

'Of course, she will. That dog enclosure is safe, and it's got more toys than the three boys combined. It's teaching the boys some responsibility, and with a grown pup to look after, it'll be another lesson.'

'What sort of dog have you got?' Jon asked as he reached for the coffee mug and one of the chocolate biscuits Braden had brought out.

'She's a pure-bred golden retriever,' Amelia answered, trying to ignore the temptation of the biscuits. 'She's just over a year old, so she's over most of the puppy chewing stage. She was abandoned in one of the small towns I travelled through and when they couldn't find an owner, I volunteered to take her. We've been great mates ever since. And she's never any trouble. Usually.' She glanced at Braden.

He laughed. 'Jon, she took a dislike to Ben Riley. He was wandering around near the dongas measuring the new concrete floors for me. She went for him.'

Amelia shook her head. 'She didn't actually bite him. She was playing and she tore his trousers. He flared up and he took it the wrong way. She wants to be everyone's friend.'

'Anyway, she's welcome to stay in the run with the other three whenever you have to head out. We do have some late nights here.'

Jon put his cup down. 'Are you more comfortable on horseback or bike? We've got a couple of all-terrain four-wheelers too.' He glanced nervously at Braden, but he was checking a message on his phone.

'Either or,' Amelia said. 'I'm experienced, and comfortable on both, and I'm a competent horsewoman.'

'We use helicopters to muster, and sometimes to survey the livestock and the watering points that are way out. Any questions?'

'No all good. I'm looking forward to getting to work. Tomorrow?'

Braden looked up and shook his head. 'Monday. That way you can go into town with Callie and the boys for the dog obedience class.' He held her gaze, and Amelia's mouth dropped open but she shut it before any argument could come out.

She swallowed and then nodded. 'Okay, that sounds like a plan. Thanks again.'

'I'll just finish up here with Braden and I'll meet you over at the shed near the horse paddock,' Jon said. 'Do you know where that is?'

'I do.'

'Okay, give me about twenty minutes and we'll saddle up for an hour or two.' He frowned. 'As long as that's okay with you.'

'Suits me fine. It'll be great to be on horseback. It's been a few weeks.' Amelia stood and pushed the chair in. 'I took a bit of a break on the way down from the Gulf.'

As she walked out, she wondered why Braden was so keen to get her and Chilli into those dog obedience classes. It sort of felt like a setup but she couldn't object, because he'd been so good with letting her bring Chilli to the station, and then the offer to let her stay with the three other pet dogs when she was working had been so unexpected.

She'd appreciated his kindness, what was one afternoon in town at a dog obedience class?

***

Braden waited until Amelia was out of earshot. 'So, you think she'll work out?'

'If she's anything like her brothers and her father, you'll want to hang onto her.'

'You know them?' Braden raised his eyebrows.

'I worked on Granite Springs for a few months a couple of years ago.'

'Amelia didn't remember you?'

Jon shook his head as he reached for the coffee pot. 'She was away when I was there. Overseas, I think. But she has a reputation as a formidable horsewoman.' He chuckled. 'Apparently, she has no fear, and is as tough as they come.'

'You sure wouldn't get that from looking at her.'

'Don't let appearances deceive you, Braden, although I know what you mean. I'll never forget the first time Fallon took me up in the chopper, and I misjudged her. Amelia's a tiny thing, but according to her brothers, she swears like a trooper and can outride any of them. She has the look of her father, but by God, he was a tough boss. Not popular with the stock manager or any of the ringers, or to be honest, his boys. If she's as feisty as they say, I can imagine she would have clashed with Greg Foley.'

'Interesting. I like her. She joined in with our celebration last night. Ben Riley was here too.'

'Celebration?' Jon looked curiously at his boss.

'Callie's agreed to marry me. And Kent and Sophie got engaged too.'

Jon stood and held out his hand to Braden. 'Congratulations, mate. That's great news. I'm happy for you.'

Braden shook his hand and grinned at him. 'Thanks, mate. I think Callie was going to ring Fallon today and tell her. We're having a bit of a formal do in town in a couple of weeks. Would love to see you there. How is Fallon? Keeping well?'

'She is, but she's sick of herself. The doc's sending her to Charleville for another scan next week.' Jon shook his head. 'He suspects twins.'

'Holy hell, that's pretty special.'

Jon nodded. 'Pretty scary. I would think one's enough of a challenge.'

'Mate, trust me. An old hand here. You'll be fine. After a few days, it's just like you've always had a kid.' He lowered his voice. 'I'd like to think Callie and I will have kids.'

'We could almost start our own school out here.' Jon started to walk to the door. 'That reminds me. What's the go with Amelia's dog and puppy school? Is it a terror?'

'No, Chilli's a great dog.' Braden's grin was wide. 'I'm just helping a mate along. There was a definite spark between Amelia and Ben last night, but she put some barriers up. I'm—'

'You're playing matchmaker.'

'Possibly. Are you heading into town this afternoon?'

'Yeah, Fallon's got an appointment with the new doctor.'

'New doctor? What happened to Doc Henry? He's not crook, is he?'

'No, but he doesn't want to do the commute from Charleville anymore, so the board advertised and appointed a new doc last week. Harry Higgins. Seems like a nice enough bloke. Bit quiet, but came with a great reputation.'

'Wife and kids?'

'Nah, came by himself from all accounts.'

'I'll have to drop in and say gidday. Listen, while you're in town, do me a favour?'

'What's that, mate?'

'If you see Ben, tell him to give his mother a night off from the puppy school. He'll understand why.'

'You really are matchmaking. I'm glad I'm settled now. You're a bad man, Braden Cartwright.'

'Just like to see everyone happy.'

It's good to see you happy, mate.' Jon thumped him on the arm on the way out.

Chapter 8

Friday afternoon
Amelia

Amelia sat in the front with Callie, the four dogs were tied up and lying on a blanket on the back seat. They were remarkably quiet and when Amelia glanced over the back, she could see that Chilli had gone to sleep.

'It's a big day for the boys. I don't work Fridays so Braden drives them to school,' Callie said. 'Petie does half a day at kindy and then Fallon's mum picks him up. The other two go to her place after school and stay there until I go in and get them. Ruth adores them. She's going to make a fabulous granny.'

Amelia knew she must have looked blank when Callie hurried on with an explanation.

'You probably don't know Fallon?'

Amelia shook her head.

'She's Jon's fiancée. They're having their first bub in about three months. Fallon came to town about the same time Jon came back to the district to work with Braden. I'd been here a couple of weeks, and I was still feeling my way around. Fallon and I hit it off and we've become good friends. Her mum and dad came to town when they discovered they were going to be grandparents.'

'Where from?' Amelia asked. She couldn't imagine her mum and dad following her to Augathella. She hid a smile as Callie answered.

'Brisbane. But there's some family connection. They're cleaning out an old uncle's house ready to put on the market.'

Amelia's interest quickened. 'Any land around it?'

'A few acres I think.'

'Is it in town?'

'Just on the edge, I think. Why? Are you looking for a place?'

'If the right place came up, maybe. But I want to suss out the area first. I love the thought of working on Kilcoy Station, but I haven't seen much of town yet. When I first hit Augathella at Easter, it was packed, and I'm guessing that's unusual.'

Callie shook her head. 'I've been surprised how many tourists come out this way. There's always something happening in one of the towns. The new shire mayor is a real dynamo, and he's getting all the towns connected. Charleville, Morven, Augathella and

Cooladdi. He even does a Facebook video every week to let the shire know what's going on. I thought I was coming out to the sticks to a sleepy country town, but there's more to do here than I ever did in Brisbane.' She grinned at Amelia. 'Who ever would have guessed I'd be happy living in the remote outback? My friends in Brisbane can't believe it, and they're sending Jen, my best friend, out here to make sure I'm not off my rocker. If anyone had told me six months ago I'd be driving along a dirt outback road with four dogs in the back and heading to a little town to go to puppy school, I would have thought they were mad.'

'So, tell me how you got out here, Callie. Why does everyone think you're mad? Did you meet Braden when you were out here on holidays? Or did you meet him in Brisbane?'

'It's a long story, Amelia.'

'I love a good story. But if you'd prefer not to share. . .'

'No, it's okay. It took a while but I'm fine about it now. Being out here in the wide-open spaces makes some things seem trivial. In the city, everything seems magnified. Out here, you know what matters. And when I met Braden and the boys and realised what they'd been through—his wife died in an accident in a storm.'

'Oh, how sad. Such little boys.'

'Yes, adorable little boys who are coping remarkably well these days. Sophie was a godsend for Braden, and when she went away, he advertised for a nanny.'

'And you applied?'

'I was looking for a job, any job, as long as I got as far away from Brisbane as I could.'

'That doesn't sound good.'

'Actually, it was my own fault. I was sort of engaged to this guy I worked with.'

'Sort of?'

'Yes, I was too trusting. I was a presenter on the weather channel at one at the networks in Brisbane. Unbeknown to me, he was doing the dirty behind my back and naive me thought we were about to get engaged no matter what his excuses were. I was after a stable relationship. He was after my property and investments.'

'Oh, no!'

Callie nodded and rolled her eyes. 'To cut a long story short he proposed to his other woman on national television. I saw red and I didn't realise the cameras were still rolling. I went over and shoved him on his bum. And it was seen by millions of viewers.'

'Sounds like he got everything he deserved.'

'That may be the case, but it went viral on TikTok and I was absolutely mortified. So, I went looking for a job as a school teacher—I trained and worked as a teacher for a few years before I met Greg. But I'll be forever grateful that I found the nanny job out at Kilcoy Station.' She took her eyes off the road for a second and glanced at Amelia. 'And here I am six months later, engaged to Braden and about to become a step mum. Three gorgeous little boys who I already adore. So that's enough about me. Tell me how you ended up at Augathella.' She smiled and gestured over to the backseat. 'I mean how did you and Chilli Girl end up at Augathella?'

Chilli heard her name and gave a soft woof from the back seat. Amelia turned around, reached out and gave her a quick pat. 'Nearly there. You've been such a good girl.' She turned back around in her seat. 'My story's not as exciting as yours. I grew up on the Gulf of Carpentaria on a cattle station.'

'So, you're a genuine outback girl.'

'Not really. I haven't spent a lot of time there since I was about ten.'

'How come? Is it still your home?' Callie slowed as an emu appeared in the paddock on the passenger side.

'It is, but my father doesn't believe women should have a place out on the land, but ever since I was a little girl, I've loved station life. The cattle, the horses, outback life. He did everything he could to turn me into a lady.'

'I think you're very ladylike,' Callie said as she sped up again.

'My mum was the same too. Mum is so old school she still gets changed and puts makeup on before Dad comes in from the station in the afternoon.' Amelia rolled her eyes as she thought of home. 'Would you believe she even hosts garden parties in the middle of nowhere?'

'Who for?' Callie frowned. 'If you are so isolated, I mean.'

'Oh, it's a weekend event for the Gulf Country. Every spring, the Foley garden party is an event not to be missed. Families fly and drive in. Hundreds of kilometres.'

'Wow, sounds pretty special.'

Amelia shook her head. 'Not really. I don't think Mum's even aware that most people in the twenty-first century don't even know what a garden party is.'

'Actually, I do.' Callie flicked her a glance. 'There's a garden party in Augathella the weekend after next. Ben's mum apparently has one in autumn and spring each year.'

'Save me,' Amelia said, but she smiled. 'Anyway, to cut a long story short I didn't fit in as the daughter they wanted. I was sent to boarding school, then secretarial college, and when finishing school in Switzerland was discussed, I bailed. Dad wouldn't let me work on the place, even though I am more than capable. He thought my five brothers were enough. Although there's only four there now because Josh, my younger brother, and Dad didn't get on, but that's another story.'

'So, you set off to find your own way?'

'I did. I packed up and travelled around for a little while and came across my Chilli Girl up near Longreach. I needed the company, and she was there, and then a few months after travelling the west, I saw the job advertised here at Kilcoy Station.'

'And we're glad you did. I think you'll fit right in, Amelia. This place gets into your heart. The locals are lovely, and there's so much to do.'

'So far, I love everything. Everyone I've met has been so welcoming. Even the old guy I met at the pub at Augathella when I was watching the billy cart races before I met you guys was fun. We had a lovely chat about the age of the artesian bore water. I must follow him up when I'm in town and see if he looked it up on Google.'

Callie chuckled. 'Old Reg is a town institution. You won't have any trouble finding him if you do go looking. Always at the same table outside the pub, day in, day out.'

'I'll make sure I go and talk to him again.'

'That's sweet of you. You'll do well here, Amelia. It's great to have you in Augathella.'

As they approached the turnoff into town, Callie slowed and put the indicator on. 'Are you and Chilli ready for puppy school?'

'We are.'

'We'll call in and pick the boys up at Ruth's place. It'll give you a chance to have a look at the property if you really are interested. I know it's coming on the market soon. Then I'll drop you and the three boys at puppy school. I'm going to go to school and do some photocopying for my lessons tomorrow.'

'Puppy school,' Amelia echoed. 'Why do I have a bad feeling about this?'

***

Ben jumped as a squeal came from behind him in the hallway.

'Gawd, Mum, you frightened ten years growth out of me with that squeal. What's wrong?'

'*You* scared me! I didn't know you were home, love. I didn't see your car out the front. I would have got some afternoon tea ready for you if I'd known you were coming home early. I was watering the back garden and didn't hear your car. Have you got a gig with Kent tonight?'

'No, I came home early because I'm running an extra puppy school class tonight, I meant to tell you. Did anyone ring?'

'No, she didn't.' His mother frowned. 'An extra one? An extra class? What for? We've never done that before.'

'Ah . . . um . . . the Cartwright boys have got three new dogs and I thought it would be good to have them all together by themselves rather than mixed in with the usual whole class. Plus, there's a new girl out there at Kilcoy Station and she's got a golden retriever that needs a bit of work, so I offered for them to come in together this afternoon.'

Mum raised her eyebrows, and a smile twitched at her lips. 'And you've showered and shaved. Is there something you're not telling me? You *never* shave in the afternoon, Benny boy.'

'Like what?' Ben reached for another towel and rubbed his hair. 'Tell you what?'

'I don't know. I thought you were busy at work. And I didn't think you wanted to have much to do with the obedience school anymore.'

'Well, to be honest, the girl out there who has the dog, she went for me.'

'The girl?'

'No, the retriever. I told her in my role as shire inspector that she had to come to obedience school.'

'You told the dog?'

'No, Mum.' Ben tried to keep his voice patient. He knew when his mother was trying to wind him up and he wasn't going to bite. 'I told the *owner* that the dog would have to come to obedience school.'

'What? You can't do that. You're the shire inspector, not the shire ranger.'

'Okay. But if you do happen to meet her, her name is Amelia and please don't mention that.'

'Mention what?'

'My role. My job. What I do.'

His mother frowned. 'I suppose it's a bit of a worry if the retriever is dangerous, around the little kids out there at Kilcoy. Is it a rescue dog? Maybe it—did you say Chilli Girl? Maybe she has a problem with men? You never know where rescue dogs have been and what treatment they've had. Remember that little rescue Maltese Terrier that come through here with those grey nomies last year? She hated little girls.'

'No, Mum, I wasn't here last year. Remember?'

His mother waved her hand, still encased in a gardening glove. 'Well, whatever. You know what I mean. A lot of them have problems, and we have to work extra hard with them. They're all redeemable, poor little pets. It's not their fault.'

'Well, Chilli's not exactly dangerous. I think she was just protecting her owner. I gave them both a fright when I came around the side of the building.'

A slow smile spread across his mother's face. 'Hmm. So, there's another side to the story, my lad, is there? I'm guessing this Amelia is a pretty young lady.'

'Yeah, she's okay.' Ben tried to sound nonchalant. 'Not bad.'

'Ben, I know you well. There's no reason why you would ever run an extra puppy school after a day at work unless you had an ulterior motive. Last I heard you were complaining about not having enough time to help me. Now you've started up a class of your own? I smell a rat.'

'Okay. So, she's cute and I asked her out but she said no, so I figured if she brought Chilli Girl into puppy school, I'd get a second chance.'

'You *must* be interested. I didn't think you were hanging around here long enough to get involved with anyone?'

'A coffee or a drink is not getting involved. I don't intend marrying the girl, Mum. Sheesh.'

'Okay, who is she?'

'She's a new station hand out at Braden's place.'

Mum screwed up her face. 'She's got a golden retriever out there? That's not a working dog.'

'Yeah, I thought that too, but I think Chilli is more of a companion to her than a working dog.'

'She sounds interesting. I must meet her and invite her to the garden party.'

'No, Mum. For goodness' sake.' Ben held his temper, all the more determined to move out of his childhood home as soon as he could. He felt about fifteen.

'No, everyone's coming and I can invite who I want to. Which reminds me. Your father is going to bowls that weekend so can I depend on you for a hand?'

'Of course, you can, Mother dear. You know I won't let you down.'

'Good. Thank you.'

Ben knew why Dad wasn't staying home. His father would rather spend his weekend watching the footie or playing bowls, and not serving champagne at a garden party.

'And the same goes for you. Don't you let me down. If you do happen to meet Amelia. You just take care of what you say.'

'I'll just say one thing. It would be so nice if she turned out to be "the one" and you settle here.'

'Mum.' Ben's voice held a warning note but as usual, his mother didn't take heed.

'No, let me have my say. For the life of me, I don't know why you're hellbent on moving away. There's nothing wrong with Augathella.'

'No, there's nothing wrong with Augathella, but I'm a big boy now and I can make my own choices in life.'

The sound that came from his mother's mouth as she turned and strode down to the kitchen was extremely rude.

'Mum!'

'Not now, Ben, I'm busy. I have to go and prune the…' The back door slammed before she finished her sentence and Ben shook his head. How the heck had he managed to say so little and get Mum on his case? She did it every time; she always managed to prise every little detail out of him without him twigging to it. He'd never been able to hide anything from her, ever since he was a little tacker. The sooner he moved away, the quicker he could have some peace and quiet in his life.

He pushed away the thought that he hadn't been very content when he was living away either.

Ben went in search of a clean pair of jeans in his chest of drawers. One advantage of living at home. He didn't have to worry about washing and ironing.

The back door opened as he reached for his jeans, and his mother's voice called down the hall.

'I forgot to tell you I heard something today I thought you might be interested in.'

'What's that, Mum?'

'I had coffee with Ruth Malone.'

'Who?'

'You know, Fallon's mum.'

'Oh yeah, I know who she is. I've seen her around with Fallon. Fallon hasn't had the baby, has she?'

'No of course not, she's still got around three months to go.'

Ben zipped up his denim jeans and shrugged as he stepped into the hall. His mother was standing there with her arms folded.

'What did you hear?'

'Do you know old George Malone?'

'Yep, I remember him. The grumpy old fellow who used to live in the last house in the street on the edge of town. Where I used to go to cricket training.'

'That's the one. He's Fallon's uncle, or great uncle. Well, he went into aged care a few months ago. Fallon lived there when she first came to town. Now that she and Jon are living out at the back of Kilcoy Station, Ruth and her hubby have come to town to be close by when the baby's born, and they've all been cleaning out George's house.'

'Is there a point to this?' Ben looked pointedly at the clock at the end of the hall.

'Yes, there is. Don't be rude.'

'And the point is? Hurry up, Mum. I want to be down there by five.'

'You've got plenty of time. Just listen to me. Anyway, Ruth and Fallon have talked to George and he wants to sell the place.'

Ben stilled. 'The Malone place? It's got a bit of land with it, hasn't it?'

'Yes, I think it's got about ten acres,' his mother said. She looked innocent and he stared at her.

'So, you thought I might be interested, Mum?'

'Well, even if you insist on going away *again*, it wouldn't be bad to have a base here for when you do come home.' She grinned. 'You wouldn't have to live with your old mum and dad, and have me putting your clothes out and watching your every move.' Her lips twitched again, and he knew she had reeled him in, hook, line and sinker.

'You know I don't mind living here, Mum.'

'I know, my sweet, but you're thirty-two years old and you *shouldn't* be living with your parents.'

'Are you saying you don't want me here? I'll pack up tonight.'

'Temper, temper. You are so like your father. Of course, I'm not saying that. If you had your own place here, with your good job and all your friends here, plus you and Kent are making a real go of this singing, it would be easier for you. I just thought it might be something for you to think about.'

Ben pulled a face. 'As much as I hate saying it, Mum, okay, you've got me interested. Who should I see? Fallon, or her mum and dad?'

'I'm not sure. It wouldn't hurt to call around there one afternoon.' Her expression reminded him of Barney, Mum's spoiled cat when he beat Ben to the chair near the fire in the living room.

'I might call around tonight after puppy school.'

His mother's grin widened and her eyes were bright. 'You *are* keen, are you? I knew it would be perfect for you.'

'No. I'm just interested in seeing what's going.'

'Excellent. Now, hurry up, Ben, or you'll be late.'

'What time is it?'

'Five to five.'

'Oh shit.' This time, Ben did roll his eyes as he raced back to the Star Wars poster-covered bedroom he'd grown up in. Rummaging through his wardrobe he searched for his Guns and Roses T-shirt. He didn't want to look too formal; he probably looked a bit officious in his work clothes carrying his clipboard the other day.

He wanted to look more like himself, although Amelia had been at the concert the other night so she had seen him in his black gear and his Akubra when he was up there playing with Kent.

Maybe Craig Wilson should have had him as a raffle prize too. Ben pulled himself up short as he wrangled the T-shirt over his head. *Jeez, get over yourself, mate.*

Although he did have a suspicion that the raffle prize of a date with Kent had been rigged, set up by Craig especially to get Kent and Sophie together.

It had worked. He was mighty pleased about that; Kent was happy, but the last thing Ben wanted to do was settle down. He had a lot of Queensland to see before he set up a home although the Malone house being for sale was very tempting.

He grabbed his keys and wallet and then changed his mind and rushed into the kitchen, taking the van keys off the hook near the back door.

'Mum,' he yelled out the back door. 'I'm taking your van. All the gear's in it.'

Ben was thoughtful as he hurried out to his mother's van. He knew the Malone property well; he used to go down there when he was a kid and play cricket at the back of George Malone's house. There was a crowd of boys there, enough for two teams most summer afternoons. The land was dead flat and the lawn had made a great cricket pitch; there'd been lots of fours hit across that rolling lawn on those afternoons. Old George even had a roller to roll the pitch for the boys back in those days. He'd been the president of the senior and junior cricket clubs for about twenty-five years. His name took up most of the board in the sports club.

It was a damn good property and there weren't many like it that would come on the market in Augathella. A suburban street with a solid house, but best of all were the ten acres at the back.

He had to go to Charleville for a meeting on Monday, so he'd call in and see the bank when he was there. Just an enquiry, though. Nothing more.

Even though there'd be no trouble getting a loan, he had to think if it really was a wise move to put his savings into real estate in Augathella. He'd managed to whack a fair bit of money away over the last few years. It all came down to how much it was going to sell for.

Plus, now that he was living at home again and had a local government ute, his entire pay packet stayed in the bank every fortnight. A couple of beers on a Friday night with the blokes down at the pub, and the occasional hamburger on the weekend at the footie were his only expenses. He'd tried to give Mum some board money, but she waved him off.

He and Kent had also been surprised that the local clubs were happy to pay for them to perform, and the bookings had been filling up as the word got around. Next weekend they were up at the pub at Tambo where the crowds would be gathering for the famous chicken races.

Ben was thoughtful as he pulled up at the showground. Actually, living back at Augathella was turning out better than he'd expected.

Chapter 9

As Callie turned into a street at the back of the small town, a red vintage ute drove across the intersection in front of them.

'Oh, good stuff! Fallon's in town,' Callie said. 'She must be visiting Ruth. I'm so pleased you're going to meet her. Both of them, actually. Fallon's an interesting person, I think you'll get on like a house on fire. You've met Jon, haven't you?'

'Yes, I had a meeting with Jon and Braden this morning, and Jon showed me around. I think I'm going to enjoy working at the station.' Amelia watched with interest as the old red ute pulled up in the driveway of the house.

Callie parked on the street outside the small weatherboard house. The front garden was neat and tidy, and the house looked to be in pretty good condition. Lush green paddocks behind the house caught her attention; a huge expense of land disappeared down behind the house and was dotted with a few fat and shiny steers. In the distance, she could see the glint of the river.

'You don't know how much land there is here, do you?' she asked as she opened the door, keen to see the house.

'Ruth and Fallon will be able to tell you. Come on in and you can meet them.'

Amelia reached down for Chilli's lead, and Callie lifted the three leads for the boys' dogs from the console before she climbed out of the driver's side. Amelia went around to open the door on Chilli's side just as the door of the red ute opened.

A tall, very attractive, very pregnant woman climbed carefully out of the ute and Amelia's eyes widened; Fallon was a lot bigger than she'd expected to see. Not that she knew much about pregnancy, but her stomach was *huge*. The boys came running out behind her.

'Wow, this is a welcoming committee,' Fallon said as she walked across to them. 'Hi, you must be Amelia. Jon told me all about you. Welcome to Augathella, or probably more to the point, welcome to Kilcoy Station.'

'Thank you, it's good to be here. I enjoyed talking to Jon this morning. And I like Augathella too.'

'Holy hell, Fallon. You like look like you're just about ready to pop this bub out,' Callie put her hand on Fallon's stomach, keeping one eye on the boys as they secured the leads to the dogs' collars.

'Ages to go yet. Besides, we're not ready for him yet. We've still got a lot of painting and tiling to do.'

'Him?' Callie said.

'Yep, not a secret. Not twins either. Can't see the point in keeping it quiet.'

'The boys will be excited. And you're well?' Callie asked.

'Fit as a fiddle.' Fallon laughed. 'But a fat fiddle.'

They all walked across the footpath to the front gate. Rory, Nigel, and Petie were holding the dogs' leads and Chilli barked as if to say "wait for me" as they ran ahead through the gate. Amelia knew her eyes were wide as she looked around. The house had such a welcoming and homely feel to it.

'Amelia wants to know a little bit about your uncle's place,' Callie said.

'Uncle George's place?' Fallon rolled her eyes. 'We've been cleaning it out for ages. I'm just so glad Mum and Dad turned up to help. Dad's been helping Jon sort out the sheds. We've taken so much to the op shop in town, I swear Val locks the door when she sees us coming!'

'Did your uncle pass away recently?' Amelia asked.

'No, he's in the aged care facility up the road. He actually wanted me to move into the old place. Said he'd leave it to me.'

'And you're not moving in?' Amelia looked around the garden.

'No. I find being in town claustrophobic. We're happy out on the land. But I didn't say no to Uncle George's fabulous ute. I told him to sell the place and make some money while he's still alive. But he said he's got no need for it. Mum and Dad don't want to move out here. They're going back to Brisbane in a little while, so we talked to George and he's agreed to sell the place.' She looked curiously at Amelia. 'Are you really interested? It'll go for a song. It's pretty hard to sell places out here now. Everyone's moving away, even if it's only to Charleville.'

'I am looking to settle somewhere,' Amelia said, not wanting to sound too keen. 'I'm not quite sure where yet, but Augathella is looking good so far. I've had a really good impression of the town and what's on. It's such a friendly place. The local cattle industry seems to be booming so there'll always be lots of work, but I'm looking for a place of my own. A house that's got enough land that I can run a few cattle of my own and bring my horse down from the Gulf.'

'The Gulf? Were you working up there?' Fallon asked.

'Yeah, sort of. My Mum and Dad own Granite Springs.'

'I know it. I did some mustering not far from there a couple of years back. It's one of the biggest spreads up there.' The look Fallon was giving her now was full of interest.

'Do you work on the land too?' Amelia asked, just as interested in Fallon's background.

'I'm a helicopter pilot,' Fallon replied. 'I did aerial mustering up in the Territory and North Queensland for a few years before I moved down here late last year.' Fallon patted her stomach. 'Long story short. I fell in love with the boss, and we've moved in together. But there won't be any helicopter flying at the moment, and probably not for a while after the bub.'

'Do you miss it?' Amelia asked.

'I do but not as much as I expected. I'm keeping busy. Jon and I are doing up the old house we're living in at the back of Kilcoy Station.'

'It's the house that Braden and Sophie grew up in,' Callie said.

'Yeah, the original homestead. We're doing the work in exchange for Braden letting us stay there.'

Fallon opened the front gate, Callie and Amelia behind her and the boys came running over.

'Callie, Callie. Guess what Ruth made for us? Some pink lamingtons and we're allowed to have lemonade too, in little cups called tumblers.' Petie's words tumbled over each other. 'If you say yes, we can, she said.'

Amelia looked up at the older woman who walked out of the house with a sheepish smile on her face.

'I hope that was alright, Callie.'

'Of course, it is. It doesn't hurt the boys to have a treat occasionally. I won't tell you they had Tim Tams and potato chips for dinner the other night amid all the excitement.'

Ruth laughed. 'The night you get engaged is a pretty special night.'

Callie rolled her eyes. 'Don't tell me the news has got to town already?'

Ruth's smile was wide. 'Sweetie, you'll get used to a small country town, quick smart. Nothing stays private here for very long.' She turned to Amelia who was hanging back as they all chatted. 'Hello, and welcome, don't be shy,' she said. 'You must be Amelia.

I heard you were coming in with Callie. Welcome to Augathella, although I can't really say that because I'm not a true local myself, although a semi-local, I suppose. I used to come out and visit George when I was a young girl.'

Fallon glanced over at her mum. 'Amelia might be interested in having a look at the place. Have you listed it with the real estate agent yet?'

'No,' Ruth said. 'I haven't got around to it yet, but Amelia, if you're serious, you're more than welcome to have a look around.'

'How much land is there?' Amelia asked.

'Ah, I think there's around ten acres from the back of the house to the boundary near the river, but I can find out exactly if you want.'

Amelia's eyes grew wide. 'Ten acres? Wow, that sounds great.'

'Anyway, you can have a look around the place and have a think about it. I think most people in town think we're waiting for poor George to pass on before we sell it. It certainly hasn't been advertised yet and I don't know that it's going to sell very quickly. But one thing I'd hate is to see someone come out from the city and play at being a country farmer.'

Amelia saw the hurt look on Callie's face, and Ruth must have noticed too.

'Ah Callie, I don't mean you, I know how much you love it out here.'

'I know that, Ruth.'

Ruth held the small iron gate open as the girls walked through. Callie and Fallon were chatting ahead of her, and Amelia smiled her thanks as she walked through with Chilli Girl. The minute she stepped onto the path edged by two narrow gardens a shiver ran down her back. Not an unpleasant shiver, at all. She looked around at the neatly mown and fenced yard, the edges of the path trimmed and the gardens free of weeds. It appealed to her so much, she wasn't game to look at the house in case she was disappointed.

'What do you think, Chilli Girl? It's a lovely big garden, isn't it? How good would it be to play ball here?'

Chilli barked and Amelia smiled at her. 'Yes, girl, I think it would be fun too.'

Typical Amelia, she could just hear her father saying. *No thought, no logic, just go with the flow of what you want at the time. Don't you, girlie?*

The "girlie" was always said in the same disparaging tone.

Maybe she was adopted?

Maybe Mum had had an affair with a station hand, and that cranky old man wasn't even her father.

'Amelia?'

'Oh sorry, Ruth. I was miles away.'

'I asked if would you like a cup of tea or coffee? Callie said you've got an hour or so before you have to be at the showground.'

'Yes, please. Coffee would be great.'

'Come on in. It's a bit warmer in the kitchen. You must find it cold here after the Gulf.'

'The past few mornings have been cool. Chilli climbed up in the van with me the other morning before we moved out to the station, poor baby.' Amelia swallowed as she followed Ruth over to the back door. Callie and Fallon were near the fence with the three boys and the pups.

'There's a hen sitting on eggs over there. Petie's been keeping guard since he came here from kindy.'

'Oh. Will Chilli be all right out here? I'd better stay out with her.'

'It's fine. Look, Petie and the boys have a handle on the situation.'

Amelia smiled as she looked over there. True enough the three boys had formed a wall at the edge of the garden.

'Won't the ground be too cold now that the cold weather's coming?'

Ruth chuckled. 'My husband's been putting a gas heater out there each night. It's the most spoiled chook in Augathella. They're not far off hatching and then we can bring them inside.'

'I like that. How thoughtful of him.'

Ruth laughed again. 'We're not country people by a long shot, but Fallon's been teaching us. Come in, come in. Your dog will be fine.'

Amelia took a deep breath and followed Ruth. The screen door was an old-fashioned one. A rectangle of gauze was tacked onto a green-painted timber frame. The door squeaked as it swung shut behind them.

A cosy kitchen filled with the smell of fresh baking, and the accompanying warmth from a combustion stove greeted them. Trays of biscuits lined the benches as well as the pink lamingtons that the boys had mentioned. Pretty red and white checked curtains framed the window that overlooked the back garden and out over the acres that stretched as far as she could see. Amelia's eyes widened and warmth filled her as she imagined living here. She shook herself out of her daydream when she realised Ruth was watching her with a smile on her face.

'You've been busy, Ruth,' Amelia said. 'It smells wonderful.'

'I'm helping out with the cooking for the garden party that's coming up. A fundraiser for the RFDS. Most of this lot will go in the deep freeze.'

'That's good of you. They'll sell on aroma alone.' Amelia pulled a face. 'Very different to our place. Mum's garden parties are catered for by fly-in caterers from Darwin.'

The more Amelia heard about this town, the more she liked it, and the more she thought maybe she could settle here. 'May I look through the rest of the house?' she asked timidly. 'Would that be okay?'

'Of course, sweetie. Feel free to have a wander through and poke in all the rooms. We're just caretaking for a while, so have a good look. Most of the stuff in the rooms is George's, and we have to decide whether to keep or give it away. Mind you, it looks a lot better now than it did three months ago. Take your time, I'll put the jug on.'

As Amelia stepped into the wide hallway, she heard the back door open and Ruth tell the others she was looking around the house.

The voices and the smell of home baking faded as she stepped through the house. The carpet was old and faded but clean. The bathroom had a pink bathtub and old-fashioned vanity basin, but she loved it. Three bedrooms, all with large proportions came off the hallway and at the front, a glassed-in porch looked out over the quiet street, and then across to more paddocks. The house reminded her of Gran's house in Normanton, where no one ever came to the front door. Everyone was welcomed through the kitchen.

She turned around and went back to the kitchen where the three women were sitting around the red Laminex kitchen table.

'Have a seat, Amelia. Your coffee's there, and there's milk and sugar in the pink jugs.' Ruth pointed to the mug in front of the empty chair.

'Oh, how lovely. My gran had that same jug with the cow face. Now I really feel like I'm at home.'

Fallon and Ruth shared a hopeful look and Amelia smiled.

'I'd really love to come back and have a good look. Perhaps you could let me know when I do how much you would be asking?'

Chapter 10

Callie looked at her phone.

'Time we went to the showground. Jenny will be waiting for us.'

'Thanks so much for the coffee and lamingtons, Ruth,' Amelia said. 'It was so good to see the house. My dad always tells me that I rush into things, but I'll come into town when I have my first day off. Does that suit your schedule or are you in a rush to sell?'

'Sweetie, this is Augathella,' Ruth said with a wide smile. 'An old place might take quite a while to sell, although the land might be of interest to some. I'd hate to see the old house knocked down for the land.'

'Oh no. Do you think that could happen?' Amelia decided to get back as fast as she could. Maybe even after she'd knocked off one afternoon? It all depended on what Jon had lined up for her, and whether she'd be out on the property in a swag at night.

'Well, like I said, I'm interested, but I guess if you have an offer before I get the chance to have a better look and get my finances organised, you just have to take the first offer. I'd hate you to wait around and then I decided it wasn't for me, so just take note that I'm interested but if someone else is, just let me know maybe.'

Amelia followed Callie outside and Callie called the boys. They'd gone back outside with the dogs. 'Come on, kids, it's time to go to puppy school and see Jenny.'

Amelia followed slowly. The house was sweet and she loved the land around it. It just felt right; it was as though the house had been waiting for her to come to Augathella. She'd stayed in a few places on her way south but none had welcomed her as much as this little town.

With ten acres she could run a few cattle and have a chook pen. She could get her horse from home and there was enough work around at the surrounding properties that she could still get work after her contract at Kilcoy Station was completed. Maybe she'd stay there; Braden and Callie seemed to like her so far, but she guessed it would depend on whether Braden and Jon were happy with her work. She had no doubt she could prove herself.

Callie must have read her thoughts. 'It would be so good to have you in town, Amelia.'

'I think it would be good to be here.'

Callie looked at her curiously, probably wondering why someone of her age was looking to resettle by herself, but she didn't ask.

'Heaps of us here you can be friends with, so you won't be lonely if you buy the property.'

'I don't want to rush in, but between you and me, I'm really keen.' Amelia crouched down as Chilli came running over to her. 'Have you been a good girl? Are you going to be a good girl at puppy school?' She turned to Callie who was hurrying the boys up. 'Do you know who runs the puppy school Callie?' she asked.

'Yes, it's Mrs Riley. She's lovely.'

'Riley?' Amelia frowned. 'Is she related to Ben?'

'I'm pretty sure she's his mum. I'm still new enough in town to be learning who's related to who. I met her in town once. She happened to be putting the poster up on the community noticeboard and I asked about it. I'm glad you told me it was tonight because I thought it was on Saturday afternoons.' She lowered her voice as the boys climbed into the four-wheel drive. 'Between you and me, I'll be really interested to see how the boys go. The pups have got a bit out of hand. It'll be good for the boys to learn some structure. I'm not much good. I've never had a dog. And Braden's been too busy to teach them.'

'This should be good for them. I really don't know why *we* have to be here though. Chilli has good habits and is obedient, but Mr High and Mighty Riley decreed we had to come. I hope his mum is nicer than he is.'

'She is. She's a lovely lady, friends with Ruth, she said. I met her again at Fallon and Jon's engagement drink at the pub. I'm pretty sure she is his mum, but I could be wrong. They are related though, I think. He wasn't there that night. He and Kent were singing down in Charleville.'

'Engaged? I thought they were married?'

'They are. They slipped away and got married quietly a couple of months ago. Just the two of them, with her parents as witnesses. Fallon's not one for fuss and bother.'

'That's a shame. If I ever get married, I want the full works. The big white wedding in a church.' She grinned but sadness tugged at her. 'I can't see my father giving me away. He already has.'

'What do you mean?'

'Me and Dad? That's a long story. One for over a drink one night. Actually, he'd probably be really pleased to give me away to someone. To get me out of his hair once and for all.'

'We'll have that drinks' night. It's probably time to organise another girls' night out, and you can meet some of the others. You know, I've socialised more in Augathella than I ever did in Brisbane.' Callie held the dogs' leads as the boys climbed into the four-wheel drive. 'I've been telling my best friend in Brissie about this town, and she's going to bring her kids out for a visit. She's also going to be the matron of honour at the wedding. Mind you, I think it's more to do with checking out Braden! So, don't worry, there's plenty for you to do here. You'll never be bored.'

'I like my own company, and now I've got Chilli, I've got someone to talk to. I'd be quite happy living in old George's house on the edge of town. I could be a happy spinster looking after some chooks, and cows.'

'Don't speak too soon, sweetie. That was my philosophy up till six months ago when my almost fiancé at the time did the dirty on me. Look at me now! Engaged and about to become a step mum to three fabulous little boys.'

'When's the wedding?'

Callie smiled. 'That's the next thing we have to decide. Life is so busy!' She opened the back of the Landcruiser station wagon and lifted the three puppies in. 'Put Chilli in the front with us. We only have a short way to go.'

Amelia put her arms beneath Chilli and lifted her up. 'Oh my God, girl, I think I need to put you on a diet. You're growing way too fast.' Amelia climbed in after her and looped her fingers through Chilli's collar. 'So where are we going? I mean where is it held? Inside or outside?'

'Well, it used to be at the showground but now that you mention it, I'm not sure whether it's there or at the park. I'll give Ben a call. His number's in my phone.'

Callie started the car and put the phone on speaker as she pulled out onto the road and turned the corner towards the main street.

'Ben Riley.'

Amelia turned away as *his* voice came over the speaker.

'Hey Ben, how's it going? It's Callie Young here. We're on our way to puppy school with your mum and I'm not sure where it's being held. At the showground or the park?'

Amelia's heart took a leap and she tried not to listen as Ben's voice came over the car audio. 'Hey, Callie. It's at the showground. I'm looking forward to seeing the boys there.'

Amelia widened her eyes and her fingers tightened automatically on Chilli's collar. *He* was going to be there too.

'Okay, see you there in five. We're not far away.'

'See ya.'

Amelia turned to Callie. 'Did you know Ben was going to be there tonight too?'

Callie turned a wide-eyed innocent look in her direction. 'I think Ben helps out sometimes.'

'So this is a bit of a setup, is it?' Amelia folded her arms. 'I don't even know why he insisted that I bring Chilli in.'

'A setup? No, not at all. Chilli bit Ben, so he's right saying she needs some obedience lessons.' Callie followed the main street along and followed the sign to the showground.

'She didn't bite him. She just tore his trousers a little bit.'

Callie raised her eyebrows, but she didn't comment.

Amelia pulled out her bag and took out a comb, loosened the scrunchie around her ponytail and brushed her hair back and re-tied it. She glanced over at Callie, but she was innocently watching the road ahead.

Surreptitiously, Amelia reached into her bag and twisted the lid off a small pot of lip gloss and put a little bit on her finger and rubbed it on her lips. Pinching her cheeks until she knew her fair skin would have some colour she sat back and smoothed her T-shirt down over her jeans. If she had to see Mr Riley, she'd look tidy.

***

Ben drove towards the showground resisting the temptation of turning down Jane Street for a quick look at George Malone's place. He didn't have time. He wanted to be set up before his class arrived.

He cursed under his breath as he parked behind Braden's Landcruiser on Roselyn Road. They'd got there before him. He jumped out and quickly walked around and opened the back of the van and pulled out the six plastic chairs and the dog mats.

Callie and the boys were in the middle of the show ring with Amelia and Chilli Girl. The boys' yells were punctuated by Chilli's deep woof as they chased three small but energetic dogs around.

Once he had the chairs and mats set up, he walked around to the back of the wagon and pulled out a bag of pigs' ears and some liver treats.

Amelia and the boys and the dogs stayed out in the middle of the field.

Callie spotted him setting up and walked over, 'Hi, Ben. Your mum's not here yet?' She looked across at the van.

'Mum's not coming tonight. I decided to do an extra class so we could keep you all together.'

'Thanks for that. The boys are really excited. Will I get them over now?'

'Yep, if we start now, we'll have a good hour before dark.'

Ben grinned as Callie put her hand to her mouth and let out a sharp whistle. She gestured to the group in the middle and the boys took off towards them, followed closely by the three dogs, and more slowly by Amelia who had her hand on Chilli's collar.

'I've got some things to do at school. Are you okay if I leave you with the boys and Amelia and the four dogs, or would you rather I hung around?'

'No, that's fine, you do whatever you have to do.'

'About an hour you said?'

'Yes, we'll just do the basics tonight and let the dogs settle in. Have the boys' dogs learned any skills yet?'

Callie shook her head. 'They've got some pretty bad habits. The boys spoil them rotten. Braden's always roaring at them and telling them to make them sit down and stay and do things like that, but the boys and the pups all do what they want. He's taking it slowly with them—the boys I mean—but it's going to come to a head soon. He found Cottie asleep with Petie in his bed the other morning.'

'Okay, I'll stress to the boys that the pups need a routine.'

'You've got your work cut out, I think.'

'Not a problem. Been there, done that. I know what to do. It'll probably take the six sessions to see a difference, but if you can get the boys practising at home it'll reinforce it.'

'With both the dogs and the boys.' Callie laughed. 'Braden's finally realising that he doesn't have to go so soft on them. It's not doing them any favours; they're getting out of line.'

'It's been a hard time for all of you,' Ben said, glancing across as Amelia stood back waiting for them to finish talking. Her dark hair was pulled back in a high ponytail and her fair cheeks had that rosy glow. She really was a pretty woman.

Callie saw him looking at Amelia and a smile played around her lips.

'And you're right with Amelia and Chilli too?'

'Yeah, all good. I guess Amelia wasn't real keen on coming. Has Chilli behaved with the other dogs?'

'She loves them, and the boys. She hasn't been aggressive at all, although she did tear your trousers the other day.'

'Yeah. She wasn't happy to see me. I'll be watching her.'

The dog under discussion sat sedately beside her mistress.

'As far as I can see, she's placid and she seems to do what she's told. I've got no idea why she bit you that day.'

'I think she thought I was threatening Amelia. I did come up very suddenly from behind the building and it's not a bad thing that a dog will protect their mistress like that.'

'So, there's no need for Chilli to be here at puppy school?' This time Callie grinned and they shared a look.

'There is a need,' Ben replied. 'We'll wait and see how she goes.'

'Okay, I'll see you in an hour or so.'

Callie crouched down next to the boys and Amelia continued to stand back. Ben waited as Callie gave the boys instructions.

'Now, you all listen carefully to Ben and do what he says. I'll be back soon, okay?'

They all nodded and Ben waited until Callie was in the car before he turned to greet them. For some reason he felt nervous; strange because it hadn't been that long since he'd run a class.

Amelia was watching him with a closed expression.

'Welcome boys, and hello, Amelia.'

She nodded without speaking.

'Now I'd like you all to introduce me to your dogs and I'll show you the right way to greet a dog you haven't met before.'

Ben turned over his right hand and held it out as Rory walked over with a reddish-brown dog. Ben glanced across at the other two; it looked like they were all from the same litter.

He crouched down as the small dog hesitantly sniffed at the back of his hand. 'What's his name, Rory?'

'His name is Bumper. I called him that because when I lay down on the ground with him when he was a little pup, he liked to bump my head.'

'An excellent name,' he said. Glancing up, Ben finally caught the glimmer of a smile from Amelia.

Nigel ran over, his dog nipping at his heels.

A bad habit, Ben thought.

'This is Tweedle. He's my dog,' Nigel said puffing his chest out as the dog licked Ben's hand and then turned to roll over with Bumper. 'Tweedle Dee is his full name.'

'From the story?' Ben asked.

'No.' Nigel screwed his face up. 'It's from a nursery rhyme that Aunty Sophie made up for us.'

This time Ben and Amelia's eyes connected and her smile was wide. She came over to Nigel and put her hand on his shoulder. 'There's a Tweedle Dee and Tweedle Dum in one of my favourite stories about a girl called Alice.'

'I don't like girl stories,' Nigel said with a pout. 'Actually, I don't like girls very much. They're a bit silly. They giggle and Callie gets cross at them in the playground.'

'You might change your mind when you get a bit older, mate.' Ben was pleased to see that Amelia looked a bit more relaxed, but she was still hanging tightly onto Chilli.

Nigel shrugged and Ben turned to little Petie 'Now Petie's turn. Introduce me to your pup.'

'This is my Cottie and she's the bestest behaved dog in our family.' Petie leaned over and cupped his hand over Ben's ear, his breath warm on his cheek. 'Dad said that's because I look after her the bestest, but don't tell Nigel and Rory that.'

Ben lowered his voice. 'I won't tell.'

'Now boys, while I meet Amelia's dog, I'd like you to sit on the chairs and get your pups on the mat in front of your feet. If they won't stay there, you can get one treat each out of the bag and give it to them to get them to sit quietly. Can you do that?'

The three boys nodded and did as they were asked, and Ben finally turned to Amelia. 'Hello, Amelia, I'm pleased to see you here.'

Her chin lifted a fraction, but his gaze honed in on her pink lips, shiny with gloss. For a moment his thoughts left him, and he shook his head to try to remember what he'd been going to say.

Finally, his head cleared. 'May I talk to Chilli?'

She nodded. 'You may.'

He moved across to stand in front of the dog who stood quietly next to her mistress. Holding his handout, he said quietly. 'Hello, Chilli Girl.'

The golden Labrador looked at him with something akin to adoration in her eyes and Ben grinned.

'That's a much nicer welcome, Chilli.' He lifted his head and caught a strange look on Amelia's face as he met her eyes. 'Come on over and sit down, and see if Chilli will sit in front of you,' he said.

Her eyebrows rose. 'Chilli will do whatever I tell her to. There is no need for us to be here.'

Ben shook his head. 'I beg to differ. Even though she seems happy to see me tonight, there was still her reaction the other day. We have to understand what caused that.'

Amelia's lips pursed and she moved across to one of the empty chairs. She pointed to the mat, and didn't even speak. The look she flashed him as Chilli sat quietly at her feet was triumphant.

Ben surveyed his class with a smile. Three little boys and one pretty woman sat on the chairs with four well behaved dogs sitting at their feet. Granted, Tweedle and Bumper had needed a treat to sit down, but Petie's Cottie, and Chilli, had obeyed the simple instruction.

Ben settled into the class and began to enjoy himself, forgetting for a while that it was Amelia sitting there. Over the hour, she seemed to relax and he was pleased to hear her laugh at one point. The only downside was Nigel's reluctance to follow instructions.

A couple of times Ben stood close to Amelia as he taught her some quick tricks to get Chilli's attention, and a waft of something floral surrounded him.

Too soon the sound of a vehicle caught his attention, and he looked up as a car door slammed. Callie was walking across to them.

Petie let go of Cottie's lead and ran across to meet her. Ben smiled as he wrapped his arms around Callie's jean-clad legs. 'Oh, Callie, we've had the bestest time, and Cottie was the bestest dog.'

'He was not.' Nigel's face reddened with anger as he almost yelled. 'You're just a baby, Petie. What would you know about dogs!'

Ben went to intervene but held back when Amelia caught his eye and shook her head slightly. Callie walked over to Nigel and put her hand on his shoulder. 'That wasn't very nice, Nigel. I want you to say sorry to Petie.'

Nigel glared up at her. 'No.'

'Nigel, you are—'

'You're not my mother and you can't tell me what to do.'

Ben and Amelia looked at each other, and Ben felt sorry for Callie and more than a bit helpless. He didn't know whether to intervene or leave it to Callie to handle the situation. He decided to stay quiet and not give in to Nigel's demand for attention.

Callie's teacher training came to the fore as she defused the situation and took the attention off Nigel. 'Rory, Petie, say thank you to Ben and then take Bumper and Cottie and get in the car and wait for us please.' She ignored Nigel who stared after his brothers as they thanked Ben and ran off to the car. When the boys were in the car, Ben was surprised when Amelia turned to him and held her hand out.

'Thank you, Ben. I've learned a lot tonight.'

He took her hand and shook it gently, maybe holding on for longer than necessary. Finally, he let go and she dropped her gaze.

'Same time next week suit?' he asked.

'Um, I'm not sure. I'll be at work by then, and I could be out on the property but we'll sort something.' With a quick smile, she tugged on Chilli's lead and they headed off to the car.

Callie put her hand on Nigel's shoulder. 'Right, young man, your turn.'

'My turn to what?' came the sullen reply.

'To say what we're waiting for.'

'What?'

'You know, Nigel. Manners please.'

Nigel lifted his chin and the look he shot Callie was full of venom. 'Okay. I'll say it. Petie is a little turd and I hate you.'

Ben couldn't help himself. 'Nigel! I'm very disappointed in you.'

Callie shook her head. 'Thanks, Ben, we'll get going now. I'll give you a call about next week.' Her eyes were awash with tears and Ben's heart broke for her. Nigel was still carrying a lot of grief inside, the poor little bloke, and Ben hoped that the situation wouldn't impact on Braden and Callie's relationship.

He put his hand out to Callie, and she dropped her gaze as she took it briefly before she let go and took hold of Nigel's shoulder.

'You take care, Callie.'

'I will, Ben. Now, to the car, Nigel.'

To Ben's relief, the little boy bent down and picked up Tweedle and took off towards the car.

After they had driven off, he packed up the chairs and mats and carried them to the car.

He wondered how they could help Nigel, and then his thoughts turned to Amelia. She had responded to him tonight and that had made him all the more determined to ask her out. He wondered whether she was just being polite, although they had seemed to connect a few times.

Hopefully, he'd get a yes this time.

Chapter 11

'Mummy. Nigel pinched me.'

Amelia froze as Petie's plaintive little cry filled the car.

Mummy? That was guaranteed to stir Nigel up even more.

'*She's* not our mother. Our mother's dead. We don't need a new mother. We've got Aunty Sophie. I want you to go away.'

Petie started to cry and Amelia glanced at Callie. Her eyes were full of tears and her hands were white as she gripped the steering wheel. The journey up until now had been quiet and Amelia judged they were past halfway back to the station.

Assistance came from an unexpected quarter. 'Nigel, shut up. You're being mean.' Rory leaned forward from the back seat and put his hand on Callie's shoulder. 'Don't cry, Callie. Petie and I both love you lots. And if Petie wants to call you Mummy, I think that's okay too. I was even thinking about that last night, when you and Daddy get married. It's going to be good. When are you going to get married? It would be cool if it was soon. I think that would make Dad really happy.'

Amelia didn't know what to say or where to look. Callie's shoulders were shaking and tears rolled down her cheeks.

Amelia spoke quietly. 'Would you like me to drive, Callie?'

Callie shook her head and she took one hand from the steering wheel and brushed the back of her hand over her eyes. 'I'm okay, but thank you.'

Amelia half-turned in the passenger seat and looked over into the back. Nigel's face was bright red and he stared out the window chewing at his lip. Rory had his arm around little Petie who'd stopped crying.

'Who knows how to play I Spy?' she said brightly.

##

Keeping the kids focused on the I Spy game—even Nigel eventually joined in—and keeping an eye on Callie took all of Amelia's energy on the way home. Dusk had come in quickly and it was too dark to see past the headlights now. Callie was watching the road carefully and Amelia kept her eyes peeled for wildlife. The trip seemed to take forever; her heart went out to Callie; she looked so upset.

As they approached the main gate of Kilcoy Station, Callie finally spoke. Her voice was husky and full of tears. 'Amelia, could I ask you not to say anything about what's been said here? I need to think before I talk to Braden. I need to decide what to do.'

'Okay, your turn, Rory,' Amelia said brightly. The boys were making enough noise in the back to cover their conversation in the front.

'Dead tree,' Nigel yelled.

'Donga,' Petie said. For a pre-schooler, she was impressed with how well he knew his letters.

'Dark! You're both wrong. And Petie there's no dongas out here.'

Amelia turned to Callie. 'I won't say anything,' she said quietly. 'But promise me you won't do anything silly like taking off in the middle of the night.'

Callie's smile was sad. 'Are you a mind reader? I've already done that once. I've run away before. But I thought that had had a happy ending. Maybe not.'

Amelia shook her head. 'Callie, there's obviously more behind this. I'm no child psychologist, but Nigel is hurting. He's been fine since I arrived. Something's happened to bring this on, and you're his target to make him feel better.' She shook her head. 'Trust me, I know how cruel kids can be in an attempt to make themselves feel better. Please don't do anything rash. Sit down and talk to Braden tonight.'

Callie's head shake was emphatic. 'I can't make him choose. He shouldn't have to choose between me and his kids. If I go, he'll get over it. He must put his boys first.'

Amelia held back a sigh. She felt totally useless. 'Well, just promise me that if you do decide to do anything like that, you'll tell me. Promise?'

Callie nodded. 'Okay.' She took one hand off the steering wheel and reached over and squeezed Amelia's hand. 'And thank you. I'm sorry you've been brought into our troubles. You've only been here five minutes and you've been drawn into it.'

'Things will get better. There's always a solution and I'm sure you and Braden can get to the bottom of it together.'

'I'll do what needs to be done. What's best for Braden and the boys.'

Amelia stared at Callie and her voice was firm. 'Don't you leave yourself out of the equation. Your happiness is important too, Callie. And I've seen how you and Braden are together. Your love for each other shines out, and the boys will all be a part of that.'

Callie lowered her voice as the noise in the back had reduced slightly. 'I think Braden and I got engaged too soon. But thanks for caring, Amelia. It's good to have you here. As a friend.'

Amelia chuckled in an attempt to lighten the heavy atmosphere. 'I'm glad, because I feel like an imposter at the moment. I haven't done any work yet, and Braden put me on the payroll from today.'

'It's the nature of this town, the whole area, I've found. And you've been helping! It may not be cattle work, but you've already put your stamp on the place. I'm very pleased you're here. Thank you for caring.'

It was dark when they drove into the house yard towards the shed, but the back lights illuminated the path to the gate. Braden came out of the house.

Callie pulled up but left the motor running. 'You all get out here, and I'll put the car away.'

Amelia opened her door and then went to the passenger door at the back. As she lifted Petie out, Braden came across and opened the other side. She was pleased to see that Nigel was more subdued, but Braden looked at his middle son; Nigel's eyes were noticeably red.

'How did you all go? Do we have obedient dogs now?' He smiled at Amelia.

Rory scrambled out and headed around to the back to let the dogs out. 'We have to do lots of practice, Dad.' He looked at his two brothers as Braden lifted the small dogs down. 'Nigel and Petie, you go and put the dogs away and give them their tea.' He lowered his voice. 'I need to talk to Dad.'

Nigel shot him a sour look as Amelia reached for Chilli's lead and helped her down.

'Thanks for taking me in,' she called out to Callie as the car began to move towards the big shed.

Callie gave her a wave. 'No problem.'

'Come on, Chilli, we'll go and get you settled for the night.'

'To save you cooking, Amelia, would you like to join us for dinner? I've got the barbie heating up,' Braden asked.

Rory tugged at his arm. 'Dad, I have to talk to you before Callie comes back.' The other two had disappeared towards the dog pens.

'Thanks for the offer, but I'll take a rain check, Braden. A bowl of soup and some toast will do me. It's been a big day. I'll see you all tomorrow.'

'Okay, if you need anything, just yell out. Our freezers are full,' Braden said. 'And thank you. I'm sure you helped out with these three terrors.'

As Amelia walked away, she heard Braden talk to Rory. 'What's up, mate?'

'Dad, Nigel was really, really mean to Callie and she was crying. Can you fix it, please? I don't want her to go away like Mummy did.'

Amelia picked up the pace before she could hear what Braden said. As sad as she was for them, it wasn't her business.

She heard Braden tell the boys to go inside, and he ran over to the shed, his shoulders sagging, his strides long as he made his way over to the shed and Callie.

Chapter 12

Amelia poured a can of tomato soup into a bowl and put it in the microwave. While it heated, she made some toast, and when the soup was hot, she loaded a tray and headed out to the back porch of the donga. Even though it was well and truly dark, she loved sitting out there, watching the sky, and listening to the comforting sounds of the bush. She was far enough away from the main house so that she couldn't see the lights or hear any sound from it. So far, she hadn't seen anyone in the donga next to hers. There had been some activity close by during the day where three more dongas were being built. Between the building works, the kids and the dogs, there was always something happening at Kilcoy Station.

The soup was warming and her wool poncho protected her from the chill wind. The lowing and snuffling of cattle in the paddock closest to the dongas carried on the wind and made her feel at home. As she ate her thoughts turned to the events of the day.

She hoped that Braden had given Nigel a good talking to, although maybe he needed to be shown he was loved more than getting into trouble. It was a hard call, and one she knew she wouldn't be able to make. Since she'd set off from home, her future seemed so uncertain. She had no desire to settle down with a partner, and until she'd met the three little Cartwright boys and discovered that she was a natural talking to them—and enjoyed it—the thought of having kids in the foreseeable future had never once crossed her mind.

Then she had to decide what to do about that house. Logic—not that she had much of that if she listened to Dad—well, logic told her it would be a stupid thing to do. She'd arrived in this town to work with cattle, and not to go looking at houses.

But oh, how she'd loved it. And how her heart was telling her to go ahead and buy it. There was no place for logic; it was your heart you had to follow.

Her face scrunched up as Ben Riley came into her thoughts.

Now there was something her heart—well maybe not so much her heart, but parts of her that were located a tiny bit lower than her heart—were telling her to take notice of their cries.

Her sex life was pretty non-existent, and that long-neglected part of her had only flared to life because Ben Riley was such an attractive guy.

Okay, so she hadn't noticed it before. When he'd been on the stage at that Easter concert, he'd been in black in the background while Kent took the front of the stage with his singing.

And then when he'd rocked up near the donga the other day and Chilli had gone for him—although that was a harsh way to put it—all she'd seen was an officious cranky man carrying a clipboard.

The Ben Riley of tonight had set her hormones clamouring for attention. His well-muscled arms in that sexy tight T-shirt, his kindness and patience with the boys, not to mention the times she'd snagged his gaze and could have drowned in those dark brown eyes, had hit her for six, and that was not on.

She was here to work. She'd already knocked back the offer of a date, and she would continue to do so.

As if on cue, her phone rang. She jumped up and hurried inside and picked it up, but it was an unknown number.

'Hello?' she said tentatively, waiting for someone to try to sell her solar panels or life insurance.

'Hey, Amelia, it's Ben.' Her traitorous body jumped straight to attention. 'I hope you don't mind; I got your number from Braden. I had to persuade him though.'

She smiled. 'That's okay. What's up? Was Chilli too hard for you to handle tonight?'

'No, she was great. I . . .um. . . I was hoping you'd come out to dinner with me tomorrow night.' He rushed on before she could answer. 'I haven't had many weekends free lately, because Kent and I are getting a few gigs. He asked for this weekend off because he's taking Sophie away, so I wondered if I could take you to dinner. To apologise for being such a jerk when we first met.'

Her words seemed to be creating themselves and Amelia surprised herself when they left her lips almost before he'd stopped talking. 'I'd love to.'

Where did that come from?

'You would?'

'Yeah, a night out would be good before I start work next week. Where to?'

She could hear the smile in his voice.

'Well, there's the pub or the—'

'Or the pub,' she finished for him.

His chuckle gave her goosebumps. Nice ones.

'Yep, the pub, unless you want to drive to Charleville. There's a great pub there. Lots of history and great meals.'

'The local pub will be fine. I don't want to go too far yet. I'm still learning the local district.'

'Trust me, that won't take too long. Great. I'll pick you up at five tomorrow.'

'There's no need to come out of town. I can drive in.'

'No. If I have a date, I insist on being a gentleman.'

Her common sense came to the fore.

About time.

'It's not a date, Ben. It's an apology.'

He laughed again and those damn goosebumps danced up and down her spine. 'Okay, I'll pick you up for my apology. See you tomorrow night.'

'Okay, I'll call you if something comes up.'

'See you tomorrow, Amelia.'

The call disconnected before she could say another word, but there was a smile on her face.

Whoever would have thought the shire inspector who'd pushed her buttons a few days ago was now pushing them in a very different way?

Amelia picked up her plates and spoon and headed inside. The wind had picked up and she was getting cold. As she rinsed her plates, her phone rang again, and she smiled.

What did he want now?

'Hello again,' she answered and then straightened as a female voice replied.

'Amelia, it's Callie. I hope I didn't wake you?'

'Heck no, I've just had dinner. Been sitting out the back enjoying the landscape. Everything okay?'

'Yes, all good, but I have a huge favour to ask. If you can't or don't want to, just say no, and we'll change our plans.'

'What do you need?'

'We've had a big heart-to-heart here, and we're still worried about Nigel. He's got himself in a real state. Braden rang the doctor, but he's away, and the new doctor answered. He wants us to come in first thing in the morning. I called Sophie but she and Kent are going away for the weekend. We just need someone to watch the other two boys. I know it's not your role here—'

'Stop right now. Of course, I will. I'm free all day. And forget about roles, it's what friends do. And I love those boys already. We'll have a great time.'

Callie's voice shook. 'You're a sweetheart. Amelia. Thanks so much. The appointment's for eight-thirty, so we'll have to leave a bit after seven. Sorry to get you up so early.'

'Callie, when I start work next week, I'll be up at five most days. I'll be over at the house by seven.'

***

Ben hummed under his breath as he stepped out of the bathroom towelling his hair.

She said yes!

He'd gone really close to not calling Amelia tonight, but he figured nothing ventured, nothing gained. He almost fell over when she'd said yes straight up.

So, he hadn't imagined that look in her eyes a couple of times this afternoon when their gazes had connected over Chilli.

'I take it the puppy school went well.' The dry voice came from behind as he walked up the hall.

'Jeez, Mum, give a man a heart attack. I thought you were in bed. You're up late.'

'I've been on the phone to your father trying to talk him into coming to the garden party but I was wasting my breath. You won't let me down, will you, Ben?'

'No, Mother dear. I gave you my word and I'll be there. It's for a good cause. But knowing what an event you put on, you'll need some more helpers. How about I ask Braden and Kent to help me set up the tables and chairs for you?'

'That would be greatly appreciated. It's the setting up that's the problem. The catering's well under control and I can get some of the young girls in town to come and serve and help clean up.'

'Sounds like it's all under control.' He leaned over and dropped a kiss on the top of his mother's head. 'Good night, mother dear. Don't sit up too late.'

Her eyes widened and she shook her head as he headed toward his room. 'You didn't tell me how the puppy school went.' She chuckled. 'But I guess there's no need to. Someone's in a very good mood.'

'Night, Mum,' he called as he went to close the door. He hesitated and pulled it open and poked his head around. 'Don't go cooking dinner for me tomorrow night. I'll be out.'

'Night, Ben. Sweet dreams.'

The smile stayed on his face after he was in bed and drifting off to sleep.

Chapter 13

Amelia headed over to the house a few minutes before seven. She tapped on the screen door, and Braden was there in an instant opening it for her.

'Thanks so much Amelia, we owe you.'

She smiled. 'My pleasure. The boys and I will have fun.'

'We all had a late night. It was a bit of a tough one, so we put a movie on and watched it until after ten. Petie and Rory are still sound asleep, so make yourself at home here until they wander out. Callie's just having a quick shower and we'll be off. Come into the kitchen and I'll show you where everything is.'

Amelia followed him into the kitchen. Nigel was sitting at the table, a bowl of Weet Bix in front of him. His eyes stayed closed as he spooned the cereal into his mouth, making odd little grunting noises with each mouthful.

She frowned as she looked at Braden, but he chuckled. 'Don't worry, that's Nigel. He eats his brekky like that every day. He's not a morning person. He'll wake up in a minute and turn back into the Nigel we all know and love.' He ruffled his son's hair as he walked over to the long bench under the window. 'Won't you, mate?'

Another grunt.

'Coffee maker is on. Just drop a pod into it when you're ready. Cereal is under here. They all have something different. Toaster, there, and jam and butter in the fridge.'

Callie came in and put her handbag on the table. 'Thanks, Amelia. We should be back by lunchtime. If there's anything you need, just give us a call.'

Five minutes later, she was standing at the window watching the family Landcruiser drive out the gate. The house was silent, only the ticking of the kitchen clock breaking the silence. The wind had picked up overnight and swirling willies of red dust spiralled along the road. It wasn't going to be a very nice day outside. She'd let the boys sleep as long as they wanted.

Chapter 14

The first thing that Ben did on Saturday morning was jump in his car and go around to George Malone's place. He looked around the neat and tidy garden as he walked up to the front door. The green timber door had a frosted glass panel at the top and one of those old-fashioned metal door ringers that you turned to make the bell ring. He tried to turn the ringer but it wouldn't turn; the door looked as though it hadn't been open for a long time. He wiped the rust off his fingers onto the side of his jeans.

Remembering his mother's habit of always welcoming guests at the back door, he stepped off the front porch and headed around the side towards the back of the house, past rose gardens fat with buds.

'Hello,' he called as he spotted an older woman hanging sheets on the old-fashioned clothes prop; pre-Hills Hoist days, it had two timber posts that tilted and lowered the line that she was throwing sheets over.

'Hello there. I'll be with you in a minute.'

As Ben watched, the line flew up on the other side and a strong gust of wind blew the sheet the woman was trying to drape over the wire onto the grass.

'Can I give you a hand?' he said as he walked over.

'That'd be a great help. Thank you. I haven't hung washing on a line like this since I used to stay with my grandmother back in the 1960s!' She laughed as he held the line steady while she retrieved the wet sheet off the grass. When it was draped over the line, she lifted the cane washing basket onto her hip and turned to him. 'What can I do for you?'

'I'm Ben Riley and I spent a lot of time here when I was a boy. Cricket practice.'

'Are you Jenny's boy?'

'I am.' There was no getting away from your country roots in a town this size. When he'd been working in the larger towns, Ben had appreciated the anonymity that had come with living there. It hadn't bothered him at all being referred to as a blow-in.

'I'm Ruth. I guess your mum told you the place was for sale? I bumped into her at IGA yesterday. She said she knew someone who might be interested.'

'Hi Ruth, nice to meet you. I met Fallon and Jon at Easter.'

'You're the singer, aren't you?'

Before he could answer she headed off across the lawn to the house. 'Come on in and we'll have a chat over a cuppa. I'm past due for one, been fighting with that clothesline all morning. But I'm done now. I don't know what possessed me to decide to wash everything in the linen press! It's all going to go to the op shop in the long run anyway.'

Ben held the screen door open for Ruth, and she disappeared into the laundry that was off to one side. He'd been in there a few times as a kid, to get a drink of water on hot afternoons, and the place smelled exactly the same. A damp concrete smell brought the memories rushing back.

Ruth hurried out and gestured to the kitchen. 'Sit down, I put the jug on before I went outside. Now, are you a tea drinker?' She lifted a teapot off the bench top.

'Tea's fine, thank you.'

A few minutes later, Ruth poured tea into a huge mug, and then put a plate of lamingtons on the table. 'Don't tell your mum, but I kept a few of these back from the CWA stall. My husband loves them and I never get a chance to cook when we're home in Brisbane.'

'I'm pleased you did.' He took a sip of burning hot tea and put the mug down on the table. 'So, is Mum right? Is this place for sale? I didn't see a For Sale sign when I came in.'

'The word sure got around,' Ruth said. 'We haven't seen the agent yet, but there's already a bit of interest. I'm surprised actually. I thought it would sit here for months. So, would you like to have a look through?'

'I would. If that's okay before it's on the market?'

'Of course it is. Anyway, from the interest so far, it might not even be advertised. Have another lamington, and you can have a wander while I fight with that old washing machine. Can you believe George still has an old wringer?'

Ben laughed. 'I don't even know what a wringer is.'

'Get away with you. Take your cup of tea and have a look around. Then if you're interested. just let me know and I'll talk to Fallon.'

Ben was careful as he walked up the dark hall carrying the mug of tea. Ruth's welcome had been friendly and she'd made him smile a few times as they'd chatted. He paused and looked into every room. It was obvious that they were cleaning out. Some rooms were empty and some had boxes in the corner. Despite being an old house, it was in good condition, and the rooms were a fair size with high ceilings. He could easily imagine living here.

For a while that was, and then when he moved away, he could rent it. His financial adviser was always telling him to put some of his money into property. There was no sign of Ruth when he rinsed his mug in the kitchen sink. He pushed open the back door and spotted her in a small vegie garden near the back fence.

'Thanks for letting me look around, Ruth. I'll get back to you within a week or so. Do you know how much it will go on the market for yet?'

'No. But I think we'll get it valued in the next few days. Fallon's going down to Charleville tomorrow to do some business, so I'll get her to make some enquiries.'

'Thanks, I'll call in and see you in a week or two if that suits?'

'No rush, Ben. Just let us know if you are seriously interested.'

'I will. Say hello to Fallon for me.'

Chapter 15

Amelia leaned back in the chair and put her hands on the table in front of her. Since she hadn't been working with cattle for a few months her nails had grown and her hands were a lot softer. She'd painted her fingernails tonight—the first time in a couple of years. She'd also gone to a bit more effort with what she wore, and with her hair. As she'd waited for Ben, she'd wondered why she had.

Ben had gone over to the bar to order their meals. He'd had one beer and was changing to Coke now and, Amelia had said no to another wine; deciding one white wine would last her a while.

Being a Saturday night, the pub was busy and full of noise and happy voices, and she relaxed, thinking how nice it was to see more of the town and how it fitted together. A few couples with small children sat out in the beer garden, the restaurant was quite full—most of the customers looked like grey nomies, but she recognised three couples who she'd seen at the Easter events sitting at a large table under the window. Spending most of her time alone or now with Chilli since she had got here—Amelia took an interest in people. She was enjoying the buzz of happiness around her and contentment seeped through her.

She loved this little town.

Chilli was home in the pen with the three pups and had seemed quite happy when she'd left.

Braden and Callie and Nigel had come home just after lunch and Amelia had had the afternoon to herself. She'd checked if Chilli would be okay, and there'd been no problem. When she'd said she was going out for a meal with Ben, Braden and Callie had both smiled.

The effort Amelia had put into getting herself ready to go out had been well worth it from the look on his face when he'd knocked at her door about an hour ago. His eyes were full of admiration and a warm flush went up her neck into her cheeks. No need to pinch her cheeks to get a bit of colour into them tonight.

The trip into town had gone quickly as they chatted the whole way. Amelia had tried hard not to give into her normal nervous habit of talking to fill the silence.

Ben had been full of questions about where she grew up and where she'd travelled, what she was doing here and how she spent her spare time. The conversation was easy as they travelled into town.

As soon as they crossed the road from where Ben had parked, the old man sitting at the table outside the main door of the hotel sat straight.

'Well, hello there, Missy. I've missed you,' he said.

'Gidday, Reg. How have you been?'

'Fair to middling, love. Fair to middling. Come back and have a chat with me later.'

'I will.' Amelia turned to Ben as they walked inside. 'That doesn't sound good. He must have been sick.'

Ben chuckled. 'You'll get to know old Reg. Fair to middling is a good day.'

Amelia got some curious looks as Ben guided her ahead of him. Everyone seemed to know Ben and there were lots of greetings as they crossed to the bistro.

'Gidday, Ben.'

'Good to see you back in town, mate.'

Ben nodded and smiled but didn't stop. The only hello Amelia received was the one from old Reg.

Ben pulled out a chair at the table he'd reserved. 'What would you like to drink?' he asked.

'A small white wine would be great, thanks. If you want to order our meal, I'm happy with a chicken parmi.'

He grinned at her. 'My meal of choice too.

After he walked back to the bar and waited at the counter with his back to her, chatting to the man beside him Amelia took the opportunity to really check Ben out.

For the life of her, she couldn't understand how she had gone from thinking he was a total jerk on their first meeting and really disliking him, to doing a full switch around sitting here thinking what a good-looking man he was, and what a nice guy. She felt totally at ease in his company.

With a slight frown, she tried to ignore that surge of attraction that was making her all warm and fuzzy inside.

Think about what your father would say, she reminded herself.

That'd be right, Amelia. Just rush into everything. Don't think about the consequences, then again you just don't think at all, do you? You just do what you want to.

Dad's criticism stung, even though it was only in her head. She sat up straight and pushed away her thoughts. What consequences could come from having a nice dinner with a very pleasant man? It wasn't as though she was going to hop into bed with him on the way home.

Then again, it had been a long time since she'd hopped into bed with anyone. With a soft sigh, Amelia waited for her new friend to come back.

***

'No gig, tonight, Ben?' Craig Wilson picked up his beer and leaned back on the bar counter.

'No, mate, Kent wanted the weekend off. We've been booked up since the concert out at your place.'

'The word got around, hey. Anyway, it should, I reckon you pair could be the new Keith Urban.'

Ben chuckled. 'Don't think so mate. Sure not going to replace the day job.'

'Good to have you back in town. I'll get you to come out to my place one day when I'm not out on the station. Need a bit of advice. I've seen what Braden's doing with his new accommodation, and I'd like you to have a look at where I'm thinking about building something similar.'

'Sure, how about Wednesday?' Ben swiped his credit card over the EFTPOS as his drinks were charged. Mack, the barman he'd gone to school with handed him a buzzer for their meals.

'Yep, that suits. You'd better go over and give your friend some company. New in town? Although she looks familiar.'

'Yep. She was at the concert at your place.'

'Ah, I remember. The new station hand out at Braden's. I'll have to ask him where he hires. There are a few agencies around these days. None of my blokes are lookers like she is.'

Ben felt uncomfortable discussing Amelia. 'I'll see you Wednesday, Craig.' With a nod, he picked up the drinks and the buzzer and headed back to their table.

He put the drinks on the table carefully and then placed the buzzer in the middle of the table before he sat down.

'It's busy in here tonight. I haven't seen the place humming like this for a few months. Lots of tourists. Good to see.'

'I love this town, so much atmosphere,' Amelia said.

Ben raised his eyebrows. 'Atmosphere? You must have had a very quiet life.'

'Not much happens in the Gulf on the cattle stations and there are no towns like this anywhere close. The only visitors we really had were those who flew in, and then I was away at school most of the time so I can't say it was terribly exciting.'

'I guess that's why you think this is exciting then. How would you go in the big smoke?'

'Oh no.' Amelia shook her head. 'I was in Longreach for a few weeks. Actually, that's where I got Chilli. I'll tell you that story later. I couldn't handle the traffic and the crowds and the noise. So many different people around you. Give me a quiet country town like this any day.'

'We're total opposites,' Ben said with a grin. 'I worked in a Longreach for a while.'

'Inspector?' she asked.

'No, engineer. I did engineering at uni. Came back home for a while and then I got a job in Longreach, and then a promotion to the shire in Charters Towers. I suppose they're not cities, but they're both big enough towns. Then I moved to St George. A bit closer to home.'

'And then you ended up back in Augathella where you grew up. You must have been pleased about that.'

'Not one little bit.' He pulled a face. 'I did my study and became an engineer so I could spread my wings and move somewhere interesting. I applied for a transfer to St George and I wasn't aware they had a reciprocal agreement with Morweh Shire and guess where I ended up? At Augathella as inspector!'

'And you're not happy about it, I'd say?' She raised a quizzical eyebrow.

'My mum is. But how many thirty-something-year-olds still live at home with their mum getting their washing and ironing done?'

'Half your luck. Mind you,' she said with a grin, as a warm shiver ran down Ben's back. 'I wash but I don't iron. There's not a lot of demand for pressed clothes in the paddock.'

'You're lucky. I've got the ironed shirts and the tie. The boss likes us to look professional.'

'Nothing wrong with that. But you really don't want to be here? That's a shame.'

'It's only a temporary trade,' he said. 'A year or so, but I have the option to choose where I end up. And it won't be here. What about you? Are you on contract?'

'Yes, I am, but I really love this place. I'm looking to settle somewhere and I reckon Augathella might be it.'

'But why Augathella?' he asked, bemused that someone young would really consider moving here.

'It's just the impression I've had. I've only been here a couple of weeks.'

'I thought you'd only been at Kilcoy Station for a few days.'

'No, I arrived just before Easter.' Her grin was cheeky. 'I was at the Easter concert where there was this really good duo playing.'

Ben flushed. 'So, not the time I made a fool of myself with my overreaction to Chilli Girl.'

'No, that was the second time I saw you. I wasn't impressed that the cool singer dude was a jerk.' She hurried on. 'I don't think that now though. Your apology has been very nice, thank you.'

'So, tell me what's contributed to this impression of Augathella that feels so good to you?'

'It just feels right. Kilcoy Station is a great property. I know I haven't been out and looked at most of it yet, but I can tell by looking at the cattle. It's a very well-run property. Jon is taking me out next week to show me what I'll be doing. And as far as the town goes, I've made more friends here than I've made anywhere in such a short time. I've been welcomed to town so warmly.' She gestured outside. 'Even old Reg was extra friendly.'

Ben lowered his voice and looked at her animated expression. 'I'd like to spend more time with you, Amelia. Can you fit in another friend?'

'I can. I'd like to be your friend too.'

Their eyes met and held, and Ben was lost. The spell was broken as the buzzer vibrated on the tabletop between them.

'Guess our dinner is ready,' Ben said looking away and feeling flustered.

What had happened then? He'd never had that strange jolt before. 'Stay there, I'll collect them.'

A couple of minutes later and he'd regained his composure as he carried two meals of chicken parmi back.

'Oh yum, that looks amazing,' Amelia said. 'It's my favourite.'

'I thought you'd be a steak girl.'

She chuckled and her eyes lit up as he sat opposite her and passed over the cutlery. 'Would you believe I don't eat red meat?'

The evening went quickly as they ate and chatted. Amelia watched on quietly as several locals stopped at the table to say hello to him and be introduced to Amelia. Her expression was interested and friendly, and Ben found it hard to take his eyes off her. Eventually, he stood and pushed in his chair.

'It's getting late. Last drinks soon. Are you right to go?'

'Sure,' she replied. He walked around and held her chair as she stood. 'You are a true gentleman, Ben Riley.'

'My mum has always taught me good manners.'

'And that includes picking up a girl and then taking her home?'

'That's exactly right.' It felt right as she slipped her arm through the crook of his elbow as they walked out through the pub.

'Won't be long getting back to Mum,' he thought as Mrs Jenkins smiled at him and nudged her husband in the ribs.

The drive home went quickly as they kept talking. The main house was in darkness when he pulled up outside her donga.

'Thank you, Ben. I'll be right. You go, it's late. I'll just go and check on Chilli.'

'No, I'll come with you and I'll see you to your door. That's what a gentleman does.'

He could see her smile in the darkness as he got out and came around to open the passenger door.

'I could get used to this,' she said as he took her hand and she slid down to the ground.

Ben didn't move as she stood next to him and he kept hold of her hand in the comfortable silence. Eventually, she squeezed his fingers. 'Come on, we'll go over and check if Chilli's happy. If she's settled, I'll leave her there. It's good practice for her for when I have to do overnight work out on the station.'

'Has she been behaving?' Ben asked quietly as they walked over.

Amelia nodded as they walked over to the dog pen behind the shed adjacent to the main house. Chilli came out and licked both their hands, wagging her tail madly as Ben crouched down at the fence.

'Hello, Chill Girl,' he said quietly. There was no sign of the other dogs. Chilli stretched and went back into her kennel at Amelia's command. Amelia turned and beckoned Ben away quietly. Nothing stirred. The night was still, the wind had dropped and the cattle were quiet. The night sky was brilliant, full of diamond stars.

'It's so beautiful, out here, isn't it?' Amelia whispered as they reached her donga. Ben stopped, held her gently and turned her to him.

'It's not the only beautiful thing out here, tonight, Amelia. I hope you don't mind if I kiss you goodnight,' he said as he lowered his head.

Chapter 16

'I don't mind at all,' Amelia whispered. His kiss was beautiful. Softly at first, his lips touched her cheek and then slid slowly to the crease at the edge of her mouth.

'Are you sure?' he murmured.

'I'm sure,' she said quietly, as warm anticipation coursed through her veins. His lips slid gently onto hers and her knees trembled, but Ben's arms held her close as he deepened the kiss. Amelia kept her eyes closed, not wanting it to end.

Finally, he lifted his head and she slowly opened her eyes.

'That was very nice,' she said.

'It was. I have a question for you.' His voice was low and husky.

For a moment she worried that he wanted to stay the night. No matter how good the kiss had been or how much she liked Ben, sex on a first date wasn't something she did.

No matter *how* tempted she was.

'Y . . .e . . .s?' she asked slowly as he turned towards her donga and held her hand.

'I have to go to Charleville tomorrow. I was hoping you'd keep me company. Unless you've got other plans already.'

Amelia shook her head, and his face fell in disappointment.

She squeezed his fingers. 'I have no plans. I'd love to. I haven't been to Charleville yet.'

'Excellent. I just have to make one quick stop and then I'll take you on the tourist trail, and then we'll have lunch at my favourite pub.'

'I hope there's lots of walking involved after that huge dinner I had tonight.'

'There can be. Or I could pack a picnic and we could sit by the river.'

'Or I could buy hamburgers or fish and chips. My turn to shout you. So, tell me about the tourist trail.'

'More red dirt, solar flares, great camping, bilbies, damper, secret WW2 bases, great coffee and star gazing. Wear jeans and walking shoes and I'll show you the sights.'

'All in one day? I'll look forward to it.'

They had reached the bottom step of her donga.

Ben glanced at this watch. 'I guess I'd better get going. Thank you for a great night.'

Again, Amelia was tempted to invite him in for coffee, but she knew if she did, that was giving a signal she wasn't ready for yet. 'Thank you. I'll drive in and meet you in town. What time?'

Ben shook his head. 'No, I'll come and pick you up. My invite, I drive. What about Chilli? Do you want to bring her?'

'I'll check with Callie in the morning to see if she can stay in the pen. I'll get up early and take her for a walk if she stays home.'

'She can come too if you want. We can take her to most places we'll be going. Especially if we have a picnic. Would she be okay in the car for a few minutes now and then?'

'That's very kind of you. And yes, she's used to that.'

'Hey, I love dogs. Even ones that have bitten me.' He laughed and she smiled up at him. 'I'll pick you up at nine. Unless that's too early on a Sunday morning.'

'Nine is good. I'll go over and see Callie early.' Amelia stood on her toes—Ben was tall—and reached up and brushed her lips over his. 'Now get going. I'll see you tomorrow.'

His arms went around her waist and it was a good ten minutes later that Amelia stood watching the tail lights of his four-wheel drive disappear down the road.

She put her fingers to her lips and walked inside, a huge smile on her face. Her feet were almost walking on air.

Or that's what it felt like anyway.

Whoever would have thought it?

Another reason to love Augathella. The only problem was it sounded as though Ben wouldn't be here long.

##

The next morning Amelia was up bright and early. She pulled on her old work clothes and hurried across to the dog pen with Chilli's lead. Chilli had been made so welcome by Callie and the Cartwrights that the least she could do was feed the dogs and clean up the pen.

Chilli came wandering out, stretched and came over for a cuddle.

'Hello, my beautiful girl. Have you been good? I didn't hear a peep out of you all night. Or did I sleep too soundly?' Her sleep had been full of delicious dreams. Each one involved Ben Riley, and she was looking forward to spending more time with him today.

Amelia filled the bowls with kibble and supervised to make sure they all stayed at their own bowl. She filled up the water bowls and then after removing the hessian beds and hanging them on the fence she washed out the concrete pen with the hose. As she turned the tap off, the screen door of the house opened, and Callie came out with a basket of washing on her hip.

'Morning, Amelia,' Callie said glancing across at the pen. 'Oh, thanks so much for doing that. We all slept in.'

'So did the dogs.' Amelia grinned. Happiness was bursting out of her. It was a beautiful day, despite the chill of the autumn wind making her nose cold. 'How did things go yesterday?'

'Really, really good. The new doctor at the hospital, Doctor Higgins, was really thorough and even though he has a brisk and cool manner, Nigel warmed to him straight away. He talked to us with Nigel there first, and then he spent an hour with Nigel. He obviously said the right things, because the first thing Nigel did when he came out was put his arms around and say sorry to me.' Callie blinked. 'I cried.'

'That's progress,' Amelia said. 'I felt so sorry for you yesterday, and poor little Nigel.'

'Yes, as time passes, he's not dealing with Julia's loss as well as Rory and Petie. Dr Higgins has referred him to a child psychologist in Charleville. Thanks so much for looking after the other two. We seem to have imposed on you so much.'

'Not at all. That's what friends are for. Did you need me for anything today?'

'No, of course not. It's Sunday and I know Jon will be here bright and early to take you out to see the station tomorrow. You relax today.' Callie gestured to the dog pen. 'You've already done a day's work there.'

'I was, um, thinking about going to Charleville myself. Ben has to go in and he invited me to go with him.'

Callie looked at her quizzically, and then she smiled when Amelia's cheeks heated.

'Then I guess the dinner date went well?'

'It did. We talked for hours. And I mean we *both* did. I managed not to talk too much for a change. My mum always says I can talk the hind leg off a donkey. Ben is great. He's taking me on the tourist trail of Charleville today.'

'What about Chilli?'

'He said I could bring her.'

'Why don't you leave her here? She's no trouble and the pups and the boys love her.'

'Would that really be all right? I hate imposing. I really do.'

'Of course, it's okay! Now you go and get ready. Leave Chilli's lead here. The boys can take her for a walk later. And don't rush home, although make sure you watch out for roos if you're home after dark. They were pretty bad last night.'

'Ben's coming out to pick me up. And drop me home.'

Callie's eyebrows rose. 'Wow, I'm impressed. He must be smitten. He's a really nice guy.'

'He is.' Amelia felt her cheeks heat again. 'Anyway, we won't be too late because I have an early start tomorrow. Jon said we'd be heading out at six.'

'Okay, you have a good day. Oh, and while I think of it, another station hand will be moving into the second donga today, so don't worry if you see a light there. His name's Charlie Cavanagh. One of our regulars. He usually camps out in a swag, but he's finally admitted he's too old to sleep on the ground.'

'Okay, thanks. I wondered if there was someone there.'

'Soon. He's a real character. Now go make yourself beautiful, girlfriend!'

Amelia crouched down and gave Chilli Girl a pat and a hug as Callie headed to the clothesline. 'You be a good girl, and I'll see you this afternoon.'

***

Ben wandered out to the kitchen still in his PJs and covered a yawn with the back of his hand.

'Morning, Mum,' he said.

'Morning, sweetheart. You look tired. You had a late night last night, didn't you?'

'I did and I've got to head off to Charleville this morning. What are your plans for the day?'

'I'm spending the whole day in the garden. I've got a lot of pruning to do and I want to mulch the rose garden and I'd like to—'

'Do you need your car today?' Ben interrupted. He knew Mum could talk forever about what her plans were in the garden.

'No, I don't have any intentions of going anywhere today. Do you want to borrow it?'

'I do. I'm off to Charleville. Billy Hanna called me last week. He's got a new guitar in stock and I said I couldn't get down through the week so he's taken it home and I said I'd call in today.'

'So, you need my car to bring home a new guitar? If you buy it.'

'Not exactly. I'm . . .ah . . . taking someone with me for the drive.' He tried to keep a casual tone but Mum honed right in.

'Would that be the pretty girl you had dinner with at the hotel last night?'

Ben rolled his eyes. 'God, Mum, this is why I hate living in Augathella. Nothing's private. You can't even take a leak without someone knowing.'

'No need to be crude. It's one of the reasons you should love living in a town like this. People like you, people care about you, and people are interested in what you do. Everyone is so pleased to see you back in town and everyone is saying what a great job you're doing on the shire.

'Well, it would be nice to have somewhere different to go for dinner and not have the whole town know the next morning where you've been and what you ate.'

'And how was the chicken parmi?' Jenny chuckled and put her hands up. 'And no. No one told me what you had for dinner. I just know you well, my boy. Mind you, I remember when I was teaching at the high school and some of the kids had after-school jobs. I did hate that everybody in town knew what you and your father and I were having for dinner every night when I used to go to IGA on the way home.'

'Then you know exactly what I'm saying.'

'I do, but don't change the subject. Tell me who you were having dinner with. From all accounts, she's very pretty.'

'You're incorrigible, Mum. She's a new station hand out at Braden's property. I met her a week or so ago when I was out there looking at the concrete for his new dongas

'Oh, she was the one whose dog bit you and you did the puppy school with on Friday night. Quick work, son. Friday night puppy school Saturday night dinner, Sunday Charleville. Hmmm.'

'That's enough hmming from you Mum. We're simply friends and I thought she might like to see Charleville while I'm down there. There's lots to see. I haven't been to the World War II site yet.'

'That's fine, take my car. I won't need it but you might like to give it a bit of a sweep out first because I brought home some fertiliser the other day and it spilt in the backseat. There's a bit of a smell in there.'

'In your Audi? You put chook poo in the Audi? For goodness' sake, Mum, next time put it in the boot or ask me and I'll pick it up in my ute.'

'It's okay. It'll clean. I'll dig out some air freshener So is she coming in and meeting you here? I'd better get out of my dressing gown. A mother never wants to meet her son's—'

'Mum!'

'I was going to say meet her son's friends in her dressing gown.' But her smile was devious.

'No. I'm going to take my ute out and pick her up at Kilcoy Station and then we'll call in here and swap cars over. I guess if you're home, you'd like to meet Amelia. She likes Augathella.'

'An excellent influence on you. And I'd love to meet her. That's what this town needs. More young blood moving in. Have you heard about the new young couple in town with the organic vegie crops?'

'I have.' Ben was relieved she'd finally got off the subject of meeting Amelia.

'One thing I will say if you are interested in George Malone's house, I'd get a move on. There are a few newbies in town. There might be a bit of interest.'

'I'll think about it.' He wasn't going to let on he'd already looked at the house but it seemed that nugget of news hadn't got back to Mum yet. That was a first.

She tipped her head to one side. 'First time I've known you to take someone out for quite a long time.'

'Mum, you've got no idea what I've been doing while I've been in Longreach and Charters Towers and St George.'

'I know. That's why it's so good to have you home and I do know what's happening.' She giggled, more like a teenager than a fifty-five-year-old. 'What are you going to wear today? Your dark brown long-sleeved shirt is ironed. It brings out the colour of your eyes. You've got your father's eyes. They always sucked me in when we were courting.'

'Mum! I am not courting! And if I was, I wouldn't tell you. Now get out in that garden, Mother. I'm going to have a shower.' Ben ruffled her hair on his way out as she sat at the kitchen table drinking her cup of tea.

Chapter 17

'Your mum's lovely.'

Ben smiled as they turned onto the highway towards Charleville.

'She was certainly on her best behaviour. I don't think she was game to be anything else,' he chuckled.

'Beautiful garden. I envy her. It's one thing I want to do. I'd love to have a yard where I can grow my flowers.'

'You'd like to settle one day?'

'I would. I'd love to have my own place with a bit of land. I could bring my horse down. I do miss her.'

For some reason, Amelia didn't want to say that she was looking at a place in Augathella because she knew how much Ben wanted to get out; she worried that he would judge her. That she was rushing in before she really knew the town, or before she had a permanent job, not just a contract. He didn't need to know that money wasn't an issue for her.

'Me too. I'd like to have my own place. I just don't know where yet. I certainly don't want to be living with my parents for the rest of my life.' He pulled a face and she grinned at him.

'Tell me where we're going today,' she said. 'What this tourist trail tour is.'

'Well, if you don't mind the first thing, I have to do is to call in and see a mate and pick up a guitar I've bought.'

'No problem at all. I'm in your hands.' The look he gave her was cheeky.

'Nice,' he said.

'Don't be rude,' Amelia said but her smile stayed.

'Then it's your choice. You tell me what you'd like to do. There are a lot of things to see. Are you into stars?'

'What sort of stars? Movie stars or sky stars? Or astrology stars? I had my tarot cards read at the van park in Longreach.'

The banter continued between them for the next hour or so and in the end, they decided to begin the tour at the Cosmos Centre after Ben had picked up his guitar.

Amelia sat in the car and sent her weekly text home while she waited; she'd forgotten to do it earlier. She shook her head with a grin. She'd been too excited waiting for Ben to come and collect her for their day out. She called home only on rare occasions, and her parents never rang her.

A door closed and she watched Ben as he came out of the house carefully carrying a guitar case. He placed it almost reverently on the back seat.

'She's a beauty. Emerald green and she sings. Can't wait to play her at our next gig.'

'A singing guitar? I've never seen one of them,' she teased. 'You'll have to tell me where it is. I'd love to hear you both again.'

'We're up at Tambo at the pub next weekend. Sunday afternoon gig.'

'I'll see if I'm working. How far is it?'

'About an hour north,' he said. 'You could come with me if you wanted.'

'I'll see what happens. I can't go leaving Chilli all the time. That's not why I got her.'

'Dogs are allowed at the pub there.'

'I'll see.'

'Okay.'

Ben obviously picked up not to push her.

'I really enjoyed listening to you and Kent performing at the Easter concert. You did sing a little bit that night, didn't you?'

'Sometimes, but Kent's the one with the voice. I just love to play guitar.'

'Do you play any other instruments?'

'Yeah, the piano, and I've got a drum set back in the garage at home. What about you?'

'I love listening to music but I'm pretty much tone deaf. Can't sing, don't play any instruments, unless you count the recorder at school. The teachers used to despair of me at boarding school. I couldn't even play that well.'

'Boarding school? High school?'

'No. From when I was ten.'

'Was that hard?'

'Sure was. I missed being out on the land. And I missed my horse.'

He glanced at her and she realised she hadn't said anything about her family.

'Oh, and my brothers, of course.'

Amelia was pleased when he changed the subject.

'Any other hobbies?'

'Riding. I know that's work, but it's also a passion of mine. I so miss my horse. I left Brinny at home. It'll be good to be on horseback tomorrow. When I do settle somewhere I'll bring her down. She smiled and looked out of the car. 'Are we going to sit and chat all day or are we going to see the stars now?'

'We are.' Ben started the Audi and pulled out onto the road. 'That's the railway station. We can come back here later for the bilby show. I rang up and checked what time it was on. If you still want to go, that is.'

'I do. I tell you what though. I'd love a coffee. Is there a café where we're going?'

'I'm not sure, but there are a few good coffee places in town. You're a woman after my own heart. I love a good coffee. Plus, I'm hungry.'

Amelia nodded. 'I should be embarrassed to admit it, but so am I. Coffee and cake sound good to me.'

'Well, that's at least one thing we have in common,' Ben said. 'And you've got a big week of work ahead, I guess.'

'I do. What about you?'

'I've got a bit of travelling this week. I'll be out at Kilcoy for a meeting with Braden sometime, but I guess you'll be out on the station.'

'Text me and let me know when you'll be there. I might be able to give you a coffee if it's late in the day.' She put on a smug smile. 'I have a very good coffeemaker for coffee snobs.'

'I will. Have you got next weekend off? And what about Friday night for Chilli's puppy class?'

'I'll know more tomorrow.' She looked down as Ben reached over and touched her hand briefly.

'Stay in touch through the week?'

'If you'd like me to.'

'I would,' he said as he turned into an area that looked like the main business centre. He took a right and parked outside an old house that had been turned into a historical museum.

'Good.'

'You could be sorry you asked that. You might find me totally painful today after you show me around.'

'I don't think that's a possibility. I'm getting to know you. And I like what I see.'

Chapter 18

The next week flew past with only one minor incident, but that solved the mystery of poor Chilli's initial incident with Ben. After two days out on horseback with Jon, Amelia spent Wednesday in the main shed with him, learning more about the property and her role over the next few months. Charlie, the other new arrival had gone to join the team mustering in the far paddocks. Amelia was pleased that to begin with she would be mostly on horseback, mustering and looking after steers that needed attention and would be held in a paddock not far from the homestead.

When Ben texted on Wednesday to say he would be calling in to see Braden at about four-thirty, she was able to respond she would be home and would have the coffee on.

Callie was in the house garden when Amelia walked back from the shed just after three.

'Hey,' she called out. 'How's your week been, Amelia? You've had a couple of long days.'

'I have but I've loved every minute of it. Kilcoy Station is so well run.'

Callie smiled. 'I'm more up to date with education than agriculture or cattle work but I'm pleased you're happy.'

'I have a huge favour to ask, but feel free to say no.'

'What can I do for you?

Amelia looked around. 'The boys aren't home from school yet?'

'No. It's my other day at home, and Braden took them in. He had to go down to Charleville for the day but he's at the school getting them now. He's not long called. They're coming straight home because he's got a meeting here with Ben around four. Why? What's up?'

'I really hope I'm not overstepping, but Ben's going to have a coffee with me, and I haven't been shopping. I don't even have a dry biscuit in the donga. Would you mind if I baked a cake in your kitchen and I'll just take a couple of slices and the boys can have the rest for afternoon tea? I'll pay for the ingredients.'

'Of course, you can. And you're not paying for anything. Come in now and we'll have a cuppa while you get started.'

'I'll just race back and have a wash and get changed.'

Callie grinned. 'I'm sure Ben will like you just the way you are.'

Amelia grinned back. 'Give me five.' She hurried to her donga, had a quick wash, got rid of the cattle smell, and slipped into a pair of clean jeans and a plain T-shirt She didn't want to look like she'd made too much of an effort.

Half an hour later, she and Callie were sitting on the veranda with a coffee and the aroma of the sultana cake baking in the oven drifting out through the doorway. Chilli and the three pups were playing chase on the lawn inside the house fence.

'I meant to ask you before. Are you free on Saturday night?' Callie asked. 'Sophie called me to invite us all to dinner. Kent was going to ask Ben, but they weren't sure whether you pair were a couple or what. So, she asked me to invite you, and he's going to invite Ben.'

Amelia flushed. 'Um, we get on well, and we enjoy each other's company. The day we spent in Charleville was great and we ended up having a late one because Ben took me to the Corones Hotel for an early dinner. I'm going to Tambo with him and Kent on Sunday, but Saturday's free.'

'Sounds pretty good to me,' Callie said.

'But we're just friends,' Amelia insisted.

'So far.' Callie winked. 'Look there's a car coming. Too soon for Braden. It must be Ben. I'll go and check that sultana cake for you.'

Amelia stood and went to the gate yard so Ben would see she was at the house.

He waved and parked the shire ute over near the shed. She waited until he came across, and Chilli ran over to her for a pat.

She crouched down and hugged her dog. 'You've been such a good girl.' She was rewarded with a wet lick on her cheek. They'd been practising the instructions that Ben had taught them last Friday night. She laughed as the other three pups came over and sat when she commanded them to while Ben stood at the gate.

He smiled at her and a warm fuzzy feeling ran through her. His eyes stayed on hers as he lifted the latch.

Would he kiss her hello? Or was it too public?

Or were they just friends?

Ben looked down as Chilli began to creep towards the gate, a low growl emanating from her throat.

'Chilli!' Amelia commanded. 'Sit. Now!'

She leaned forward to hold Chilli's collar, but her dog took off before she could grab her.

Ben stood stock still as Chill bounded towards him, barking, and the bark held a menace. Amelia dived after her and finally caught her just before she reached the gate, her growl deepening and her teeth bared.

'Ben, shut the gate, quick,' she yelled as she tried to hold Chilli back.

Finally, the angry dog settled once Ben was behind the gate again. Amelia frowned as she looked down at her usually docile dog.

She looked up at Ben, and he shrugged, and then she looked back down at Chilli who had started to whimper.

Crouching down, she held the pup's chin firmly in her hand. 'What is it, sweetie? What's wrong?'

Callie opened the door and walked down the steps. 'Hi, Ben, come on in. Cake's ready, Amelia.'

'I'll be there in a minute. Thanks,' Ben called back.

Amelia bit her lip. Chilli was looking at Ben and shaking.

Callie came over to the gate. 'What's wrong?'

'Chilli tried to go for Ben again.'

'But she's been okay with him since last week, hasn't she?'

'She has. She loved him at puppy school last week.'

'What's happened?'

'Nothing.' Amelia looked up at Ben, her heart breaking. If Chilli didn't like Ben, she couldn't keep seeing him. She'd already been through one lot of trauma and been abandoned. Amelia wouldn't do that to her again.

'Can you hold her for me please? I'll go over and talk to Ben.' She handed the lead to Callie. But hold her tight. She's strong.'

As she handed the lead to Callie, Ben called her name.

'Amelia, wait. I think I know what the problem is. Let me try something.'

She and Callie stood back and watched as Ben turned his back for a minute.

When he turned around, Chilli Girl looked up and wagged her tail. He hadn't moved or spoken and hadn't greeted her. Amelia looked on in amazement.

It was as much as if she was saying, 'Ben, it's you!'

Ben opened the gate and with a happy woof, Chilli ran over to him and as he crouched down, Amelia could see what he'd done.

'Well, will you look at that,' she said to Callie.

He'd taken his tie off, and his name tag, and rolled up his long sleeves. The official look had gone and now he just looked like Ben.

Amelia walked over to the gate and stood beside them. Without paying any regard to Callie, he leaned over and kissed Amelia on the lips.

'Hello.'

'Hello, you,' she said against his warm mouth.

Callie was smiling when they turned to her.

'I know what we have to work on with Chilli,' Ben said. 'The authority look. She's obviously been hurt by someone looking official.'

'Can you work with her on that?' Amelia asked anxiously.

'I can but it will mean spending a lot more time with Chilli and her owner.'

'Excellent. Good work, Ben! Now that's sorted do you want cake and coffee here or over at Amelia's place?' Callie said.

Amelia looked at Ben, and Ben looked at Callie.

'Do you have real coffee, Callie? I know Amelia's fussy.'

'I know who's fussy,' she said. 'And despite that I made you a cake!'

'I'll go and grind the beans and leave you two to argue,' Callie said with a wide grin. 'But be quick because I can see the dust from Braden's car. You'll get no peace once the boys are home.'

Ben opened his arms and Amelia stepped into them.

And there wasn't one peep out of Chilli Girl.

Chapter 19
Saturday night

As usual Ben had insisted on driving out to Kilcoy Station to pick Amelia up for the dinner at the pub on Saturday night. Sophie and Kent had organised the dinner, and apparently, a large group was going.

Ruth Malone was minding the boys so Callie and Braden could have a night out. They left for town before Ben arrived.

Amelia was strangely nervous; she'd tried to chase the feeling away as she'd walked back from the dog pen where Chilli had settled happily for the night.

Why did she feel so strange?

Wasn't this what she'd wanted?

To become part of a community?

She fussed about what to wear and fiddled with her hair. Tying it back, leaving it loose and then tying it up again.

When she heard Ben's ute pull up outside, she ran to the mirror and a pale face looked back at her. She pinched her cheeks until they had some colour, smoothed her hand down her skirt, and slipped her knee-length boots on over her tights.

Had she fallen into this relationship too quickly? Was she doing everything that Dad always said she did? Rushed in, no thought?

Like she had when she had rescued Chilli Girl? Like she had when she'd seen the job at Kilcoy Station and applied without thinking twice?

At least she'd pulled back on buying the Malone house. That would have been too much of a rush with the financial outlay. So, see, Dad, she could be sensible.

But with Ben, all sense flew out the window.

She'd lost it when Ben had kissed her the first time.

There had been many kisses since then, but that's where they'd left it for the time being. But she knew if Ben had had his own place, things would have moved much more quickly.

Had she got in too deep too fast?

Amelia put a shaking hand to her face as his footsteps on the stairs shook the flimsy donga. She opened the door and a long wolf whistle came from the verandah of the other donga.

Charlie Cavanagh was out there having a smoke. 'Looking good, girlie. Sorry, Ben,' he chuckled. 'Just admiring, not stepping on your toes, mate.'

Ben gave him a wave and held his other hand out to Amelia.

'You look drop-dead gorgeous.' His dark eyes snagged hers and she drew a quick breath.

She held her breath at his expression, and her doubts fled in an instant. 'You don't look too bad yourself,' she said reaching up to kiss him and that brought another whistle from Charlie.

Ben put his arm around her. 'Hurry up and get in the car. That westerly wind has come early.'

She climbed into the warmth of the cabin, and Ben hurried around and opened his door. Once in, he sat there for a moment and didn't start the car.

'What's wrong?' she asked.

'I wanted to tell you something. A couple of things actually. Before we get to the pub and the grapevine kicks into gear.'

She drew another quick breath. 'You're leaving town?'

Ben stared at her for a long minute. 'Do you think I could?' he finally said.

'I know you want to.'

'I wanted to leave the life I had here. But I've grown to love it here a lot more in the last few weeks. Since a certain dog tried to bite me.'

'But?'

'But I've also met someone I want to get to know a lot better. I'm not going to rush you, Amelia. We have all the time in the world to explore where this is taking us.'

'But you hate living at home. And you don't like your job.'

'I do like my job.' His expression held a lot of satisfaction. 'My new job. I didn't tell you I applied for another one. Meet the new shire engineer for Morweh Council. Not a new job, but I was asked if I was interested in a promotion. I got the nod today.'

'So, you're moving to Charleville?'

'No, I'm moving out of home, but not that far. A little bit closer to Charleville.' He smiled at her. 'About a kilometre closer.'

'Stop teasing me. Where to?'

He folded his arms and looked very satisfied. 'I've bought a house. It has land and it could do with a horse there if you know anyone who's looking for a place to leave their horse.'

'Oh, my goodness,' she exclaimed. 'Did you buy George Malone's house?'

His face was a picture. 'Do you know George? How did you know his house was for sale?'

'Because I looked through it and fell in love with it, and thought about buying it myself!'

'So, you wouldn't mind living on the edge of town. Maybe one day?'

'If the right offer was made one day, I'd certainly consider it. Like you said, Ben, we have all the time in the world.'

It was quite a while before Ben drove them into town.

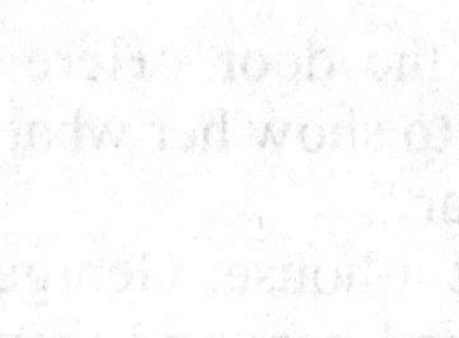

Epilogue
The pub

Braden put his arm around Callie's shoulder and he looked around, satisfied. His little sister, Sophie, caught his eye and her smile was wide as she looked back at him. Her fiancé, Kent, was deep in conversation with Jon Ingram, and Fallon was sitting at the end of the table, one hand on her very pregnant stomach. Kent's sister, Jacinta, was sitting beside Sophie's best friend, Kimberly, and a couple of their teacher friends from the primary school were at the other end of the table with their partners, all local cattlemen Braden had worked with.

The queue at the bistro was growing quickly and Callie leaned into him. 'Do you think we should wait for Ben and Amelia, or should we order?'

Braden gestured to the door. 'Here they are now. I'd say Ben took Amelia for a drive to show her what he's bought.'

'Has he got a new car?'

'Nope. He's bought a house. George Malone's place. Ruth and her husband have finished here and they're going back to Brisbane for a couple of months until the baby's born.'

Callie elbowed him in the ribs. 'How come I work in town but you know more gossip than I do?'

'Because I'm a local.' He pressed his lips close to her ear.' And you could be too, if you agreed to set a wedding date.'

He felt Callie's withdrawal and a chill ran through him. He just hoped it wasn't a premonition.

'Don't push, Bray. I agreed to stay engaged, but we won't get married until we're sure it's the right thing for the boys.'

'I'm sorry, sweetheart. I love you, and I want you to be my wife.'

'And I've said yes, but when Nigel's better.'

Kent stood up and dinged a spoon on the side of his beer glass. It was barely heard over the noise in the bistro, so he put two fingers to his mouth and whistled.

There was instant silence, not only at their table but in the whole bistro.

'Ssh everyone, Kent's gonna sing us a song, came a quavering voice from the bar.

'I'll sing you a song, Reggie,' he replied with a laugh. 'Thanks for coming, everyone. Sophie and I just wanted to say a few words while we had you all together, and before we all start eating.'

Sophie stood up and took Kent's hand and satisfaction filled Braden. His sister was settled, and she had a good man.

'Thanks, everyone,' Sophie echoed Kent's words. 'Kent and I have set a wedding date.'

Cheers and clapping filled the room, and she waited for the noise to subside before she continued. 'September three, the first Saturday in spring. And three lovely ladies have agreed to be my bridesmaids. Stand up, girls!'

Kimberly Riordan was the first to stand and another cheer went up. Kent's sister, Jacinta stood slowly, her cheeks flushed with embarrassment. Braden felt sorry for her; where Kent was an outgoing performer, Jacinta was an introvert.

Another round of clapping ensued, and Braden was surprised when Callie lifted his arm and she too stood. She grinned down at him and he grinned back.

'Well, I never,' he said.

'A bridesmaid, my dear, not a matron of honour,' she whispered.

'I'll bring you round,' he said.

Things had been tough lately. Since Nigel's meltdown, Callie had moved into the spare room, and he worried that it was the start of a division between them.

The new doctor, Harry Higgins, had assured him that it was a wise move, to give Nigel time to adjust to Callie being their step mum. Braden was torn; he wanted the best for Nigel, but he also didn't want to let Callie go.

If he'd been a stronger man when Julia had died and kept the boys, maybe Nigel would have been better.

'Patience, my darling.' Callie's lips brushing across his cheek made him feel a little better. 'I'll go and order for us. You grab yourself another beer.'

At least Callie had agreed to stay in a room at the pub tonight and the boys were sleeping over at the Malone's house.

'The usual steak with mushroom sauce?' she asked. 'And garlic bread?'

'You know me well.'

As Callie walked across to the counter with Sophie, Braden saw Kent half-rise in his chair, his face leached of all colour. He was staring at the door that led out to the street.

Braden turned with a frown and for a moment his heart stopped. *Julia?*

And then sense kicked in. Julia was in the local cemetery, and this woman was a lot taller than his wife had been. But the shock of seeing a face almost identical to Julia's had him standing without even thinking about it.

He gripped the back of his chair as she walked over to him.

'Hello, Braden.' Her tone was cold and her accent plummy, and he suddenly realised who it was.

'Laura,' he whispered.

'Yes, Braden. It looks like all I've heard is true. You and your new woman are out drinking while those three motherless boys are where?' She looked around. 'Out in the beer garden? Or home alone? Nothing would surprise me from you.'

Braden took her arm and tried to lead her outside before she made a scene. Julia had always told him what a loose cannon his sister-in-law was, and despite being married to Julia for almost seven years, he'd never met Laura Adnum. As far as he'd known she still lived in the UK.

What on earth was she doing here in Augathella?

THE END

**The stories continue in
The Augathella Girls: Volume 2**

The last four books in the bestselling Augathella Girls series in
one volume. Over a year, eight women make their way to the
Augathella region in outback Queensland.
The magic of the landscape, new friendships, and new loves give
each of them a new beginning.

If you would like to stay up to date with Annie's releases, subscribe to her newsletter here:
http://www.annieseaton.net

OTHER BOOKS from ANNIE

Daughters of the Darling

From Across the Sea
Over the River (2024)

Porter Sisters Series

Kakadu Sunset
Daintree
Diamond Sky
Hidden Valley
Larapinta
Kakadu Dawn

Pentecost Island Series

Pippa
Eliza
Nell
Tamsin
Evie
Cherry
Odessa
Sienna
Tess
Isla

The Augathella Girls Series

Outback Roads
Outback Sky
Outback Escape
Outback Wind
Outback Dawn
Outback Moonlight
Outback Dust
Outback Hope
The Augathella Girls: Volume 1
The Augathella Girls: Volume 2

Augathella Short and Sweet

An Augathella Surprise
An Augathella Baby
An Augathella Spring
An Augathella Christmas
An Augathella Wedding
An Augathella Easter

Others
Whitsunday Dawn
Undara
Osprey Reef
East of Alice
Four Seasons Short and Sweet
Follow the Sun
Ten Days in Paradise
Deadly Secrets
Adventures in Time
Silver Valley Witch
The Emerald Necklace
A Clever Christmas
Christmas with the Boss
Her Christmas Star

About the Author

Annie lives in Australia, on the beautiful north coast of New South Wales. She sits in her writing chair and looks out over the tranquil Pacific Ocean.

She writes contemporary romance and loves telling stories that always have a happily ever after. She lives with her very own hero of many years and they share their home with Toby, the naughtiest dog in the universe, and Barney, the ragdoll puss, who hides when the four grandchildren come to visit.

Stay up to date with her latest releases at her website: http://www.annieseaton.net

Awards

2023: Winner of the long contemporary RUBY award for Larapinta

Finalist for the NZ KORU Award 2018 and 2020.

Winner ...Best Established Author of the Year 2017 AUSROM

Longlisted for the Sisters in Crime Davitt Awards 2016, 2017, 2018, 2019

Finalist in Book of the Year, Long Romance, RWA Ruby Awards 2016 Kakadu Sunset

Winner ...Best Established Author of the Year 2015 AUSROM

Winner ...Author of the Year 2014 AUSROM

Best Established Author, Ausrom Readers' Choice 2017